REBEL TRAIN

A CIVIL WAR NOVEL

DAVID HEALEY

REBEL TRAIN

By David Healey

Cover design by Juan Padron.

The title page image is from an illustration by Frank Schoonover. Used by permission of the Schoonover family. The artist, born in 1877 in Oxford, New Jersey, was a student of Howard Pyle at Drexel Institute of Art, Science, and Industry (now Drexel University.) He became an artist and illustrator working in Wilmington, Delaware, and Bushkill, Pennsylvania, from 1900-1965, creating over 2,500 major works of art. Schoonover's works illustrated over 150 books and hundreds of magazine articles. He died in 1972 at age 95.

BISAC Subject Headings:

FIC014000 FICTION/Historical

FIC032000 FICTION/War & Military

CHAPTER 1

Gettysburg, Pennsylvania • Autumn 1863

WHEN THE FALL RAINS CAME, so did the bones. Liberated from their shallow graves across the battlefield, skeletons wearing tattered uniforms and rotting leather boots appeared in backyards and pastures. Hollow-eyed stares and grinning yellow teeth became a common sight. On a few occasions, a dog or a pig got hold of a leg bone and dragged it through the streets.

Among the citizens of Gettysburg, it was decided that something needed to be done. It was neither sanitary nor dignified treatment for the soldiers on both sides who had fought so hard and given so much.

A young lawyer in town took it upon himself to plan a cemetery for the war dead. Land near the battlefield was surveyed. Graves would be laid out in neat sections according to the home states of the fallen, even the Confederates. One day a central monument would be built, lit with an eternal flame to honor the souls lost on the battlefield.

It was an ambitious plan and one that was rapidly carried out. A date was set for the official dedication of the cemetery. The keynote speaker would be Edward Everett, a popular orator and former governor of Massachusetts. It was also fitting to invite the president of the United States, Abraham Lincoln. After all, Gettysburg was a relatively short train ride from the nation's capital at Washington City. It was generally expected that President Lincoln would be traveling on the Northern Central Railroad that connected Baltimore to Gettysburg. Citizens of the small towns along the route readied flags and banners to wave at the president as his train passed by. Excitement grew as the great day drew near.

* * *

ON A STORMY FALL NIGHT, a lone man walked down a country road outside Gettysburg, wind and rain whipping his face. Damned if he wasn't a fool for being out on a night like this, he told himself, feet slipping in the muddy road. He stepped into a wheel rut and nearly lost a shoe in the muck. He longed for the warm fire at home and almost turned back, then thought better of it. Spying was not the sort of work that could be done in broad daylight.

The spy was wet and miserable, but he stumbled on through the storm. He had seen and heard things that must be told. He knew he would be paid well for his information, more than enough to make it worthwhile to brave the stormy November night.

Up ahead, through the blowing rain, he spotted the lights of the tavern. The Blue Lantern. Aside from a few farmhouses and barns, it was the only tavern for miles around Gettysburg. He knew there would be a roaring fire in the hearth, along with a drink of whiskey to warm his bones. And there would be money. The one-eyed man would see to that.

Wind stripped the last of the leaves from the oaks and maples along the road, hurling them like giant snowflakes in the gusts. A black, dirty night to be out. The tavern was set back from the Baltimore Turnpike, and he trudged the last one hundred feet across the muddy yard, toward the yellow light that shined from the windows.

His chilled hand gripped the handle and he swung the door open.

The tavern was full. Inside, the air was hazy with wood and tobacco smoke. There were few places to stay on the road from Baltimore, and the storm had driven travelers to whatever shelter they could find. The spy shut the door behind him, then stood for a moment, blinking in the sudden light. Conversations trailed off as the tavern's customers eyed the newcomer.

"Is that a man or a muskrat?" someone shouted. That brought laughter, and the men at the tables turned back to their food and drink. The spy wasn't the first man that night to wander in out of the storm.

The tavern keeper recognized him and nodded, then jerked his head at a man sitting alone by the fire. The spy moved toward a narrow-shouldered figure hunkered down on a bench, his hands toward the fire. He looked up as the spy approached, and smiled. The spy smiled back, trying not to stare at the black patch where the man's left eye used to be. He had never summoned the courage to ask what had happened to the man's eye. Some claimed he was blinded in a knife fight while others said his jealous wife had burned it out with a hot iron one night while he slept. In any case, it gave him a sinister and frightening appearance.

"You're a good man to come out on a night like this," the one-eyed man said quietly.

"I'm a friend to the Cause."

The man nodded, then flicked a bony finger at the bench across from him. He spoke in a low voice so that only the spy could hear. "Not all are friends here. I wouldn't go talking about Causes if I were you."

The spy shrugged out of his heavy coat and took off his hat, glad of the fire. He sat on the bench. After a few minutes his wet clothes began to steam.

The one-eyed man was watching him. The spy did not know his name, just that he could be found at the tavern most nights, and that whenever he had information he passed it on to this fellow on the bench. He supposed the man then took the train to Baltimore, or passed word to someone on the train. In any case, there was always a bit of money in it, which was why he had learned to keep his ears and eyes open. The spy really didn't care which side won the war. Times were hard because of the war and a few dollars were welcome. The Confederates always paid more. Pennsylvania was a Union state, so whatever they learned about the enemy was welcome.

"What I got is worth something," the spy said, surprised at the excitement in his own voice, the loudness of it.

The man winced and held out his hands. "Quietly, if you please. I'm sure we'd be better off if everyone in the place didn't hear what you have to say." The man flashed yellow teeth and the spy was reminded of the corpses that had plagued the town all summer and fall.

"Lincoln's going to Gettysburg," the spy said. "On November seventeenth. He's staying the night at the home of a lawyer in town and then there's going to be a big ceremony the next day to dedicate the new cemetery for all them dead Yankees."

"I've heard about the ceremony," the man said, leaning toward the spy. His one eye glittered. "Are you sure about Lincoln?"

"It's just been decided," the spy said. "He's going to give a speech when they dedicate the cemetery."

"Lincoln." The man said the name and fell silent, thinking it over. After a few moments he looked up again, glanced over his shoulder, then turned to the spy. "The whole country will know before long that he's going to Gettysburg. It's not worth anything to me."

On the other side of the tavern, three men were struggling into their heavy coats. They went out the door into the rain, and the spy thought they must be fools to trade the tavern's smoky warmth for the autumn storm.

It was the spy's turn to smile as he leaned in close to the man across from him. "I reckon the whole country will know before long about Mr. Lincoln going to Gettysburg. It will be in the newspapers next week. But now you know before everybody else. That's good information."

The man with the eye patch shrugged. The truth was, he knew all about Lincoln's planned trip to Gettysburg. He had even helped Colonel Norris, head of the Confederate Secret Service in Richmond, set up an ambush for the train on the tracks north of Baltimore. He didn't tell any of this to the spy.

"Well," the spy continued, "I guess it really ain't much of a secret. Hell, Lincoln wants everyone to know about it."

"What are you talking about?"

He motioned for the man to lean closer. "How do you think Mr. Lincoln's travelin' to Gettysburg?"

The man humored him. "Why, on the train, I should think."

"Which one?"

The man appeared to think it over. "Washington to Gettysburg? He'll take a train to Baltimore, then take the Northern Central Railroad north to Hanover. There's a spur there that runs to Gettysburg."

It was the spy's turn to smile. "Well, that's just what the Yankees want you to think, ain't it? Lincoln ain't goin' to be on that train, though."

"What do you mean?"

"I've got ears, don't I?" the spy said. He was grinning now, enjoying himself. "How many ears do you think Mr. Lincoln's got? Why, lots and lots, I reckon. He's heard all about your plans. That's why he ain't goin' to be on that train."

The man stared keenly at the spy, suddenly interested. "What plans are you talking about?"

"Them guns. A whole battery of artillery. I heard about how you're planning to ambush the train. Hell, you'll be able to blow Abe Lincoln to Kingdom Come and back. Shame he ain't goin' to be on the train, though."

The man with the eye patch went very still. "Tell me what you mean by all this," he hissed.

"Mr. Lincoln is leavin' Washington on November seventeenth, then he's goin' to Baltimore, only he ain't goin' to take the Northern Central to Pennsylvania. No, not Honest Abe. He'll be gettin' on a Baltimore and Ohio Railroad car headed west. Nobody knows about this, mind you. Then at Weverton he's taking the Hagerstown spur, and from there he's going to Gettysburg. The roundabout way, only it's a secret. Safer that way and he gets there all the same. Like I said, he's done heard all about your plans."

"What about the train he's supposed to be on?" the man asked.

"Oh, I reckon it will leave Baltimore in fine style, only they'll say Mr. Lincoln has pressing concerns or he's tired and can't be bothered in his car. Ain't nobody goin' to see him again till Gettysburg."

The one-eyed man sat quietly for a minute, considering what he had just heard. The spy's clothes were steaming nicely, the grease in the wool giving off a pungent scent. Finally, he gave a short laugh.

"Surely this can't be true," he said.

"It is." The spy screwed up his face in a wise expression.

"Though you won't hear it around half the countryside, I reckon."

"Where did you hear it?"

"Never mattered to you before, did it?" The spy shrugged. "I got my sources."

The man with the eye patch smiled again, flashing his yellow teeth, and put a hand inside his coat. He produced a wad of greenbacks, and pressed it into the spy's hands. It was more money than the spy had ever received before, and he gripped it tightly in his hand, staring down in wonder. Then the bills disappeared inside his damp coat.

"A drink to the Cause?" the man asked quietly.

"I reckon that would be good."

They shared three whiskeys there by the fire, neither of them saying much. It was strong liquor, and the spy swayed when he stood up to leave. He wasn't looking forward to walking home in the storm, but his wife was waiting for him. It was just three miles he had to go, but it would take him well over an hour on a night like this. No one paid much attention as he left, except the man by the fire, who stared after him as the spy launched himself into the night.

The cold air sobered him at once. The storm had grown worse. Sleet now stung his face as he leaned into the wind and picked his way between the wagon ruts. Up ahead, the spy thought he saw something move, but he didn't pay much attention. Probably just the wind blowing a gust of rain. No man or beast would be out on a night such as this, at least, not if they had any sense. He tugged his collar tighter at his throat, glad for the whiskey's warmth inside him.

He shivered, although the thought of the money in his pocket more than made up for a little cold and wet. What would he do with all that money? Bring home a few bottles of the tavern's whiskey, for one thing. Maybe get himself a new coat, too, one that kept off the rain.

Above the howl of the storm, he heard someone splashing up the road behind him. Before he could turn, someone grabbed him and the spy felt a powerful arm around his throat. Instinctively, he reached behind him, found a face, gouged at the eyes. He heard a muffled curse and the grip loosened.

As he spun to face his attacker, he felt something hot and sharp bite into his side. The pain was terrible, paralyzing. As if in a dream, he caught a glimpse of a long knife blade as it pulled free, bloody and dripping, before it plunged again deep into his side. He felt steel twist in his kidneys.

He screamed.

The spy hoped someone in the tavern would hear. But the wind and wet night swallowed up his cries. The blade stabbed in again and the spy fell to his knees in the mud. The coppery taste of his own blood welled up from inside him and filled his mouth, dribbling from his lips. The pain was awful.

"Bastard almost put my eye out," a gruff voice said.

Then someone grabbed him under the arms and dragged him off the road into the muddy cornfield nearby. He felt hands search his pockets until they found the roll of greenbacks. He wanted to protest, but no words would come from his mouth, only gurgling sounds.

"No," he finally managed to moan through the terrible pain. He had the odd sensation of being able to feel every raindrop, every grain of dirt in the mud between his fingers. Then all the color went out of the world.

"Finish him off," the gruff voice said.

"He's done for. Let's get out of here before someone comes along. He squealed like a stuck pig."

The gruff-voiced one kicked the spy. "Hell, of course he can squeal. Squeals to the Rebs every time he hears some news, don't he? Well, that was the last time."

Footsteps splashed away, and the spy lay there as his blood

pumped out to mingle with the rainwater in the furrows. He tried to crawl back to the road where there might be a chance that someone would find him, but he only slipped deeper into a plowed rut. His face was in a puddle but he didn't have the strength to raise it. A few bubbles rose up. After a minute, the bubbles stopped. The spy was dead, drowned in a puddle of muddy water streaked red with blood.

But the assassins were too late to stop him from sharing his secret. Lincoln was coming to Gettysburg, just not the way anyone expected.

CHAPTER 2

Baltimore • November 6, 1863

"TICKETS, PLEASE!"

As the locomotive swept into a long curve, the sudden shift in direction made the passenger car roll like a ship riding the ocean's swells. Bad leg or not, Conductor George Greer kept his balance as easily as any sea captain. He had ridden this route so many times that he knew every bump in the rails.

He squinted into the autumn sunlight, saw the blue shadows of the Allegheny Mountains on the horizon. Despite repeated raids by Confederate cavalry in the mountains and the Shenandoah Valley, the Baltimore & Ohio Railroad remained one of the busiest railways in the nation. The tracks gleamed like knives stabbing into the distance.

The great locomotive spewed a cloud of smoke and sparks as the *Chesapeake* spun along the iron rails. Sunlight reflected off the locomotive's massive black bulk, glinted on the brass bell and the glass windows that enclosed the cab. The driving wheels, two on each side and taller than a man, churned in a blur of iron as the locomotive roared at sixty miles per hour across the gently rolling farmland west of Baltimore.

The train was traveling faster than it should have, but Greer had always been reckless when it came to speed. He knew what his locomotive could do. In fact, he knew every piston and rod and valve. Greer was thirty-three years old, blue-eyed, with brown hair and a serious, determined face. The corners of his eyes and mouth drooped slightly to give him a doleful look, like a bloodhound. He was short but powerfully built, with strong arms, broad shoulders and a barrel chest. A bulldog of a man. Even with a limp, Greer looked as if he could back up the authority in his voice. When he gave an order aboard his train, crew and passengers alike did as they were told.

At the battle of Bull Run in 1861, a Confederate bullet had left him with the limp and a deep hatred of the secessionists who had divided the nation and brought on the bloodshed. Greer had not thought twice about joining the fight, considering his grandfather had been one of the defenders of Fort McHenry during the War of 1812 and his great-grandfather had fought in the Revolution. Greers always had fought for the United States of America.

However, the embarrassing defeat of the Union army at Bull Run had been his first and last taste of war. His wound had put him out of the army for good. Greer had happily returned to his old job on the railroad. He had been a brakeman and engineer before the war broke out, and his war service, brief though it had been, had soon brought him a promotion to conductor.

"Tickets, please!" he repeated. Greer was friendly in an officious way as he passed through the car. He puffed out his chest as he paraded the aisles in his blue conductor's uniform with its bright, brass buttons. It was as fancy as any general's uniform. He nodded at the men, tipped his hat to the women.

His eye lingered longer than usual on the couple who

occupied the last seat. The two had come aboard at Mount Clare Station in Baltimore with tickets for Cumberland, a tall, muscular man with a pretty young woman on his arm. They wore flashy clothes — the man a bowler hat with a red silk tie at his neck, the woman wearing a wide hoop skirt that rustled with expensive crinoline petticoats. The front of the dress was cut low enough to reveal the milky white tops of her breasts, and the silk fabric was a bright, racy green — hardly the sort of clothes most women wore for traveling. They had the look of people who had worn their best clothes and were flaunting their finery like peacocks. Greer sensed they were trouble as soon as he laid eyes on them.

The man caught Greer studying him and returned the look with a taunting stare. He had a tough face, Greer decided, hard black eyes and oiled, dark hair. Everything about him was cocky. Greer had seen his kind often enough in the gangs of toughs known as Plug Uglies who hung around the wharves in Baltimore. Troublemakers. The city was full of thieves and copperheads who sympathized with the Confederate cause.

"Do you have your ticket, sir?" Greer asked. He could have moved on, but he didn't like the way the man was sneering at him.

"You ought to know," the man muttered. "You checked it yourself back in Baltimore."

Greer didn't like surly passengers. He wasn't having any nonsense on *his* train. He did not move, but stood waiting in the aisle, and the passenger knew well enough it was the conductor's right to check tickets because the train stopped at every station and new people were constantly coming aboard. He thrust the ticket at the conductor.

Greer gave the piece of paper a long look, then handed it back. "Thank you, sir."

He walked on, feeling the man's eyes boring into his back.

Greer wasn't afraid of anybody, but he also knew it wasn't his job to pick fights with the passengers. The B&O didn't pay him for that. Still, it didn't mean he couldn't put an uppity passenger in his place.

He opened the back door of the car and stepped out onto the platform where the wind blew with sudden force. Clamping his round conductor's cap onto his head with one hand, he crossed to the next car and went in. As soon as the conductor shut the door behind him, the woman in the green dress whispered harshly to her companion, "Charlie, what are you trying to do, ruin the whole plan?"

"The son of a bitch was giving me a hard look, Nellie."

The woman shook her head angrily. "We're here to ride the train, Charlie Gilmore. That's all. We want to get a feel for it. We need to learn the routine. Next time we ride this train you can shoot that conductor if you want, but for now you'd better smile at him. Don't cause trouble."

"Don't tell me what to do," the man said, raising his voice just enough that he attracted the attention of the other passengers. He glared at them until they looked away.

Nellie leaned close so that only he could hear what she said. She smiled as she spoke, although her low voice was cold and steely. "Behave or I'll put a knife in your ribs and save that conductor the trouble of putting you off at the next station."

"You'd do it, too, wouldn't you, Nell?"

In answer, he felt the sharp point of a blade between his ribs. One thrust and the steel would bury itself deep in his heart. He held himself very still. A man could never be sure what Nellie Jones would do next. She was a dangerous woman. Crazy, some said. At the moment, he had to agree.

Just as quickly as it had appeared, the knife vanished into the sleeve of her dress. No one else had seen because Nellie was pressed up close against him. Anyone watching would think they were lovers.

He forced a laugh to show he hadn't been afraid. "You wouldn't stab me, now would you, Nell?"

"I want to be rich," she whispered. "And you're not going to stop me. Now sit up straight and act proper."

The door to the car opened again and the conductor reappeared. He gave the couple from Baltimore a quick glance and continued down the aisle.

Gilmore watched the conductor closely. "He's damn full of himself," he grumbled. "The man runs a train and acts like he owns the world. He must think he's a general instead of a two-bit railroad conductor."

Beside him, Nellie squeezed his arm. "You just wait," she said. "If we pull this off you can buy your own goddamn train."

CHAPTER 3

Confederate Secret Service, Richmond • November 8, 1863

COLONEL WILLIAM NORRIS worked through the pile of dispatches on his desk. Most contained routine intelligence and he glanced at the messages, then put them aside. It wasn't until he was nearly at the bottom of the pile that he came across a report that made him sit up very straight at his desk and begin giving the message a close second look. He stared at the words on the page, scarcely able to believe what he was reading. Was it possible?

"Fletcher!"

Boots sounded in the hall and a young captain in an immaculately tailored uniform entered the office. He snapped to attention.

"Sir?"

Norris handed him the sheet of paper. "Who sent this dispatch?"

"One of our agents in Pennsylvania. He has always been highly reliable in the past."

Norris smiled. He had the sort of grin that seemed to make the air in the room grow cold. Fletcher shifted uneasily from foot to foot, making the leather of his highly polished boots squeak.

"We need to be very sure of what this says, Captain Fletcher. I want you to make certain there were no mistakes in decoding the cipher."

"Yes, sir."

Fletcher hurried out as Norris lit a cigar and tried to make some sense of the spy's report.

The Confederate Secret Service in Richmond was virtually unknown to most people, except those with some stake in the war fought over information, far beyond the battlefield. Officially, Norris was chief of the Confederate Signal Bureau. On paper, the Secret Service he directed did not even exist.

Norris was a West Point graduate who had resigned from the United States Army to fight for his native Virginia. Early in the war, he had developed the system known as "semaphore," which enabled military units to communicate over long distances using signal flags. Once the equipment had been developed and men trained, Norris had turned his attention to an altogether different kind of communication.

To all appearances, he was a quiet and intelligent man whom few would have suspected of directing the Confederacy's vast network of spies. Norris was also ruthless, and more than one of the bloated bodies found in the James River or in the stinking wastelands surrounding the Tredegar Iron Works was a result of his long reach.

The work was not nearly as exciting as it might seem. Most of what Norris did was collect dispatches from various spies scattered from Virginia to Canada. Some of what he received was quite useless or even inaccurate. He thought of it as a process not unlike distilling sour mash into whiskey. Norris did his best to sort through it all and then pass the information along to the appropriate commanders and political leaders. When necessary, he took matters into his own hands.

Norris had known for some time that the Yankee president, Abraham Lincoln, planned to take part in the ceremony dedicating the new cemetery for the Union dead at the Gettysburg battlefield. That information was hardly news because a president took part in similar public events on a regular basis. But Norris had anticipated an opportunity. He had sent a small band of saboteurs to ambush Lincoln's train on its way to Gettysburg.

There were many in the Confederacy who opposed such means of winning the war. But if Norris had learned anything in nearly three years of war, it was that the South had to exploit every Union weakness it could find if the Confederacy was to survive.

However, the dispatch he had just read changed everything. That Scottish zealot Alan Pinkerton, who ran the Union's network of spies, had rooted out the saboteurs. Still, to avoid any further danger to the president the Yankees proposed to do something quite daring and extraordinary. It also presented Norris with a great opportunity. He could make the Yankees' cleverness work against them.

Norris paused to light another cigar. He puffed a blue cloud of tobacco smoke toward the ceiling, thinking. Several minutes passed before he suddenly called out in annoyance, "Fletcher! Where the hell are you?"

The captain hurried back in. "No mistakes, sir. The dispatch is accurate. I would stake my life on it."

Leaning back in his chair, Norris kept his eyes focused on the ceiling. "Would you? I'll keep that in mind. Now tell me, is that fellow Arthur Percy still in Richmond? Or has the general shot him?"

"Percy?" Fletcher didn't want to show that he listened to

common gossip, so he pretended not to know the name, even though the whole city had heard the scandal.

"Don't be difficult, Fletcher. I'm talking about the one who was philandering with the general's wife."

"Oh. I suppose just about everyone has heard of *that* Colonel Percy." Fletcher sneered. "Not a very respectable sort, from what I understand."

"He's just the one I want," Norris said. "He's a good cavalry officer and a very brave man, no matter what else is being said about him. Find him and bring him here, Fletcher. He's about to undertake a mission for me."

Fletcher saluted and began to leave. Norris called him back. "While you're at it, Fletcher, find Tom Flynn as well."

"*Flynn*, sir?" Fletcher made no pretense about not knowing that name. He curled a disdainful upper lip in disgust. "The Irishman."

"I take it you don't like him, Captain?"

"No, sir. He's a lowborn immigrant."

"Why don't you point that out to him, the next time you see him?"

Fletcher cleared his throat nervously, plainly uncomfortable. "Flynn isn't worth the effort, sir."

"Go find them for me, Fletcher. Find Colonel Percy and the Irishman. They're just the men for the job I have in mind."

"Yes, sir."

Norris smiled again with a grin that could freeze water, not to mention the blood in Fletcher's veins. "Who knows? There might even be something in it for you, Captain."

CHAPTER 4

Richmond • November 8, 1863

"FORBES HAS GOT to be here somewhere," Colonel Arthur Percy said.

"Last time I seen him was on this street with that woman," Bill Hazlett replied, then leaned over to spit tobacco juice. "Ugly bitch. Tits like a goat."

"You see, boys, I told you women are nothing but trouble," Percy said, lecturing the small band of soldiers who walked with him down one of Richmond's most wretched streets.

"You would know, wouldn't you, Colonel?" asked Hazlett, a tall, evil-looking man with a nasty scar under his right cheekbone. He smiled, revealing long, unevenly spaced teeth that resembled fangs. Sergeant's stripes slashed across the arm of his tattered Confederate uniform.

The others laughed and Percy joined in, even though Hazlett's comments irritated him. Hazlett had a way of making salty remarks that marched right up to the edge of insulting. Most officers would not have tolerated insubordinate talk from a mere sergeant, but Hazlett was family, more or less. He was capable enough as a sergeant, but the real reason he wore stripes was because he was married — badly — to one of Percy's cousins. Twice the poor woman had shown up at the Percys' big house with bruises and a black eye. There might even have been trouble between Percy and Hazlett if the war hadn't broken out.

It was hard to pull rank on your cousin-in-law. Most of the time, Percy tried to treat Hazlett like an equal. The last thing he needed was a feud from back home to haunt them now. Still, he suspected that Hazlett despised him behind his back.

It did not help that Percy's recently ended affair with a prominent general's young wife was still feeding the gossip mills of Richmond. Everyone expected a duel as soon as the hot-headed general returned to the capital. The colonel had a nonchalant attitude toward all the talk. A Yankee bullet or the general's— it was all the same to him.

"Do as I say, but not as I do," Percy added in a fatherly tone when the laughter died away. "A truly wise man — wiser than any of *you*, at least — learns from the mistakes of others, not his own."

"Hell, Colonel, a wise man would have made damn sure her husband didn't find out," a soldier named John Cook said, and once more the group erupted in laughter.

Percy laughed with them. Even though he was an officer, he had been with these men too long for anything but an easy familiarity. He had even grown up with a few of them. They would all be neighbors again back home, if they survived the war.

Percy was thirty-five years old, sandy haired and blue-eyed. Every inch of his lean, six-foot frame looked the part of Southern hero. He was one of those dashing men the South had a gift for producing: a cavalier at home on horseback, who rode with a sword in one hand and a revolver in the other. He could shoot, he could ride, and he wasn't afraid of anything or anyone — especially not the Yankees who had invaded his homeland.

Percy didn't like regular soldiering with its "Yes sirs" and "No sirs" and gallant charges into the mouths of cannons. Percy liked playing the fox. Outsmarting Yankees. Beating the odds. His raids behind Yankee lines had made him famous when accounts of his deeds had appeared in newspapers in the North and South. Then his luck began to run out. A Yankee bullet had put him in a Richmond hospital.

It was in the Confederate capital that Percy had met the general's wife. She had been his undoing, a raven-haired, green-eyed beauty too young to be safely left alone while her older and esteemed husband was off leading his troops in Mississippi. The general was a violent and jealous man, and society as a whole did not approve of men who seduced wives while their husbands were away doing their duty and serving the Confederacy.

Percy had already been threatened by several of the general's friends in Richmond, and was almost shot outright by one of them, until his lover had interfered. Percy expected he would have to fight a duel when the general returned to Richmond, and it was a duel Percy might not win because the general was known as a particularly vengeful bastard.

Not that Percy gave a damn either way. What really mattered was that few general officers wanted him in their units after such a scandal, including his old commander, who had already sent Percy a terse note declining his services. Percy waited to be reassigned to some unit, somewhere. Meanwhile, he found there was never a dull moment for a soldier on leave in Richmond.

* * *

A FEW PEOPLE stared from the doorways as Percy and his ragtag band passed. This was a rough part of the city and any one of the soldiers alone might have been in danger. But the seven together were a tough-looking and battle-hardened bunch, lean as a pack of wolves. Heavy revolvers hung in holsters at their sides, the iron and leather looking worn as a workman's well-used tools.

Five of the men wore threadbare cavalry uniforms, the gray fabric stained with sweat, dirt and blood. Percy's uniform had the golden "chicken guts" braiding of an officer reaching above the elbows of his uniform coat while another man, Silas Cater, wore the less ornate insignia of a lieutenant.

In addition to Lieutenant Cater and Hazlett, there was a tall, whip-thin man named Douglas Pettibone who wore the double stripes of a corporal. John Cook was also a corporal. Private Johnny Benjamin, who was hardly more than a boy, was on furlough after being released from the hospital. Although he wasn't part of their old regiment, some of the other men had taken the boy under their wing.

The seventh man in the group wore no weapon or uniform. He was Percy's servant, a huge black man named Hudson. At six feet, four inches tall, he was the biggest member of the group, powerfully built, and his dark, African face answered the stares from the doorways with an open defiance that made even these unsavory Richmond residents look away.

Hazlett came to a stop and nodded at a ramshackle dwelling a few doors ahead. "This is the place."

Percy made a disapproving noise. "You would think Forbes could have done better," he said.

"He was drunk, sir," explained Corporal Pettibone, who also had been with Forbes the night he disappeared.

"When isn't he drunk?" Percy pointed out.

As a soldier, Willie Forbes functioned well enough even

when he was awash with liquor, and he always managed to get away with things that a sober man couldn't. Only this time he'd gone on a binge in Richmond's seedier streets, which were not kind to drunken soldiers. So his comrades had gone to rescue him, or what was left of Forbes after a two-day drunk with rotgut whiskey and a cheap whore.

Percy took charge. He felt responsible. The five cavalrymen were on furlough from the regiment and had come to Richmond to visit their colonel just out of the hospital — and to have a good time with the ample food, liquor and women the city had to offer. It was the last two temptations that had landed Forbes in trouble. As for Percy, he had already recovered from the minié ball that had pierced his upper arm and had found his own difficulties in the form of the general's wife. Richmond was a city of sin and decadence, as far as he could tell. He was eager to return to the war.

"That's the place, sir," said Pettibone, who had seen Forbes disappear with the woman on his arm.

Percy sighed. "Bastard will have the pox," he muttered.

They were looking at a shabby, two-story house that was hardly fifteen feet wide. The gray, unpainted clapboards had long since splintered and cracked, and the whole house, like many others on the street, gave the impression that it might blow down in the next strong wind.

Hazlett leaned over and spat. "Ain't much of a place."

"All right," Percy said. "Let's go get him."

Percy shoved open the door. A thickset man was sitting inside at a table, and he blinked up in surprise at the sudden appearance of the tall officer in his doorway.

"What the hell—"

As the man started to get up, Percy put a hand on his shoulder and shoved him back down.

"Where is he?" Percy asked, keeping the man pinned

firmly in his chair. A cunning look came into the man's eyes. "Who?"

It was not the answer Percy wanted. He nodded at the doorway and suddenly the room filled with soldiers. John Cook stayed outside to serve as a lookout. Percy crinkled his nose. The whole place stank of stale liquor, lamp fumes and sweat.

"Shut the door," Percy ordered. "We don't want the provost guard in here causing trouble. That is, if they even bother to patrol this part of the city."

"Who are you?" blustered the man at the table as he struggled to get up. Hudson went over and held the man's other shoulder and a look of genuine fear crossed his face at the powerful grip of the black man's hands. He strained one last time, then gave up.

"Never mind who we are," Percy said. "We just want our friend back."

The proprietor of the flophouse nodded toward a back room. "He's in there, if it's that little scrub of a cavalryman you're lookin' for."

Percy turned to Sergeant Hazlett. "Get him."

Hazlett disappeared into the back room. There was the sound of a woman cursing, and they heard a man moaning in pain.

"Leave me be," he groaned. "I want to die here, in my true love's arms."

"You dumb son of a bitch," Hazlett growled. "Put your damn clothes on."

Hazlett soon emerged, shoving a half-dressed Forbes in front of him. A slattern of a woman followed them out. She looked as drunk as Forbes, her hair greasy and tangled. She had managed to get just one arm into a sleeve of her dress. One breast hung out, a gray, lumpen thing with a nipple the color of old leather.

"Jesus," Percy heard one of the men gasp at the sight of her.

"You can have him," the whore said, plucking at the dress and finally succeeding in covering herself. She slurred her words. "No-good bastard's a drunk. Nothin' but a no-good drunk soldier!"

She swayed, then collapsed into a chair at the same table where the proprietor of the house sat.

"How many in here?" Percy asked.

"She's downstairs. Two upstairs," the man replied.

Forbes was so drunk he could only fumble with his buttons as if his fingers were thick as sausages. Pettibone went over and helped him. Forbes's uniform was in an awful state: muddy, wrinkled, and reeking of whiskey. A dried crust of what appeared to be vomit clung to one sleeve.

"Colonel," Forbes said, and attempted a salute. He reeled and nearly fell over.

"Forbes, you are a sorry excuse for a soldier," Percy said. "And your taste in women leaves something to be desired. Now let's go."

"He owes me ten dollars for the whiskey he drank," the proprietor said, then jerked his head toward the awful-looking woman. "And for her."

Percy shrugged. "Very well. Hud, pay the man."

Hudson drove a massive fist into the fat man's belly. The man's breath rushed out and he collapsed on the floor and lay there gasping like a huge, bloated fish. The whore shrieked. In the tiny room, the noise was like a shell exploding.

"Let's go, boys, just in case that fool has friends in the neighborhood," Percy said. "Frank and Johnny, prop Forbes up in between you there and make him walk. That'll sober him up. Does he have anything left in his pockets?"

"They picked him clean, sir."

"Come on, then."

They went back the way they had come as quickly as they could. It was not a good neighborhood in which to linger because Percy's concerns about the flophouse proprietor's friends were not without good reason. Also, Percy didn't want any trouble with the Richmond provost guard because he knew well enough that many of Richmond's more important citizens who would like nothing better than a good excuse to put him in jail—at least until the general could shoot him.

"I reckon you had yourself a good time, Willie," Hazlett said as he helped half-drag, half-carry Forbes along the muddy street. "We went to a lot of goddamn trouble to find you."

"Good thing you was drunk," Pettibone chipped in. "She was powerful ugly."

Forbes staggered along under the abuse of his comrades. "You can say what you want, boys, but she was a fine woman. Hell, I might just marry her!"

"Ain't you already married?"

"Why, I reckon I am, boys. Promise me you won't tell my wife?"

They were all laughing so hard that they almost didn't notice the officer and two soldiers standing in the street ahead, directly in their path. Percy squinted, trying to see who it was, but he didn't recognize the man. The group came to a stop and watched the officer expectantly.

"Excuse me," the officer said. His stern voice and immaculate uniform could only mean trouble. Although he was just a captain, only an officer of some importance on one of Richmond's administrative staffs would have such a splendid uniform. *Dandy* was the word that came to Percy's mind.

"Damn headquarters peacock," Hazlett muttered, loud enough for the officer to hear.

"Can I help you?" Percy asked. He eyed the officer warily. Although they had reached a better part of town where several bands of soldiers roamed the street, the captain appeared to have been waiting just for them. Not a good sign. Percy wondered if he was being arrested.

"Are you Colonel Arthur Percy?"

"Yes. What can I do for you?"

"I am Captain Fletcher. You are to come with me. Colonel Norris's orders." Fletcher sniffed, then added, "Sir."

Percy thought quickly. He had never heard of any Colonel Norris. Not that it mattered. As a field officer, Percy knew well enough that he was nearly ignorant of Richmond's military bureaucracy. That was just the way he liked it.

Colonel Norris, whoever he was, must be a man of some importance if he sent well-dressed fools like this arrogant captain to run his errands. At any rate, the summons did not appear to include his men, a fact for which Percy was grateful. He didn't know what this was about, but it couldn't be good.

"All right, Fletcher, lead the way," Percy said. "Hudson, you come with me. I'll see you men later. See that you stay out of trouble."

Captain Fletcher looked Hudson up and down, making no effort to hide his displeasure. "Who is this darkie?"

"He's my servant and he goes where I go," Percy said. "And that reminds me, Fletcher. Isn't it customary for a captain to salute a colonel? Or don't you bother with that sort of thing in Richmond?"

Fletcher's eyes filled with sudden venom. It was obvious the well-groomed captain thought it beneath him to salute a ragged colonel.

"Very well, *Colonel*." Fletcher managed a half-hearted salute.

Percy smiled. "Lead on, Captain Fletcher."

CHAPTER 5

CAPTAIN FLETCHER HAD a carriage waiting around the corner. Percy and the captain climbed inside while the two soldiers pulled themselves up to share the buckboard with the driver. Hudson clung to the back of the carriage.

Percy wondered if he had made a mistake in bringing Hudson along, considering he didn't know what any of this was about. Although Fletcher hadn't placed him under arrest, the soldiers bore an uncomfortable resemblance to guards.

"Where are we going, Captain?" Percy asked as cheerfully as he could under the circumstances. "And who is this Colonel Norris?"

Fletcher raised an eyebrow, as if amazed that someone had not heard of Norris. "He's chief of the Confederate Signal Bureau," Fletcher said haughtily. "Which is, of course, where we're going?"

"The Signal Bureau?" Percy couldn't imagine what in the world someone from the Signal Bureau wanted of him. He had never even heard of it.

Fletcher smiled at his confusion. "Let's just say things aren't always as they seem, Colonel."

Percy could see any conversation with Fletcher was going to be antagonistic, so he gave up and stared out the window. What he saw did not inspire great hope in the future of the Confederacy. The muddy streets were strewn with garbage. Most of the buildings they passed, homes and businesses alike, needed a coat of paint. Knots of ragged soldiers drifted by, looking haggard and dirty, and the civilians he saw, mostly women, children and old men, wore threadbare clothes. Only a few appeared to have done well by the war, and they were the whores, whoremasters, and black market traders who paraded the streets, flaunting their ill-gotten finery in the faces of proper Richmond society.

As the carriage passed, Percy caught the eye of a pretty and garishly dressed young lady. She couldn't have been more than eighteen years old, but the elaborate silk dress she wore made no secret of her trade. The girl smiled and Percy tipped his hat and grinned wolfishly out the carriage window.

"Nobody knew the war would fill the city with whores," Fletcher said, sounding disgusted. The truth was, he was a regular at many of Richmond's whorehouses, but he liked to pretend otherwise.

Percy laughed. "Hell, Captain. Every country girl with a pretty face and some ambition is making her fortune. It's better than being wife to some farmer and spending her days feeding chickens and raising children. Besides," he said, staring after the girl, who in turn stood with a pout, watching the carriage as it rolled away. "That one might just be worth a month's pay."

"I should have known a man of your reputation—" Fletcher began to say, then stopped himself upon noticing Percy's expression.

"What reputation might that be, Captain?" Percy asked, his voice dangerously brittle. The girl was gone from sight and he gave Fletcher his full attention. His eyes appeared to change color from clear blue to the color of mountains before a storm.

"Well ... I misspoke, Colonel," Fletcher sputtered. "Please forgive me."

They rode the rest of the way in silence. Percy was unimpressed when they arrived. There was nothing about the building that housed the Confederate Signal Bureau to indicate its real purpose. Fletcher led the way to Norris's office and introduced Percy, then disappeared, shutting the door discreetly behind him.

Colonel Norris did not look sinister, Percy thought. If anything, he resembled a strict school teacher. Norris had a medium build and was of average height, with thick brown hair and a full beard through which small, even teeth flashed in a smile. Although his uniform wasn't tattered like a field officer's, it was plain enough. Unlike many administrative officers, including the obnoxious Captain Fletcher, Norris obviously did not hold gold braid or fancy tailoring in high regard.

"Thank you for coming, Colonel," Norris said.

"Did I really have any choice?"

Norris laughed. "We all have choices. As a matter of fact, Colonel, I'm about to offer you one."

An uneasy feeling took hold in Percy's belly. "What might that be?"

"In due time, Colonel. In due time. Let me explain my position."

Norris paused to offer Percy a cigar. He accepted, and tobacco smoke soon drifted in great clouds toward the high, plaster ceiling.

"You've heard of the Andrews train raid, Colonel?"

"Who hasn't?"

It had been one of the Union's most daring feats of the war. In April 1862, a Yankee spy and contraband trader named James Andrews had slipped South with twenty-two men.

They seized a Confederate train outside Atlanta and raced north toward Chattanooga, wrecking tracks as they went, to prevent the Confederates from sending reinforcements to the Tennessee city as the Union army attacked. The raiders were eventually caught and most of them hanged. The incident had been in all the newspapers.

"I propose doing something of the same sort, Colonel Percy. And I need your help."

Percy eyed Norris suspiciously. "What is this place?" he asked. "Who are you?"

Norris waved the cigar in his hand as he spoke. "Officially, this place is the Signal Bureau. In reality, it's headquarters for the Confederate Secret Service. The war is fought in many ways, Colonel Percy. Not just on the battlefield. There are spies, of course. Subtle acts of allowing misleading information to fall into enemy hands."

"And you're the commander of this army of spies?" Percy asked. "I take it that you also arrange train raids?"

"Just this one, so far."

Percy shook his head. "Well, I'm not interested."

He stood, ready to take his leave. Norris did not appear the least bit perturbed. "Thank you for the cigar, sir. But you'll have to steal this train without me.""At least hear me out, Colonel."

"Sorry." Percy stood up and turned to go.

Behind him, he heard Norris sigh. "I had really hoped you might agree to do this great service for our new nation and the Cause for which we all fight. If you walk out, Colonel, I'll have Captain Fletcher arrest you. I'm sure it would give him a certain amount of pleasure."

"Arrest me for what?" Percy glared down at the man behind the desk. Even as he said it, Percy had a nagging suspicion that Norris was capable of many things, hidden away in this old building like a spider in a web.

"Espionage, perhaps? Being a traitor to the Confederacy? Certain letters will be found in your possession ..."

"I don't have any letters!"

"But you will, Colonel." Norris spoke cheerfully. "Don't you see? Unfortunately, I'm afraid the penalty for spying is rather severe. It involves rope and scaffolding."

Norris smiled, and for the first time, Percy realized what a cold and deliberate man sat before him. He also felt uneasy, because he sensed that the threat was within Norris's power to carry out.

"I don't think you'll find much support if you are arrested," Norris went on. "You do have an excellent war record, but I believe your recent affair with the general's wife has won you more enemies than friends here in Richmond."

Defeated, Percy sank back into his chair. He was no coward, but he felt helpless in the face of this kind of threat. He also knew that when a man had you on a leash like a dog, it was best to go along until you found the best time to bite him.

"Maybe I'd rather be hanged than go on some train raid," he said.

"I doubt that, Colonel," Norris said. "Besides, if you agree to help me—to help your country, really—I will fix things up for you with the general. He's a proud man, but he'll listen to reason in the matter of his wife. You will have your military career back."

"If the Yankees don't catch me first and hang me as a spy."

"There's always that possibility. But you're better than that, Colonel. You have a particular talent for quick and daring operations like this. The Buckley Courthouse raid, for instance. You and your men captured eighty Yankees. Eighty! Not to mention ten wagons and sixty horses. And one slumbering general who even today remains at Libby Prison. That's very impressive."

"The fools should have posted a guard."

"Don't you see why we need you?"

"I'm still not convinced." Percy took another step toward the door.

"Well, there are always your men to consider. Several of them are here in Richmond, aren't they?"

Percy gripped the arms of the chair so hard his knuckles turned white. Norris had his full attention.

"What about them?"

"We can't have deserters running about the capital."

"They're not deserters, damn you!" Percy jumped up, but Norris didn't look concerned.

"They can be anything I want," Norris said.

Percy returned to his chair and slumped into it. "What must I do?" he asked.

Knowing he had won, Norris smiled. The room seemed to grow colder. He stood and walked to a shelf, then took down a map and unrolled it on his desk. Percy joined him in studying it.

"Maryland?"

"It all starts here for you," Norris said, placing his finger on the map beside a crossroads town a few miles miles west of Baltimore and twenty-five miles north of Washington.

"Ellicott Mills, Colonel. Let me tell you about it. You see, you're going there to capture President Abraham Lincoln."

"What?"

Norris laughed. "Listen, Colonel. Let me explain."

At first, Percy couldn't believe what he was hearing. But as he heard Norris give details of the plan, he began to feel less beaten, mainly because the very idea of kidnapping Lincoln was so outrageous it just might work. By the time Norris finished, Percy was surprised that he was interested in spite of the circumstances. Capture Lincoln? His heart began to race with excitement.

"It's really quite simple," Norris said. "The Yankee president intends to avoid the northern train route from Baltimore, where rumor has it that loyal Maryland Confederates may be plotting an ambush. They plan on bypassing the Northern Central Railroad altogether.

"Instead, Lincoln plans to secretly switch trains in Baltimore. The president's train will continue toward Gettysburg, but Lincoln won't be on it. Instead, he will be aboard a westbound train of the Baltimore and Ohio Railroad."

"How do you know this?" Percy asked.

"We have our spies, Colonel," Norris said. "This information comes from more than one source. I would say it's highly reliable."

The train would steam the length of the long, narrow border state of Maryland. At a town called Weverton, shortly before the train reached Harpers Ferry, Lincoln would veer north on the Washington County Railroad, a spur from the B&O line to the city of Hagerstown. From that western Maryland city, train tracks stretched north toward Gettysburg.

It was a more roundabout route from Baltimore to Gettysburg than a traveler would normally take because most would opt for the more direct and thus faster northern route. However, Lincoln would get there all the same via the western route without placing himself in any grave danger. The president had used a similar subterfuge to avoid assassins at least once before, when first arriving by train to take office in Washington. The subterfuge had earned him some ridicule at the time, but it had also kept him safe from harm.

The key to the success of Lincoln's plan was secrecy. Norris's network of spies had already breached that, although the Yankees apparently didn't know yet. Because Lincoln would of necessity be traveling with few guards, it created an opportunity to capture him. Having the Yankee president as a prisoner would change the outcome of the war, Norris believed, and in any case it would be a highly embarrassing situation for the Union. It might even prompt England to finally recognize the Confederate States of America as a sovereign nation.

"You and your men will leave Richmond in two smaller groups and slip across the Potomac River into Maryland," Norris continued. "From there, you must travel thirty more miles to Ellicott Mills. That town is the real starting point on the B&O's westward route."

Percy's raiders would assemble there after slipping through enemy territory. Lincoln's train had to stop in the same town, and Percy's men, who would purchase tickets to various towns along the B&O line, would board the train.

"He'll have too many guards," Percy interrupted. "We'll never get near that train."

Norris shook his head. "He'll be doing this secretly, remember? He'll have one car and only a small number of guards. Lincoln has never shown much concern for his personal safety in the past."

Percy still wasn't convinced. He had been a soldier too long to believe the odds were ever good, or that anything ever went according to plan.

"All right," he said. "But how do a handful of men commandeer a train? There will be passengers, maybe even soldiers traveling home or back to their posts, not to mention Lincoln's guards. We can't overpower them all."

"That's where breakfast comes in," Norris said. He tapped the map with a tobacco-stained finger. "The train is scheduled to stop briefly in a town called Sykesville, a few miles from Ellicott Mills. Most of the crew and passengers will get off to eat breakfast at a hotel near the tracks. At that point you'll take the train and run for the Shenandoah Valley. You should have just enough daylight to make it."

Percy suddenly remembered. The Andrews raid! That was where Norris had gotten the idea. The Yankees had stolen the train when the crew stopped for breakfast at a station outside Atlanta. The crew had left her under steam and gone inside the station house to eat, never thinking there was any danger of the train being stolen.

It had worked once before, Percy thought. It might just work again. The whole damn thing might work. Norris gave him the rest of the plan. Once they had the train, they would run like greased lightning across Maryland, cross the Potomac River at Harpers Ferry, and head for the Allegheny Mountains.

Percy interrupted again. "If you want us to head south into the Shenandoah Valley, why wouldn't we take this branch?" he asked, letting his finger on the map trace the route of the Winchester and Potomac Railroad than ran south from Harpers Ferry to Winchester, Virginia.

Norris shook his head. "It would be faster—if Winchester weren't crawling with Union troops. There's no way we can get cavalry there to escort you to Richmond. The Yankees have had a firm grip on Winchester since Stonewall Jackson left the valley."

Percy nodded in agreement, and Norris continued to outline his plan. Once the train had gone deep into the mountains, some of General Jubal Early's men would be detailed to meet it near the town of Romney and help spirit Abraham Lincoln down the valley to Richmond, where the Union president would become a prisoner of war.

"That is, if you can take him alive," Norris said. "If not, you'll have to kill him."

"He's a civilian," Percy pointed out.

"He's commander in chief of the Union Army. Civilian or not, that makes him the enemy. Kill him if you must."

"What's to stop the Yankees from doing the same to Jefferson Davis?"

Norris shrugged. "There are those who might say we'd be better off without him."

Percy chose not to acknowledge the last remark, just in case Norris was testing his loyalty. "Who do I take with me?"

"The men you have with you in Richmond will do," Norris said.

Percy started to protest. "This is too risky."

Norris held up a hand to interrupt him. He smiled wickedly again. "If I could have you arrested, Colonel, think of what I could do to them. Take your men."

"You're a bastard, Norris."

The chief of the Signal Bureau calmly puffed his cigar, ignoring the insult. "Oh, and you'll be taking Fletcher, too."

Percy couldn't believe what he was hearing. "What? Look here, Colonel—"

"Fletcher goes with you," Norris said. "I want two of my own men on this raid. Fletcher will serve as an official representative of the army. He's also from Maryland, which might prove useful."

"He does look good in a uniform." Percy smirked. "Who's the other man?"

"His name is Flynn."

"Does he have a nice uniform, too?"

"Flynn doesn't wear a uniform, Colonel. He's not the type. In point of fact, he's not even a soldier."

"Then what's he got to do with this raid?"

"I'm sending Flynn along to kill you if you change your mind about the raid once you get to Maryland."

"What? I can't do this thing with some murderous bastard waiting every moment to shoot me."

Norris laughed around his cigar. "Flynn isn't that way, Colonel. I think you'll like him, in spite of yourself. But make no mistake, Flynn does as he is told. I pay him very well for that."

"You mean this isn't his first time?"

"Exactly."

Percy shrugged. The whole plan was already outrageous. Adding Captain Fletcher to the mix couldn't make things much worse, he decided. But who was this Flynn? The last thing Percy needed was someone waiting to shoot him in the back when things weren't going right.

They discussed a few more details such as the number of raiders, weapons and cash for train tickets. Then Norris stood and extended his hand. "Good luck, Colonel."

Percy made no effort to take Norris's hand. "I would rather shake with the Devil," he said.

Norris simply shrugged and sat down to busy himself with paperwork.

Head spinning, Percy practically ran from the room. In the hallway, he paused to take a deep breath. Captain Fletcher worked at his desk in the hall, pointedly ignoring both Percy and his servant, who sat in a chair near Norris's door. It made sense, of course, that Norris wanted two of his own men along for the raid, although Fletcher was the last man Percy would have picked for the mission.

Hudson looked at Percy expectantly, but the colonel only shook his head, not wanting to take the time yet to explain what had happened. He just wanted to be out of that dark, dismal building. The place had an unwholesome air.

"Come on," he said, and Hudson got up from his chair and followed Percy out.

On the street, Percy paused to get his bearings. He actually felt dizzy. *This was madness.* A plan to end the war, or at least to strike a terrible blow against the Yankees. He decided then that he would go on this mission not because of Norris' threats but out of his own sense of duty. He knew that if they brought President Lincoln to Richmond as a prisoner, it would be a blow to the Union worth more than a thousand Buckley Courthouse raids.

Percy nearly laughed in spite of the circumstances. The plan was just crazy enough to work.

CHAPTER 6

Caswell's Rooming House, Richmond • November 10, 1863

TOM FLYNN STOOD in front of the rooming house that served as the headquarters for Colonel Percy's train raiders. *Poor bastards*, he thought, watching the three men who lounged on the porch. In just five days they would cross the Potomac, probably never to return. Flynn felt even sorrier for himself because he would be going with them. Silently, he cursed Colonel Norris. The colonel was mad if he thought they could capture Abraham Lincoln with a handful of raiders.

He climbed the porch steps as the three men watched him warily.

"I'm looking for Colonel Percy."

"You're not welcome here," said one of the men, who wore a lieutenant's insignia.

"That's no way to treat a stranger," Flynn said, thickening his accent until he sounded like an Irishman fresh from the bog. He knew it was the quickest way to render himself harmless in the soldiers' eyes. "What's the world comin' to?"

"Hud, you best go fetch the colonel," the lieutenant said.

The biggest of the men, who looked as hard and dark as

oiled locust wood, finally stood. Flynn shifted the heavy satchel that hung from his shoulder, ready for anything. But the enormous black man only looked him over for a moment, then disappeared into the house.

Flynn sighed and promptly collapsed into the old chair the guard had been using. The other two men just stared, like dogs deciding whether or not they would bite. He ignored them. After all, he had not been expecting a warm reception. He settled down to wait.

* * *

FLYNN HAD COME to America in 1847, the black year when the famine was at its worst in Ireland. Hundreds of thousands of Irish were starving to death due to the failure of the potato crop but Flynn managed to escape thanks to an aunt who scraped together the money to buy his passage from Cobh Harbor. Unlike many of the Irish refugees who sailed to New York or Boston or Newfoundland, his famine ship arrived in Baltimore.

"There it is, lad," one of the deckhands said, pointing out the brick fort standing guard at the harbor entrance. "That's Fort McHenry, where the British met their match against the Americans."

"I'm going to be an American now," the boy said proudly. Like most of the Irish, he hated the British who were slowly starving his people.

"Aye." But the deckhand shook his head sadly. "So much for Ireland, laddy. There's no doubt your future lies here now."

Baltimore was a seafaring city where ships arrived from around the world full of goods and immigrants hoping for a better life. Along with the Irish came Polish and Germans, each living in their own squalid neighborhoods ringing the harbor.

Flynn's new home was in the cellar of a decrepit row house, where he shared the damp quarters with an extended family headed by a distant cousin. They took him in because they had to, but there was no joy in greeting the young boy from home.

"He's a big 'un," he overhead the cousin telling his wife late one night when they thought Flynn and the other children were asleep, tumbled among each other under the dirty blankets. "Another gob to feed."

"He's plenty big enough to work," the wife said. "He can earn what he eats."

So Flynn was sent to the docks and the breweries and the stables, wherever a strong young boy was needed. His wages were paid to the cousin. In return, Flynn got scraps of bread and salt pork.

Life was hard and the boy might have been worked to death before that first winter was out. But his fate changed one day when the parish priest hired the boy's services to muck out the stables. After hours of shoveling, Flynn sat eating a bowl of soup at the table in the rectory kitchen when the priest came in with a newspaper. He put the paper down on the table and proceeded to talk with the cook. Flynn sneaked a look at the paper and glanced up a minute later, mortified, to find the priest staring at him.

"You can read, boy?"

"Yes, Father."

At a time when most of the Irish immigrants still spoke Gaelic, a boy who could read was rare. But his aunt had taught him in Ireland, holding lessons in front of the peat fire, telling him it was the way of the future.

Impressed, the priest put an end to Flynn's laboring. Flynn became an altar boy and an errand runner for the priest. Father McGlynn was a rough and belligerent working man's priest who drank too much whiskey, but he made certain that Flynn got his lessons. "Reading and writing and thinking are what separate us from the dumb beasts," the old priest grumped. "Now copy out that damned page like I told you."

By the time he was a teenager, the penniless immigrant boy could read and write as well as anyone, even in Latin.

He could have gone into the priesthood or found some job clerking in an office, but that was not the life for Flynn. He found that quick wits were useful, but quick fists even better. He went to work in the adventurous world that was America in the 1850s. When the war broke out, he found himself on the Southern side when the lines were drawn. Briefly, he shouldered a musket in the Confederate ranks but discovered that soldiering wasn't for him. One dark night he deserted and fled to Richmond.

He soon found himself employed by Colonel Norris. From smuggling messages and quinine to helping Confederate agents cross the Potomac, Flynn had done more to help the Cause than he ever had in the ranks of General Joseph Johnston's ragtag army.

As for Colonel Norris, his stern demeanor and severity reminded Flynn of Father McGlynn. But Flynn did not believe in the Southern Cause, just as he had not believed in old McGlynn's unrelenting Catholicism. Flynn was in this war for himself, just as he had always done everything for himself. It was the way of the future.

* * *

FLYNN WAS STILL SPRAWLED in the chair a few minutes later when Colonel Percy came out onto the porch with the massive guard. Flynn made a show of clumsily scrambling to his feet and saluting awkwardly. The tall, sandy-bearded colonel squinted at him. He was about Flynn's height but with a lean build. In fact, his clothes hung loosely, as if he had lost weight. Flynn seemed to remember something about the colonel having been wounded.

"I'm Percy," he said. "Who are you?"

"Thomas Flynn, sir. Sergeant Flynn." Flynn promoted himself; he had only been a private when he last wore a uniform.

"You're the one Norris sent," Percy said. His look was not friendly. "You're the one who's going to shoot me."

"Well, I'm not in any hurry."

"What if I shoot you first?"

"That could happen." Flynn shrugged. "The truth is that I'm against shooting either one of us. I propose we go get Mr. Lincoln like Colonel Norris wants and make that the end of it."

Percy still looked hostile. Evidently, he had already told his men what Flynn's role was to be on the raid. The big guard had huge hands that he kept flexing as if he couldn't wait to fit them around Flynn's throat. Two other men had appeared in the doorway, the first a tall, lank-haired fellow with bad teeth and a wicked scar under his cheekbone. The second man was pale-eyed and whip thin, and his hand rested on a revolver in a hip holster.

"This could end right here," Percy said.

Flynn nodded. "Sure, and you think Colonel Norris would let you get away with that? He's a vengeful bastard and if he doesn't find you, he will find your men. Or maybe even your home and your family. Fauquier County, isn't it?"

"You son of a bitch," Percy hissed, taking a step toward him.

Flynn held his ground. "It's not me you should be mad at, Colonel," he said, realizing that things had gone as wrong as they could. Percy's men circled him like wolves. "It's Norris. I'm stuck with you as much as you're stuck with me, don't you see? There's things I'd rather do than drag me arse to Maryland. Besides, I'm kinder than anyone else Norris could have sent. Or might still. I'll only use one bullet."

Percy smiled slightly, and Flynn decided that the colonel understood him, even if he couldn't like him. His men seemed to sense the tension ease and drifted away. Flynn really hadn't known what to expect when Norris had sent him to join these soldiers. And Flynn hadn't been exaggerating about Norris' long reach. There was no betraying him unless a man wanted to find himself dragged out of bed late at night and dumped into the James River with a hundred pounds of iron chain around his ankles. Flynn himself had performed those exact services for the spymaster.

Considering the company Norris kept, Flynn had expected Percy to be an altogether different man from the gentlemanly, handsome, likable officer he found. Percy looked every bit the dashing Southern hero and Flynn would not be surprised if the man even wore a plume in his hat. He would regret killing him, if it came to that.

"Let's get off the street," Percy said, interrupting his thoughts "This is the sort of discussion we should be having indoors."

Percy led the way into the house, followed by Flynn and then the two who had come out on the porch. The huge black man stayed behind to keep a lookout.

"That was Hudson on the porch," Percy explained as they entered a high-ceilinged parlor to the left of the front door.

"Oh? I thought it was Samson, guarding the temple."

Percy chuckled. "Hudson does not have much faith in humanity. You wouldn't, either, if you had been born a slave."

"I'm Irish. That's close enough."

The colonel nodded at the group of men now staring at

Flynn. "You've already met Lieutenant Cater, I believe. This is the rest of the bunch."

The room was crowded with soldiers. Flynn could see at once that they were all veterans, except for one young fellow who was trying to look fierce, but not quite succeeding. The soldiers shared that same sharp, wary look about the eyes that men who have been in combat frequently develop. These hard-eyed men were all watching Flynn, as was Percy. It was not a friendly welcome.

Flynn smiled at them.

"Well, Sergeant Flynn," Percy said in his no-nonsense officer's voice. "I take it you already know Captain Fletcher?"

The young, arrogant captain, well-dressed as usual, stepped in from another room. He saw Flynn and frowned.

"Why, if it ain't Colonel Norris's bootlick."

"Sergeant," Percy said sharply. "You are speaking to an officer."

"All right. Why, if it ain't *Captain* Bootlick."

That brought laughter from the men in the room. Even Percy couldn't suppress a smile. It was easy to see Fletcher was less-than-popular with the other raiders.

"A pleasure to see you, too, Flynn," said Fletcher, scowling.

Only the man with the bad teeth didn't laugh. He spoke up: "I don't believe we need any more hands on this trip, Colonel," he said, not taking his eyes off Flynn. "Not with this boy Benjamin along. We sure don't need no damn Irishmen who wander in off the street."

"That's Sergeant Hazlett," Percy said.

Flynn forced himself to smile, even though he wanted nothing better than to smash a fist into Hazlett's ugly face. He had always found it the quickest way to settle any questions about the Irish being an inferior race. But he was here to join the raid, not start brawls. Besides, Hazlett was surrounded by friends and Flynn was not eager to take on a room full of soldiers.

"It's not polite to insult strangers, lad," Flynn said, an edge coming into his voice in spite of himself.

Sensing trouble, Colonel Percy raised a hand. "Save it for the Yankees, boys. There will be no fighting here. We don't need the Provost Guard snooping around ... or Colonel Norris, either. We're stuck with Flynn and Fletcher, and they're stuck with us."

Fletcher muttered something under his breath and disappeared into another room. Flynn hefted the strap of the leather satchel off his shoulder and placed the bag on a nearby table with a heavy sound.

"What's in there?" Percy asked.

Flynn turned around. Percy was squinting at him again. Did the man need spectacles? Hazlett was glaring, but Flynn ignored him. "I thought you'd never ask."

Flynn unlatched the satchel's leather flap, then reached inside. He took out a bundled, oily cloth, then unwrapped it to reveal a new, six-shot Colt Navy revolver.

He gave the handgun to Percy and the colonel smiled as he inspected the weapon.

"How did you know we needed guns?" Percy asked.

"Colonel Norris said you might. I happened to know where to find some." It wasn't the truth, but Flynn figured the more he could do to make himself look good, the better.

Percy took the revolver, hefted it, and sighted down the barrel. "At least you're more useful than Fletcher," he said.

Flynn managed to look hurt. "A man hardly knows what to say to such a compliment. Now, what if I were to tell you I knew something about the part of Maryland we'll be riding through?"

"What part?"

"Out beyond Harpers Ferry. I worked on the Chesapeake

and Ohio Canal. Backbreaking work, I can tell you. Nothing but rocks in that soil. As you know, Colonel, the tracks of that train you'll be riding run right along the canal most of the way to the city of Cumberland."

Percy stroked his beard as Flynn waited. Norris had told him that Percy lacked a guide. Of course, Norris was sending Fletcher because the captain was from Maryland—not that Flynn had much faith in Fletcher's abilities as a guide. In any case, Norris hadn't been overly concerned. He pointed out that once Percy and his men were aboard that train, all they had to do was keep the engine stoked and they would end up where they were supposed to rendezvous with the Confederate cavalry. Flynn knew it wouldn't be that easy.

"We don't need no damn Paddy to guide us," Hazlett said. "I reckon we can find our own way."

Colonel Percy held up a hand to silence him. He stared hard at Flynn, who was taken aback by the sudden, flinty expression. Percy, he realized, was not a man to be taken lightly.

"Where we're going, Hazlett, we'll need all the help we can get," Percy said. "If Sergeant Flynn here knows the territory, that's all the better. At least we won't be traveling blind. And you seem to have certain persuasive talents, Flynn."

" 'Tis a gift, sir."

"I've heard that about the Irish. Well, we might need all the gifts we have to get us across Maryland and aboard that train." Percy lowered his voice so the others couldn't hear. "I won't say I'm glad you're here, Flynn, considering you might shoot me in the back at any moment. Don't forget, of course, that we might do the same to you."

"Like I said, let's just do what Norris wants and we'll all get back home alive," Flynn said.

Percy nodded, and turned away. Flynn realized he had been dismissed. He gathered up his satchel.

He found Fletcher in the next room and clapped the captain on the arm so hard he winced. "Looks like we're partners, Captain," Flynn said.

Curling his lip in distaste, Fletcher moved out from under Flynn's hand. "Don't make things worse between us, Flynn. I told these men you were coming, and why."

"That would explain the warm welcome," Flynn said.

Fletcher smiled wanly. "From what I've heard, I'd say you could use all the friends you can get, Sergeant."

For once, Flynn thought, Fletcher had a point.

Flynn left the room, and Hazlett walked over to Captain Fletcher. He had sensed the animosity between the two men and his face wore a sly look that quickly vanished as the captain turned around.

"He's an uppity son of a bitch, ain't he?" Hazlett said. "He ain't got no right to treat a man like you that way, Captain."

Fletcher blinked in surprise. So far, Percy's men had hardly spoken to him. He studied the lean, scarred face and thought that Hazlett looked to be a particularly hard man. A good man to have on your side.

Up close, Hazlett appeared even more terrifying. He was taller than Fletcher by a head, with long, lank brown hair. The scar made him look evil. His smile revealed oddly spaced teeth that resembled fangs.

"Flynn doesn't respect his betters," the captain replied.

"That's the Irish for you," Hazlett said with real venom in his voice. He did not like the Irish because he had seen so many of them come to Virginia before the war and rise to success on their farms or with their small businesses. Meanwhile, Hazlett's own circumstances had hardly improved, despite marrying Percy's cousin. "People got to know their place. Trash like the Irish and the negroes has got to be kept down."

Fletcher agreed completely, although he was surprised to

hear someone like Hazlett put into words the very thoughts that had been going through Fletcher's mind.

"He's uppity, all right," Fletcher said.

"I'll put that Paddy in his place. Don't you worry none about that, sir," Hazlett said, then saluted the captain and walked away.

Fletcher, feeling puffed up by Hazlett's compliments, believed he had just found an ally among the raiders.

CHAPTER 7

IN THE MORNING, Colonel Percy had his band of men walk nearly two miles out of Richmond. The city fell away, replaced by small farms that looked dusty and worn out. Weeds grew in most of the fields they passed and the cattle were all slat-ribbed. Finally, Percy led the men to a meadow ringed with trees and they spread out in an uneasy half-circle, wondering why the colonel had brought them there.

"This morning we're going to have some shooting practice," Percy said.

A couple of the men laughed. "Hell, Colonel, you think we're gettin' rusty here in Richmond?"

Percy turned to Flynn. "Show 'em what you brought along, Sergeant."

Flynn lifted the leather satchel off his shoulder, spread a cloth on a fallen log, and one by one placed several new revolvers on it. The polished wooden grips gleamed in the sun and the well-oiled pistols left a bitter metallic smell in the morning air.

"Colt Navy revolvers," Flynn said. "Brand new, from the armory in Connecticut."

"Yankee guns," Hazlett said. He didn't sound happy about it.

"Some of the best ever made," Percy replied. "Six shots, thirty-six caliber. Small enough to fit in a coat pocket if necessary. And this way we'll all have the same weapons and can use each other's ammunition if necessary."

"Makes sense to me, Colonel," said Silas Cater, walking over to the log and selecting one of the revolvers. "It's got a nice feel to it."

Although all of the cavalrymen had pistols, the problem was that almost all of them carried different models, from Kerr revolvers manufactured in London to Griswold & Gunnison six-shooters made by slaves at a factory in Georgia. Each man was always scrambling to find enough ammunition for his particular weapon.

Hudson had also carried a sack out from Richmond, and he placed it now on the ground next to the log.

"We have holsters for the revolvers here," Flynn said, then reached into the sack and took out a box of cartridges. The box read: *Six cartridges for Colt's Navy Pistol, made at the Laboratory of Confederate States Army, Richmond, Va.* "Plenty of ammunition, too."

Flynn took up one of the revolvers and proceeded to load it, explaining the process as he went: "Pull back the hammer to half-cock to free the cylinder. Put a cartridge in each cylinder, tamp it down with the loading lever, then put percussion caps on each chamber. That's six dead Yankees for you."

Lieutenant Cater deftly loaded a revolver and sighted down the barrel. "Very nice," he said.

"Don't say I never done nothing for you," Flynn said.

Percy took one of the revolvers and loaded it. "All right, boys, let's see how you shoot."

"We're two guns short," Flynn pointed out. "That's all they gave us."

Of course, that wasn't quite true. Back in Richmond, the Confederate Secret Service had supplied him with a revolver for each raider, but he had traded two on the black market for several excellent bottles of whiskey.

Hudson and the downy-faced soldier, Johnny Benjamin, were the two without guns.

"If someone on this side of the Potomac sees Hudson carrying a gun there will only be trouble," Percy said. "I'll give him one once we're on the train. Johnny, you take my Colt for now until we can get you a pistol."

"A darkie sure as hell don't need no gun," Hazlett agreed.

Flynn glanced at Hudson to see how he would react, but his ebony face was stoic. He busied himself sorting the ammunition in the bag.

"Willie, give me your hat," Percy ordered.

Forbes handed it over, and Percy strode through the tall grass of the meadow to a stump about fifty feet away. The stump was cut high, nearly as tall as Percy, and he placed the hat on top. "That there's the enemy," he explained, walking back over to the men. "Just don't shoot any holes in Willie's hat. Aim for the stump. Lieutenant Cater, you go first."

Cater stepped forward, raised the revolver, and fired. At the sound of the gunshot, a flock of crows flew off from the field, cawing in alarm. As they wheeled away, Flynn counted ten birds, exactly the number in their own group. He fought the urge to cross himself as they flew out of sight. He didn't know what the crows meant exactly, but it couldn't be anything good.

The second shot also missed the stump. Hitting a target with a pistol relied more on instinct and experience than using a rifle did. There was no rear sight as with a rifle so you focused on the front sight at the end of the barrel and tried to get a feel for how to aim. It took practice to hit anything that wasn't in spitting distance.

Cater fired again. This time, bark flew from the stump. The next three shots also hit their mark.

Cater turned to Flynn. "You want to practice?"

"Oh, I already did that when I first got the guns," he said, hoping nobody would press it. The truth was, Flynn couldn't shoot worth a damn. He preferred using his fists to settle any differences.

One by one, the other men tested their new Colts. Like Cater, most missed the first two or three shots. Captain Fletcher missed all six. The others laughed out loud.

"That's enough!" Percy shouted. "I haven't seen any of you do much better."

Then came Johnny Benjamin's turn. The boy took the Colt and stepped forward.

"I hope that gun ain't too heavy for you, son. Better use two hands," Hazlett taunted. "I reckon you ought to be old enough to shave before you can shoot."

Ignoring Hazlett, the boy didn't bother to aim the revolver but held the Colt at waist level and quickly fired off six shots that skinned bark off the stump. The last bullet flicked the hat away and sent it rolling through the field.

"Damn it all!" Willie Forbes shouted. "Don't go shooting my hat."

The boy was grinning as he handed Percy back the pistol. "Six shots, six dead Yankees," Benjamin said. "I reckon that's a pretty good start."

"We'll see," Percy said.

* * *

"YOU WILL BE TRAVELING in two groups," Percy explained that afternoon in the crowded parlor of the rooming house. "We don't want to attract attention, which we surely would moving together."

"Where do we meet up?" Pettibone asked.

"Each group will go its own way and cross the Potomac at different points," Percy said. "That should increase the changes that some of us will get through. As long as at least one group arrives at the rendezvous, we can still carry out the mission."

Captain Fletcher stepped forward. "I just wanted to clarify one point, sir, that as the next highest-ranking officer and as Colonel Norris's representative I am second in command."

"No."

Fletcher appeared shocked. "What do you mean?"

"You may be a captain, Fletcher, but on this raid Lieutenant Cater is my official second in command. He knows how to handle himself and he knows what needs to be done. Is that clear to everyone?"

The others nodded approval. Fletcher sputtered something in protest but nobody paid him any mind.

"Let's continue." The colonel went on outlining his plan. Hazlett, Forbes, Lieutenant Cater and John Cook were in the first group. Percy assigned himself to Hudson and Corporal Pettibone. The men he grouped together were all from his old regiment and they were now all on special duty thanks to Colonel Norris.

That left Flynn and Captain Fletcher, along with Johnny Benjamin and two railroad men: an engineer named Cephas Wilson and a fireman, Hank Cunningham. Percy had taken a lesson from last year's failed Andrews train raid in recruiting two men who knew something about locomotives. Andrews hadn't brought any experienced railroaders with him and this had resulted in some difficulty in operating the captured train. Percy didn't want to make the same mistake. It would be up to Wilson and Cunningham to keep the locomotive running all the way from Baltimore to Confederate territory in the Shenandoah Valley. Both men were older than the others, their hair streaked with gray. Their hands were work-hardened and seemed to be permanently stained with soot and oil. Standing among Percy's seasoned veterans, it was clear they were not soldiers.

"You two go with Lieutenant Cater," Percy said to the rail-road men. "If anyone can get you across the Potomac, he can."

Wilson and Cunningham moved off to join their group. Flynn, Fletcher, Pettibone and Benjamin were left standing by themselves in the parlor.

Flynn spoke up. "Looks like I'll be going with you, Colonel. I guess you don't want to let me out of your sight."

"My daddy always told me to keep my friends close and my enemies closer, so I could keep any eye on them."

Hazlett said, "Hell, Irish, the Colonel just reckoned you'd get lost unless you went with him. You and that snot-nose boy. I might just lose you on purpose, if you was to go with me."

"Hell, if Irish and the boy ain't at the rendezvous, it's no great loss," Cook said from the back of the room. "The rest of us will get ourselves there, one way or another."

Beside him, Flynn felt the boy go tense at the remark. He put a hand on Benjamin's shoulder and winked at him, then turned to Hazlett. He had met Hazlett's kind before, men who hated the Irish and other immigrants because they thought the newcomers were crowding them out and robbing them of opportunity. Flynn wasn't one to accept insults lightly, but this wasn't the place for a fight. He decided he would settle accounts with Hazlett when the time came. For the moment, he hid his anger behind a laugh.

"We'll be there before you, Hazlett," he said lightly. "I'll bet you a bottle of good whiskey that this lad and I are waiting for you at the rendezvous."

"It's not a race," Percy interrupted. "You are to reach Elli-cott Mills without any trouble. Go as quietly and as quickly as you can. The real mission doesn't start until that train rolls into town."

The men shuffled impatiently, waiting for him to continue. Percy smiled and produced a thick sheaf of paper money from inside his coat.

"Yankee greenbacks," he said. "You'll each get enough for food and lodging to get you to Ellicott Mills, and to buy tickets for the train. You won't get enough money to buy whiskey or whores, or to play cards. You're on duty from this point on. Consider yourselves as being in the field, not in Richmond."

"I reckon the furlough's over," Forbes said.

"It is," Percy said. "That means no whiskey for you, Forbes. From now on, if you want to get drunk, you have to ask my permission."

Forbes started to protest. "We're still in Richmond, Colonel — "

"Not one drop," Percy said sternly. "For you or anyone else."

"Yes, sir."

Percy counted out a few Yankee dollars to each man. The face of Treasury Secretary Salmon P. Chase appeared on each bill like an omen. Their palms held what seemed like a small amount of money compared to the stacks of Confederate currency needed to buy anything in Richmond. "Don't lose that money now, boys," Percy said. "You're going to need it."

Each man had memorized the route from the Potomac to the little crossroads town of Ellicott Mills, and each also knew which town along the B&O's route he was to buy a ticket for once he had reached the rendezvous. Percy didn't want all the men to buy tickets for Cumberland, thus drawing the ticket clerk's attention.

Willie Forbes spoke up. "What do you think our chances are, Colonel?"

Percy looked around the room at all the faces in front of him. Most belonged to men he had shared many dangers and adventures with since the first days of the war. Good men, all of them, and Percy didn't like the thought that he might be leading them into disaster. Kidnap the president of the United States? It was a risky adventure, at best. When he first spoke the idea out loud it sounded impossible. But now, after thinking about it, the possibilities of it all had taken hold. Percy had been a soldier long enough to know that sometimes the most brash and daring ideas were the ones that worked best of all. His own success during the war had been the result of gambling heavily with his men. But the odds this time were against them.

"All I know is that we're either going to be famous—or dead," Percy said. "Any other questions?"

He looked around at the knot of men in the room. Some faces were stony, some grinning, but no one spoke up. It was as if they were going into battle.

Percy nodded. "Let's go catch us a president, boys."

CHAPTER 8

"You sure do talk a lot," Pettibone finally said to Flynn, who hadn't been quiet for a moment since leaving Richmond.

"That's because you lads haven't got anything to say."

"What's there to talk about?" Pettibone said. "We know what we got to do once we get across the river. I just hope there's something decent to eat in Maryland. Lord, what I wouldn't do for a nice bit of ham."

"All I want is a chance to kill some Yankees," Benjamin said.

Flynn raised his eyes theatrically to heaven. "Help me, Lord. One man thinks of his belly, the other is thirsty for blood."

The raiders had split up early that morning, striking out in their separate groups for the river that marked boundary between North and South.

"So you want to kill Yankees, do you now, Johnny lad?" Flynn asked.

"I reckon I do. I done got wounded down in Tennessee before I could even fire my rifle."

"Well, I hope Colonel Percy gave you a decent pistol,"

Flynn said. "The way you were shooting yesterday, he should have given you one of the new Colts."

Benjamin pushed back his long coat to reveal an unwieldy and old-fashioned looking Model 1842 Horse Pistol. "I reckon this will do just fine."

Flynn pulled his horse up short. He looked shocked. "Percy sent you on this raid with *that*? An old single-shot pistol? Why, lad, I believe General Washington himself carried one of those."

Flynn drew his own Colt Navy revolver and handed it to Benjamin. "Here you go, lad. You'll make better use of it than me, I'm sure."

Pettibone watched the exchange with amusement. "That's mighty generous of you, Flynn. But what are you going to do if we run into some Yankees—talk them to death?"

"Sure, and I'll be using my other gun." Flynn patted his pocket. "A Le Mat revolver imported all the way from Paris. It fires nine shots and a shotgun blast to boot."

Pettibone nodded. "I reckon that ought do the trick."

"What should I do with this old horse pistol?" Benjamin asked.

"Give it to me, lad."

"What are you going to do with it?" Pettibone asked.

"I'll use it as a backup gun. Besides, one shot is all I need," Flynn said. "When I shoot a man, I'm generally close enough that I can stick the barrel in the bastard's belly." He slipped the old pistol into his pocket. "This one will do me just fine."

Pettibone snorted. "You're an odd one, Flynn."

"That's been said before."

"I reckon you're touched in the head, all right, to come with us," Pettibone said. "This is a fool's mission."

"The decision wasn't entirely mine. Besides, I do what I'm told because I know who butters my bread," Flynn said. He then asked as idly as possible, "Don't you have confidence in Colonel Percy?"

"Flynn, I'd follow the colonel to hell and back," Pettibone said. "Come to think of it, I reckon I already have, in some ways. But think of what we're asked to do. The devil himself couldn't pull this off. Kidnap Abraham Lincoln? That's like trying to steal Christ off the cross."

"Don't blaspheme the Lord. It's bad luck," Flynn said.

"You still goin' to shoot Percy?" Pettibone asked. "I have to tell you, Flynn, that I'll kill you first."

"Whatever happens is up to Colonel Percy now," Flynn said, not eager to argue the point with Pettibone. He sensed that the rawboned corporal was one of the few raiders who didn't seem eager to shoot him in the back first chance he got. He looked over at Benjamin, who was busy sighting his new Colt at trees and stumps they rode past, one eye squinted. "The odds don't seem to bother this lad at all. Tell me, Johnny lad, how did you get mixed up with this bunch? What would your poor mother say?"

Benjamin holstered the Colt. "Well, I didn't know nobody in Richmond after I got out of the hospital. I done had me a furlough pass for a few days, but not enough to get home. I just fell in with these fellers, got to drinkin' with 'em, you know, and Colonel Percy fixed up a transfer so I could go on the raid."

"You're a fool to come with us, boy," Pettibone said. "Won't be many comin' back."

"Maybe I'm a fool, but at least I'll be famous."

They laughed. Flynn didn't let the silence afterwards last long. "Tell me about the others," he said.

"Ain't much to tell," Pettibone said. Still, he shrugged, and started to talk.

* * *

ASIDE FROM FLYNN, Benjamin, and the two railroaders, Percy's men were all from Fauquier County in Virginia. They had known each other practically since birth. Silas Cater, for instance, was actually a cousin of Percy's. He had been off at Washington College studying philosophy when the war broke out. He was competent enough at making sure the guard was posted or at holding a flank, but he could never have replaced Percy. Still, he made a good captain and worshipped his older cousin.

Willie Forbes was a hopeless drunk. He drank in prodigious quantities at every opportunity and no amount of punishment could curb his taste for liquor. Oddly enough, he was a good soldier and he was never too drunk to ride. Besides, sober or drunk, he was a good man in a fight.

Bill Hazlett was a son of a bitch but they all put up with him. Most of the men were afraid of him. Percy had made him a sergeant mainly because of family connections. Hazlett, after all, was married to a cousin. However, he was competent enough and inspired a certain amount of fear in new recruits, especially the ones they had been getting recently to fill their regiment's battle- and disease-depleted ranks. Hazlett had a mean streak wider than the Potomac River.

"Why doesn't he like Irishmen?" Flynn asked. "I don't think anyone's been as hostile to an Irishman since Oliver Cromwell showed up at the gates of Drogheda."

"I don't know about this Cromwell you mentioned, but I do know Hazlett," Pettibone said. "It's best to keep on his good side."

"He's a pain in the arse," Flynn said irritably. "I can promise you that he'll be sorry if he ever sees my bad side."

"How did he get his scar?" Benjamin asked. "I reckon it was in a knife fight."

Pettibone snorted. "Not hardly, boy. He come home drunk one night and his wife hit him with a poker."

John Cook had been a farmer back home. Not a very good one, though. When a cow or pig turned up missing, there was a chance you could find it in Cook's pasture—or in his smokehouse. Still, he was a good-enough cavalryman, even if you couldn't leave anything valuable lying about when he was around.

"What about you, Pettibone?" Flynn asked.

Pettibone shrugged. "Well, I ain't that much different from the rest of 'em, I reckon. Got me a little farm, a wife and two young 'uns back home. Them Yankees got my dander up back in sixty-one, and I thought I'd sign up, fight the war, and be back home in two months. Here I am, over two years later."

Flynn laughed. "Sure, and it's better than farming."

"I don't know about that," Pettibone said. "I don't, indeed."

Pettibone had hardly said more than two or three words all at once before he had explained his fellow Virginians to Flynn. They spent the rest of the afternoon swapping stories and talking about what they would do after the war. At nightfall, they stopped at a crossroads tavern and used some of the money Norris had given them to secure a room. Once again, Fletcher kept to himself, and the colonel and his servant went off alone.

Although Flynn didn't let on, he knew the inn well. It was a common stopover for travelers between Virginia and Maryland, even though, officially, there wasn't supposed to be travel between the two warring nations. The innkeeper recognized Flynn, although he knew better than to acknowledge him with anything more than a slight nod.

Once they were settled for the night, Flynn slipped away from his companions long enough to use a pencil to scratch a note on a piece of paper. It surprised some people that Flynn

could write—in fact, he could read and write very well—
although it was a skill he usually kept to himself.

* * *

Nov. 15
   Colonel,
   Fine bunch of misfits you have assembled. They seem very capable. We'll be crossing the Potomac in the morning. Then the fun begins.
   Flynn

* * *

NORRIS HAD INSISTED that Flynn stay in touch with him,
although Flynn himself didn't see the point. What would he
write to Norris about, the weather? But while he was in
Virginia, he would follow Norris's wishes, because the
spymaster had a long arm. Once they crossed the Potomac
into Maryland, Flynn planned to make his own rules—or
some of them, at least.

When he was finished, he gave the envelope to the
innkeeper. The man accepted the note and the Yankee green-
back wrapped around it with the same nod he had given
Flynn earlier.

The envelope was addressed to Colonel William Norris,
Confederate Signal Bureau.

"Send it along to that bastard," Flynn said. Colonel Percy
had since retired to his room, so Flynn bought a bottle of
cheap whiskey, gave Benjamin a cupful, and then he and Pettibone got drunk together in a corner of the inn.

CHAPTER 9

Potomac River, Virginia Shore • November 16, 1863 • 2 a.m.

THE SMUGGLERS WAITED for the raiders in the shelter of a narrow creek that emptied into the Potomac River. The two men were short and wiry, with hands like leather and arms well-muscled from working the oars. The smugglers stood quietly, smoking pipes in the darkness, watching as the raiders stumbled toward them down the steep bank.

These smugglers had made many midnight crossings, ferrying people and goods between the Confederacy and Union. One of Colonel Norris's agents had made the arrangements for that night's services.

However, the smugglers had never carried a black man across the river. They looked sullenly at Hudson's dark face, which shone like ebony in the moonlight.

"Is there a problem?" Percy asked, noticing the men's silence.

"He can row hisself," one of the smugglers said, jerking his chin at Hudson. He coughed up something from deep in his throat and spat into the creek.

Percy, having just traveled at breakneck speed from Richmond to this isolated cove, was in no mood to argue. Mission be damned, he thought, and opened his mouth to tell these water rats what he thought of them. Before he could make a sound, Flynn slipped past him and swatted the smuggler with a powerful blow that knocked the man off his feet.

"That man's an officer," Flynn said, his voice low and harsh. "You best show him some respect."

There might have been more trouble if Hudson hadn't slipped into the skiff, folding his huge frame into the craft with such cat-like grace that not so much as a ripple disturbed the glassy midnight stillness of the creek. He settled himself and tested a pair of oars in their locks.

Unnerved by the swiftness with which the huge black man had moved, not to mention Flynn's bullying, the two smugglers set to work. One motioned the raiders into the skiff. They all slipped into the skiff quietly enough, except for Captain Fletcher, who only managed to climb aboard after noisily thumping his riding boots in the belly of the boat. The noise echoed like a drumbeat across the water.

One of the smugglers swore under his breath and growled at Fletcher, "Hell, boy, there's Yankees all up and down this river. Why don't you just blow a bugle and let 'me know we're about to come over?"

"I hate boats," was all that Fletcher muttered in reply.

Once Fletcher was settled, one smuggler took up the second pair of oars while the other shoved the skiff toward the center of the creek before jumping in and landing soundlessly.

"Don't fall overboard, Fletcher," Percy warned in a whisper. "Those fancy boots of yours will fill with water and pull you down like stones."

Fletcher, chastised on all sides, hunkered even lower in the boat. "That's just as well," he said. "I can't swim, anyhow."

With Hudson and the two oarsmen rowing, and Flynn at the tiller, they soon swept out onto the Potomac.

After the darkness of the creek, which was overhung with trees, the sudden vastness of the big river was stunning. Stars shone overhead, wind moaned, and the black water gurgled around the skiff's wooden skin. The tall banks opposite them looked impossibly far away, but the skiff cut quickly through the river.

"What happens if we see any Yankees?" Percy asked the smugglers.

One of the men snorted. "It's best to row like hell and hope we don't see none."

Percy settled in his seat, feeling naked and exposed on the open river. Cold wind numbed his cheeks and ears. He longed to be on horseback instead of being in this small skiff in the middle of the river. At least on a horse a man had a chance.

He and his men were crossing the Potomac farther south than the second group of raiders led by Captain Cater. Washington would be just a short walk from the opposite shore, if they cared to visit the Union capital. However, this was no sight-seeing trip. Instead, Percy planned to angle northeast as quickly as possible and rendezvous with the other raiders at Ellicott Mills. Percy's small band would have forty miles to cover, but he was sure they could reach the rendezvous in two days.

The shafts of the oars were covered in rawhide to keep them from knocking in the oarlocks, which were themselves greased with lard for silence. A successful crossing depended upon slipping across the river while no Yankee gunboats were in sight. It also required that no unfriendly ears or eyes noticed them from the United States side of the river.

The river was empty as they first launched onto it from the creek's shelter. Each sweep of the oars carried them closer to the safety of the far shore. They were halfway there when there was a distant flash upriver. It took Percy a moment to realize he was seeing moonlight reflecting on a glistening paddle wheel.

"It's a goddamn gunboat!"

Sure enough, a vessel was rounding the bend upriver, its paddle wheel churning through the water and shattering the stillness of the night.

Fletcher drew his revolver.

"Put that away," Percy snapped. "If you fire a single shot, they'll open up on us with their bow gun and blow us out of the water."

The skiff surged ahead as Hudson and the other oarsmen rowed hard. Flynn found a paddle under his seat.

"Take the tiller, Pettibone," Flynn said, and began to dig frantically at the water. Their only hope was to reach shore before the gunboat came closer. Pettibone scooted back and reached for the tiller, pointing the boat toward the river's edge ahead, which lay deep in shadow.

The river crossing had become a race against time. Speed was everything. If the gunboat passed between them and the Northern shore, they would be spotted and cut off. There was no chance of outrunning a paddle wheeler. If the gunboat passed behind them, they still might be able to hide themselves in the shadows cast across the river by the high banks of the Maryland shore. Unfortunately, the current and paddle wheel were carrying the Yankee gunboat toward them at an alarming rate of speed.

"If they spot us, jump over the side," panted one of the smugglers. "Their gun will turn this skiff into kindling but they can't hit a man in the water."

Percy did not like the thought of taking to the cold water with the opposite shore still so far away. He and Hudson were both strong swimmers, but he wasn't sure about the others. The river had November's chill and the current was swift.

"I can't swim," Fletcher protested.

"I can't, either," Benjamin said quietly.

"Then stay with the boat and get blown to pieces, you damn fools," a smuggler snapped at them.

"We'll all stay with the boat," Percy said. "None of us will make it to shore if we don't stay together."

The gunboat swept toward them, looming larger all the time. At the last possible instant, one of the smugglers hissed, "Get down!" and all the men hunkered in the skiff, hoping that in the darkness the Yankees might mistake the boat for a drifting log.

They were so close they could hear two of the men aboard talking and laughing. The Rebels held their breath and prayed. With luck, the Yankee gunboat would sweep past them.

The laughter aboard the gunboat stopped. "What's that in the water, Bill?" came a Yankee's voice, sounding like it was right on top of them.

"It's a log, I guess."

"Hell, that's a boat!" The Yankee sailor raised his voice. "You in the boat, what the hell you doin' on this river? Best state your business."

Crouched in the boat, Percy looked at the smuggler whose face was only yards away from his own. He could smell the rich tobacco smoke from the Yankee's pipe.

"Now what?" Percy hissed.

"I reckon we row like hell," the smuggler whispered back. "It ain't far to shore."

"All right," Percy said, and felt for the butt of his pistol. "Now!"

The men in the skiff sat up and grabbed the oars. They were now in a race for their lives.

"They're running'!" came a shout from the gunboat.

"Halt or we'll fire!"

"Aw, hell," the other smuggler said. "Time to go over the side."

"No, goddamnit," Percy barked at him. "Row, you damn coward. We have to get across this river."

Fortunately for the raiders, surprise was on their side. It took maybe thirty seconds for the Yankee crew members to swivel their gun around and prime it. The gun was only a six-pounder, but it was powerful enough to smash them to pieces if the skiff took a direct hit. Hudson and the two smugglers worked the oars like demons, trying to put as much distance as possible between the gunboat and the skiff before the gun was ready.

"Fire!"

A jet of flame rolled across the river's surface, illuminating the night like lightning, with a thunderclap to match. The cannonball passed so close to the skiff that they all felt the rush of air and heat as it hurtled past, then skimmed the river like a skipped stone.

"Row, row!" Pettibone shouted as he steered the skiff. Fletcher was flopping around in the bottom of the boat like a freshly caught fish, trying to pull off his boots in case they had to swim for it. Percy and Benjamin fired their revolvers at the Yankees, although their guns seemed to do about as much harm as flicking pebbles at the gunboat.

A second shot crashed into the river no more than a foot from the skiff's bow. Cold water showered Hudson in the front of the skiff.

"Hud, you all right?" Percy called.

"Never better, Mr. Arthur," Hudson replied, rowing on without so much as breaking his rhythm. The skiff surged ahead with each powerful stroke.

"Bastards have us in range now," Percy growled. Aboard the gunboat, he could see the Yankees silhouetted against the moonlit sky as they scrambled to reload the swivel gun. He held his breath. They wouldn't miss again.

And then the skiff was in shadow, swallowed up by the darkness cast by the cliffs of the Maryland shore, hidden from the Yankee gunners. A third shot spewed flames and thunder across the river's surface, but the ball threw up a gout of spray several yards to their left. The darkness protected them better than any armor, and the gunboat wouldn't dare chase them close to shore for fear of hidden snags and shallow water.

"Looks like we lost them," Percy said, peering back over his shoulder. He could see the gunboat clearly in the starlight, its lamps shining and the water shimmering as it cascaded off the paddle wheel. On deck, men were cursing, throwing taunts at the night. Smugglers and Yankee patrols played a constant, deadly game here on the navigable portion of the Potomac, and this time, the smugglers had won.

"That was terribly close," Fletcher said in a quavering voice.

Percy suppressed a laugh. He almost felt sorry for Fletcher, who had seen no combat in the service of the Confederate Signal Bureau. He supposed Fletcher was trying to master the fear that gripped most men the first time guns were fired at them.

"We'll be lucky if the Yankees let us off as easy as that the next time," Percy said. "Now let's find a place to land this skiff and get moving before some Yankee patrol shows up on shore to see what all the noise was about."

* * *

IN HIS OFFICE at the Confederate Secret Service, William Norris read the note from Flynn and smiled at the Irishman's description. *Fine group of misfits*. He couldn't have said it better himself.

"The Irish do have a way with words," he murmured to the empty room.

A fire crackled in the small fireplace, making shadows dance on the walls. The only other light came from a single candle on the spymaster's desk. Neither the fireplace nor the candle did much to light the room, and they certainly didn't keep off the cold. Norris was bundled in a shawl against the November chill, with only his hands exposed for writing. The only sound besides the shifting coals came from the scratching of his pen. A glass of bourbon was within reach. His cigar had long since gone out, but Norris kept it clenched between his long yellow teeth.

He stood and walked over to the fire, then dropped Flynn's letter into the flames. It curled up and turned to ash.

Better that there was no record of this mission, he thought. By now the raiders would be in Union territory and if they succeeded, they might help win the war. If they failed, the world might be ready to condemn them for undertaking something as dishonorable as trying to kidnap a president.

Norris walked back to his desk, reached for the glass of bourbon, and raised it toward the flames. "To my fine group of misfits," he said. "You might just hold the fate of the Confederacy in your hands."

CHAPTER 10

Ellicott Mills, Maryland • November 17, 1863

No one paid much attention to the six men who walked down Main Street toward the train station at the edge of the Patapsco River, which seemed like a stream compared to the mighty Potomac. The old granite building was the oldest train station in America on either side of the Mason-Dixon Line.

"Remember that all of us have a different destination," Percy reminded them outside. "And don't stand around talking once you're in there. No sense making anyone suspicious."

With that, the colonel disappeared into the stone build-ing. He emerged a few minutes later after buying tickets for himself and Hudson, then nodded at Benjamin. Nervously, the boy entered the dark interior of the station. Several minutes passed.

"What the hell is taking that boy so long?" Percy wondered out loud. He looked sharply at Captain Fletcher. "Fletcher, get in there and find out what's going on. At least you sound like you're from goddamn Baltimore when you talk. The rest of us sound too much like Southerners."

Fletcher entered the station. It was cool, dark and spot-lessly clean. He saw Benjamin at the ticket counter, fidgeting nervously from foot to foot. One of the B&O ticket agents had come out from behind the counter and was standing between Benjamin and the doorway, as if to block his exit.

Something was obviously wrong.

Fletcher hesitated, near panic, wondering what to do. If there was trouble this early in the mission, it would only mean disaster for them all. He remembered what Percy had said about him being the only one of the raiders who sounded like a Baltimorean, took a deep breath, and called out, "Johnny! Where the hell are those tickets?"

His voice in the empty station echoed like a gunshot and both B&O agents looked up, startled.

"I want to know where those tickets are, boy. I'm waiting."

The ticket agent looked at Benjamin. "I thought you said you only wanted one ticket to Cumberland."

"One ticket?" Fletcher interrupted, sounding exasperated. "Boy, what are you playing at? I distinctly said to buy two tickets."

"Yes, sir," Benjamin said, sounding dreadfully Southern, with the "sir" drawled out as *suhh*. Fletcher knew immediately why the ticket agents were suspicious. All through the war, Marylanders who sympathized with the Confederacy had been trickling South. After all, Fletcher had done the same thing himself when it became clear that Maryland would not leave the Union, mainly because it had become occupied by blue-coated soldiers and its pro-Southern leaders had been arrested. A train trip west to the Shenandoah Valley would be the perfect way to join up with Confederate forces.

"Who might you be?" the agent demanded.

Fletcher straightened his back, threw out his chest and put one hand on his hip. If there was one thing he was good at, it was sounding haughty. He was glad he had worn his best pre-war suit on this journey. "I am Robert Fletcher," he paused to let the name sink in for effect. "Of the Baltimore Fletchers. And if you don't immediately sell my manservant here two tickets to Cumberland I shall report you to John Garrett."

It was as if Fletcher had snapped a whip. John Garrett was president of the B&O Railroad. Fletcher's tone, and the mention of the B&O president, had the agent scrambling to produce the tickets. Fletcher felt pleased that he had once met Garrett before the war and consequently remembered his name.

"We thought the boy might be a Reb," the ticket agent explained hastily. "He sure sounds like one."

"He's from the Eastern Shore," Fletcher said. That was the distant part of Maryland that lay across the Chesapeake Bay and where Southern-style plantation life flourished. "Kent County. They have a Southern inflection there."

The agent obviously didn't know what Fletcher meant, but he agreed, nodding and adding, "Yes, sir."

"Good day," Fletcher huffed, sounding for all the world like the society man he had been. Together, he and Benjamin walked out of the station.

"You was awful uppity in there, Captain," Benjamin said, sounding annoyed. "I ain't never been nobody's servant."

Fletcher ignored him. They crossed the street and went right to Percy.

"That was close," Fletcher said to the colonel. "It was the accent. You'd better have Flynn buy Pettibone's ticket. Those two won't mind an Irishman, but if they hear that drawl of Pettibone's they're going to be suspicious all over again."

Percy turned to Flynn. "You heard him. Buy two."

"Yes, sir."

Flynn soon returned, tickets in hand, and they settled down to wait for the others.

* * *

It was late in the afternoon when the rest of the raiders arrived. Flynn, with a mischievous grin on his face, was waiting on a bench outside the B&O ticket office in Ellicott Mills when Hazlett appeared.

Hazlett glared at him. The sergeant looked tired and dirty after the hard journey from Richmond. His fists clenched and unclenched at his sides when he saw Flynn grinning at him.

"You Irish bastard," Hazlett hissed as loudly as he dared on the station platform. "What are you lookin' at?"

"Is that any way to talk to someone you owe a bottle of whiskey to?" Flynn said. "Store-bought whiskey, too, if you don't mind. My stomach don't take kindly to rotgut."

"I'll be damned if I'd give you a bottle of piss, Paddy, let alone good whiskey." Hazlett practically spat the words.

The smile left Flynn's face, and the eyes that had been twinkling a moment before turned iron gray and cold. The change in expression was so sudden and complete that Hazlett was startled. "I don't want the goddamn whiskey, Hazlett," Flynn said quietly. "In fact, I'd as soon drink piss than take anything of yours, you son of a bitch. And if you call me 'Paddy' again, I'm going to kill you and piss on your goddamn grave."

Hazlett's face turned red with rage, and he stepped toward Flynn.

"That's enough," snapped Colonel Percy, who appeared out of nowhere to step between the two men. "You want to get us all hanged?"

Despite their anger, both Hazlett and Flynn knew the colonel was right. After all, they were deep in enemy territory, and starting a fight now could jeopardize everything if the local constable took an interest. Already, a handful of bystanders had gathered, smelling a fight. Disappointed, they drifted away.

"This ain't the end of it," Hazlett said. He gave Flynn a look of pure malice, then pushed on past into the office to buy his ticket. Percy followed him in.

Pettibone and Benjamin were standing a few feet away and had witnessed the confrontation.

"You've just bought yourself trouble," Pettibone said in his matter-of-fact way. "Hazlett ain't one to let things lie."

Flynn smiled icily. "Neither am I."

"Hazlett don't fight fair," Pettibone warned. "Hell, I reckon I shouldn't even care, considerin' why you're here. But if I was you, I'd watch my back."

Benjamin stepped forward. "I'll stand with you in a fight," he said. He flipped back the tails of his long coat to reveal the Colt revolver in its holster. "Hazlett ain't nothin'."

"Lad, if there's a fight, you keep out of it," Flynn said. "I'll deal with Hazlett when the time comes. I gave you that gun for shooting Yankees, and Yankees alone. And keep that damn gun out of sight. Percy's right, the last thing we need is any more attention."

Despite Colonel Percy's orders to the contrary, Willie Forbes bought a bottle of whiskey. He, Hazlett and Cook sat near the river and drank it. If Percy caught them, he would be furious, especially after the incident between Hazlett and Flynn, but from where they sat they had a clear view up Main Street of anyone coming toward the river. In the distance, they could see Flynn on the sidewalk, talking with a young woman.

"That goddamn Flynn is plenty full of himself," Hazlett said, then took a long pull from the bottle.

"I reckon we're drinking his whiskey, by rights," Forbes said.

"Shut up, Willie," Hazlett said. "You want me to tell Percy you got a drunk on? He'll skin you alive."

Forbes snickered. He was a small man, and the whiskey was already going to his head. "He'll be madder than hell."

"Then you best shut up."

Hazlett watched Flynn cross Main Street in the distance. He hated uppity Irishmen. To him, the Irish were a threat. They came here with nothing and worked for next to nothing, taking jobs from decent Americans. And some of them were smart, oh so goddamn smart, like that bastard Flynn. He didn't know his place. Already, it was easy to see how much the colonel favored him.

Hazlett had an idea. He flipped a coin at Forbes.

"Willie, go get me another bottle of whiskey."

"If the colonel finds out— "

"You let me worry about the colonel."

Forbes scurried off, and Hazlett smiled. He had an idea that would take Flynn down a notch or two.

CHAPTER 11

Ellicott Mills Station • November 18, 1863 • 6 a.m.

PERCY'S MEN were waiting at dawn when the *Chesapeake* steamed into town.

Earlier, they had seen another train come through—just a locomotive and tender. The locomotive had slowed, but had not stopped. The station master had come out to watch it pass.

"That's the *Lord Baltimore*," the man said, admiring the locomotive. He lifted a hand in greeting and the engineer waved back. "She just came out of the factory and she's on her maiden run."

"Where's the passenger train?" Percy asked.

"Should be along any minute now," the station master said, consulting a large, gold pocket watch. "She always runs right on time."

The new locomotive disappeared, and the raiders stood around in the crisp morning air. They could hear the train long before it arrived in Ellicott Mills. Finally, it came into sight, huffing clouds of smoke as it followed the bend in the Patapsco River and slowed for the station. It was a short train, only made up of the locomotive, a tender car loaded with firewood, two passenger cars, a baggage car and a fourth, private car at the rear.

"Don't look like much," Pettibone muttered.

"Sure, and that's just what the Yankees want you to think," Flynn said. "Did you think they'd have flags flapping and trumpets blowing? Lincoln is traveling in secret, don't forget."

Nearby, Hazlett hawked and spat to show what he thought of Flynn's opinions.

Percy was in no mood to listen to anyone's speculations. "Shut up and pay attention," he grumbled at his men. "It's all about to begin."

Willie Forbes moved toward the tracks for a better look. He wasn't watching where he was going and bumped right into Flynn. Briefly, he got tangled in Flynn's long coat.

"Steady, lad," Flynn said, catching a whiff of stale whiskey. "What you need is a drink."

Forbes laughed nervously and moved away.

The train, glinting in the dawn light, looked no different from the others that had passed through town the previous day. Certainly, it wasn't as fancy as the *Lord Baltimore*. Percy felt a nagging doubt. Was the Yankee president really on board? He couldn't help but wonder if Norris, back in his office in Richmond, hadn't made some mistake and sent them all on a perilous journey into enemy territory for no good reason.

Whatever misgivings Percy felt, he couldn't reveal any doubts in front of his men. They had come too far for that. He squared his shoulders and turned to the raiders gathered on the platform. They stood a little apart from the half dozen other passengers waiting to catch the train. Behind Percy, the train rolled closer and a ripple of wind carried the smell of grease, smoke and iron toward them.

"Remember," Percy spoke in a harsh, urgent voice. "Don't

get on in a bunch. Mix yourselves in with the other passengers and use both cars."

Flynn was first in line, and he made sure Benjamin was second. The boy might be full of bravado when it came to threatening to shoot Yankees, but he was also a farm boy who didn't know the first thing about being a passenger on a train.

"Follow me, lad," Flynn said quietly. "Let the conductor punch your ticket, then we'll find a seat."

Finally, the train coasted to a stop in front of the station with a burst of steam and a squeal of brakes. Flynn practically had to pull Benjamin up the steps after him.

"Come on, lad," he said, and led the way through the car to an empty seat.

Flynn glanced around at his fellow passengers. Much to his relief, there were few young men and no Union uniforms. They would be better off without any hot-blooded heroes. Mostly the car was filled with white-haired gentlemen whose folded hands rested securely on their paunches, and matronly women who held baskets of food for the trip.

The exception was a couple across the aisle from where he and Benjamin sat. The woman was slim, dark, and pretty, and the man was dressed in flashy clothes like a gambler. The dandy's arms and broad shoulders strained against the fabric of the suit, which looked to be a size too small for him, and he had a crooked nose that had been broken at some point and badly set.

Flynn had dealt with enough riffraff in Richmond to know the fellow wasn't any businessman, and the woman wasn't any lady in the proper sense. They would bear watching, Flynn decided.

He swiveled in his seat to look around. Pettibone and Fletcher were two seats behind him, and their eyes met his, then glanced away. Cephas Wilson, the engineer, was already in conversation with a portly gentleman. Percy was the last of the raiders to board, and he appeared in the car's doorway and casually walked up the aisle, nodding to Flynn and Benjamin in the same way he nodded to everyone else on the train.

Hudson was nowhere in sight. Maryland might be part of the Union, but that didn't mean a black man could travel with the white passengers. He was riding in the baggage car. The rest of the raiders were in the other passenger car.

"This ain't what I expected," Benjamin grumbled in a low voice. "I thought there would be soldiers around, not old men and ladies. I don't want to kill none of them, even if they are Yankees."

"The longer it takes to pull a gun on this train, the better off we'll be," Flynn muttered in reply. He didn't tell the boy, but he was sure they would have a lot more than old men and ladies to worry about before the day was through.

Aside from Percy's men, only a few passengers got on at the station. Soon, the train lurched forward, and the locomotive up ahead emitted a powerful chug. The noise came faster and faster. Before long the scenery of Ellicott Mills was slipping by and cinders from the smokestack began to clink against the window glass like sleet.

Well, thought Flynn. *It's begun.*

The door of the car opened, and the conductor walked in. He was a bulldog of a man, of average height and stout through the middle. His blue B&O uniform was crisp and the brass buttons gleamed. It made Flynn painfully aware of his own somewhat ragged state after the headlong journey from Richmond.

"Tickets, please," the conductor announced, and began to make his way down the aisle. He took his time, checking tickets, nodding officiously, and answering questions. Flynn recalled the dark car that held Lincoln at the end of the train.

How could the man be so calm knowing such an important passenger was aboard?

He doesn't know, Flynn realized. *Oh, that's lovely for us.*

The conductor was soon at their seat. Beside him, Flynn felt Benjamin go stiff as a bird dog. He touched the boy's knee to calm him.

"Tickets," the conductor said, and Flynn handed over both his own and Benjamin's. The man looked from the tickets to the two men in the seat. "Cumberland. Well. Not many folks headed that way in these times. You hardly know from one day to the next whether it's a Union city or Confederate."

"Let's hope it's Union at the moment," Flynn said. "I've had my fill of fighting those damn Rebs."

Beside him, Benjamin stiffened. Flynn prodded him with the toe of his boot.

"You're a veteran, are you?" the conductor asked with sudden interest.

"Took a bullet at Gettysburg on the third day," Flynn said. "Now that I'm out of the hospital down there to Washington City, I'm on my way to visit my people."

The conductor nodded sympathetically. "I took my bullet at First Bull Run," he said. "That was enough of the war for me. I've been running trains since then."

As he handed back the tickets, the conductor stopped and scowled.

"I don't allow drinking on my train," he said gruffly and loudly enough for the other passengers to hear. "Veteran or not, I don't play favorites."

Startled, Flynn realized the conductor was staring at the neck of a pint bottle of whiskey poking from his coat pocket. Flynn had no idea how the bottle had gotten there. As the conductor moved on with a disapproving air, Flynn felt Colonel Percy's eyes upon him. He looked up and met Percy's angry glare. The colonel had forbidden any drinking—they were soldiers on duty—and the steely eyes held a promise of wrath to come. Besides, the whiskey bottle had attracted unnecessary attention to Flynn.

He was still stumped as to how it had appeared in his pocket. And then he remembered Willie Forbes bumping into him on the station platform. Of course! It was an old pickpocket's trick, only Forbes had used it to put something in Flynn's pocket, not steal something out of it.

Why would Forbes do that?

Hazlett. He must have put Forbes up to it. Forbes would do anything the sergeant told him. Pettibone had warned him Hazlett was a sly bastard. From now on, Flynn knew he would have to watch his back.

Flynn noticed the conductor had nothing but an unfriendly look for the dandy across the aisle. "You again," Flynn overheard the conductor saying to the man. "I remember you from last month. I won't trouble you about your tickets this time."

As the conductor moved on, the man stared at his back, muttered something, and flipped open his jacket to reveal the butt of a revolver.

"Charles," the woman whispered harshly, just loudly enough for Flynn to overhear, and flipped the jacket back over the handgun.

Flynn wondered what it was all about. He was careful, though, not to appear too curious.

The conductor finished checking all the tickets, then moved on to the next car.

"You didn't have to go making friends with him," Benjamin said. "If he hadn't seen that whiskey bottle, I reckon he might have invited you home to supper."

Flynn laughed. "Always make friends when you can, lad. There's more profit in it than in making enemies. After all, when you meet a strange dog, don't you give him your hand to smell first? It will be hard for him to bite it later. It's the same with men."

Outside, the scenery rushed past. It was rough, hilly country, and the leaves were mostly gone from the trees, leaving the landscape bare and brown. The tracks followed the Patapsco River, which twisted and turned through the valley as it led deeper into the countryside. There were far too many curves for the train to move with any real speed, so the raiders bided their time, each mile feeling like an eternity.

As the train rolled on, the raiders in the car exchanged anxious glances.

"Not long now, lad," Flynn whispered to Benjamin.

* * *

Sykesville, Maryland • 8 a.m.

At last, they steamed into a sleepy town ringed by more of the same rough terrain, with houses built into the hills rising above the river. A main street ran perpendicular to the Patapsco, crossing the river at a newly built bridge. J.E.B. Stuart's cavalry had burned the old bridge a few months before on their roundabout ride to Gettysburg.

The biggest building in town was Sykes's Hotel, a four-story tavern near the banks of the river that served as an unofficial train station. The train halted more or less in front of the hotel and the passengers began to get off and amble toward the establishment, which offered hot coffee and buttermilk biscuits with ham to hungry travelers.

"Breakfast!" the conductor called, bursting into the car and striding down the aisle. "Last stop we'll make between here and Harpers Ferry! We leave again in half an hour. Don't be late, ladies and gentlemen."

The conductor himself was soon hurrying toward the hotel with his engineer and fireman.

Flynn leaned close to Benjamin. "Best get ready, lad. It's beginning. Just don't shoot anyone you don't have to."

Not everyone got off the train. Some thrifty passengers had brought their own food, while others appeared content to go without. Flynn noticed the dapper couple from Baltimore stayed put, their breakfast consisting of a few quick nips from a flask passed between them.

Flynn's eyes slid to Percy. He was expecting some sign from the colonel. Benjamin fidgeted on the seat beside him, nervous as a damn puppy. The other passengers talked among themselves or produced their breakfasts from baskets and bags: biscuits, apples, a cold chicken drumstick or two.

"I believe I'll get some air," Percy announced to no one in particular, but loudly enough for all the raiders in the car to hear. "Sykesville, is it? A lovely town."

He stepped out the door.

"What's he playing at?" Benjamin hissed so loudly the dandified couple looked his way. The man had tiny scars at the corners of his eyes, a sign that he had been in his share of fights. He'll be a tough bastard, Flynn thought. Once again, he wondered what the couple was doing aboard the train.

He didn't spend much time wondering, though. He turned to Benjamin. "Do as Percy says, lad," Flynn said quietly. He stood up, stretched, sniffed. "Take the air like a proper gentleman."

"I wish I knew what in hell was going on," Benjamin whispered.

"You will, lad, soon enough."

They left the train and joined Percy on the platform, or what there was of one. Sykesville was not a big town and its train station was minimal, especially considering that the damage J.E.B. Stuart's men had done while riding through last summer had yet to be completely repaired. There was a platform of rough-sawn boards so passengers could get on and off the train without stepping in the mud. The railroad had come to town in 1831, but the closest thing to a train station was Sykes's Hotel.

Outside on the platform, Percy was staring off to the other side of the river. Flynn followed his gaze and what he saw made his breath come out in a gasp.

"Sweet Jesus," he muttered.

"Damn," said Benjamin, seeing it, too.

Flynn realized he had been so busy studying the town as the train arrived that he hadn't bothered to look across the river.

Percy just stared. Captain Cater was now on the platform, as were Wilson and Pettibone. They were soon joined by Forbes and Hazlett.

All of them fixed their eyes on the meadow beyond the riverbank, where a full regiment of Yankees was camped. Across the river, several bored soldiers eyed the train. All of them had rifles in their hands.

Pettibone spat. "At least it ain't cavalry."

But there were nearly a thousand infantrymen, and the Patapsco River separating them from the railroad tracks was so shallow after a hot, dry autumn that the soldiers could easily splash across at the first alarm. The platform was well within range of the enemy's Springfield rifles, although it was doubtful the Yankees would open fire with civilian passengers still aboard the train. The raiders had counted on the *Chesapeake* stopping for breakfast, but not on a regiment of Yankees using the town as a campground.

That wasn't the worst of it. Three soldiers swung down from the baggage car and walked out onto the platform. All three carried rifles with fixed bayonets. They eyed the men on the platform suspiciously. Hudson came out of the car and sat on the iron steps. Behind the soldiers' backs, he held up three fingers, pointed at the Yankees, then pointed at the car and made a circle with his fingers to indicate no one else was inside.

"Who the hell are they?" Forbes asked.

"Guards," Percy said. "Lincoln's on the train, remember? It makes sense they didn't send him entirely alone."

"Now what?" Pettibone wondered out loud, speaking for all of them. They hadn't planned on hijacking the train in plain view of a Yankee regiment.

Percy just stared across the river, thinking

CHAPTER 12

"Look at all them Yankees," Hazlett said. "We can't steal the damn train now. Ain't that right, Colonel?"

Percy appeared not to have heard. He was busy studying the Yankee camp across the river. When he finally spoke, it was to give orders: "Captain Cater, take Private Cook with you and go to the rear of the train and get up on the last car. If anyone chases us, they'll try to jump on the back. Don't let them."

"That's Mr. Lincoln's car, sir."

"Yes, but don't worry yourself about that. Lincoln and whoever else is with him will stay holed up in that car like gophers, which is just where we want them. No one is supposed to know they're aboard, remember? Lincoln isn't about to show himself."

Percy quickly gave the rest of his orders. He sent Cephas Wilson and Hank Cunningham to the locomotive and told them to get the train underway. He ordered Hazlett, Forbes and Pettibone aboard the tender, to help the railroad men in any way they needed.

"If there's any shooting that needs doing, you men take care of it and let those two run the train," Percy said.

"What about us, Colonel, sir?" Flynn asked when he found that he, Benjamin and Fletcher were the only ones left on the platform with Percy.

"Fletcher, you and I will take the first passenger car," Percy said. He nodded at Flynn and Benjamin. "You two take the second car. If any of the passengers cause trouble, shoot them."

"All right," Flynn said. He looked toward the Yankee soldiers on the platform. "What about the guards?"

"Hudson will take care of them."

The massive driving wheels of the *Chesapeake* began to move, and a fresh gout of smoke filled the air. Inside the locomotive's cab, Cunningham opened the blower and increased the air flow to the locomotive's firebox so the wood could burn hotter.

The train was still under steam, and using both hands, Wilson took hold of the Johnson bar, which was about three feet tall and jutted straight up from the floor of the locomotive right beside the engineer's seat. He shoved it forward, putting his weight into it, and the train began to roll.

He pulled back the two-foot long throttle lever, gave the locomotive a burst of steam, then shoved the throttle forward again, shutting off the steam. He repeated this action three times, which got the locomotive rolling more effectively than opening the throttle wide open. That would only have caused the wheels to slip uselessly on the rails. Still, the driving wheels spun as they sought purchase on the well-polished rails. Wilson reached up and pulled a handle at the end of a long bar which ran the length of the locomotive to the sand box atop the forward end. Tubes ran down the sides of the locomotive, spitting sand on the rails just in front of the wheels to give them traction.

As the train began to move, Flynn ran for the second car with Benjamin close behind him. The boy had already pulled out the Colt Navy revolver, and Flynn stopped and gently laid a hand on the gun before they reentered the coach.

"Remember, lad, I gave you that gun to shoot soldiers, not old ladies. Best put it away till you need it. And need it you will, before the day is out."

"Goddamnit, Flynn— "

Flynn glared at him. "That's Sergeant Flynn to you, lad, and I'm tellin' you to put that gun away. No use in causing trouble just yet."

Benjamin gave him a sullen look, but did as he was told. They returned to the car they had ridden out from Ellicott Mills. Already the train was moving, groaning, shuffling ahead like an old man.

As the train began to roll, the three soldiers on the platform ran for the baggage car.

"It's leavin' without us, fellas," one of the men shouted.

The guards had no reason to think the train was being stolen, so they did not shout for help to the soldiers across the river. Hudson was no longer sitting on the steps, but was waiting just inside the open doorway of the car. As the three guards crowded onto the narrow walkway at the front of the car, Hudson jumped out and used his massive arms to grab up all three startled guards in a bear hug. He hurled them off the train before they could even cry out in protest.

The guards landed in a heap on the far side of the train, out of sight of the encamped soldiers. One man writhed on the ground in pain, holding an arm that was twisted at an odd angle. Another guard jumped up and ran at Hudson, but he kicked the man neatly in the jaw and the soldier flopped to the ground.

The third man ran toward the train, bayonet at the ready, but he backed off when he saw the Colt revolver in Hudson's hand. The guard raised his rifle to fire, but the train was picking up speed, and Hudson was already out of sight, giving the guard the side of the car as a target.

"Thieves!" he shouted, although the train drowned him out as it rolled away from the platform. "Thieves!"

* * *

"Biscuits and coffee for us," George Greer said to Mrs. Sykes, scooting his chair closer to the table in the dining room of Sykes's Hotel.

"Lots of coffee *und* butter for the biscuits," added Oscar Schmidt, the engineer. He still had a hint of his German accent, even though he had lived in Baltimore for twenty years, and pronounced his "W's" as "V's." "It *vill* be a long journey to Cumberland."

"Hungry work," agreed Walter Frost, the fireman. It was his job to keep water in the *Chesapeake's* boiler and a steady supply of wood in the firebox. He was not a large man but he was sinewy and muscular. His hands were like leather, the fingers square-tipped stubs from handling cordwood all day. He had washed before entering the hotel, but ash still clung to the creases in his face and to his hair.

The three railroad men had made the run to western Maryland many times. Greer and Schmidt had worked together for years and knew each other almost as well as they knew their own wives. Frost wasn't married, although there was a war widow he got on well with in Baltimore.

"What do you reckon is in that last car?" Frost asked. It had been attached to their train in the early morning hours as they left the city. An officer had told them it was being added to their train and that they should leave the car alone. He had been emphatic about that.

Greer shrugged. "Army business," he said.

He was just as curious as Frost, of course, but he knew better than to be too inquisitive where the military was concerned. B&O officials assisted the military whenever possible, because they counted on the army to guard the tracks against marauding Confederates. Consequently, his bosses would not look kindly upon a nosy conductor.

It was bad enough that they were carrying the payroll for the Cumberland garrison. Greer guessed the mysterious car held nothing more interesting than good whiskey for the general at Cumberland, or possibly even a couple of Baltimore whores for the officers. He had heard of such things, and while he didn't necessarily approve, he knew better than to question them out loud.

Schmidt spread butter on a biscuit, wolfed it down, then slurped noisily at his coffee.

"Damn *goot*," he said. "This should hold me until lunch in Harpers Ferry."

Greer laughed. "Always thinking of your belly, aren't you, Oscar?"

"A man can't work on an empty stomach."

The three men laughed and went on eating.

As Greer went to take another sip of coffee, his gaze settled on the train across the river. He stopped laughing, and his coffee cup froze halfway to his mouth.

"What is wrong?" Schmidt asked.

Greer barely heard him. He was busy watching a plume of thick, black smoke coming from the *Chesapeake's* funnel, a telltale sign that someone was stoking the firebox.

"Look at that," he said, aghast. His two companions turned, just in time to see the train lurch ahead, then start down the tracks.

Schmidt swore. "Someone's taking our train!"

In the distance, they could barely hear someone shouting, "Thieves! Brigands!"

Suddenly the dining room exploded into action as the three men jumped up from the table. Coffee spilled, chairs fell over and a plate of biscuits clattered to the floor.

"Where are ya'll goin' ?" called Mrs. Sykes, running from the kitchen in alarm, but the railroad men were already out the door, sprinting for the bridge across the Patapsco.

* * *

ABOARD THE TRAIN, the passengers appeared only mildly concerned that the *Chesapeake* was slowly rolling out of Sykesville, even though several of their fellow passengers were still having breakfast at Sykes's Hotel.

"What's going on?" a fat matron demanded of Flynn, who had just come from outside.

"Not to worry, ma'am," he said, tipping his hat. "I believe there's something to load on the last car, and the engineer had to pull the train ahead a few feet to bring the car even with the platform."

Flynn spoke in a voice loud enough for the other passengers to hear, and his explanation seemed to satisfy the woman, who settled back down in her seat.

"Well, we're going awfully fast," she huffed.

The train gathered speed. Flynn expected at any moment to hear the shooting begin, but all was quiet except for the growing noise of the iron wheels turning ever faster on the rails beneath them.

"Young man, I don't believe we're going to stop," the matron spoke up, sounding annoyed, as if she knew Flynn had misled her.

"The engineer must be drunk," he said lamely. "It's been known to happen."

No one took exception to that. It seemed as good an explanation as any. Flynn looked out the window. They were moving much faster. The train rolled past a man on foot, quickly outpacing him. Trees flickered past. The brown autumn grass was a blur.

Flynn thought of all those Yankee soldiers nearby and expected at any moment to hear gunshots. Seconds passed, and the only sound was the scrape and clatter of iron wheels on the rails. He realized his armpits were damp and his palms sweaty.

Damn, he thought. We did it.

"Stay here, lad, and don't move until I tell you," he ordered Benjamin, and stepped out into the aisle. He made his way to the front of the car. Flynn didn't want any of the passengers to leave the car, but he also didn't want to make it seem as if he were guarding the door. That would come soon enough. He stood by the stove in the corner of the car and spent some time fishing a cigar out of his pocket, then patting down his coat in a search for matches.

"Someone ought to go up and tell that engineer to stop," the fat matron said. "People have been left behind at the station."

Flynn didn't volunteer.

She cleared her throat loudly. "Young man— "

"I'm sure the engineer knows what he's doing, ma'am," he said easily, although he felt his armpits become more damp. Trouble was starting.

She turned to her husband, a white-haired gentleman beside her. "Alfred, pull the signal cord. That engineer must stop this train."

The signal cord was suspended by straps from the ceiling of the passenger car. The cord ran the length of the train, all the way to the locomotive, and was used when the conductor wished to signal the engineer. Tugging on the cord sounded a bell up in the locomotive's cab. This system saved the conductor from making a somewhat perilous trip across the tender to the locomotive itself.

From the resigned way in which her husband silently complied, it was easy to see he knew better than to argue with his wife. He was past sixty, paunchy, and puffed a bit as he stood up and reached for the signal cord overhead.

Flynn gave his pockets a final pat, then let his hand rest beneath his coat on the butt of his Le Mat revolver.

"I'm afraid you'll have to sit back down, sir," said Flynn, as he walked down the aisle and came up beside the man.

"What are you talking about?"

"Conductor's orders, sir. Please sit down."

"I'll do no such thing." The old man was as stubborn as his wife. "Now, if you'll kindly step aside— "

Almost casually, Flynn pulled out the Le Mat and leveled it at the man's belly. The old man's eyes grew wide in disbelief. "What's all this about?"

"Sit down."

Wide-eyed, the old fellow retreated to his seat. His back had blocked Flynn's gun from view of most of the passengers, but some up front had seen the huge revolver. A woman gasped. A man cried out, "Now see here— "

"Shut up," Flynn said harshly, and he moved down the aisle, the brutal-looking Le Mat revolver in plain view. "Listen up everyone. I am a Confederate soldier. Several of us on board have commandeered this train. We're taking it west. Now, we're not in the business of shooting civilians, but we will if we must. The best way not to get shot is to stay in your seat and keep quiet."

The portly matron began muttering indignantly. "This is a travesty. Where's your uniform? Soldiers? I doubt it! You're nothing but common thieves."

Flynn moved toward her.

"Shut up, Henrietta," her husband said, clapping a hand over her mouth. "He's an outlaw. He'll shoot you."

"That's right, sir. I'll shoot her if she opens that big mouth of hers again." He winked. "From the looks of it, I may be doing you a favor."

No one else spoke. The train was moving even faster. Flynn was just beginning to think everything was going well when two hard-looking men who were sharing a seat stood up.

Damn, thought Flynn. Quickly, he glanced at Benjamin, who nodded and quietly slipped his own revolver from a coat pocket.

One of the men spoke up. "Way I see it, they ain't but one of you," said one of the men. He smiled. "And they's two of us."

"Don't do it, lads," Flynn said.

Everything seemed to happen in slow motion. Both men clumsily drew revolvers. Someone screamed.

Flynn fired. His bullet missed and blew out one of the windows at the back of the car. He fired again and his bullet ricocheted off the stove pipe in a flash of sparks. More women were wailing. A bullet snicked past his ear.

To his right, Johnny Benjamin jumped up and shot one of the men through the head. Flynn got off another shot, and this time he was dead-on, the Le Mat's .40-caliber slug knocking the remaining man into the seat behind him.

"Nobody move!" Flynn shouted.

The gunfight had lasted only seconds. Flynn's ears rang. The car was filled with bluish smoke and stank of sulfur. A woman cried hysterically, while a terrified hush had fallen over the other passengers.

"Stop that wailing," Flynn shouted at the crying woman. He raised the Le Mat and swung the muzzle around the car, demanding, "Any other Yankees present?"

No one moved. Finally, a bald, bespectacled man spoke up. "This one's still alive," he said. He was bent over the man Flynn had shot. There was a ragged hole in the wounded man's chest that was making ugly, bubbling noises. Pink froth showed at the man's lips and his eyes flicked desperately around the car. Flynn had seen enough men lung shot to know that the man had just minutes to live.

"Help me drag him out," Flynn said to the man with the glasses.

"He shouldn't be moved— "

"Shut up and grab his feet, you four-eyed son of a bitch, or I'll shoot you, too."

The man hurried to grab the feet.

Flynn turned to Benjamin. For all his talk about shooting Yankees, the boy was white as a boiled shirt. Flynn clapped him on the arm to snap him out of it. "Keep an eye on the passengers," Flynn said, speaking loudly so everyone in the car could hear. "Shoot anyone who moves."

Benjamin managed to nod, but kept his lips drawn into a tight line.

The door opened and Captain Fletcher appeared. "Colonel Percy sent me to see what all the shooting was about."

"Nothing we can't handle, Fletcher, unless you want to give us a hand with these bodies?"

Fletcher gave him a horrified look, then withdrew.

Flynn and the passenger carried the dead man out first, laying him on the small platform outside the car.

"What's your name?" Flynn asked the passenger.

"William Prescott."

"What do you do, Mr. Prescott? Obviously, you're not a soldier."

"I'm a lawyer," he said. "I have a practice in Baltimore."

Flynn smirked. "It's a shame you couldn't have gotten a bit of business from these two writing their wills. Too bad."

They went back for the wounded man. He was still alive, wheezing hard, his mouth ringed with pink froth from his lung wound. They laid him next to the dead man.

"He needs help or he's going to die," Prescott said.

"Oh, he's going to die, all right."

Then, as Prescott watched in horror, Flynn kicked first the corpse and then the wounded man off the platform. The train was moving at a good speed and the bodies bounced and tumbled, then flopped in the brush along the tracks.

"Oh my God," Prescott stammered. "You killed him."

"That was the idea," Flynn said, enjoying himself just a little too much. "Lung-shot like that, he had a minute or two to live before he drowned in his own blood. We did the fellow a favor. Now shut up and sit back down—unless you want me to throw you off the train, too."

White-faced, the fat lawyer scurried back into the car, and Flynn followed, wondering how long it would be before he had to shoot someone else.

CHAPTER 13

GREER DASHED across the bridge and raced down the tracks after the *Chesapeake*.

"Come on!" he shouted over his shoulder at Frost and Schmidt, who were already falling behind. Schmidt's huge belly flopped like a tub of raw sausages as he ran and Frost wasn't much faster than the big German.

But someone was stealing his train, and blind rage was enough to propel Greer in a sprint down the tracks. The uneven railroad ties threatened to trip him at every stride and his leg ached from his old battle wound, but Greer stuck out his chin, pumped his arms, and ran for all he was worth.

Up ahead, he could just see the last car of the train, where two men stood on the platform. They were rapidly disappearing from sight.

Greer knew damn well that a man on foot couldn't overtake a train. However, he was counting on the train stopping before long. It was one thing to get a locomotive rolling—with a little luck, almost anyone could do it if there was still a head of steam in the boiler—but it was another thing altogether to keep it moving. He was sure they would find the train around the next bend.

He took a quick look over his shoulder and saw Schmidt and Frost still lagging behind. Greer had hoped a few soldiers would join the chase, but so far only the engineer and fireman were in sight.

"Run!" he shouted at them. "We've got to catch that train!"

* * *

INSIDE THE PASSENGER CAR, Flynn saw that Benjamin still had his Colt at the ready, and the lad was keeping a close eye on the passengers. He looked pale, but the hand that held his revolver was steady enough. The passengers themselves were coping by various degrees. Some sat stone-faced, others cried, a couple of men looked angry enough to try something foolish, but Flynn decided they must be unarmed, or else they would have acted along with the two men he and Benjamin had been forced to shoot.

The blustery old couple, Alfred and Henrietta, looked indignant and rumpled, like hens caught in the rain. The image made Flynn smile, but his grin faded when he noticed the Baltimore tough and his woman. There was not the slightest hint of fear on their faces. Among all these hens, they had the look of foxes, Flynn thought. Cunning. The gunfight hadn't scared them a bit.

He touched Benjamin's arm. "Keep an eye on those two," he whispered. "They'll be the next to make a move."

"All right," the boy said.

He gave Benjamin's arm a squeeze. "You did good, lad," Flynn spoke quietly. "Those men didn't give us any choice."

"I know."

"If it comes to using your gun again, lad, don't hesitate,"

Flynn warned him. "If you do, you'll be the dead man next time. Shoot first, think later."

Benjamin nodded, as if he understood. Flynn hoped the boy did, because he was sure many more shots would be fired before the day was through.

* * *

GREER'S ARMS felt as if they were on fire and his legs were heavy as logs, but he would be damned if someone was going to steal his train and get away with it. He kept running.

Slow as the train had started, it quickly gathered speed. The harder Greer ran, the further ahead the train seemed to get. Soon he watched it disappear around a bend, and he staggered to a halt, doubled over, and gasped for breath. Frost and Schmidt ran up behind him. They hadn't been running nearly as hard and weren't as winded, and they had brought along a young captain astride a chestnut mare. No other soldiers were in sight.

"Where were you five minutes ago?" Greer panted, glaring at the mounted officer. He hawked and spat, trying to catch his breath. "You could have caught them on that horse."

"What seems to be the trouble?" the captain asked. He was no more than twenty-one or two, young and arrogant.

"Deserters stole my train," Greer snapped, the captain's nonchalance beginning to gall him. "That's the trouble."

"What deserters?" the captain asked.

"From your regiment, most likely."

"We don't have any deserters that I know of."

Greer scowled, but the captain appeared not to notice. Greer started over from the beginning. In the distance, he could hear the sound of the train—*his* train—receding and finally being lost in the noise made by the nearby Patapsco as it gurgled over the rocky riverbed.

"Someone took our train," he said. "If you send ten men with me, I'm sure before long we'll find the train stopped down the tracks a mile or two from here, and your boys can arrest— "

The captain held up a gloved hand. "That train is your concern."

"But deserters— "

The captain wheeled his mare and started back toward the station. He called back over his shoulder: "Maybe deserters took your train, but they weren't ours. It's none of my concern."

Greer cursed as the captain rode off. He couldn't believe the officer wouldn't help. Someone had stolen the train, and the captain didn't give a damn. With officers like that, no wonder it was taking so long to win the war. He was just like all the rest of the fools back at First Bull Run who had gotten him wounded and then lost the battle.

"Come on," he growled at Frost and Schmidt. "We'll find our own goddamn train."

Greer started off down the tracks at a jog. Frost and Schmidt were right behind him.

"This doesn't look good," Schmidt said. "We let our train be stolen. If anything happens to the *Chesapeake*, we can say goodbye to our jobs on the railroad."

They ran a little faster.

* * *

COLONEL PERCY LEFT the first passenger car and climbed toward the engine, sending Cook, Hazlett and Forbes back to join Captain Fletcher in keeping watch over the passengers. He didn't trust Fletcher on his own. None of the passengers in their car had given them any trouble when they announced the takeover of the train. Of course, the Colt revolvers in the raiders' hands had not encouraged the passengers to speak up.

Pettibone stayed to guard the engine. Percy climbed over the tender—an open car stacked high with wood—and onto the locomotive itself, where Cephas Wilson and Hank Cunningham worked like madmen to wring more speed out of the *Chesapeake*.

Wilson sat in the engineer's seat to the extreme right of the cab. He had the throttle wide open, but he was now working the Johnson bar back toward the neutral position.

"Give me a hand, Colonel," Wilson said by way of greeting. Because of all the steam pressure, the Johnson bar was incredibly difficult to move. Wilson had straddled the bar, with one foot on an iron stirrup and the other on a wooden chock. Both footholds had been put there to give an engineer leverage when wrestling the bar forward or backward. Percy grabbed hold, and the two men managed to work the bar back until it was nearly straight up and down.

"Don't you want this all the way forward?" Percy asked. The Johnson bar was basically a combination of gear shift and throttle. Pushed all the way forward, the locomotive went at its greatest speed, while the middle position left the engine virtually in neutral.

"We're rolling along pretty good now," Wilson explained. "With the reverse lever in that position we'll save wood and water and still make good time."

The engine had been slow getting out of Sykesville and Percy was concerned that unless they built up speed and put some distance between the town and themselves, cavalry might catch them if they slowed down for any reason.

"How is she running?" he shouted over the roaring engine.

Wilson answered with a wide grin. "She can roll, yes sir, she can. With the throttle wide open she'll maybe do sixty miles an hour on a level stretch."

"How fast are we going?" Percy shouted.

Wilson looked out the window at the ground. Any experienced engineer could tell within ten miles per hour how fast his train was going by how blurred the ground below looked.

"About forty," he said.

"Can we go faster?"

Wilson laughed and jerked his chin at the tracks ahead. The bright steel rails closely followed the river bed, twisting and turning with the narrow Patapsco.

"You want us to end up in the river? She won't stay on the tracks at sixty. Not here, anyway. I'll keep her at forty, Colonel. There's still not a horse that can catch us."

"All right," Percy agreed. He would have liked to run faster, but he had to admit that even forty seemed like a reckless speed as the gray, leafless trees flickered past.

"We'll open her up once we get beyond the Patapsco," Wilson said. "It's good, flat country up ahead."

Hank Cunningham shoved by with an armload of wood. His coat was off, his sleeves rolled up, and sweat stood out on his face as he threw open the door to the firebox and tossed a chunk of wood into the glowing red maw. He was careful to keep the wood in an even layer several inches deep so that it created an even heat inside the firebox.

Turning, Percy leaned out from the locomotive's cab as far as he dared and looked back at the tracks leading to Sykesville. There was no sign of pursuit. Of course, they were traveling so fast that no cavalry squadron could keep up, especially over the rough, uneven footing of the track bed. Still, Percy thought it was a good thing that it had been infantry, not cavalry, camped back in Sykesville.

"Wilson, we'll be crossing the Washington Road in about three miles," Percy said. "I want you to stop, and I'll have Willie Forbes shimmy up the telegraph poles to cut the wires. We can outrun cavalry, but we can't outrun the telegraph and

we don't want the Yankees to put a barrier across the tracks
somewhere ahead of us."

"Yes, sir," Wilson said. He eased the throttle open a notch
wider, and they roared along the twisting tracks as quickly as
they dared.

* * *

GREER FOUND the first body lying face down across the
tracks.

"Lord have mercy," he said, stopping to flip the man over
with the toe of his boot. From the man's face, he recognized
him as one of the passengers from the *Chesapeake*. There was
an ugly purple bullet hole in the man's temple.

He felt a wave of nausea wash over him. The sight of the
bullet wound brought back memories of the terrible things he
had seen on the battlefield at Bull Run. He forced himself to
look away from the dead man.

A shout from Schmidt interrupted his thoughts. "Greer,
up ahead!" Schmidt shouted.

Another body was sprawled alongside the tracks. Blood
stained the front of the dead man's shirt.

"They're shooting the passengers," Greer said in disbelief.
The situation was even worse than he had imagined.

"Maybe these two tried to stop them," Schmidt pointed
out.

"If that's what happened, then we're dealing with murderers, not just train thieves," Greer said. His horror at the sight
of the dead men had turned to anger. He clenched and
unclenched his fists. "Whoever is doing this needs to be
brought to justice."

"It ain't right," Frost agreed.

"Let's go."

Greer set off at a run down the tracks, cursing at his engineer and fireman to keep up the pace. Frost was young enough that he hardly broke a sweat as they moved through the dappled November sunshine. He was in good shape from hauling wood from tender to firebox. Greer decided Frost could most likely run all day long, but he only seemed to have one speed and it wasn't fast enough.

Schmidt was another matter. He was fond of his German wife's cooking, and he washed down his schnitzel and sauerkraut with great quantities of beer from Baltimore's breweries. His huge belly bounced as he ran and his lungs chugged like the steam locomotive he normally operated on these same tracks.

"*Mein Gott*," he panted. "Let them have the damn train."

"Shut up and save your wind," Greer snapped. "We've got to catch these damn thieves."

"What will we do if we catch them?" Schmidt huffed. "They killed two passengers. What do you think they'll do to us? We don't even have a gun."

Before finding the bodies, it hadn't occurred to Greer that the train thieves probably had guns. Neither he, Schmidt nor Frost were armed. Well, he decided, they would worry about that when they found the train. With any luck, the thieves would abandon the train as soon as it ground to a halt.

Greer thought they would have found the *Chesapeake* by now. They were already three or four miles out of Sykesville. There might have been enough steam left in the boiler to get the train moving, but someone aboard knew something about running trains to get her this far.

He still believed that deserters had taken the train, even if the surly young captain back in Sykesville had claimed otherwise. Many men were making a career of signing on for the bonus money offered new recruits, then deserting and signing up yet again to collect more money. A train would be a handy means of escape for men like that. Deserters might also be desperate enough to commit murder, knowing that a hangman's rope or a firing squad most likely awaited them if they were caught.

One of the deserters must have had some knowledge of trains to keep the *Chesapeake* running this far. Still, at any moment, Greer expected to come across the train stopped on the tracks. He braced himself to deal with the irate passengers who would be spilling out from the cars, wondering what had happened.

The train thieves would be long-gone, and Greer would have to back the *Chesapeake* the few miles into town to pick up the passengers left behind at Sykes's Hotel. The incident would be embarrassing, but not disastrous.

They ran another mile, but there was no train. Not even a sign of the *Chesapeake*. No screech ahead of wheels on iron rails. No plume of smoke above the treetops. The train had vanished.

"Bastards," Greer cursed the thieves. He was sure the owners of the B&O Railroad might just be inclined to fire a train crew who had allowed a locomotive and several cars to be stolen, all because they had stopped for breakfast. "Why would they take my train?"

"Payroll money," panted Frost, struggling to keep up. "Must have been several thousand dollars in that baggage car."

Greer dismissed the idea. "If thieves wanted the payroll money, it stands to reason they would have taken the money, not the entire train," he said. "Besides, the baggage car had been well-guarded."

It never occurred to any of them that the last car, mysteriously attached to the train during the night, had anything to do with the morning's events.

"Whatever the reason, the directors of the B&O Railroad

aren't going to be happy about what had happened," he added.

Anger gave him new strength and he ran faster, determined to find the *Chesapeake*. He knew it was the only hope of redemption he, Schmidt and Frost had.

"Nobody steals my goddamn train," he panted.

"For pity's sake, Greer," Schmidt gasped, sounding close to collapse. "I can't keep this up much longer."

"Shut up and run," Greer growled.

CHAPTER 14

Hood's Mill, Maryland • 8:45 a.m.

A FEW MILES up the tracks, the *Chesapeake* was coming to a halt, not because it had run out of steam, but because Colonel Percy had ordered it. The train crept across the Washington Road and stopped.

"Keep her under steam," Percy told Wilson. "We'll only be here a few minutes, just long enough to cut the telegraph wires."

Percy jumped down from the locomotive and ran back to the cars. He was anxious to get as far as possible before there was any sign of pursuit, but he hoped cutting the wires would increase their chances of escape. Several of the raiders were leaning out the windows to see what was going on.

"Keep one man in each car to guard the passengers and the rest of you get down here," Percy shouted. "We have work to do. Forbes! Where the hell are you?"

A head appeared in a window. "Here, sir!"

"Get out here. I have a job for you."

The raiders quickly jumped down and gathered near the locomotive. Lieutenant Cater came running up from the last car, the one that held Lincoln, but Percy waved him back.

"All right, boys, we're going to do two things while we're stopped—cut the telegraph wires and pull up a couple of rails in case the Yankees send a train after us. First, I want to know how the passengers are behaving."

Flynn spoke up. "Well, sir, we had to shoot two of them."

Percy blinked in surprise. "Dead?"

"Yes, sir. I got one and the lad got the other."

"I hope you had good reason."

"They hauled out guns and decided they weren't going to put up with the likes of us. They were Yankee veterans, Colonel, acting brave."

Percy nodded. Nearby, Hazlett sneered, as if Flynn had failed somehow.

"All right," Percy said bitterly. "What's done is done. Let's try not to shoot anyone else. I hadn't counted on there being so many people on board."

"They look just like cattle," Hazlett muttered in disgust, staring back at the passengers watching from the windows.

Percy wasn't finished. He turned to Flynn with a steely glare. "And I better not catch you drinking any goddamn whiskey, Flynn. You sure as hell set off that conductor back there—you could have put us all in danger. I know you were sent to keep an eye on me, Sergeant, but I'm in command of this raid, and you'll do as I tell you."

"I hear you."

That was as good a dressing down as he'd ever had in his previous short career as a soldier. Flynn realized he still had the whiskey bottle in his coat pocket, and he pulled it out and pitched it away. He knew trying to explain to Percy how the bottle had ended up in his pocket was pointless. Flynn glanced at Hazlett, and noticed the sergeant was grinning.

Forbes watched with greedy eyes as the bottle landed with a thud in the bushes, unbroken.

"We could put all the passengers off right here, sir," Pettibone suggested.

"They would have the Yankees onto us in no time," Flynn said. "This is a settled area and we're sitting on one of the major roads out of Washington City. There's another road just three miles south of here that carries all the traffic going west out of Baltimore. Cavalry passes all the time on both these roads."

"Flynn's right," Percy said. "Nobody but the passengers knows who we are, so let's keep it that way for a while."

"We could just let Flynn shoot them," Hazlett said. His gap-toothed smile made him look more wicked than usual.

Percy ignored him. "Let's get moving. If Flynn's right about this road we don't want to meet any soldiers, so the less time spent sitting here, the better. Forbes, borrow that big Bowie knife off Hazlett and cut the wires on those poles." Percy pointed out the two sets of telegraph wires, one running east-west, the other north-south. "Cut the one going west first, since that's the way we're going. Pettibone, you help him. The rest of us are going to pull up some rails."

"With what?" Flynn asked.

"With ... hell, I don't know. Our fingers if we have to." Percy turned toward the engine and shouted, "Wilson, you got and pry bars in there?"

The engineer bent down, reappeared with a hammer in his hand. "That's all there is, Colonel. This and some small tools for the locomotive."

Percy swore. Wrenching an iron rail free of the cross ties was no easy task, especially without a pry bar to give a man leverage. "This is a fine time to be thinking about tools."

"Let's just cut the wires and be gone," Flynn said. "Otherwise we'll only be wasting time. All we have to pull up those rails is rocks and our hands, and that's not enough. Trust me,

Colonel. I've put a few rails down in my time so I know something about pulling them up."

Forbes and Pettibone went off to cut the telegraph wires. Forbes was a slightly built man, no more than five-feet, five-inches tall and 110 pounds. Perfect size for a cavalryman, and even better for shimmying up telegraph poles.

Percy turned to Hazlett. "Sergeant, you keep an eye out up and down this road for any Yankee cavalry. No shooting, if you can help it."

"Yes, sir. I'll shout if I see anyone." He looked toward the dirt road which climbed steeply on both sides of the river. "There should be enough dust to give us fair warning."

"Good. Flynn, you come with me."

Together, Flynn and the colonel started down the length of the train. Both men were aware of the passengers watching them out the windows.

"How's Benjamin holding up?" Percy asked.

"He's a bit green to this sort of work, but he'll be all right."

"That's why I put him with you." Percy seemed to have forgotten all about reprimanding Flynn over the whiskey.

"Why not with Hazlett?" Flynn thought he already knew the answer, but he asked the question anyway.

"Hazlett is not an easy man to work with," Percy said. "We go back long before the war. He's a good man to have in a fight, though. Sometimes the best soldiers are the same men you'd want watching your back in a tavern brawl. You of all people should know that, Flynn. I sense you've had some experience in such matters."

"*Och*, I've cleared out a room or two in my day."

But tavern brawls weren't Percy's style, Flynn knew, and he couldn't help wondering why Percy seemed so loyal to someone like Hazlett. The colonel was tough in his own way, but Flynn could see that he was also a romantic. What some might call a "Southern Gentleman." Virginia was full of men like that who got caught up in the Confederacy's hopeless cause.

Hazlett was none of those things. He was what well-bred Southerners like Percy called "white trash," that class who caught and whipped the runaway slaves or maybe made moonshine out in the woods. The man was downright vicious.

As if reading Flynn's mind, Percy went on, "I suppose I should tell you, Flynn, that Hazlett is married to my cousin. The less illustrious branch of the Percys, but family none-theless."

"I thought it might be something like that." Flynn suppressed a smile. He was sure now that Percy did not like Hazlett, but only tolerated him. Blood ran thicker than water, and Percy would be too much of a gentleman to allow personal feelings to overrule the Southern obligations of family. "He may be your cousin's wife, but as soon as this raid is over, I'm going to shoot him."

Percy laughed. "If he doesn't shoot you first, you mean."

"We'll see about that."

The grin left Percy's face. "You know I'm doing the best I can with this damned raid, Flynn. Norris sent us on a mission that's damn near impossible."

"Some might even call it a fool's errand," Flynn added. "But here we are, and if you don't mind me saying so, Colonel, if anyone can pull this off it's you."

"Does this mean you're not going to shoot me?"

"You don't have to watch your back with me," Flynn said. "There's some things I am, and some I'm not. One of those is a backstabber."

"If I thought you were the kind of man who would do that, I would have had Hudson toss you in the Potomac River once we were halfway across—or maybe I would have shot you myself as soon as we got into Maryland."

"At this point, Colonel, I think we're all going to have enough trouble getting home alive with Abraham Lincoln that we can pretty much forget about any need to shoot each other. Besides, it's pretty clear to me you intend to see this thing through."

"I do."

"You know, I always thought the Irish were the craziest people in the world, but I was wrong. You Virginians have us beat."

They hurried toward the last car. Hudson jumped down from the baggage car to join them. Lieutenant Cater and Private Cook were on the ground, waiting, revolvers in their hands.

"Anything going on in there?" Percy asked.

"Quiet as a church, sir," Cater said. "I reckon President Lincoln has slept through all the ruckus—if there's even anyone in there."

The car that supposedly held Lincoln resembled a miniature fortress on wheels. It was painted black and well-built, but lacked any ornament that befitted a president. The windows were placed high up the sides of the car, designed to let light in rather than to let passengers look out. There was one door made of thick oak and bound with iron that opened onto a small platform skirted with a plain iron railing. Lincoln and his bodyguard—he must surely have at least one other man inside with him—could make an effective last stand firing down from the high windows. The car's walls, sturdy as they were, could not have withstood return fire from Springfield rifles, but against the less heavy caliber revolvers carried by the raiders, those walls would be like iron.

"Any noise from inside?"

"No, sir," the lieutenant said.

"What are you thinking?" Flynn asked.

"I wonder if there is anyone inside," Percy said. "Imagine if the Yankees spun this whole crazy scheme about Lincoln sneaking into Gettysburg the back way, fed it to Norris down in Richmond, and meanwhile Lincoln is safely aboard the presidential train on the Northern Central after all, eating smoked oysters, smoking cigars, and listening to a bunch of fat Yankee carpetbaggers decide how they'll carve up the South after the war."

"The joke is on us, then?" Flynn asked, amazed. Percy's scenario suddenly made sense. "I suppose we'll have to find out if Lincoln is in there. No sense going through with this if he's not."

The thought of being in the middle of Maryland with just a handful of men and a stolen train was not appealing to anyone. Not when every crossroads threatened to bring an encounter with Yankee troops.

"Colonel, you want me to knock on the door?" Lieutenant Cater asked.

"Let Flynn do it," Percy said. "If there is someone inside and they shoot through the door, we can afford to lose him better than you." He smiled, as if to show he was only joking. Flynn didn't find the humor in it.

"Let's get your cousin-in-law to do it."

"Go knock on the goddamn door, Flynn," Percy snapped. "And make sure you stand to one side so you don't get shot."

Flynn climbed the iron steps, wondering how he got into these situations. He should have been back in Richmond, drinking good black market whiskey, thumping heads, and taking his pick of the whores. Instead, he might be about to get his insides filled with lead.

"Remember," Percy hissed after him. "You're not supposed to know it's Lincoln."

Flynn sighed. How was he supposed to find out if President Lincoln was inside if he couldn't ask for him by name? He knocked on the door and shouted, "Anybody in there?"

No answer. He pounded on the door again.

Finally, a gruff voice answered from within. "What do you want?"

"The conductor wants to know if everything is all right," Flynn said. "We've had trouble with raiders."

No answer.

"Rebels," Flynn added helpfully.

"Will there be any delay?"

"That depends."

"On what?"

"On how soon the engineer can get this train moving again."

"Then you had better tell him to get to work. We have a schedule to keep."

Flynn looked at the door, then over to Percy. The colonel raised his eyebrows in question. Flynn shrugged in reply. He still didn't know if Lincoln was inside the car.

"Aw, hell," he muttered, and knocked on the door again.

"What do you want now?" the voice demanded impatiently.

Flynn took a deep breath and decided to take a chance. "I'm looking for President Lincoln."

This time there was a long, long pause. Flynn was on the verge of repeating his question, just in case it hadn't been heard, when the voice spoke on the other side of the door.

"Who wants to know?"

Flynn decided there was no longer any point in being anything but direct. "This is Sergeant Thomas Flynn of the Confederate States of America. The train has been captured by Colonel Arthur Percy, and you are now prisoners of the Confederacy."

The silence stretched long moments before someone

spoke up. "I'm Major Rathbone, the president's assistant," said the voice. "What do you intend to do with us?"

"We're taking you to Richmond," Flynn replied. "Is President Lincoln really in there?"

A new voice spoke up. Not as deep as Rathbone's. A tired-sounding voice. "I'm Lincoln."

Flynn heard hands fumbling at the bolt on the other side of the door, then a hushed voice say, "No, sir. It could be a trap." The fumbling stopped.

"I'm afraid I have no sword to surrender, Sergeant Flynn," Lincoln said. "Therefore I won't open the door."

"Then have a good trip, sir," Flynn said.

"I trust you will have a good journey as well, Sergeant." He thought he heard Lincoln chuckle. "You realize, of course, that you're still in the middle of Maryland. There are cavalry patrols all around. Infantry guards all the major railroad bridges and stations. Richmond is a long way off."

"Yes, sir," was all Flynn could think to say.

Lincoln was right, of course. They would need God himself on their side to make it to Richmond. "If you need anything, sir, there will be guards outside your car."

"I believe we shall be just fine, Sergeant."

Flynn climbed down and joined Percy, who had edged closer, hoping to hear some of the conversation. "Well, is it Lincoln or isn't it?" Percy asked.

"It's Lincoln, all right," Flynn said. "In fact, I believe he would have come out and had a drink with us, but some fellow in there named Major Rathbone wouldn't let him open the door."

Percy nodded. "I've heard of Rathbone. He's Lincoln's bodyguard. It makes sense that he'd be traveling to Gettysburg with the president."

"I guess that settles it," Flynn said. He smiled. "You've got your president, Colonel. Now what?"

"On to Richmond, of course."

The lieutenant and Private Cook returned to their post guarding the president's car, while Percy, Flynn and Hudson started back toward the engine. They had barely come even with the baggage car when Hazlett shouted a warning. Someone was coming.

"Come on," Percy said, and the three men started running for the front of the train.

CHAPTER 15

"GET READY, BOYS!" Percy shouted as he ran. "Here come the Yankees!"

Flynn drew the Le Mat revolver and sprinted after Percy, whose long legs easily covered the distance to the front of the train. Forbes finished cutting the second telegraph wire and slid down the pole. As the others ran past, Forbes dropped the last few feet, nearly landing on top of Pettibone, who jumped out of the way just in time, cursing.

Benjamin poked his head out the window. "What's all the commotion about?" he shouted.

"Cavalry, I reckon," Flynn yelled back. "Keep an eye on those passengers, lad. If something starts with the Yankees, they're sure to cause trouble."

Flynn fully expected to see a troop of blue-coated cavalry coming down the Washington Road. He knew the raiders wouldn't stand a chance, not with the train stopped. A squadron of any size would outnumber them. The best they could hope for was to hold the Yankees off long enough for the train to reach a decent speed, and then outrun them.

He wasn't prepared for what he did see, which was a hand

car carrying a crew of four startled workmen. They rolled out of the woods to the west on the opposite track.

"Hold your fire," Percy snapped at his men.

Although the crew's arrival was more welcome than cavalry, Percy knew they still presented a problem, for here were four men who could quickly spread word of the raid if they learned what was going on. If the workers found them out, the raiders would have no choice but to take the men prisoner, or shoot them.

"What do we do about them?" Hazlett wondered out loud.

"Let me do the talking," Percy muttered to the knot of men who still ringed the engine, revolvers at the ready. "And put those guns away. If we start shooting, it's only going to attract attention if there are any soldiers on the road."

Percy approached the crew, who looked suspiciously at the *Chesapeake*, standing under steam at the Washington Road crossing. It was unusual for a westbound train to be stopped there. One of the crew gripped an old shotgun, which Percy supposed they kept for killing snakes

"Where's Greer?" the man holding the shotgun asked. He was bigger than the others, and Percy took him to be the foreman.

"He took sick," said Percy, which was the first thing that came to mind. He wondered who Greer might be.

The man stared at Percy for several long moments. Finally, he leaned to one side and spat a stream of brown tobacco juice, expertly hitting the rail. "Hell, it ain't like Greer to let someone else run his train. That locomotive there is his pride and joy. He must be on his deathbed."

"Well, it's not his train, is it? It's the B&O Railroad's," Percy pointed out. He was losing patience.

"I didn't catch your name," the foreman said.

"Arthur Percy."

The crew foreman looked long and hard at the colonel. Behind him, Percy could sense his own men begin to grow uneasy, like a shifting in the wind.

"Never heard of no Percy," the foreman said. "I know most everyone who works for the railroad, I reckon."

"Well, I suppose you just haven't heard of me." This time, there was nothing friendly in Percy's voice. "It's good you came along. We'll be needing your tools."

"What are you talking about?" the foreman asked. "You don't need tools on an engine. Not pry bars and shovels, at least."

"There are raiders up ahead, and the tools will help put back the track they've torn up."

"That why you boys all have your guns out?" the foreman asked. Percy sensed the tension going out of his men. "You reckoned we was Rebels?"

"That's right," Percy said. "We thought you were Rebels."

"Hell!" The foreman suddenly laughed, harder and harder, until he nearly choked. Then he paused to cough up phlegm, which he spat to the ground in a long, ropy stream. "Rebels."

"Well, you can't be too careful in times like these."

"Ain't that God's honest truth," the foreman said. He added without any enthusiasm, "You want us to ride along to do the work for you?"

"I reckon we can handle it," Percy said.

The foreman looked relieved.

They soon had all the workers' tools loaded into the tender. Any fears that the men might be suspicious were dispelled when one of the crew climbed down the river bank and produced a stone jug from a hiding place in the Patapsco's shallows. The men sat on the push car, drinking their chilled whiskey, and watched as the *Chesapeake* got underway again.

"I'll be damned," Percy said once the engine was chugging

on toward Cumberland. "If the Yankees are all that easy to
fool, we'll have Lincoln in Richmond in two days' time."

* * *

GREER, Frost and Schmidt jogged up the tracks, badly
winded. The sight of the hand car rolling toward them was
like an answered prayer.

"Thank *Gott*," Schmidt wheezed. "Now we won't have to
walk back to Baltimore."

"We're not going back," Greer growled. "We're going after
our train."

Schmidt was too tired to argue. The three men stopped
and caught their breath as the hand car rolled closer and
coasted to a stop.

"George Greer!" shouted a man named Jones, whom
Greer recognized as the crew foreman. The man's leathery
face wore a puzzled expression. "You ain't laid up?"

"Hell no! Does it look like I am?"

The foreman jerked a thumb over his shoulder. "The
conductor back there said you was sick, so he was running
your train. Some fellow name of Percy. I thought it all seemed
awful strange."

"Conductor? He's a thief! The son of a bitch stole my
train."

Excitement swept over the workmen. Greer could smell
whiskey on their breath, which was no surprise. Track
workers were the bottom rung of the railroad hierarchy, and
he was in no mood to waste time on these drunken fools.
"Why the hell didn't you stop them?" he snapped.

"We didn't know they was thieves. Besides, there was a lot
of 'em and they had guns."

"Guns?"

"Told us there was trouble on the tracks west of here.

Hell, Greer, you know as well as I do that the Rebs jump over into Maryland every chance they get to play hell with the tracks."

It was true enough. The Harpers Ferry bridge, for instance, had been burned and rebuilt so many times that Greer could no longer keep count. But he wasn't ready to let the foreman and his men off the hook too easily.

"You could have asked more questions and drank less whiskey."

"Goddamnit, Greer, I'm tellin' you they had guns— "

"Where are your tools?" Greer asked, suddenly noticing the bed of the hand car was empty.

"They took 'em," the foreman said. "They said the tracks ahead might need to be repaired on account of the Rebs."

Now it was Greer's turn to swear. He cussed till he was breathless and sputtering, and when he finished, the workmen's mouths gaped open in various degree of astonishment.

Greer spat out a final oath and glared at the men. "What do you think the Rebs are going to do with those tools, you jackasses? They're going to tear up track! That's what. You fools gave them just what they need to do it."

"We didn't know." The foreman made a half-hearted attempt to defend himself. "Not much we could have done, anyhow."

Greer had heard enough. "Get the hell out of my way," he said. "We'll take the hand car and go after them."

The foreman protested. "It's four miles into town—"

"You'll walk it, goddamnit," Greer snapped. He climbed aboard the push car and grabbed one end of the lever. "Frost, Schmidt, get on up here."

"You'll never catch up to a train on that contraption, Greer," the foreman said.

"Let me worry about that. Now, when you get into town, tell Sykes at the hotel to wire ahead that the train's been stolen. You got that? Someone might be able to stop them at the next station."

The foreman shook his head. "I hope so, because you ain't goin' to catch them on no hand car."

Greer ground his teeth. "Shut up, you damn fool. You leave it to us to see how much catchin' up we can do."

The work gang, now on foot, turned and headed east toward Sykesville. They had left a canteen behind, and the three men gratefully drank the water. Then Greer, Schmidt and Frost got the hand car moving. It was slow work starting from a dead stop, so Schmidt jumped off and began to push, grunting with the effort. The heavy crossbar moved up and down, faster and faster, and when the car began to pick up speed, Schmidt jumped aboard. As the three men began to work the crossbar in earnest, sweat broke out on their faces despite the fact that it was mid-November.

Greer couldn't help thinking of the *Chesapeake's* dual, five-foot tall driving wheels and the powerful steam engine that drove those wheels. The locomotive could do a mile a minute on level ground. A steam locomotive running at full throttle was an awesome sight to behold, and the muscle-powered hand car seemed too hopelessly slow to ever catch the *Chesapeake*.

Schmidt spoke the same thought out loud. "We're too far behind. Let's just turn back and let someone stop her at the next station."

"Just put your back into it, Oscar," Greer grunted as he shoved down the handle, powering the car along the tracks. "We're going after our train."

* * *

A FEW MILES AHEAD, the *Chesapeake* was steaming along just the way her pursuers imagined. The steam pistons churned with a powerful rhythm, and a long plume of black smoke streamed behind her, creating a smudge on the otherwise brilliant blue autumn sky. The locomotive was a beautiful sight, spinning along the bright ribbon of track that cut through the golden fields of autumn.

Hank Cunningham stood up tall on the tender and let the wind stream around him. He threw back his head and let out a long, blood-curdling Rebel yell.

"You sound like a goddamn Indian," Wilson complained good-naturedly as he worked the *Chesapeake's* controls. He pulled a lever on the floor behind him to release more water into the locomotive's boiler, then opened the throttle a little wider. Operating a steam locomotive was part art, part instinct. There were few gauges, so an engineer relied on the feel of an engine, its sound, and his own experience.

Percy shared the cramped cab of the locomotive with Wilson. Whenever they came to a curve, the colonel leaned out, looking as far behind them as he could. He was watching for the telltale plume of smoke that would mean an engine was pursuing them. So far, there had been no sign that anyone was chasing them, and the Yankees hadn't attempted to block the tracks ahead, either.

Their luck, Percy thought, had been unbelievable so far. If it held out, they would soon have the Yankee president spirited into Confederate-held territory as a prisoner of war.

Abraham Lincoln. It was a name that could conjure political magic for the struggling Confederacy. The very thought that they had Lincoln as a prisoner was intoxicating. Capturing the president would do more to help the Cause than a score of battlefield victories.

Percy's thoughts were interrupted as Hank Cunningham pushed past with another load of wood for the firebox. They were burning cordwood at a terrific rate to maintain the

Chesapeake's speed. Cunningham worked like a fiend to feed the hungry maw of the firebox.

"How are we set on wood and water?" Percy asked.

Wilson looked at Cunningham, who shrugged. "Well, we might not have enough water to make it to Harpers Ferry, if that's what you mean, sir. We'll have to stop at Frederick Junction on the Monocacy River to take on wood and water both. This train hasn't been refueled since it left Baltimore this morning."

Percy was disappointed—and a little uneasy. The Monocacy was still well within Maryland. On the other hand, Harpers Ferry would be a major milestone, not in the least because the former United States arsenal was heavily guarded by Union soldiers and artillery.

Once they crossed the Potomac River and made it through Harpers Ferry, they would still be traveling through Union territory, but the Yankees' hold on the new state of West Virginia was not nearly as strong as it was on this side of the river. Each mile would bring them closer to the safety of the Shenandoah Valley, where Confederate troops would help them carry Lincoln south.

Still, Percy wasn't taking any chances.

"Run another ten minutes at full throttle and then stop," Percy ordered, shouting to be heard over the roar of the locomotive. He smiled. "We need to leave a little something to slow down anybody who tries to follow us."

"Yes, sir."

Percy grinned. "You know what 'Shenandoah' means, Wilson? It's an Indian word."

"No, Colonel." Wilson was distracted, busy working a lever.

"It means, 'Daughter of the Stars,' " Percy said. "I like the sound of that. Now let's get ourselves to the Shenandoah Valley just as fast as we can."

CHAPTER 16

Richmond

COLONEL WILLIAM NORRIS read the latest news in a smuggled copy of *The Washington Star* and nodded his approval. So, Lincoln was still expected at Gettysburg. Reading the Northern newspapers was almost as productive as spying. Early in the war he had learned a great deal about troop movements and even strategy until the Federal government had begun to censor the news.

Then again, you didn't see everything in the newspapers. There was no news of his raiders, for example. The note from Flynn had been his last update.

Norris stood and walked to the fire to warm himself. His fingers had grown stiff with cold. He was about to call for Fletcher when he caught himself. Well, so much for that. Fletcher had served his purpose but Norris did not trust him to keep his mouth closed about the secret business that went on at the Confederate Signal Bureau. Sending him on the raid seemed like a good way to rid himself of a liability. Of course, there was always the off chance that Captain Fletcher might survive and return.

And the others? It would not do for Colonel Percy and his

band to receive a hero's welcome in Richmond. Like Fletcher, he did not trust them to keep their secrets.

Norris sighed and stalked back to his desk. He took out a fresh sheet of paper and dipped his pen into the inkwell. Then he began to write out an order for the immediate arrest of Colonel Arthur Percy and all those accompanying him. The reason? Norris paused with his pen above the blank sheet, thinking of a good charge. *Treason.* There. He wrote it down. When the time came, he could engineer the details.

* * *

Woodbine, Maryland • 9:45 a.m.

FLYNN AND BENJAMIN stood side by side at the front of the car, keeping watch over the passengers. Captain Fletcher guarded the back door.

"I don't like it one bit, lad," Flynn whispered to Benjamin. "It's been too damn easy so far."

"Ain't that good?" Benjamin asked.

"Nothing worth doing is ever easy, lad. Just remember that. I have a bad feelin' that this won't turn out quite the way we hoped."

"Then why did you come along?"

"Why, for the fun, boy." That couldn't be further from the truth, but Benjamin didn't need to know that. Besides, it was too late for any of them to turn back now. Their only hope was to run for the valley.

Nearby, the passengers strained to hear what was being said. Flynn gave them an impish grin. "Why don't you pull up a chair?"

The matronly woman sniffed. "If we thought there was anything intelligent being said, we might."

Flynn tried to appear shocked. "Do you hear the insults she's hurling at us, lad?"

Her husband spoke up. "There's no need to go picking on women."

Flynn ignored him. "I don't believe we've been introduced, ma'am."

"Mrs. Henrietta Parker." She turned to her husband. "This is Alfred, my husband."

Flynn winked at Benjamin and made his way down the aisle to where the Parkers sat. He transferred the Le Mat revolver to his left hand and offered his right to Alfred Parker, who, in confusion, gripped it in a weak handshake. "Sergeant Thomas Flynn at your service," he said as they shook. "The young fellow there is Private Johnny Benjamin and that's Billy Fletcher in the back."

"Captain William Fletcher," the officer corrected him, sounding annoyed.

Flynn turned to the lawyer from Baltimore. The man still appeared shocked at having seen Flynn kick the bodies off the train because he regarded the raider with the sort of nervous look reserved for wild beasts and Indians. "The captain there has been wondering if you could write a will for him, Mr. Lawyer."

"A will?" Mrs. Henrietta Parker sniffed again. "I dare say you'll all be needing one of those. I can only hope this outrage ends with several hangings. It's the best end for cheap Rebel trash."

"Why, Mrs. Parker," Flynn said, winking. "That's not very Christian of you. Now mind you keep quiet, or I'll hang you out the window."

He turned his back on the indignant noises the woman was making and went to stand beside Benjamin near the stove. He kept the Le Mat in plain view of the passengers, hoping that the sight of the huge revolver would discourage any more bravery like the episode which had already left two men dead.

He stopped in front of the couple from Baltimore, the dandy and the woman. The woman stiffened and the man scowled.

"Can't you find another train to steal?" he said.

"We like this one," Flynn said.

"Goddamn Johnny Rebs."

The woman gripped her partner's arm. "Charlie Gilmore," she said sharply. "Leave it alone."

"Listen to the woman, Charlie."

Flynn moved on. The car was not entirely full, but Flynn was aware of the many eyes fixed hatefully upon him. Some of the eyes held fear, others anger, which was fine with Flynn. However, the eyes of the couple from Baltimore were filled with contempt, a far more dangerous emotion. People who were afraid could be told what to do. People who were angry could be intimidated by the big Le Mat pistol. But there was no controlling contempt. It was a rebellious emotion. As far as Flynn was concerned, the sooner they unloaded the passengers, the better.

Flynn leaned toward Benjamin. "Keep your eyes on those two," he whispered. The boy stared at the couple. "They're trouble, lad. Maybe not for us, but they're trouble in general."

Benjamin nodded. At the back of the car, Captain Fletcher kept watch, his eyes going everywhere, self-important as always. He looked the part of an officer right down to his immaculate uniform, but Fletcher wouldn't be worth a damn if there was any shooting.

Flynn cast a sideways glance at Benjamin. The boy had been looking pale since that morning's gunfight. Killing was never easy work, Flynn thought.

He motioned Benjamin out of earshot of the passengers. "Listen, lad," he whispered. "That was good work this morning. Now I know why I gave you that new Colt. You saved the day. That was just a lucky shot I got off. I can't hit a damn thing with a pistol."

The boy shrugged.

"Now, I've noticed you've been kind of quiet. I'm thinking it may be the first time you killed a man."

Benjamin shrugged. "I reckon," he finally said.

Flynn nodded. "It's no easy thing, killing a man. It's not like killing a chicken or a pig or a goat. Not at all like that. The priests will tell you it's a mortal sin, except in war, when you get a dispensation from the church for killing, although I sometimes wonder if God takes the same view. Killing some men isn't a sin at all, because some bastards deserve it. Now, if those two heroes this morning hadn't tried to be brave and foolish, they would still be alive. Don't you think?"

"I suppose they would be."

"Now, the real question to ask yourself is whether or not you'll hesitate next time before you shoot. Don't freeze up. That's war for you, lad. Hesitate, give the other fellow a chance, and you're a dead man. I don't know about you, lad, but I'd much rather be alive and feeling guilty than dead. Any day, lad. Any day it's better to pull the trigger and stay alive. Remember that."

Benjamin was silent for a moment, then asked, "You know something, Flynn?"

"What's that?"

"Pettibone's right. You talk too damn much."

But he was smiling when he said it, so Flynn knew the boy would be all right.

Just then the whistle blew one short, sharp blast and the train began to slow. In the car, raiders and captives alike looked at each other uneasily, as if to ask, "What next?"

* * *

Twin Arch Bridge, Watersville, Maryland • 10 a.m.

Colonel Percy jumped down from the engine, shouting as soon as his feet touched the ground. "Hazlett! Flynn! Leave one man to guard the passengers and the rest of you get out here. We have work to do."

Moments later, Percy gave his orders. The raiders swarmed toward the locomotive for the tools they had commandeered from the repair crew. They grabbed up the crowbars and mauls, then headed for the tracks at the end of the train. The tracks crossed a road and creek below using a stone, twin-arched bridge, with one span for the road and the other for the waterway. The railroad bed leading to the bridge was very high and steep. Deep ravines filled with rocks and brush bordered the tracks.

"Just two rails is all you need to pull up," Percy said. "Two rails on each side and anyone following us will go right off the track into that ravine."

The raiders set to work. Crowbars slipped under the rails. Hazlett and Hudson alternately pushed down and pulled until the veins stood out like wires in their necks. Pettibone grabbed a maul. Flynn fitted the slotted end of a crowbar to the head of a spike and tugged and twisted, trying to work it free.

While the others worked, Captain Fletcher only stood and watched. Even Percy had grabbed hold of a maul and was pounding at a rail, sweating and cursing with his men.

"Pitch in any time, Fletcher," Percy called out.

"I'm an officer," Fletcher sniffed. "I don't work with my hands."

Percy straightened up and handed his maul to another man. "Is that so?"

"Yes, Colonel, that's my right."

Percy stood, staring for a moment at the priggish captain.

Then his hand casually drifted to the hip holster that held his Colt revolver. He drew the weapon, cocked it, advanced a few steps toward Fletcher, and shoved the muzzle into the captain's face.

"Fletcher, get to work or I'll blow your goddamn head off." Percy's voice was brittle, like broken glass. "I have no patience with shirkers."

Fletcher's face blanched with fear. He began to stammer some protest, thought better of it, and edged around the gun to join Hazlett and Hudson, who were straining to free a rail.

"That's better," Percy said, holstering his pistol.

The spikes holding a rail in place gave all at once with a shriek as they ripped from the wooden tie, nearly pitching the men over backward. Forbes whooped as he lost his balance and plunked down on his backside. The men grabbed the loose rail and pitched it into the ravine twenty feet below. They joined the others sweating and cursing over the second rail and soon had that one free as well.

"Sure, and that will be a fine surprise for anyone coming after us," said Flynn, looking down at the twin rails now gleaming in the brush.

"I don't believe you mean that, Irish," Hazlett said. He was standing a few feet away, a crowbar over one shoulder. "Maybe you want them to catch us. Hell, you might just be a Yankee yourself. Lord knows there's enough potato-eaters wearing blue."

"Hazlett, you don't know your arse from a potato, much less a Yankee from a Reb."

Hazlett snarled and in one, smooth motion, he planted his feet and swung the iron bar at Flynn's head. The Irishman ducked and the bar swished harmlessly through the air. Forbes, standing next to Flynn, couldn't get out of the way fast enough and the crow bar struck him a glancing blow on the upper arm. He howled and swore.

Flynn went at Hazlett from a crouch, thumping hard fists deep into his belly. Hazlett slashed down with the crow bar. Flynn dodged a second too late. The iron bar missed his head but the flattened tip ripped a bloody furrow along his jawbone.

Flynn ignored the pain and danced back out of reach. The two men circled each other. Hazlett's dark eyes burned with hatred as he sneered at Flynn.

"I'm goin' to do you good, Irish."

"Anytime you're ready."

Colonel Percy stepped between them. "I will not have this!" he shouted, reaching for the iron bar in Hazlett's hands. Hazlett didn't let go. For a moment, it looked as if he might even attack Percy. Then, reluctantly, he let Percy have the crowbar. "There will be no fighting among ourselves. Flynn, Hazlett, do you hear me?"

Percy's face had turned red, his grip on the crowbar tightening until his knuckles showed white, and it looked as if he might swing it at the sergeants. His voice was shrill. "Do you hear me?"

"I hear you." Flynn spoke first. He relaxed, went out of a fighter's stance, and gingerly touched the wound on his chin. His fingertips came away bloody and he glared at Hazlett. "I understand."

"Hazlett?"

"All right, Colonel."

"We move again in five minutes."

The men drifted away. Some found a spring near the tracks and drank deeply. They pulled biscuits and cold fried chicken from their pockets and ate it standing near the train. A soldier learned to eat and drink when he could.

"I could use some coffee," John Cook said wistfully. "Real coffee like we had this morning, not what we're used to drinking back home that's made out of chicory."

"Ain't no time for making coffee."

"I just said it would be nice, is all," Cook said, then stared hungrily at the bundle of food the other man had taken from his pocket and unwrapped. "You gonna eat that biscuit?"

Further down the tracks, Colonel Percy fell into step beside Pettibone.

"What's with those two?" Percy asked. "I think they would have killed each other."

"It's like two roosters in a barnyard, Colonel," Pettibone said philosophically. "Sooner or later, they's goin' to fight. This ain't the end of it, neither."

"But why those two?" Percy wondered aloud. If there was trouble between his men, he wanted to know the cause.

"Hazlett is a son-of-a-bitch and a no-good troublemaker," Pettibone said, then added, "Sir. I know he's married to your cousin. But he always was a bully back home, and a man like that thrives in army life, 'specially if he wears stripes. Now Flynn, he won't abide a man like that. He's quick to make a joke, I reckon, but make no mistake, he's a hard man. Someone like him stands up to a piece of horse shit like Hazlett. And Hazlett don't like that."

Percy shook his head. He supposed he had known as much all along. "It ain't enough that the Yankees want to kill us. We have to try and kill each other, too."

Shaking his head, Percy stomped toward the locomotive. He would much rather have been on horseback, where a man felt free and easy, instead of riding this steam locomotive. Some called a locomotive an iron horse, but in Percy's mind the *Chesapeake* was as far as you could get from four hooves and a saddle. It wasn't natural. This damn train was making them all nervous.

"Colonel!"

Percy turned. Lieutenant Cater had jumped down from

the last car and was waving his arms and shouting. "Colonel! Colonel!"

Percy looked beyond Cater and saw at once what all the shouting was about. Something was coming at them down the tracks. He squinted, trying to make it out, but his near-sighted eyes saw only a distant blur.

"What is it?"

"Hand car, sir," Pettibone drawled. "Coming right at us."

"How many men on her?"

"Just three, sir."

Percy squinted again, and could begin to make out the up-and-down pumping motion. He knew his small band of raiders could easily overwhelm three men, but if his pursuers were armed, the victory might come at a bloody price.

"Everyone on the train!" he shouted. "Let's go."

He turned and ran for the engine. Wilson had already heard the commotion and pulled back the Johnson bar, getting the *Chesapeake* underway. At first, the huge drive wheels slipped uselessly on the slick, polished rails. Wilson pulled a lever, sand dropped on the rails, and the wheels caught. The train began to creep ahead, although the pursuers were gaining on them. Percy swung into the cab.

"She won't go no faster, Colonel," Wilson said, working the lever to the sandbox again. Too slowly, the locomotive was gathering speed. "There's just no traction."

"It doesn't matter," Percy said. He nodded at the gap in the rails behind them. "They won't be getting any closer."

CHAPTER 17

"WE'VE GOT THEM NOW," Greer shouted. "Faster!"

He laughed at the sight of the thieves up ahead scrambling aboard the train. Cowards, he thought, every last one of them. The *Chesapeake* was just ahead. Sweat streamed down the faces of the three railroad men and the muscles of their arms burned as they pumped harder and harder.

Greer spotted the train ahead and laughed out loud. The hand car flew over the rails, closing the distance between the pursuers and the creeping train, which was just beyond the Twin Arch Bridge.

"I knew we'd find them sooner or later," Greer crowed as they rushed closer. On the last car, he could make out two men watching them come on. Briefly, he wondered if they were armed. However, Greer's excitement over the first glimpse of his train overwhelmed his sense of caution. At this point, he really didn't give a damn if they had guns. All Greer could think about was catching up to the stolen train. By God, he would teach those train thieves a lesson.

Too late, Greer saw the missing rails ahead. Schmidt saw

it an instant later and his mouth fell open. The push car lacked brakes, so they hurtled helplessly toward disaster.

"Jump!" Greer shouted.

The three men launched themselves into thin air. The hand car hurtled on, the pump handle still beating up and down as if to invisible hands. At the gap, it ran out of rail and the front wheels churned up dirt and rocks. The car careened wildly onto its side, then flipped end over end and landed upside down in the brush lining the tracks. The four wheels went on spinning silently. If its momentum had carried it just a few more feet, the car would have sailed clear off the bridge ahead.

Greer picked himself off the ground. His left knee hurt fiercely, and his right ankle felt as if it had been twisted. He tested his legs, gradually putting his full weight on them. Nothing broken, he thought. Up ahead, he watched the train —*his* train—move faster and faster down the tracks, spouting great gouts of thick, black smoke as the locomotive picked up speed.

He clenched his fists in helpless rage. He should have known the thieves would tear up the rails. How could he have been so stupid?

"We'll never catch her now," said Schmidt, shaking himself like a bear as he crawled out of the brush lining the tracks. He uttered some choice Teutonic oaths, untangled a prickly strand of thorns from his sleeve, and dabbed at a gash on his forehead. "If we hadn't jumped, we'd have broken our necks."

They both stared down at the overturned push car. Aside from being upside down, it otherwise appeared undamaged. The wheels spun on, like a dog chasing rabbits in its dreams.

"At least it didn't go all the way down the ravine," Schmidt commented.

"We won't be getting that out of there anytime soon," Greer said. "Damn those bastards."

"Who are they, do you think?" Schmidt asked. "What do they want with our train?"

"To hell if I know. I guess it must be the payroll money they're after," Greer replied. He looked around. "Now, where the hell is Frost?"

They had been expecting him to appear out of the brush at any moment, but Frost was nowhere to be seen. Concerned, Greer and Schmidt began searching for him in the thick undergrowth that lined the tracks. The tangle of sumac, briars and poison ivy could hide a man until you stepped on him. Brush and rocks also were a favorite lair for poisonous copperhead snakes, so the two men kicked at the brush carefully.

"Frost?" Greer called. "Where in hell are you?"

"I hope he didn't break his *Gott* damn neck," Schmidt said. "I don't want to carry him all the way back to Baltimore."

"Just keep looking."

They heard a groan, and both men rushed toward the noise. Frost was on all fours, trying to extricate himself from a tangle of thorns. Schmidt reached down with a hand the size of a ham and pulled him free. Groggily, Frost got to his feet. He shook his head to clear it, coughed, and spat a stream of bloody phlegm toward the tracks. The thorns had carved a mosaic of cuts and scrapes on his face.

"Got knocked out cold," Frost said. "Must of landed on my damn head."

"Good thing it's hard," Schmidt remarked.

"You can just go to hell, Schmidt, you dumb Kraut. I damn near got killed. Hell, I believe I'm seeing double."

"All right, all right," Greer said. "Ain't none of us feeling spry at the moment. But we'd best get on after our train."

Schmidt and Frost stared at him.

"What are you two gawking at?"

"Hell, Greer, we ain't going to catch that train now."

"Not standing around we ain't. Let's get moving." He turned and started toward the overturned hand car.

"You're crazy, Greer," Schmidt said. "You know that?"

Greer wheeled, his face contorted in anger. "Let me just remind you two goddamn fools of something. I'm the conductor—" he stabbed a finger at Schmidt, then Frost "—you're the engineer, and you're the fireman of *that* train." He pointed into the distance, where they could just see a plume of black smoke moving west, away from them. "That train is our responsibility, passengers and payroll money, too, and we allowed the train to be stolen and the passengers' lives to be put in danger. I don't care if it was Rebels, horse thieves or Injuns that stole it, and the B&O Railroad ain't going to care. All that matters is that it got stolen. Now, if we catch that train, there might still be some chance of staying employed by the B&O. If we don't catch that train, we ain't going to have jobs on a train ever again. Nowhere, no how. Now, you tell me, are you jackasses going to help or not?"

Torn and bleeding, the two men looked stunned. Greer stared hard at them for a long moment, then turned abruptly and stomped over to the hand car, which lay half-buried in the weeds. He grabbed the frame and began tugging furiously at the car, trying to upright it, but it was too heavy for one man to move. Finally, Schmidt and Frost went to help. Once they raised the car enough for Schmidt to get his shoulder under it, they were able to tip the car back onto its wheels. That was the easy part. It was only after much swearing and sweating that they managed to wrestle the car back onto the tracks on the other side of the gap the raiders had made.

By then, the *Chesapeake's* smoke was gone from the sky.

Silently, the three men began pumping up and down, and the car rolled off in pursuit of the stolen train.

* * *

Near Mount Airy, Maryland • 11 a.m.

PERCY ORDERED another halt and had his men tear up more rails. Once again, the raiders found that sabotaging the tracks was far from easy, and tearing up just two rails took them much longer than it had last time.

The colonel had Willie Forbes cut the telegraph wires again, just in case the ones near Hood's Mill were repaired. Percy knew the raid's success relied heavily on surprise. If the Yankees were able to send telegraphs ahead, the train could be stopped at the next town or village by placing logs across the tracks or even by throwing a switch that would send the train onto a siding.

The colonel was so preoccupied with watching the tracks behind them that he didn't hear Flynn walk up.

"They won't be catching up to us anytime soon," Flynn said. "You saw what happened when they hit that gap back at the Twin Arch Bridge."

"That's what we officers do, Flynn," Percy said. A note of bitterness crept into his voice. "We get paid to worry."

"Then you don't get paid enough. Besides, there were only three men chasing us. It wouldn't have been much of a fight."

"Maybe, maybe not." Percy shrugged. At this point, we can't afford to lose anybody in a fight, so why take the chance? Our orders are to get Lincoln to Richmond, not fight Yankees. You should know that better than anyone."

"Then what about the passengers?" Flynn asked, ignoring Percy's attempt to chastise him. "Do we put them off the train yet?"

Percy shook his head. "Not yet. The area we're in is too densely populated. They'll have cavalry down on us in no time. We've cut the telegraph wires here, but there must be others running north-south at every crossroads town. If a warning is sent north, the Yankees will be waiting for us at Harpers Ferry. So, the passengers stay. We can't have them fanning out through the countryside, sounding the alarm. No, the passengers stay on board for now."

"Whatever you say," Flynn said. "But you can be sure there will be more trouble with the passengers before the day is through."

Percy did not appear to be listening. He was staring down the tracks. "Damn," he said. "Don't those people know when to give up?"

The hand car rolled into sight. The three men aboard pumped wildly as they raced toward the train.

"*Jaysus*, Mary and Joseph," Flynn said. "Sure, and the bastards have gumption, whoever they are. I can't believe they're still after us, after running off the tracks back at that bridge."

"You may get your fight after all, Flynn." He turned and shouted, "Back on the train! "Let's get moving."

The hand car was moving at a good clip and the engine was at a virtual standstill. It was obvious the pursuers would soon overtake the train.

"Here they come."

Percy turned and shouted a warning at Lieutenant Cater, who was leaning over the rail of the last car, revolver at the ready, Private Cook beside him. "Shoot them if they get too close," Percy yelled.

Lieutenant Cater thumbed back the hammer on the Colt and took aim. "I've got the one with his back to us," he said to Cook. "You take one of the others. Hell, if we don't get them, that gap in the rails will."

The pursuers were now so close that they could plainly see the three sweating faces of the men.

"Ready— "

At that moment, the men on the hand car quit pumping, letting the car coast. The gap in the rails was just ahead, but the car was slowing. This time there would be no spectacular derailment. The three pursuers glared defiantly at the train, which was struggling to lurch ahead.

"These Yankees don't know when to give up," Lieutenant Cater said, then pulled the trigger.

The bullet ripped the air above the pursuers, but all three men dove toward the deck of the car. Cater laughed. "Maybe they ain't such fools after all. That ought to give them something to think about."

One man jumped to his feet and shook his fist at them, yelling something unintelligible.

Cater laughed even harder and ripped another shot over their heads. The men ducked. As the raiders waited expectantly, the car rolled to a stop just in front of the spot where the rails were missing. No sooner had the car stopped than one of the men jumped down and began to run after the train. He favored one leg as he ran, but still moved quickly enough.

The *Chesapeake* gained speed slowly. As Cater watched, the man began to close the distance between them. He was short and broad, a born sprinter, and only what appeared to be a bad leg kept him from running even faster. The man's face contorted with the effort, his eyes bugged out as he gasped for air. Cater could hear him panting.

Cater leveled the pistol at him.

"That's close enough," he warned.

"You stole my train," the man managed to shout.

Cater grinned. "Ours now, Yank." He cocked the pistol. "Don't come no closer, or I'll shoot."

The sprinter didn't slow down. He was like a human locomotive.

Still, Cater couldn't bring himself to shoot the man. But if he came any closer—

With a sudden jolt, the train picked up speed. The sprinter struggled to keep up, but the train moved faster and faster until, winded and slowed by his bad leg, he began to fall behind. Finally, breathlessly, he stood with his hands on his knees, panting, then shook his fist at the train. "You ain't seen the last of me!"

Private Cook put his revolver away and gave a low whistle. "You should of shot him, Lieutenant. That man ain't goin' to give up."

Behind them, from within President Lincoln's car, a voice called through the door. Both men had forgotten all about their captive passengers and they jumped at the sound. "What's that shooting about?"

"Ain't nothing important," Cater said.

"What was it?" the voice demanded.

"Just some snakes beside the tracks," he said. "We were shooting at them."

He had been cool enough dealing with the pursuit, but he was unnerved when he thought about the presence on the other side of the oak door. The president of the United States! In all the excitement of the raid, it was easy to forget that Lincoln was even aboard the train. If they got the president to Richmond, the war might be over next week. Cater felt relieved when there were no other questions from behind the door.

"We're goin' to have quite a story to tell our grandchildren, Cook." Cater smiled and holstered his Colt. "Yes, indeed. We done captured the chief Yankee of them all. Ol' Abe Lincoln himself."

Cook was staring at the receding figure on the tracks, who

was still shaking his fist at the train and shouting, although he was too far away now for Cook to hear him. "Lot of miles between us and Richmond, Lieutenant," the private observed. "Lot of miles."

CHAPTER 18

Mount Airy, Maryland • 11:30 a.m.

GREER DID NOT WATCH the train out of sight. Cursing and gasping for breath after his futile chase, he headed back to the others. Schmidt and Frost looked about as worn out as he felt, he decided. Both men wore hangdog expressions on their faces, and they were battered and dirty. It was exhausting, working the car's handle up and down, mile after mile, as they chased the *Chesapeake*. Now they had been forced to stop at the gap in the rails and watch the train disappear once again. They were watching him, wondering what to do next.

"Well, I reckon that's that," Frost said. He sounded relieved.

"Jump down and grab a corner of the car," Greer growled. "You, too, Schmidt."

"What?"

"You heard me. We're going to carry this thing across the gap here and go after them."

"You're crazy, Greer," Frost said. "You've gone goddamn crazy on us. We ain't goin' to catch that train. Not now. Ain't that right, Oscar?"

The big German scratched his beard. "Why not?" he

finally said. "Greer is right about us letting the train be stolen. Someone will have to be punished for this, and that someone might be us if we don't catch the raiders. Otherwise, we'll never have jobs on a railroad again." He climbed off the car and claimed the back corner. "We have to go after that train. There is no other choice."

"Hell, you're both crazy."

Still, Frost jumped down and joined in as the other two men began the arduous task of moving the hand car across the gap in the rails. It was only a distance of twelve feet, but the iron and wood structure was heavy and the wheels did not roll easily over open ground. Carrying the car was out of the question because of its weight. Instead, all three men put their shoulders against the back of the car and pushed. Inch by inch, foot by foot, the car crept forward. Finally, after much heaving, sweating and cursing, they crossed the gap and lined the wheels up for the final push back onto the rails.

The *Chesapeake* was nowhere in sight. Even the telltale smoke was gone, leaving an empty, blue bowl of autumn sky.

Schmidt swore in disgust. He put his shoulder to the back of the car and single-handedly forced it onto the rails again.

Greer jumped aboard. "Come on," he said. "Let's get going."

With a sense of resignation, the other men scrambled up and took hold of the pump handle. Greer winced as he gripped the metal. Unlike Frost, whose hands were like leather from handling wood all day, Schmidt and Greer did little real labor anymore and their hands were blistered and raw. Still, Greer shoved down mightily, ignoring the pain, and the car began to roll. They took up the chase once more, although they seemed impossibly far behind, and too slow to ever hope of catching up again.

* * *

COLONEL PERCY WATCHED the scenery flash by as the *Chesapeake* built speed. Beside him in the locomotive's cab, Cephas Wilson opened the throttle even wider. Wind howled beyond the glass windows enclosing the cab as the locomotive rushed west. Hank Cunningham scurried between the firebox and tender, feeding the engine's incredible hunger for wood.

Percy laughed out loud. He was in the best spirits he'd been in since that day in Richmond when Fletcher had summoned him to Colonel Norris's office at the Confederate Secret Service. Up until now, Percy had half-expected the Yankees to catch them at any moment. Lord knows there had been enough opportunities for things to go wrong—crossing the Potomac, gathering at the train station in Ellicott Mills, even taking the train under the noses of Yankee infantry, not to mention those relentless pursuers whom they had finally lost. The stakes were high. Capture would mean death at the end of a rope for himself and his men because they would all be considered spies, not soldiers. Percy didn't plan on allowing himself or any of his men to be taken alive, if it came to that.

They had succeeded so far in spite of all the odds against them, and for the first time, Percy allowed himself to believe they might actually get Lincoln to Richmond, after all. At the moment, anything seemed possible.

"We'll make good time until the Parr's Ridge grade, sir," Wilson shouted, interrupting Percy's thoughts. "That will slow us down some. Just beyond Mount Airy is the Monocacy River. There's a bridge, and I'm sure the Yankees have it guarded." He sounded apprehensive. The crossing—known officially as Frederick Junction for the rail spur that connected the city of Frederick to the main B&O line—would have troops guarding it.

"We'll be there and gone before the Yankees know it,"

Percy said, trying to reassure Wilson. In reality, he was worried about the guard at the Monocacy crossing, but if the luck they'd had so far held, they would have surprise on their side. "We won't so much as slow down."

"We'll see about the bridge, sir." The engineer sounded doubtful. "We'll see."

"How fast are we going?" Percy asked. The ground beneath them was a blur.

"Sixty miles per hour, Colonel," Wilson said, the tone of his voice betraying some amazement. "I ain't got a stopwatch, but I reckon that's about right."

Sixty miles per hour. A mile a minute. It hardly seemed possible. Percy was amazed. The worries of the past few days slipped even further away, and he put looming problems such as the Monocacy crossing out of his mind for the moment.

"Ever run a train through Virginia this fast?"

"Yes, sir. From time to time. We've got locomotives that can manage sixty." He cracked a smile. "Mostly it's the tracks that's slow."

"These Yankees know how to build a railroad," Percy agreed. So far, all the bridges had been iron or stone, all the tracks well-tended. Far different from Virginia, with its wooden bridges and tracks left in ruins because of the war.

"Too bad these tracks don't go clear to Richmond," Percy said. "We'd be there in time for Mr. Lincoln to be Jefferson Davis's dinner guest."

"With any luck, we'll get there all the same in a few days."

Percy looked out again at the rapidly passing countryside. Beautiful country. The rolling landscape was a patchwork of woods and fields. The corn and wheat had been harvested recently, but it was easy to see this was rich farming country. He wouldn't mind coming back to spend some time here, maybe when the war was over, although it was getting so he could hardly remember when there hadn't been a war.

Compared to the bleak, untended fields in Virginia, Maryland looked like the land of plenty, even in mid-November. There were woods, too, filled with timber, and while most of the trees had lost their leaves, some still clung tenaciously to the oaks they passed. Here and there a flaming red sumac stood out defiantly against the brown and gray landscape.

"Train on the right," Wilson called, and Percy shook off his reverie in an instant.

The engine stood on a siding with four freight cars behind it. She was under steam, but had evidently pulled off the main track to let the bigger, faster *Chesapeake* pass.

It was an ugly little machine, with small wheels and a massive upright cylinder like a barrel on a wagon. The long, ungainly driving bar that powered the wheels gave the locomotive an insect-like appearance.

"What the hell is that?" Percy asked.

"It's called a Grasshopper," Wilson said. "It's an older engine that the B&O still uses for local runs. You want me to stop so we can wreck her? Some Yank might wise up and come after us on that thing."

Already, they had roared past the siding and left it behind. To stop now would cost them too much time. Percy scoffed. "Ha! That old thing? Catch us?" He waved toward the track ahead. "Go man, go! Open her up."

The *Chesapeake* roared along at an exhilarating pace, sending up a black plume of smoke, like a challenge. The Grasshopper engine was soon out of sight and forgotten.

It was all Percy could do not to whoop out loud.

* * *

FLYNN WATCHED the woods and fields fly past beyond the windows. The train was running at a terrific pace, swaying from side to side like a ship at sea. He had to admit the

Yankees would be hard-pressed to catch them now, at this speed.

An uneasy quiet had fallen over the passengers, who watched their Confederate captors sullenly. Captain Fletcher had been sent to help them guard the car, and the rhythmic motion was putting him to sleep. Flynn noticed the captain nodding off at the back of the car. How anyone could sleep just then Flynn didn't know, but it was clear the action and sleepless nights of the last forty-eight hours had caught up to Fletcher. Not that Fletcher was worth a damn awake, anyhow. They would have been better off if Colonel Percy had simply shot the man for refusing to work.

Would Percy really have shot him? Just two days ago, Flynn wouldn't have thought so, but now he wasn't so sure. He had discovered that not only was Percy a very determined individual, but there was a bit of madness about him. Percy wasn't quite crazy, but he was definitely unpredictable.

His thoughts were interrupted by a groan from Henrietta Parker. "Oh, this is terrible," she complained. "At this speed we'll run off the tracks and be killed."

Flynn moved toward her. He saw her husband touch the back of her hand, as a warning.

"Hush now, dear," Albert Parker said. "We don't want to upset these ... these *Rebels*."

Flynn grinned down wickedly at them. "That's right, ma'am. If you upset me I might have to shoot your husband."

Albert paled. His wife, however, looked furious. "I shall have a front row seat at your hanging, Sergeant."

"With any luck, Mrs. Parker, ma'am, there won't be any hangings. You said yourself the train might wreck and kill us all." At that moment, the speeding train struck an uneven spot in the rails and rocked wildly. Mrs. Parker gasped.

"That's quite enough."

Flynn turned. The fat little lawyer, Prescott, stood and

waddled up the aisle, struggling to keep his balance as the car pitched from side to side. The expression on his face wavered between fear and outrage.

Casually, Flynn leveled the Le Mat revolver at Prescott's chest. He cocked the hammer with an audible click. "Think about what you're doing, Mr. Prescott."

Prescott stopped. His doughy, white hands clenched and unclenched. "There's no call to be tormenting ladies ... Sergeant. Are you a soldier or a thug?"

Flynn was in no mood for a lecture. "At the moment I'm just a man pointing a gun at you, Mr. Prescott. Now shut the hell up and sit down."

At the back of the car, the door into the next car slammed shut with a bang. One of the passengers had slipped out. Cursing, Flynn realized Prescott's protest must have been a diversion, and he felt like a fool because he had fallen for it.

Flynn grabbed Prescott's shoulder and shoved him aside. All he could think about was going after whoever had slipped out the door. He started to shout at Benjamin, in case the boy hadn't noticed.

"Lad, we've got—"

As Prescott fell away, Flynn saw the Baltimore dandy crouched in the aisle behind the fat lawyer. He had been hidden behind Prescott's bulk. With a grunt, Charlie Gilmore launched himself at Flynn.

Caught off guard, Flynn didn't have time to react. Gilmore slugged him in the belly and Flynn doubled over in pain. The Le Mat flew from his hand. He couldn't catch his breath. A fist smashed into his chin and Flynn went down.

As Gilmore's well-shined shoe stomped down at Flynn's head, he rolled just fast enough that the heel only skidded along his temple. Flynn kicked, catching Gilmore in the knee and throwing him off balance.

Gilmore stumbled, giving Flynn time to roll to his feet. Gilmore reached for the pistol in his belt.

"You done asked for it," he snarled.

Flynn hit him before he could get the gun free, putting all the power of his shoulders into the punch. Gilmore collapsed, his pistol flying.

Benjamin jumped to help Flynn, but the lawyer flung himself at the boy. Prescott outweighed him by a good eighty pounds and the boy found himself pinned in the seat. Benjamin wriggled and squirmed but Prescott's weight bore down on him.

"Let me up!"

"Hell no!"

In the aisle, Gilmore was back on his feet and facing Flynn warily, fists at the ready. Flynn glanced around for his gun, but the Le Matt had slid out of sight.

He knew things had gone badly wrong. In another moment, all the passengers might get out of hand. They would have a mutiny, and there would be no stopping it.

Where the hell was Fletcher? To his astonishment, Flynn saw that the captain was still slumped in his seat, his eyes closed and mouth hanging open, sleeping soundly.

"Fletcher! Wake up! Shoot this son of a— "

Gilmore rushed him. Flynn tried to dodge, but the narrow aisle gave him no room. The other man grappled him around the waist and they both tumbled into the seats. A woman screamed and Flynn glimpsed Fletcher running for the door, away from the fight.

Gilmore jabbed at his kidneys with a series of rabbit punches. Flynn swatted him in the side of the head. With a snarl, Gilmore butted his head into Flynn's nose. Flynn's eyes ran and he felt a hot trickle of blood from his nose. Gilmore tried it again and Flynn bit his ear. As Gilmore howled, Flynn slammed up with the heel of his hand and caught him under the chin so hard that his teeth cracked together. Then Flynn felt himself kneed in the groin and experienced an awful, excruciating pain that took his breath away. He bit Gilmore's ear even harder.

They rolled into the aisle. Neither man could get the upper hand in such a confined space and they grappled and gouged.

Then Flynn remembered the horse pistol in his coat pocket. He fumbled for it, wondering if the thing would even fire.

As Flynn groped in his pocket, that gave Gilmore an opening, and he got both hands around Flynn's neck, digging his thumbs deep into the throat on each side of the windpipe. Flynn's vision swam with black dots. He was in trouble. His fingertips touched the pistol.

The other man had his knees on Flynn's chest now, pinning him to the floor. Flynn couldn't breathe. His hand slipped around the butt of the old pistol. He barely had the strength to drag the weapon free. He managed to pull back the hammer, wondering whether or not there was a percussion cap in place. He had never bothered to check.

The hands tightened even more on his throat and all Flynn could see was the savage face grinning down at him as if through a fog. With one final, desperate effort, he jammed the muzzle into Gilmore's side. For just an instant, Gilmore's eyes went wide, knowing what was about to happen.

And then Flynn pulled the trigger.

The .54-caliber ball ripped through the other man's body. The clothes touching the muzzle smoldered after the blast. The gory hole in his back, torn by the large ball of lead, was big enough to swallow a fist. Overhead, the ceiling was splashed with blood. Gilmore's body slumped to one side and Flynn shoved it off.

"That was close," he said. He was breathing hard. It had

been a tough fight, maybe not the toughest of his life, but he didn't want to think about what might have happened if he hadn't been able to reach the pistol in time.

Nearby, a woman was gasping in astonishment at the life-and-death struggle she had just witnessed. He could also hear Mrs. Parker. "Oh my," she kept repeating in shock. "Oh my."

"Shut up, woman," Flynn snapped. "For the love of Christ, shut up."

Mrs. Parker didn't need to be told twice. She touched her fingertips to her lips and fell silent.

A moment later, the door to the car flew open and Captain Fletcher rushed in, followed by Hazlett and Petti-bone. All three had their revolvers out. The blast from Flynn's horse pistol had left the air sulfurous and tinged with blue smoke, and the three soldiers squinted to see through the haze.

Flynn jerked his chin at a seat nearby, where Benjamin was still struggling with the ungainly bulk of the attorney. Petti-bone walked over, reversed his Colt, and clubbed Prescott behind the ear with the butt of the pistol. Prescott went limp, and Benjamin managed to wriggle out from under him.

"You should have shot that fat bastard," Hazlett said. Pettibone ignored him. Going to Gilmore's body on the floor, he rolled it all the way over with the toe of his boot.

"Yup," he drawled. "He's a dead 'un. Half his guts is on the ceiling."

Mrs. Parker whimpered again.

Hazlett grinned down maliciously at Flynn, who still on his knees in the aisle, rubbing his throat. "What's the matter, Irish, can't handle the civilians?"

"Go to hell," Flynn said wearily, and reached up to grab Pettibone's offered hand. Back on his feet, Flynn looked around and quickly assessed the situation. Gilmore was dead. Prescott was on the floor, shaking his head groggily. Terrified,

Mr. and Mrs. Parker cowered in their seat. The faces of the other passengers ran the gamut from looks of horror to blank stares as they tried not to meet the raiders' eyes.

One face, however, was not there.

"Someone's missing," Flynn said. "I saw the door open to the next car."

"It's the woman," Benjamin said. "The one who was with him. She's gone."

"She's probably planning to jump off the train," Flynn said. He limped toward the door. "I'm going after her."

"Brave man," Hazlett said sarcastically.

Flynn found the Le Mat and holstered it, thinking he wouldn't need it against a woman. He opened the door to the howling, open air. The train was still flying at a reckless speed. Seeing the ground rush past in a blur, he doubted the woman had jumped. That would be suicide. There was only one place she could be.

Flynn crossed the bucking platform toward the next car, which carried the passenger's baggage. None of the raiders had explored the freight car because they had been too busy keeping the passengers in line and ripping up rails.

Flynn tried the door. It wouldn't budge, so he hit it with his shoulder, this time throwing his weight into it. The door popped open.

He stepped inside, but couldn't see a thing. The interior was nearly pitch black. What little light there was leaked in from around the shades drawn over the windows and from the cracks under the rear door, which opened toward Lincoln's car.

Flynn squinted into the darkness. "Come out, ma'am," he said. "Save us both the trouble."

No answer came. Not that he expected one.

Swearing under his breath, Flynn stepped into the blackness. He kept the Le Mat in its holster. There had been enough bloodletting for one day, he thought, and Flynn had no intention of shooting a woman.

Carefully, he moved deeper into the car. Like a blind man, he became acutely aware of smells: oiled leather, dust, moldy canvas. The place needed a good airing out.

A sound, somewhere ahead. He paused, listened. Heard only the clacking of wheels on rails. The swaying motion inside the dark car was disorienting.

"Come out, woman," he snapped impatiently.

There. That noise again. A swishing of skirts? Sounded like it was behind him.

Flynn spun, his hand on the revolver.

Nothing.

Unnerved, he shuffled toward the windows. After what he had just been through, he was in no mood for a game of cat and mouse with the woman, whoever she was.

He reached toward a window, intending to let some light in, when he felt the cold touch of razor-sharp steel against his throat.

Flynn froze.

CHAPTER 19

"Greer!" Schmidt shouted. "Look at that!"

Ahead of them on a siding, an old Grasshopper-type engine sat under steam. The nickname fit the locomotive's insect-like appearance. The Grasshopper was small and much slower than the new locomotives, but it was one of the work-horses of the B&O, pulling freight on local routes and spurs to towns off the main line. The old locomotive was still much faster than the hand-powered car.

They coasted up to the Grasshopper. The crew was made up of old-timers, white-haired and bearded, and they watched the arrival of the hand car with curiosity.

"Greer?" said one of the men who knew the conductor. "What are you doing here? On that thing? We just saw the *Chesapeake* go by like a bat out of hell."

"My train's been stolen," Greer said, jumping down from the hand car. Quickly, he explained what had happened. Less than a minute later, Greer, Schmidt and Frost were aboard the Grasshopper locomotive, which had been uncoupled from its load of freight cars.

"Better take this," said the engineer, pressing a revolver

and a handful of cartridges on Greer. Frost was holding onto the shotgun taken from the track crew.

"Get the word out now," Greer said. "If a telegraph gets through to Frederick Junction or Harpers Ferry, they can stop the sons of bitches up ahead."

"You can count on us, Greer," the other engineer said. "I'll take this hand car in to Mount Airy. They've got a telegraph there. Now give 'em hell!"

* * *

FLYNN HELD VERY STILL as the cold knife blade touched his throat. In the dim light he could just see the gleaming steel of the stiletto, and beyond it, the flinty eyes of the woman who wielded the knife.

His hand slipped toward his revolver.

"None of that," she said, pressing the blade tight to his windpipe. "Don't move. Now tell me what happened. I heard a gunshot."

Under the circumstances, Flynn wasn't about to confess he had killed her companion. "There was a fight," he managed to say, easing each word out of his throat as if squeezing it around the knife blade.

Still, she pressed the dagger closer. He felt the outer layer of skin break, in the same way that strands of a taut rope sever at the touch of a sharp blade.

"Is Charlie alive or dead?" she demanded.

Flynn decided to tell the truth, not knowing if it would get him killed or not. "Dead," he said.

"The damn fool. I told him it would never work. That we ought to wait. But he and that lawyer got it in their heads that they could rush you. Is Prescott dead, too?"

"No."

"Well, he deserves to be."

The pressure of the knife blade against his throat eased, although the stiletto was still within a flick of a wrist of cutting his throat. Flynn was glad she didn't ask who had killed Charlie.

"That's better," he managed.

"What do you fools want with this train, anyhow?" she asked. "You're ruining everything."

"I could speak easier without that knife against my throat."

She studied him with hard, shrewd eyes. Green in this dim light, he noticed. Eyes like a cat. Or a whore.

"All right," she said. Her hand moved away, although she kept her eyes locked on Flynn's face. He shifted slightly, preparing to grab for her wrist.

But the blade was suddenly back, thrust into the space between his legs and poking up into his crotch. She grinned wickedly.

Flynn's heart leapt into his throat. He spoke, his voice an octave higher. "Mother of God, be careful, woman."

"You're the one who should be careful," she said. "Now tell me. Where are you going with the train?"

"Just south of Cumberland to a town called Romney," Flynn said. "Then we'll head down the Shenandoah Valley to Richmond on horseback."

She looked puzzled. "Why?"

"To give the Yankees hell," he explained.

It was clear she knew nothing about Abraham Lincoln being aboard the train, Flynn thought, and he wasn't about to enlighten her. Stealing a train to raise hell seemed about as good a reason as any.

"You mean you're not after the money?"

"What money?"

She didn't answer him. Instead, she said, "You're Flynn. I

overheard you telling that old busybody back there your name."

"Yes."

"I'm Nellie." The pressure of the knife eased. "So, Flynn, you like to raise hell, do you?"

"You could say that," Flynn answered, wondering what the woman was getting at.

"You're Irish," Nellie said. "The Irish are brave. And lucky."

Flynn was losing patience with this Baltimore whore. "Sure, and we piss green, too. What's your point, woman?"

"I need your help, Flynn. Charlie's dead, and I can't do it alone."

"Do what?"

Steel flashed, and the razor-edged stiletto disappeared up her sleeve. He had passed some kind of test. Flynn knew he should fetch her a good slap for nearly cutting his throat, then drag her back to the passenger car. But he was curious to know what all this was about.

"What do you think is in all these boxes around us?" she asked.

"Why don't you tell me."

She leaned toward him. "Money."

"What are you talking about?"

"It's the payroll for the Union garrison at Cumberland, Flynn. Six months of pay for 12,000 soldiers."

Flynn felt as if he had been struck. Now the guards on the train at Sykesville made sense. The soldiers weren't guarding Lincoln. They were guarding the money. "How much?"

"Charlie and I figured around four hundred thousand."

"Sweet Jesus," Flynn muttered.

For the first time, he looked more closely around him. Because of the near darkness, it was hard to distinguish much except a jumble of boxes and parcels.

"Let's let in a bit of light," he said, and pulled back a flap of canvas that covered a window. The sunlight revealed several strongboxes, built of dark oak and bound with iron. Each box was about two feet square and must have contained thousands of dollars. He counted six boxes altogether.

"They're not locked," Nellie said, reading his mind. "I guess the army doesn't worry about being robbed."

Flynn walked over and examined a strongbox. There was a hasp and clasp, but no lock. He flipped back the lid. A stack of Yankee greenbacks, neatly arranged, lay inside. He took out a bundle, fanned the edge of the stack with his thumb, then put it back.

"Look at that," he said in an awed voice. He had seen his share of black market cash in Richmond, but never so much money in one place. "There's a fortune in that one box alone."

It was indeed a fortune, far more than an honest man could ever hope to earn, considering a soldier's pay was sixteen dollars a month, and that in near-worthless Confederate scrip. Even a skilled worker in Washington City earned just two dollars per day.

Flynn's black market boss paid him well, but this was money the like of which he had never seen before. All thoughts of loyalty to anyone in Richmond evaporated at the thought of the wealth in the strongboxes.

"Let's split it, Flynn," Nellie urged. "Just me and you. That's two hundred thousand dollars apiece."

"How the hell do we get this off the train?" he wondered out loud.

"That means you'll help?"

"For two hundred thousand dollars, Nellie Jones, there's not much I wouldn't do."

"Even desert your friends?"

Flynn gave a short laugh. "They're not exactly my friends,

but that's a long story. Besides, they'll do just fine without me. I just hope none of them come in here and see these strongboxes."

She beckoned him toward the door. "First thing we have to do is get out of here. We don't want the others to come looking for us and find the money. We can talk later."

Flynn grinned wolfishly. "The lads will be suspicious anyway, me being alone with a beautiful woman."

"Then we'll have to put their minds to rest, won't we?" Before Flynn could react, Nellie gave him a hard, stinging slap that brought tears to his eyes.

"Damn you, woman!" Flynn rubbed his face.

"That will convince them, won't it?"

They crossed between the cars, Flynn's face smarting and red, and pushed through the door into the passenger car.

Thanks to the arrival of Hazlett and Pettibone, everything remained under control and the passengers sat in their seats, afraid to move. Charles Gilmore's body still lay in the aisle in a pool of blood.

All eyes were on them as they walked in. Nellie stared for a long moment at Gilmore's body, then turned to Flynn and whispered so that only he could hear: "This one's for Charlie."

She slapped him again. This time, she hit him so hard that Flynn's ears rang.

The other raiders laughed and hooted as Nellie hurried toward her seat, looking flustered. Stunned, Flynn shook his head to clear it. He had taken on prizefighters who hadn't hit him that hard.

"That'll learn you, Irish," Hazlett shouted. "Saucy women are too much for the likes of you to handle."

Flynn scowled and rubbed his aching face. Still, it was all he could do not to smile, thinking about all that money in the baggage car.

He glanced at Nellie, who was in her seat, staring straight ahead and appearing very different from the woman who just minutes before had almost cut his throat. Looking at her now, Flynn couldn't help but wonder if he had just cast his lot with the devil.

* * *

Near Parr's Ridge, Maryland • Noon

THE PLUME of smoke behind them appeared as a smudge against the blue sky. Colonel Percy had known this moment would come, but he had dreaded it all the same. They were, at last, being pursued by another locomotive.

"Looks like them Yankees finally wisened up," Hank Cunningham said, nodding at the telltale smoke as he hurried past with an armful of wood. "They found themselves a locomotive to chase us."

"Open the throttle," Percy said. They were not yet at full speed and this locomotive could do better than a mile a minute on a level track. With the lead they had, he doubted there was anything that could catch them. "We'll run for it."

"We're getting low on water," Wilson reminded him.

"I don't give a damn," Percy said. "Give her full throttle and put that Johnson bar as far forward as it will go."

"Yes, sir," Wilson said. Cunningham, hearing Percy's order, scrambled to fetch more wood for the *Chesapeake's* firebox. "One thing, sir. We're coming up on Parr's Ridge. It's quite a grade, and it's going to slow us down plenty."

"They'll have to slow down themselves," Percy said. "By then, we'll be roaring down the other side."

"Toward the Monocacy River bridge," Wilson pointed out. "But if the Yankees have any sense, they'll have men guarding the crossing. I was hoping we could take on water at Frederick Junction."

There was nothing to be done about that, Percy knew. They would find out what awaited them at the Monocacy when they reached the river. Meanwhile, they had to outrun whoever was pursuing them.

"Pour it on, boys, pour it on," Percy said. He turned to cross the tender. "I'll go pass word that things are about to get hot."

* * *

GREER SPOTTED the smoke from the *Chesapeake*. They didn't seem to be gaining on the raiders, but they weren't falling behind, either. Top speed for the little Grasshopper engine was maybe thirty miles per hour, which was much slower than the bigger *Chesapeake*, but far, far faster than the hand car.

"We'll catch them yet," Greer said. He was in high spirits for the first time that day. "Nobody steals my train and gets away with it."

It would give him great satisfaction to see the raiders captured and hanged. He just prayed they wouldn't wreck his beloved engine first.

Since climbing aboard the old locomotive, Frost and Schmidt were like different men. No longer did Greer need to berate them to continue the pursuit. They were running a locomotive again, an engine of steam and iron and fire, and the men were at home. Suddenly, they were caught up in the excitement of the chase. The Grasshopper wasn't terribly fast, but Frost and Schmidt knew their business and were wringing every possible bit of speed out of the engine.

"Now we're moving," Schmidt said, a grin crossing the big German's face. "We'll catch those sons of bitches yet, see if we don't."

"And then we'll stuff 'em in the firebox, right Oscar?" Frost laughed. "We'll burn their thieving asses."

"There are always soldiers posted at Frederick Junction," Greer added, glad that his two companions finally showed some excitement about the chase. After all, they were as tired as he was. "Let's see them get past those boys."

Greer knew the Monocacy garrison well enough because his train had passed through many times. There was a full company of infantry stationed at that vital crossing near Frederick. A battery of 12-pound Napoleon guns was trained on the bridge. The crossing was well-guarded, and with any luck, if the soldiers ahead were alert, the train thieves would be stopped, especially if a telegraph message reached the soldiers in time.

He believed the raiders were in a hopeless position. Most eastbound and westbound trains stopped at Frederick Junction to take on wood, water and passengers, along with the odd bit of freight bound for western Maryland or Baltimore. The soldiers would be suspicious if the *Chesapeake* made no sign of stopping. Of course, the train thieves wouldn't stand a chance with the sharp-eyed Yankee commander if they did stop. What lay ahead for the raiders, Greer thought with satisfaction, was a double-edged sword.

"We might catch them at Parr's Ridge," Schmidt pointed out. "This little engine, she can make the climb faster than they can with four cars."

Greer smiled and licked his lips, which tasted salty from the sweat he had worked up, first running and them helping to pump the push car in the *Chesapeake's* wake. Dimly, it registered that his leg ached from his old wound, but he ignored the pain and kept his eyes on the tracks ahead to where Parr's Ridge rose in the distance. It was also known as the Mount Airy grade, a sharp ridge in the gently rolling Piedmont plateau stretching from Chesapeake Bay to the western mountains, a hill that ran like a ripple in a blanket across an otherwise flat bed. While the tracks had followed the Patapsco River basin and then Bush Creek west to that point, on the other side they followed the Monocacy River basin to the Potomac River. Parr's Ridge was the only place where the B&O couldn't hold to the river grades.

The low, sharp ridge would slow the train racing ahead of them. They were close to catching the raiders now, very close. Greer turned and helped Frost heap wood into the raging firebox, burning now like fury itself.

* * *

THE TOWN of Gettysburg had been transformed. Red, white and blue bunting hung from the windows. Union flags flew. Everywhere you looked, houses wore new coats of white wash. It was a far cry from the war-ravaged town of the past summer.

Walking along the streets, the one-eyed man took in the crowds. The official dedication of the new national cemetery was not until tomorrow, but the festival atmosphere already had begun. While there were plenty of prayers and church services planned, the throngs in the streets were looking to forget the war and its horrors for a while. Liquor bottles were in abundance.

"Meat pies! Meat pies here!" called a man, hawking his wares. The savory smell of a gravy-filled pie in a buttery crust made the one-eyed man's stomach rumble. He bought a pie wrapped in a sheet of newsprint and devoured it on his way to the train station.

Abraham Lincoln was scheduled to arrive later that day, and he wanted to be there when the president came to town. Already, a huge crowd had gathered at the train station.

Young boys had climbed trees while their parents waved tiny hand-sewn flags.

Finally, the train came into sight, hugging along the tracks of the Northern Central Railroad that led directly to Baltimore and from there, on to Washington. The crowd grew excited. The one-eyed man was pressed from behind as more latecomers crowded in to catch a glimpse of their president.

When the train did stop in a gout of steam, a tall figure in black and wearing a stovepipe hat appeared. The crowd cheered. The president waved, then moved on to greet the local dignitaries waiting at the station. The one-eyed man watched in surprise.

Abraham Lincoln? He was puzzled. Then he found himself swept up by the crowd as it surged after the president, caught like a twig in a swirling river.

CHAPTER 20

Parr's Ridge, Maryland • 12:30 p.m.

COLONEL PERCY REACHED the passenger car just as Flynn and Pettibone carried out Charlie Gilmore's body.

"What the hell is going on?" Percy demanded.

Flynn held the feet and Pettibone carried the corpse by the shoulders, trying not to get any of Gilmore's blood and gore on his expensive civilian suit of clothes. Gilmore's eyes stared out from his head, which bumped against Pettibone's knees.

"We had a mutiny, Colonel," Flynn explained. "It was bound to happen, and it will happen again as long as we have passengers on this train."

Flynn and Pettibone balanced on the platform, swung the body between them to give it momentum—once, twice, three times—then launched it far beyond the tracks, where Gilmore's corpse rolled and flopped down a hillside.

"Goddamnit, Flynn, you've got to stop killing the passengers," Percy said, sounding annoyed.

"I only kill the ones who try to kill me first," Flynn replied.

"They'll have us in all the Northern newspapers as a bunch of bloodthirsty killers."

"Well, they're sure as hell not going to describe us as heroes in The New York Times," Flynn pointed out. "We did kidnap their president, after all."

"We can still conduct ourselves with honor," Percy said.

Flynn stared at him, surprised. "You really do believe all this business about honor and glory, don't you? Even after two years of fighting. It's all moonlight and magnolias to you, isn't it?"

"Take away everything else a man has, Flynn, and in the end all he's left with is his honor. I didn't ask to be sent on this raid but I'm going to do my duty. I'm going to see it through."

Pettibone was looking at the colonel with proud, shining eyes and Flynn thought, *there's another one*. These Southerners were consumed by their notions of honor and glory. It was what had gotten them into this war in the first place. He thought of the money hidden away in the baggage car and his plans for it, and felt just a bit ashamed.

"You're a good man, Colonel," Flynn said. "I just hope we all live to see tomorrow."

By now the locomotive had reached the foot of Parr's Ridge and the train was slowing perceptibly as the engine struggled on the steep grade. Mountains on the horizon ahead were visible as a blue blur, like distant waves.

Percy nodded behind them, where the smoke trail of the pursuing train was plainly visible. "We might have a bit more trouble soon and not just from the passengers. They've sent a train after us."

Flynn leaned out from between the cars and peered into the distance. The advance column of smoke had the look of something serious. "That they have. Will they catch us?"

"There's always a chance," Percy said. "But this locomotive is fast, and we're far ahead of them."

The three men returned to the car. Hazlett had already gone back to his own car. Captain Fletcher still had his Colt out, ready to shoot anyone who moved. As a consequence, the passengers sat rigid as stone in their seats, staring at the revolver's muzzle. Even Mrs. Henrietta Parker was no longer hysterical, but glared indignantly at the raiders while her husband murmured in her ear in the same way he might soothe a spirited horse. Somehow, he was managing to keep in check the tongue-lashing the woman obviously wanted to give her captors.

William Prescott was slumped in a seat, rubbing the back of his head and looking suitably cowed. Nellie Jones sat demurely. Flynn caught her eye and gave her a wink. She pretended not to notice.

Benjamin was massaging his side. He winced as he touched a tender spot. "I believe that fat man done cracked my ribs," he announced.

Colonel Percy took in the scene, his eyes lingering on the blood-streaked ceiling. The situation with the passengers, he thought, had gone too far. Already, three were dead. Killing innocent civilians would not play well, he knew, in the court of public opinion. To make matters worse, he knew Flynn was probably right when he said it wasn't over yet. Percy decided he would put all the passengers off the next time they stopped because there was no longer any reason to worry about them warning the Yankees. Judging by the trail of smoke behind them, the Yankees already knew. Meanwhile, he would do what he could to make certain there would be no more violence.

Percy raised his voice. "Ladies and gentlemen, listen to me. We will abide no more trouble from you. This man— " he nodded at Captain Fletcher, who looked savage enough with the pistol in his hand " — will shoot anyone who leaves his—or her—seat. Rest assured, however, that we have no desire to keep hostages. You'll all be put off the next time we stop."

"Stranded," hissed Mrs. Parker. Wide-eyed, her husband squeezed her arm to silence her. Percy stood for a moment, glaring at the woman. The tension was broken when Hank Cunningham burst through the door, his face a mask of sweat-streaked ash.

"Colonel, the engineer needs you," he said urgently.

Percy looked calmly around at the passengers. "Remember that you've been warned," he said, then turned and walked out. Once he and Cunningham were alone on the platform, Percy demanded, "What's so goddamn important that it couldn't wait, Hank?"

The fireman pointed behind them. Compared to how fast she had been going, the *Chesapeake* had slowed to what was virtually a crawl as she struggled up the Parr's Ridge grade. Smoke from the pursuing train had crept much closer.

"They're gaining on us, all right," Percy said, seeing at once why Cunningham had come to get him. "Come on."

Together, they made their way back over the tender to the engine. Wilson was busy hovering over the controls and cursing, but there was nothing he could do to make the locomotive pull any harder or faster up the slope.

"They'll catch us at this rate, Colonel."

Percy looked back. The grade was so steep he could now see the tops of the other cars below him. Suddenly, the pursuing engine came into view. He recognized the old, so-called Grasshopper engine they had passed on the siding and cursed himself for not stopping to disable it somehow. It was chugging along quickly enough, just the engine and tender, flying over the flat plain that led to Parr's Ridge.

"Damn," he said. "We may be in for trouble."

* * *

"Now we've got them!" Greer shouted into the wind as the *Chesapeake* appeared ahead, creeping up the steep slope of Parr's ridge.

Schmidt and Frost whooped with him. Finally, they had caught up to the train.

Now that the locomotive was in sight, Greer had some doubts about what to do if it came to a fight. He and Schmidt were armed with a shotgun and a revolver from the Grasshopper engine's crew, but that gave them just two guns while the raiders had revolvers—and would use them. The train thieves were killers and they had shot at Greer and his crew the last time they got close.

In their favor, however, Greer was convinced there weren't many men aboard the train. Otherwise, Greer reasoned, the thieves would have stood and fought the last time he and his men caught up. In hindsight, it was good the thieves hadn't stopped, because the fight would have been decidedly one-sided, considering the only weapon Greer had then was the shotgun. They were still lightly armed, but Greer was too exhilarated to be cautious.

"Give her everything she's got," he shouted to Schmidt, but the command was unnecessary. The engineer already had the throttle wide open. The locomotive caught the grade and the drive wheels churned up the incline, hot on the trail of the raiders.

* * *

Flynn opened a window, stuck out his head, and was immediately pelted with a hot rain of ash and cinders from the *Chesapeake's* smokestack. Still, he managed to get a glimpse of the tracks behind them and was amazed to see another, smaller locomotive right behind the *Chesapeake*.

Short of making the train go faster, there wasn't anything he could do about it. They had all known this moment might come. Flynn sauntered down the aisle, shaking cinders out of his hair, ignoring the hateful looks of the passengers. He knew that in their eyes he was a killer, a criminal and a Rebel, and they had nothing but hostility toward him. If the Yankees on that train back there caught them, Flynn was sure the passengers would be more than willing to hang him and all the rest of the raiders.

"Ma'am," Flynn said, stopping beside Nellie's seat and tipping his hat. "May I join you?"

Nellie didn't answer, but Flynn sat down anyway.

"Wee bit windy out there," he said, plucking at a piece of charcoal that had lodged under his collar. He lowered his voice so that he couldn't be overheard. "Looks like we're about to be overtaken."

Nellie stared at him, alarmed. "What do you mean?"

"There's a locomotive right behind us and it's climbing this slope better than we are, from the looks of it."

"You mean we're going to be caught?"

"Aye, Nellie lass, and all that money, too, which is the shame of it." His voice was a whisper now. "That is, unless you have some magical plan you want to share with me."

Nellie shook her head and whispered a reply. "There's no help for us here. We have to get closer to Cumberland. There is a plan, and it involves others, but it depends on the train making it to within a few miles of the city."

Flynn nodded, then sighed. "At the moment we're a long, long way from Cumberland."

"Then you better think of something."

"I was afraid you might say that. Nellie, let me ask you something. Why did you pick me out of all the others?"

"You're the one who came after me in the baggage car."

"You mean you would have asked Captain Fletcher or even Hazlett if they were the ones who'd gone after you instead?"

"No," Nellie said, thinking about it. "I would have cut their throats."

"I don't doubt it." He caught himself putting his hand to his throat, remembering the cold touch of the knife blade.

By now, the train was barely moving. Outside, someone began shouting.

Flynn stood, checked his revolver, then moved to a window and opened it. "When all else fails, shoot the bastards," he said.

* * *

GREER DUCKED as the first shots snapped overhead. The odd-looking but powerful Grasshopper locomotive chugged closer to the *Chesapeake*. Ignoring the bullets flying at them, Greer had no thought other than to overtake his stolen train.

"Come on, man, come on," he urged Schmidt.

"*Das ist vor*," Schmidt said. Frost worked like a madman, stuffing the firebox with wood.

As they roared closer, Greer could again see the two men on the last car. Both had revolvers in their hands. Somewhere in the back of his mind, Greer hoped there weren't many more raiders aboard the train. Even a handful of armed men against three with an old shotgun and a pistol hardly seemed like good odds. Still, Greer forgot all caution as they raced closer.

Briefly, he wondered why there were two armed men on the last car. Were they simply defending the train, or was there something in the last car worth guarding? If that was the case, Greer thought bitterly, then someone should have warned him that there was more aboard to worry about than the payroll money.

Greer picked up the double-barreled shotgun and leveled it at the back of the train, pulled back the twin hammers, and yanked the two triggers in rapid succession. The shotgun kicked viciously and Greer lost sight of his target in the cloud of blue smoke that billowed around him until the wind whipped it away.

A hail of buckshot shredded the air and pinged off the iron railings of Lincoln's car. Shards flew as shot ripped into the wooden sides, but none of the lead could penetrate the heavy oak.

Aboard the train, John Cook swore and clawed at his cheek, where a flying splinter of wood had embedded itself. He pulled it free, feeling the blood run down his face and soak his beard. He looked over at Lieutenant Cater, who was crouched behind the railing. The lieutenant was strangely still.

"You all right, Lieutenant?" Cook asked.

When there was no answer, Cook reached down and took Cater's shoulder. The lieutenant slumped back, revealing an ugly red gouge along his temple where buckshot had cut a deep furrow that exposed the white bone of his skull. Blood poured from the wound.

"You're goin' to be all right, Lieutenant," Cook said, although he wasn't so sure. Blood was soaking the collar of the lieutenant's coat.

Private Cook quickly pulled out the tail of his shirt and tore off a strip. Fortunately, their new civilian clothes were clean enough to serve as bandages. As he worked to tie up the wound, he kept a wary eye on the pursuing engine. It was still gaining on them, although it appeared the only weapon the men aboard carried was the shotgun, which one of the men was busy reloading. A shotgun was a poor weapon for taking on a whole trainload of Rebels, Cook thought, but it had been good enough to fell Lieutenant Cater, something even the fiercest artillery at Gettysburg had been unable to do the last time they were up north.

Cook quickly bound the wound with the rough bandage. It would at least stop the worst of the bleeding. The lieutenant needed more help than a rough bandage, but that would have to wait.

He picked up the lieutenant's revolver, so that he now held a Colt in each hand. Cook took a quick look at the door of the President's car. He was sure Lincoln and his bodyguard were safe. The wood was thick and hard as iron. It would take more than a shotgun blast to penetrate the walls. He hoped Abe Lincoln wasn't too curious about the commotion. With Lieutenant Cater wounded and the *Chesapeake* being hotly pursued, there would never be a better opportunity for the Yankee president to attempt an escape.

There was no time to worry about that. The smaller engine was right behind them, so close that Cook could clearly see the angry faces of the Yankees, one of whom had finished reloading the shotgun and was now raising it to his shoulder.

Before the man could fire, Cook lifted the revolvers and unleashed his own hail of lead.

* * *

"THOSE YANKEES ARE right on our tail and they're shooting at us," Flynn shouted, popping his head in from the window. "Fletcher, you cover the passengers. Benjamin, lad, open a window on the other side and put that fancy Colt of yours to work."

Flynn leaned out the window as far as he dared to get a

clear shot at the pursuers. He aimed the Le Mat and squeezed off a shot.

Behind him, he heard more guns open fire from Hazlett's car. A bullet snicked the air close by his ear and Flynn had to wonder if Hazlett would end their feud by shooting him in the back of the head. The thought made the hairs on the back of Flynn's neck stand on end. Flynn knew he wouldn't have been the first soldier shot in the back during battle by an enemy in his own ranks. He forced the thought from his mind. There were more immediate enemies to worry about at the moment.

* * *

FROM THE TRAIN AHEAD, THE RAIDERS' guns blazed at Greer and his crew. Bullets popped and hissed through the air and the three men took what shelter they could on the largely open deck of the grasshopper.

"Du bist schweinen!" Schmidt swore at the raiders. He was busy trying to hide his big body while still working the engine's controls. A bullet plucked at his sleeve and he tried to make himself yet smaller. Frost jumped into the tender. Nothing made men feel so helpless as being fired upon and not being able to shoot back.

Greer took the revolver and emptied it at the last car. One of the thieves was down, hit by the shotgun blast, but the remaining man fired back, a revolver in each hand. Greer ducked down and reloaded.

To Greer, it was like Bull Run all over again. Memories flooded back of being hit in the leg. There was so much pain, so many weeks in the hospital. Still, he had never been a coward, not at Bull Run and not now, either. If his time was up, it was up, and there wasn't a damn thing he could do about it. Grimly, Greer raised the revolver again.

Bullets whip-cracked around him, but he was oblivious. Greer fired. The man on the train ahead was busy loading his revolvers. He ducked down as bullet knocked chips off the car and struck sparks off the iron railing.

The two trains were now no more than fifty feet apart. They had climbed Parr's Ridge, reached the top, and run a close race across the level summit. Now that they were on level ground, Greer's locomotive couldn't pull any closer.

For all the effort it had taken to climb the ridge, it didn't offer any spectacular views. Mountains still loomed blue ahead, while harvested fields and bare woodlands dotted the rolling hills. The Monocacy River was a brown ribbon through the countryside.

Then the track began to descend, gradually at first, then at a steeper pitch. All at once the huge weight of the *Chesapeake*, which had slowed the train so much as it climbed the ridge, helped the train gather speed. The locomotive's massive driving wheels caught and spun powerfully with pent-up energy. The train surged ahead.

Up in the *Chesapeake*'s cab, a slow smile crept across Wilson's face as he saw how the tracks ahead sloped downward. "Hang on, boys," Wilson said half to himself, half out loud as he worked the locomotive's controls. "Ain't nobody can catch us now."

CHAPTER 21

"THEY'RE GETTING AWAY!" Greer shouted. Frustrated, he threw down the empty revolver and struggled to reload the shotgun. A flurry of gunfire still came from the train ahead, but he was as oblivious to the bullets as he might be of a few raindrops. "Come on, you two, pour it on!"

"She won't go any faster," Schmidt yelled in reply.

Where the climb had favored Greer's low-geared Grasshopper locomotive, gravity was now on the *Chesapeake's* side. A minute before it had appeared the pursuers were going to overtake the train, but now the gap widened. Greer cursed. Not a damn thing he could do about it, either, considering the *Chesapeake* was much larger and more powerful than the pursuing grasshopper locomotive.

A bullet pinged off a metal bar near his head, but Greer ignored it. Then the fire slackened as the raiders noticed they were pulling ahead. In frustration, Greer raised the shotgun and fired a parting blast. Already, the range was too great and the buckshot fell short. The man on the last car snapped off two shots in return, but the bullets punched at the air well above their heads.

"Was soll ich tun?" Schmidt asked. He looked clearly relieved that the shooting had stopped. Big as he was, the oddly constructed Grasshopper offered little shelter from bullets. Schmidt realized he had lapsed into German in his excitement and repeated, "What should I do?"

"Keep up our speed," Greer answered. "We need to stay with them."

"We can't keep up with the *Chesapeake*," Schmidt complained. "Not in this old locomotive. You know that."

"Just do as I say," Greer growled, still clutching the shotgun. He was in no mood to argue.

The *Chesapeake* had won the race. She was already far ahead, the powerful drive wheels churning, smoke pouring from her funnel in a thick plume bent nearly horizontal by the wind of her own passage. The land was leveling out as the dueling locomotives left Parr's Ridge behind and entered the plain that led to the Monocacy River. Just a few miles beyond lay the mighty Potomac and the crossing at Harpers Ferry.

If the raiders ever got that far. Greer was convinced the soldiers garrisoned at the Monocacy River bridge would stop the stolen train, especially if a telegraph message had reached them. And if the Monocacy garrison failed there were always the guards at Harpers Ferry. If the *Chesapeake* made it across those two bridges, however, there wasn't much that could keep them from running the train clear to Ohio if they wanted.

Damn the payroll money, Greer thought. It had to be what the train thieves were after. Then again, it didn't make sense that the raiders were still running with the train, not if they had done any planning at all. A stolen train attracted a great deal of attention. Greer thought the raiders would have been better off dividing the money between themselves, abandoning the train, and then slipping quietly away into the countryside. One thing for certain, it would mean a lot less trouble for Greer if the raiders abandoned the train.

Meanwhile, he watched helplessly as the *Chesapeake* pulled even farther ahead.

"Pile on the wood, Frost," Greer said. "Cram that firebox full. We ain't beat yet."

* * *

ABOARD THE *CHESAPEAKE*, everything was in confusion. Colonel Percy heard the shooting begin, but couldn't see what was happening from the locomotive cab.

"Hold your fire!" he shouted, hoping someone would hear.No sense wasting ammunition, he thought. They might need every round before the day was through.

The gunfire slackened as they crested Parr's Ridge, and the raiders jeered at their pursuers as they fell further behind in the older engine. One or two men took parting shots at the pursuers, but the range had become too great for the revolvers to have any effect. The passengers sat through it all, looking terrified as their captors leaned out the windows and blazed away.

At the end of the train, aboard the President's car, Private Cook knelt on the floor of the small platform, trying to make Lieutenant Cater comfortable by putting his own coat under Cater's head as a pillow. As he looked down at the unconscious lieutenant, the gold wedding band on Cater's left hand caught his attention. Unable to resist the temptation, Cook twisted the ring off the lieutenant's finger and slipped it into his own pocket.

Theft was one thing, but Cook wasn't so heartless that he wanted the lieutenant to die. He wanted to get help, but there was nothing he could do while the train was moving. The only way to reach the rest of the train was to climb the short ladder nearby and hustle across the top of Lincoln's car and down the other side, then cross through the baggage car. He had no desire to make that dangerous trip, and he didn't want to leave the lieutenant alone. Besides, Lincoln still needed guarding, and Colonel Percy would give him hell if he left his post.

With the pursuers still in sight, Cook wasn't about to signal a stop. The wounded lieutenant would have to wait for help. It was bad luck that he had been wounded, but it was a chance any soldier took.

The lieutenant was still unconscious, and Cook wondered if the bullet had done more damage than he had thought. At least the worst of the bleeding had stopped. If the lieutenant was that bad off, Cook thought, maybe the colonel could put him off with the passengers at the next stop. There might at least be a country doctor somewhere along the route who could help him. If that happened, they would leave Cater behind. Cook wouldn't have to worry about the stolen ring in his pocket being discovered.

Not that the *Chesapeake* would be stopping anytime soon. The engine rolled west, going faster every minute, racing toward the Monocacy River.

* * *

Frederick Junction on the Monocacy River • 1 p.m.

CAPTAIN THADDEUS LOWELL, who commanded the battery guarding the Monocacy River bridge, spotted the column of smoke racing toward the crossing. He was too far from Parr's Ridge to hear any of the shooting, and so wasn't expecting anything out of the ordinary.

"She's a comin' on boys," Captain Lowell said. "In a hurry, too, from the looks of it."

Guarding the river crossing was dull duty, and the passing of a train broke the monotony of staring at the Monocacy's muddy waters. Rebels were always causing trouble along the railroad's western reaches, but in central Maryland, all had been quiet since Robert E. Lee's summertime invasion months ago.

"Looks like she ain't alone, Captain," a gunner remarked.

The captain looked more closely. The soldier was right. There were two trails of smoke in sight, which was unusual, because engines almost always traveled alone. He squinted, trying to see what was going on. The trains were just visible in the distance. Out front was a bigger engine, probably the *Chesapeake*—she was due that day. The second engine was smaller and appeared to be losing ground to the first. Still, if he hadn't known better, he would have sworn the smaller engine was trying to catch the bigger one. The two trains were not traveling the safe, regulation distance apart.

"Captain?" one of the gunners asked.

"I see them," he snapped. The gun crew also had sensed something wasn't right.

He hesitated a moment before issuing orders. The captain wasn't about to have his battery open fire on any B&O Railroad locomotives, even if they did look suspicious. But there was something less drastic he could do.

"Throw the switch!" he shouted to a group of soldiers standing near the track. One of the men cupped a hand to his ear to show they hadn't heard the command. It was more likely, he thought, that they didn't understand it.

The captain mimicked a man throwing the big switch located just behind the soldiers. They stared back, obviously puzzled by his strange movements. "The switch!" he yelled.

"Lazy bastards are always playing dumb," the gunner muttered. He spat. Since Gettysburg, the ranks had been swelled with draftees and hired substitutes who were less than exemplary soldiers.

"Go tell them to throw the goddamn switch," the captain said to the gunner. He took a quick look toward the locomotives racing closer and closer. "You'd best hurry."

* * *

"No!" Greer shouted into the wind.

Disaster lay ahead. He saw at once what was going to happen. He had been expecting at any moment to hear the battery open fire on the raiders' train. But no guns fired. Roaring closer to the river, he could see the gunners standing around. To his horror, the only activity he saw was at the switch that sent trains off the main track and onto a siding.

The soldiers weren't railroad men. What they were about to do was just as deadly as unleashing the battery's guns. They didn't realize that a train traveling at full throttle would derail if it struck a turned switch. Even if it didn't jump the track, there was no way a speeding train could stop in time on the short siding before it ran out of rails. Either way, it meant disaster.

"No!" Greer shouted again, vainly trying to be heard over the engine's roar. He waved his arms wildly. The soldiers, bent at their work, didn't see him.

Up ahead, the speeding *Chesapeake* flashed past the soldiers. They had intended to stop the first engine as well, but hadn't been able to operate the switch in time. The locomotive raced toward the bridge. Even if they had wanted to, there was no way the soldiers could slew the guns around and fire in time to keep the train from reaching the bridge. Nothing in the world could stop the Rebel train now.

Greer's train wouldn't be so lucky. Heart racing, he saw

the switch being pulled down. Rails twisted out of place. He shouted at Schmidt, "Reverse! Reverse!"

Both men grabbed the Johnson bar and wrestled it backwards. But the locomotive was traveling too fast. Iron wheels slid down polished iron rails with an unearthly shriek. The engine was as unstoppable as doom itself.

"Mein Gott!" Schmidt swore, seeing what was about to happen.

The engine reached the switch. It went neither straight ahead nor down the siding, but instead launched itself clear out into the long autumn grass. Frost wailed in terror.

"Hang on!" Greer shouted.

The engine plowed across the ground, sending up clods of earth. Soldiers jumped out of the way. The tender jerked, twisted, and overturned, scattering its load of wood like a burst of shrapnel. Frost went flying.

The engine continued its sleigh ride, with Schmidt and Greer hanging on for dear life. It bounced over the rails at the end of the siding and headed for the muddy river.

"Jump!" Greer shouted. "Oscar, jump!"

Schmidt was already leaping. Greer jumped, too, and in one awful moment before he hit the ground and tumbled, he saw the engine rush on.

The locomotive careened toward the river, knocking aside telegraph poles as if they were toothpicks. Men scrambled out of the way like so many blue-coated ants. The train reached the banks of the Monocacy and plunged into the brown current, landing sideways with a tremendous splash that sent up a geyser of river water. Steam hissed and spat from the flooded engine as the river quenched the firebox. The wheels spun on, trying to grip rails that were no longer there, like a deer's legs might twitch even after the hunter's fatal shot.

Cutting through all the noise was the distant sound of the

Chesapeake's whistle. Most times a train whistle stirred something in Greer's soul. Now, he only tasted the dirt in his mouth and thought the whistle sounded triumphant, like a war cry—or even scornful. The raiders were laughing at him.

Damn them. He tried to shout, but the fall had knocked the breath from his lungs. *Damn those bastards.*

He swore he was going to see them hanged, every last one of them.

"You all right, mister?" a voice asked, and Greer looked up into the face of a young soldier who stood nearby, poking a musket at him.

He coughed. Tried to speak and couldn't. The wind was still knocked out of him. He rolled over, gasping for air. He recognized the conductor from his frequent stops at the junction.

"Hell, it's Greer," the Union captain said, hurrying over. "Point that musket somewhere else, Private, before you hurt somebody."

Hands reached for Greer and helped him up. Captain Lowell shoved a silver flask into his hands. The whiskey restored his voice. Schmidt and Frost received similar medicinal doses and were soon back on their feet. Greer thought it was a miracle that no one had been injured or killed by the runaway locomotive.

Schmidt stared at the steaming hulk of iron in the river. "*Gott*-damn thieves," the German said. "Thieving *schweinen*."

"What thieves?" the captain asked, turning to Greer, who was soon answering a flurry of questions.

* * *

WHEN THE CAPTAIN had heard enough, he shouted his orders. They would form a detail of twenty men and march west along the tracks. It would have been better to wire a warning ahead, but the train wreck had reduced the telegraph to a jumble of broken poles and snapped wires.

On foot, of course, the captain knew they would never catch the train, but there was always the chance the raiders would abandon it somewhere along the tracks. Besides, the captain welcomed anything that broke the dull routine of guarding the junction.

A downy faced lieutenant spoke up. "Sir, we're going to chase a train—on foot?"

"Lieutenant, the property of a United States business has been seized by lawless thieves," the captain said, his tone indicating he did not like to be questioned by lieutenants. He nodded at Greer. "That train was under the command of Mr. Greer here. He's a veteran wounded in the service of his country. Besides, we're going to commandeer the first train we come across and chase those raiders to hell and back if we have to. Now, let's move out!"

CHAPTER 22

Potomac River near Point of Rocks, Maryland • 1:30 p.m.

TEN MILES beyond the Monocacy River, Colonel Percy ordered a halt. They had been racing across the countryside, but there was no evidence that anyone was still giving chase. The sky behind them was clear and blue, unstained by the smoke from a pursuing locomotive.

"Keep up a full head of steam, boys, and be prepared to leave at a moment's notice," he said to the engineer and fireman. "The next bunch to come after us might have more guns."

"We're low on water, sir," Cephas Wilson reminded him.

"We'll stop the first chance we get," Percy said.

The colonel jumped down from the locomotive. He wasn't happy about stopping, but he really had no other choice. It was a gambler's call: race on toward the Potomac River crossing at Harpers Ferry, hoping everything held together, or stop and reassess. He chose the latter, mainly because they had been too lucky so far and there was no reason to stretch that luck to the breaking point. There were still many miles between them and the safety of the Shenandoah Valley.

Hazlett stuck his head out an open window and called out as Percy passed, "What's happening, Colonel?"

"Get out here, Hazlett," Percy shouted back. "Leave Pettibone to guard the passengers. I need Forbes out here, too, to cut some wires while we're stopped."

Walking a little further, Percy yelled similar instructions to Flynn. The men wasted no time getting outside the cars. Percy put Willie Forbes to work cutting telegraph wires. Considering the wreckage created when the pursuing engine derailed, the soldiers back at the Monocacy River had not likely telegraphed a warning message ahead. Still, there was no way of knowing for certain whether or not the telegraph was functional. It was in the raiders' best interest to disrupt communications whenever possible, which was what Forbes was now doing as he shimmied up a pole with a large Bowie knife clenched between his teeth.

Satisfied that Forbes was doing what he could to sever the telegraph lines, the colonel turned to Hazlett and Flynn. He noticed the two men stood some distance apart, regarding each other with barely contained hatred.Under different circumstances, he was sure they would be at each other's throats. Percy was not happy that these two men had decided to make enemies of each other, but he did not have time to play peacemaker.

"We'll put the passengers off here," Percy said. "We don't seem to be near anyplace in particular, so I doubt they can do us much harm by spreading the alarm. Harpers Ferry is only a few miles off, and once we make it across the river, the Yankees don't have much chance of catching us."

Hazlett nodded toward Forbes, high up on a pole. "We're a little late with those wires, Colonel. Those soldiers back at the Monocacy crossing will have warned the Yankees at Harpers Ferry that we're coming. They'll have quite a reception for us, to be sure."

"We haven't much choice," Percy said. "It's the only way across the Potomac. It's just a chance we'll have to take."

"Besides, we've already got their president," Flynn said. "They can try to stop the train, but we'll still be able to put a bullet in Honest Abe. Of course, that's only a last resort."

"I say kill him now and get it over with," Hazlett said, sneering. "If ever there was a Yankee that deserved killing, it's him."

"We have our orders," Percy said, wanting to put an end to the discussion. "We will do our duty."

"We'll all get killed," Hazlett replied.

"It's vital that we at least try to get President Lincoln to Richmond," Percy said, unhappy that his cousin-in-law was putting him on the defensive. "It could turn the tide of the war. The South might yet be victorious, or at least be in a position to negotiate a favorable peace with the North."

Flynn noted the tension between the two men. The colonel was intent on doing his duty but Hazlett wanted the easy way out. Of course, if the Yankees caught up with them they would have a problem even carrying out an assassination.

"You heard the colonel," he said. "We have our orders."

Hazlett snarled at him. "You damn Irishman. Just who do you think you are, to be reminding us about our orders?"

"You're the one who keeps forgetting them."

The scar on Hazlett's face flared red. If the two men had been alone, they would have come to blows, or worse. Percy didn't give them the opportunity. "All right. That's enough of that. We've got Yankees to fight, not each other."

At that moment, they heard a shout from the last car of the train. "Colonel!" It was John Cook, waving urgently.

Instinctively, all three men reached for their guns, expecting trouble.

"Come on," Percy said, and they ran to the back of the train.

There, they found Cook kneeling beside the unconscious lieutenant. The rough bandage around Cater's head was crimson with fresh blood, and the floor of the train platform was stained red.

"What happened?" Percy demanded.

"Them fools chasin' us had a shotgun, Colonel," Cook said. "Must of been loaded with buck and ball. The lieutenant done got shot in the head. He ain't come to since."

Flynn knelt beside the wounded officer. He had done his share of doctoring, both in and out of the army, and he pried up the bandage with skilled fingers to inspect the wound.

He saw an ugly gash, still oozing blood. Head wounds always bled horribly, and as bad as this wound looked, the lieutenant must have lost a lot of blood. Flynn saw none of the telltale clear liquid of a brain wound, which would likely have killed Cater outright, anyhow. The shotgun ball must have burrowed under the skin and gouged a furrow along the curve of the bone. The skull had been rapped awfully hard, maybe even fractured, which explained why Cater remained unconscious. The lieutenant moaned and Flynn took his hand away, easing the bandage back into place. A fresh rivulet of blood leaked from beneath the cloth and ran down Cater's face.

"He needs a doctor," Flynn announced. "If he doesn't get help soon, he'll die."

"Let's leave him with the passengers when we put them off," Hazlett said. "We can't be burdened with a wounded man."

"No," Percy spoke abruptly. "We'll take him with us."

Hazlett began to protest. "But Colonel—"

"Shut up, Hazlett." Percy knew he was being overly harsh, but he was in no mood to debate with the sergeant. If Hazlett

hadn't been his cousin-in-law, he would have rid himself of
such a compassionless man a long time ago. Lieutenant Cater
was like a younger brother to Percy. He would not listen to
any talk of abandoning him to the Yankees. He wouldn't be
able to face Cater's family back home in Fauquier County if
he did that, much less himself. "We're not leaving him here so
the Yankees can doctor him up, then hang him. We'll take
him with us. You two go see if there's anything in that
baggage car you can use to make a stretcher. We'll carry him
up to one of the passenger cars."

"Yes, sir," Hazlett said in an exaggerated fashion.

"Goddamnit, just get it done. We're wasting time."

Trying to control his anger at Hazlett, Percy watched the
two sergeants go. They walked carefully apart, not talking.
Side by side, the Irishman was bigger, but Hazlett had a lean
toughness about him, like a hickory post.

"There's bad blood between them two," said Cook, who
also was watching the men walk off. "Sooner or later, one is
goin' to shoot the other."

Percy grunted. Secretly, he would not mind being rid of
his cousin-in-law. The thought gave him a twinge of guilt,
thinking of all the tight places he and Hazlett had been
through. He owed the man something, for all that. He forced
all such thoughts out of his mind, however, because at the
moment he had other worries.

Damn Colonel Norris! He was safe back in Richmond,
spinning more webs of intrigue while good men like Silas
Cater lay bleeding, maybe even dying, because of this foolhardy raid. It was Norris, too, who had saddled them with
that idiot, Captain Fletcher. There was a man who was
likely to get himself and some of his fellow raiders killed
before the mission was over. Norris had also sent along
Sergeant Flynn to make certain his orders were carried out.
Percy realized that, oddly enough, once he had overcome his

initial resentment of Flynn, he had come to depend on the man.

Percy nodded at the door to Lincoln's car. "Any sound from there?" he asked Cook, keeping his voice low.

"No, sir," Cook whispered in reply. "Quiet as can be."

Percy stared at the door in wonder. It amazed him that the President of the United States was on the other side. The leader of the entire Union! For a moment, Percy was tempted to take Hazlett's advice and force his way in to shoot Lincoln, thus putting an end to this crazed race across Maryland. But, as Flynn had pointed out, those were not Norris's orders. And he could see the value of capturing Lincoln alive as a bargaining tool.

Not that Percy was worried about any implied threat on Flynn's part. Percy was, above all, a good soldier. He would follow orders not because of Norris, or Norris's watchdog, but because of his sense of duty to the Confederacy.

Even so, Hazlett had a point about Harpers Ferry. If the Yankees stopped them there, Percy would have no choice but to shoot Lincoln, because bringing the Union president to Richmond as a prize—and pawn—of war would no longer be possible.

"He's still bleeding, Colonel," Cook said despairingly. Cook was pressing hard on the bandages, trying to staunch the flow, but the lieutenant's blood soaked through and reddened Cook's hands. "It just won't stop."

Percy leaned close over the unconscious man. "Hang on, Silas," he murmured. "Hang on."

* * *

"I'LL GO HAVE a look in there," Flynn said outside the baggage car. "You best stay here and keep an eye out."

"Since when do you give me orders?" Hazlett demanded.

Flynn shrugged. "The colonel's busy tending the lieutenant and someone ought to keep watch for any trains chasing us. If you don't like it, then you go bump your way around in there and I'll keep watch."

Hazlett grinned crookedly, realizing he had the better end of the bargain, after all. "I'll stay right here, Irish."

Gritting his teeth, Flynn turned and climbed to the doorway of the baggage car. He could endure a few insults if it kept Hazlett from discovering what the baggage car really held. Flynn promised himself he would settle that damned Hazlett once and for all soon enough, but this was not the time for a fight.

He ducked into the car's dark interior. He had managed to keep Hazlett out, at least. So far, Hudson was the only other raider who had been inside, and he knew nothing about the fortune in Yankee greenbacks.

The raiders were far too busy worrying about pursuit, unruly passengers and the captive president of the United States to explore a baggage car. Only he and Nellie Jones knew it carried anything more than carpetbags stuffed with changes of drawers for the middle-aged Yankees in the passenger cars.

Flynn didn't feel guilty about not sharing his discovery of the money with the other raiders. He had helped steal the train and bring it across Maryland, after all. No one could accuse him of shirking his duty. But when the time was right, Flynn fully intended to make off with the money.

Maybe a man like Colonel Percy would condemn him for it, but Percy could afford to have ideals. He was a Virginia aristocrat. What was Flynn but an Irish immigrant who would never really be accepted? Hazlett was proof of that.

If there was one thing Flynn had learned in his hard-scrabble life, it was that a man should seize opportunity whenever it presented itself. The payroll money aboard the train was a fortune, more than he had ever dreamed of, and he would be a fool not to take it.

The question was when. Nellie had promised there would be help ahead closer to Cumberland. But he had a feeling that whoever was helping Nellie wouldn't be eager to share anything with him.

In that case, the sooner they got off the train, the better. He knew the raiders wouldn't stop to look for him because they had to spirit Lincoln out of the country. Percy was too good a man to do otherwise.

However, Flynn didn't relish the thought of being stranded in enemy territory without so much as a horse to help him carry all that money. The Yankees had thieves and cutthroats, too, and he would need someone to watch his back.

He might still be able to count on the woman to do that, of course. *Nellie.* A tough Baltimore tart if he had ever seen one. The colonel's news that he was putting all the passengers off wouldn't make her happy. Well, more money for him, even if getting it someplace safe would be harder on his own.

Still, another hand would be a good idea. Someone steady like that lad, Johnny Benjamin, although the boy might be too duty-bound to play the part of thief. None of the other raiders seemed likely. The honest ones wouldn't do it and the dishonest ones like Hazlett or even Cook or Fletcher would cut his throat and take it all for themselves the first chance they got. The boy might just be a help.

Flynn paused to check the money. He couldn't keep that bastard Hazlett waiting so long that he became curious and went looking for him. Even so, Flynn couldn't resist a quick look.

He found one of the chests filled with paper money and flipped it open to reveal the neat bundles of greenbacks. A fortune! He could buy half of Ireland with that much money and live like one of the lords. He sighed and shut the lid almost lovingly. It was a ransom fit for a king—or a president. All his for the taking, if he could only figure out how to manage it.

First, however, there were other tasks at hand. Flynn quickly scouted the car's interior for materials to make a stretcher. He found two long, narrow boards from some forgotten cargo. A sheet of canvas covering some crates would fit around them perfectly. He carried his finds outside and found Hazlett shading his eyes, staring west. Flynn turned and looked. In the distance, barely visible, was a smudge of smoke.

"Train?" Flynn wondered aloud. To the east, the direction from which they had come, the sky was empty.

"I don't know, Irish, but we best tell the colonel," Hazlett said, making no move to help Flynn carry the makings of the stretcher. "You can manage that stuff alone, can't you?"

Flynn shoved the boards into Hazlett's chest so hard he nearly knocked the man down. "You can carry those, you bastard."

"Don't tell me what to do, you immigrant son-of-a-bitch— "

The long feud between them was about to boil over. Then Colonel Percy's sharp, angry voice cut through the tension. He was on the ground beside the last car, gesturing at them to hurry up. He, too, had spotted the smoke of the approaching train.

Hazlett glared. "We'll finish this later, Irish," he said.

"Aye, that we will." Flynn's eyes were cold and hard. "That we will."

CHAPTER 23

Buckeystown, Maryland • 1:45 p.m.

GEORGE GREER HURRIED ON, his bad leg aching with each step. The more pain there was, the harder he pushed himself, refusing to let his leg slow him down.

The soldiers had been garrisoned at the Monocacy River for so long, guarding the bridge, that they were no longer in condition for marching at Greer's driven pace. The soldiers started out confidently enough, but as one mile became two became three, their enthusiasm waned. Greer had to keep looking over his shoulder and waving the soldiers on because they weren't keeping up.

"I don't know about this, Greer," the captain muttered, coming up close, out of earshot of his men. "There's no sign of your train."

"We'll catch her, all right," Greer said. "She'll likely be around the next bend."

Captain Lowell shook his head. "I doubt that. They've got an awfully good lead on us, Greer. Hell, there ain't even a sign of them."

"Then what do you call that?" Greer pointed toward the horizon.

Lowell squinted. "Hell, what's that? Smoke? By God, Greer, if they're that far ahead of us, we might as well turn around. We're never going to catch them. Not on foot, at least."

Captain Lowell stopped, and his men, glad for a break, shuffled to a halt.

Greer stood a little apart, clenching and unclenching his fists. His leg throbbed. He felt his stomach rumble and realized that because the raiders had interrupted his breakfast, he'd had nothing to eat all day but a couple of cold biscuits and some coffee back at Mount Clare station in Baltimore, long before dawn. He wasn't sure what to do, now that Captain Lowell was getting cold feet. Frost and Schmidt stood nearby, watching the two men. They, too, had sensed that Captain Lowell and his men now thought the chase was hopeless and didn't want to go any further. Greer knew he had reached a critical moment and that the chase was about to end unless he did something drastic.

He would go on, with or without them. He vowed to chase the bastards who had stolen his train to hell and back if necessary. Frost and Schmidt would come along. As conductor, they did as he told them. Even if they refused, Greer was determined to bully them into it.

Captain Lowell was another matter. Even a B&O Railroad conductor held no power over a Union officer. Besides, Greer knew well enough that the captain's duty was to protect the Monocacy River crossing, not chase train thieves. Greer had been a soldier just long enough before being wounded at Bull Run to know that an officer was best off following orders. Nothing more, nothing less.

Greer decided to take a chance. He needed the captain and the soldiers if he was going to stop the train thieves. He clenched his fists at his sides and looked the captain in the face, then raised his voice so the soldiers nearby could hear clearly: "You're a damned coward, Captain."

Captain Lowell could not have looked more surprised if the conductor had slapped him. "What did you say?"

Greer took a deep breath. "I called you a goddamn coward. You and your men."

Lowell reddened. "Look here, Mr. Greer— "

Greer raised his voice even louder to make certain all the soldiers could hear him. "You're scared of what might happen when we catch up to these train thieves. *Scared.* Scared they might turn out to have guns and that there might be a fight. Hell, most of you are conscripts who ain't worth a drink of piss. I reckon now I know why they set you to guarding a railroad bridge in the middle of nowhere." Greer sneered at them, then looked at Frost and Schmidt. "Come on, let's go."

Then Greer turned to leave.

"Wait!"

The captain took the bait. Greer spun to face him. Beyond Captain Lowell, the eyes of his men snapped with anger. No man can stand being accused of cowardice.

The captain himself was so enraged his voice shook, and he was obviously struggling to keep it under control. "You have no right to speak to me that way, Greer. I am a Union officer."

"Then act like one. The three of us are going after those train thieves. You can come or not."

Greer turned again and started off. He said a silent prayer that the soldiers would follow him. He had walked twenty feet when he finally heard the captain curse, then bark out an order. The boots of twenty men on the move behind him was music to his ears.

"Tighten it up," Lowell ordered. "Fast march. We'll move ahead another couple miles, and if we don't find anything, we'll turn around."

Greer didn't look back. He had been holding his breath, unsure of what the soldiers would do. For now, they would keep on going. Greer kept his eyes on the beacon of smoke ahead and kept moving.

* * *

JUST A FEW MILES AWAY, the Rebel raiders also had their eyes on the horizon ahead.

"It's another train," Percy said, studying the smoke. "Eastbound. We had best get going before she gets here."

Flynn nodded and took the still-unconscious Lieutenant Cater by the shoulders. "Easy," he said. "The last thing we want to do is have this wound start bleeding again."

Still unconscious, Cater groaned as they loaded him onto the makeshift stretcher.

"He looks bad, Colonel," Pettibone said.

Percy didn't say anything.

"He might come around," Flynn said, adding another strip of cloth to the blood-stained bandage. He had doctored his share of ugly wounds on the battlefield and in the back alleys of Baltimore and Richmond, and he was always amazed by how hard people were to kill. "I've seen worse, and he's a strong lad."

Colonel Percy nodded. There was a sadness about the sharp blue eyes. Already, he had lost so many good boys from back home in the war. Silas Cater was the first of his men to be wounded during this impossible mission. Percy knew they would be very lucky if the lieutenant turned out to be the only casualty.

"Carry him forward," Percy said. "Put him on the second passenger train. It's that much closer. Cook, you stay here to guard Lincoln's car until I send Hudson and Pettibone back to relieve you."

The truth was that the colonel just didn't trust John Cook. The man might have been a decent soldier, but he had also been a small-time livestock thief back home. With Cater wounded, Percy wasn't about to leave him alone. Hudson and Pettibone were far more trustworthy and capable.

With a man at each corner of the stretcher, they started forward. They moved quickly, taking care not to jostle the injured officer. Each of them kept glancing toward the smoke of the approaching train. The B&O line was double-tracked, meaning one set of rails carried trains west, the other set east, so there was no danger of a head-on collision between trains headed in opposite directions.

The oncoming train could mean one of two things, none of them good. It was possible news of the raid had somehow been telegraphed ahead, after all, and this approaching train might be loaded with soldiers, sent to head them off. In which case they would have a fight on their hands. The second possibility was simply that this was just an eastbound train bound for Baltimore. However, if the *Chesapeake* didn't get underway before the oncoming train came into sight, it would stop to see what was wrong, and there would be trouble. Even if it didn't stop, the train had spotted them and would be carrying news toward whatever pursuers trailed behind.

"Come on, boys," Percy urged them. "Hurry it up."

As they carried the stretcher aboard the passenger car, Henrietta Parker let out a gasp at the sight of the wounded lieutenant swaddled in bloody bandages.

"A wounded Rebel!" She sounded pleased.

Captain Fletcher stood, mouth wide open, and stared at Cater. He was the only one of the raiders who had never been in combat. His face was pale.

"Is he— "

"Clear a space, Captain!" Percy barked at him. "Clear a space!"

Only young Johnny Benjamin had the sense to keep an eye on the passengers, one hand resting on the handle of his holstered Colt.

They lifted Silas Cater off the stretcher and laid him on the floor between the rows of seats. Percy walked to the head of the car, turned, and faced the passengers. It was clear that the colonel was about to make a statement of some kind, and they waited expectantly.

"Contrary to what some of you may think, we are not barbarians."

Mrs. Parker made an indignant noise, which Percy quickly silenced with a glance from his steely eyes.

"We are not in the business of taking hostages," he continued. "You have been kept on this train for military purposes, not criminal ones. Those who have died did so in armed opposition to us, and suffered the consequences. Thus are the rules of war." Percy paused, his eyes lingering for a moment on the unconscious Lieutenant Cater. "However, you will be relieved to know the time has come for us to part company. Please gather your belongings and Sergeant Flynn will escort you from the train."

There was a murmur of relief from the passengers, who were more than happy to escape the train and the bloody business of the Rebel raid. Three passengers had already been killed: the two overly heroic Yankee soldiers and Charles Gilmore. The rest were glad to get off alive. At least, most of them would be, Flynn decided, thinking of Nellie's lost opportunity for a fortune in Yankee greenbacks.

Mrs. Parker spoke up, sounding alarmed. "You're putting us off here? In this wilderness? In the middle of nowhere? There's not a house, not so much as a farm— "

"That's precisely the idea, ma'am," Percy said, touching the brim of his hat in a gallant gesture.

Nellie Jones stood up. "Colonel, with your permission, I'd like to stay and care for the wounded lieutenant."

Percy appeared surprised. "That's more kindness than we could accept, ma'am."

"Please let me stay, Colonel," Nellie insisted. "Not every passenger on this train is a damn Yankee, you know."

At the remark, Mrs. Parker's eyes bugged out of her fleshy face.

Flynn suppressed a smile. He had to admire Nellie's gumption. He alone knew, of course, that her motivation came from the payroll money still undiscovered in the baggage car rather than any Rebel sympathies. The question was, would the colonel allow her to stay? If he did, Flynn knew he and the woman might just leave the train very rich indeed when the time came.

"All right, ma'am," Percy agreed. "Ordinarily I would say no, but under the circumstances we need all the help we can get." He turned to Flynn. "Sergeant, give her all the help she needs."

"Yes, sir."

Percy left and headed for the next car to make a similar speech to the passengers there.

"Well, I never," Mrs. Parker said. She scowled at Nellie. "A Rebel sympathizer in our very midst. My dear, I know you're young ... don't you realize what these soldiers will do to you once they get you alone? They can't be trusted."

Her husband interrupted. "Henrietta— "

Flynn was thinking Nellie probably knew more about soldiers—and men in general—than the matronly Mrs. Parker could ever guess.

"Get off the train, ma'am," he said.

But Mrs. Parker wasn't through with Nellie. "You'll get what you deserve if you stay with these Rebels," she said. "Why, they're vermin! Thieves! Calling themselves soldiers—"

Her husband reached for her arm. "Henrietta."

He managed to get her out to the landing, but she paused on the steps. "They'll be hanged when they're caught. Every last one of them! Strung up by their necks—"

Flynn had heard enough. He drew back his leg, put the heel of his boot in the small of Mrs. Parker's fat back, and shoved. She shrieked and landed in a heap of billowing hoop skirt and indignation. She lay on the ground, whimpering, "Oh, oh, oh—"

"Shut up, woman." He tossed the their valise after them. It hit the ground and burst open, scattering shirts and underclothes.

"Was that really necessary?" demanded a voice at his elbow. Flynn turned to face the fat lawyer, Prescott. Flynn put a hand on the huge Le Mat revolver on his hip and smiled wickedly. "How fast can you move, Mr. Prescott?"

Prescott's eyes widened with fear. He dropped his own valise and half-jumped, half-fell down the iron steps to the ground.

Flynn laughed. "You're all a bunch of cowardly Yankees." He picked up Prescott's valise and hurled it at him. Prescott gave a startled cry and weakly threw up his hands, but it wasn't enough to stop the force of the valise, which struck him in the chest and knocked him down.

"Sure, and was that really necessary, Mr. Prescott?" Flynn laughed, then turned to shout at the remaining passengers. "Get off! Get the hell off this train. I'll shoot the next one of you yellow Yankees who so much as says a word."

Thinking the sergeant had gone mad, the passengers stumbled over each other in their hurry to get down the steps to the safety of the ground. Mrs. Parker had regained her feet, and stood with hands on her hips, huffing, as her henpecked husband scurried to pick up their scattered clothes.

Captain Fletcher had witnessed all the commotion, and he stepped in front of Flynn and said in a low voice, "There's no need to torment the passengers, Flynn. They're civilians. Marylanders, too, just like me."

"Then you'd best get them off the train, Captain. Because I meant what I said about shooting the next one that squawked."

"I *am* your superior officer," Fletcher reminded him.

"Fletcher, what you *are* is Colonel Norris's boot-wipe. Now get the hell out of my way."

Fletcher hesitated a moment, taking the measure of Flynn's hard face, then did as he was told. He stared after Flynn with hateful eyes, and determined that it was the last time Flynn—or anyone else—would disrespect him.

Hazlett, who had come out the door of his own car to get the passengers there off, had witnessed the confrontation.

"That Paddy should show you some respect, sir," Hazlett said, once Flynn was out of earshot.

"Yes." Fletcher was too angry at Flynn, and at himself for not standing up to Flynn, to say more.

"I can see, Captain, that Flynn don't understand how a man in your position deserves better."

"Thank you, Sergeant." Fletcher was secretly pleased, even if Hazlett's presence unsettled him. "Now get the passengers off your car."

"Yes, sir."

Fletcher watched him set to work. Hazlett might be a crude man, he decided, but at least he understood how to respect his betters.

His wounded pride soothed, Fletcher watched the last of

the passengers get off the train. At least that one woman was staying, he thought. She was quite attractive and had a saucy look to her. Briefly, Fletcher thought how nice it would be to be left alone with her for a few minutes. With a woman like that, it was all the time he would need.

CHAPTER 24

FLYNN STALKED BACK inside the car, empty now except for Johnny Benjamin, Nellie and the wounded lieutenant. Nellie had found a rag and a bottle of water, and she was busy cleaning the caked and crusted blood from Silas Cater's face. Flynn crouched beside her. Cater's breathing was shallow and the taut skin stretched over his features was pale.

"How is he?" he asked.

"Hard to say. If he doesn't come around soon, I don't give him much of a chance. The bullet might have done more damage than we can see. His skull could be cracked."

"Too bad. He's a good lad." Flynn made sure the others were too far away to hear, then lowered his voice. "You're a clever one, Nellie. That was quick thinking on your part, offering to stay and help the wounded because you're a Rebel at heart. You were so convincing that I almost believed you myself. Not willing to give up that money, were you?"

"No," she said. "I hope you didn't think you were going to get it all to yourself."

"There's plenty enough to go around, lass. More money than one person can carry, at least. We need a plan."

Nellie nodded. "Just outside Cumberland, I have some friends who will help. They're not expecting a train filled with Confederates, of course."

Flynn raised his eyebrows. "Friends?"

She smiled. "Yes. But you said yourself, Sergeant Flynn, that there's plenty to go around."

Flynn nodded. He wondered how much more she hadn't told him. Not that he was surprised. With such a large quantity of money at stake, he should have guessed that Nellie and Gilmore had not planned the robbery alone. After all, the money had been guarded by three Yankee soldiers, and Gilmore could not have planned to take on the guards by himself. He had been cocky, but not stupid.

Fortunately, Hudson had managed to surprise and overpower the guards when the raiders seized the train. While it was convenient that the raiders had removed one of the obstacles in stealing the money, they had created a much bigger problem in that the thieves would be expecting a trio of sleepy Union guards, not a train carrying several trigger-happy Rebels. The thought was enough to make Flynn smile.

"What was your original plan?" he asked, wondering how much of the truth Nellie would actually tell him. "What were you and Gilmore going to do before things ... changed?"

"You mean, before you killed him?"

"That's not quite how I would have put it."

Nellie hesitated, then shrugged, as if deciding there wasn't any reason not to tell him. "Our friends are going to stop the train well outside of Cumberland by putting some trees across the tracks," she said. "When the train stops, the plan is to rush aboard and take the payroll money."

"What about the guards? They wouldn't have let you walk off the train with all that money without a fight."

"They would have been outnumbered," she said. "Me and

Charlie, our job was to help from the inside, any way we could. Then we would ride off with the gang."

"You would have been caught in no time at all, in the mountains," Flynn said, impressed in spite of himself. It was quite a scheme.

Nellie shook her head. "There's one or two with us who know the mountain roads like they know the laces on their boots. Nobody would ever find us. We would be long-gone."

"Back to Baltimore?"

"Why not?"

Flynn nodded. It was a good enough plan, except it wouldn't work now. "You know that if your friends stop this train then all hell's going to break loose?"

Nellie nodded. "There's got to be another way."

"We'll figure something out, even if we have to throw the money out the window and come back for it later."

Captain Fletcher entered the car and Flynn gave Nellie a wink that ended their conversation. Fletcher walked over and looked down at Lieutenant Cater, who still lay unconscious on the floor. "Well, Flynn, is he going to make it?"

"He's a strong lad." Flynn refused to address Captain Fletcher as *sir*. "There's not much more we can do for him aboard this train—except pray."

"You realize that with him wounded, I'm second in command of this raid."

Flynn crossed himself.

"What are you doing?"

"Praying," Flynn said. "Praying for the lad's life."

Fletcher scowled and stalked off.

"That man's a fool," Nellie whispered.

"Oh, he has his purpose in life, just like rats and snakes. He fetches and carries well enough back in Richmond, licks boots and kisses arses. He's a natural-born staff officer, but he's no soldier."

The train lurched, then began to creep ahead. The cars felt strangely empty without the civilians. Outside the windows, trees began to pass by as the *Chesapeake* gathered speed. The passengers they had put off stood along the tracks, watching the train roll west.

"You'll notice they didn't wave," Flynn said. "We're on our way, lass."

"Stop calling me 'lass,' *Irish*. My name is Nellie. Miss Jones, to be proper."

Flynn smiled. Between the two of them, they just might manage to steal the money, after all. But doubts nagged at Flynn. The cargo they carried was so precious: a fortune in cash, the Yankee president, the hopes of the entire Confederacy. Their odds of success were long, indeed. They still had to cross Maryland and the state was crawling with blue-coated soldiers.

"You have spirit, Miss Jones. I like that. And you'll need it before this day is through. Right now, we're like a couple of rats trying to run the length of an alley filled with stray cats. That's us, all right, little gray rats in an alley."

* * *

"Now what do we do?" Mrs. Henrietta Parker wondered out loud, a plaintive not in her voice. She paced up and down beside the tracks, hands on her hips, looking for all the world like a plump, rumpled, very angry hen. "Those Rebels abandoned us to the elements!"

"Henrietta— "

"Be quiet, Alfred! The least you and the other men on this train could have done is stand up to them."

"They had guns," Alfred pointed out. "And from what we saw, they did not hesitate to use them."

"Thieves and murderers," she said. "How dare they call themselves soldiers. Why, my honor felt threatened."

Nearby, James Prescott put his hand to his face to hide a smile. It was highly unlikely, he thought, that the raiders would have stormed the formidable fortress that was Mrs. Henrietta Parker.

The woman who had stayed aboard the train was another matter. He thought it highly imprudent for her to ride along. That attractive young lady was far more likely to find her honor threatened than was Mrs. Parker, he decided. He was a little surprised she had cast in with the train thieves, considering they had killed her traveling companion. Maybe she truly was a Rebel sympathizer. Baltimore was full of them. Then again, she appeared to be a woman who could take care of herself. She looked as if she welcomed adventure.

Did he? Not really. The truth was, he was glad they were no longer on the train, wondering from one minute to the next if the raiders would shoot them. He realized now how stupid he and Gilmore had been in trying to overpower the Rebel sergeant and the young soldier. Even if they had succeeded, what then? Prescott knew he was lucky to be alive, considering what had happened to Gilmore. The man had paid for their foolishness with his life.

In spite of all that, Prescott felt some pangs of regret as he watched the train disappear. There went an adventure, he thought, going on without him. Somehow, the fact that the young woman had chosen to ride the train while he had been eager to get off made him feel like less of a man.

A shout interrupted his thoughts. "Look!" someone cried. "There's smoke on the horizon. Must be a train coming."

"Flag it down!"

"No, no, no," Mrs. Parker sputtered. "It could be the Rebels coming back! Alfred, tell them, tell them!"

"Shut up, Henrietta," Alfred said wearily. "The Rebels are

not coming back this way. Now get over here and start waving."

Prescott joined the group that pressed up to the tracks. Some of the men took off their coats and flapped them up and down, the better to catch the engineer's attention. Prescott thought it unlikely the engineer wouldn't notice a crowd of people standing along the tracks in the middle of nowhere.

He could see it now, too, a column of smoke approaching from the west. Well, he thought, maybe the adventure wasn't over quite yet. He made up his mind that he was going along for the chase, if there was one.

* * *

Near Weverton, Maryland • 2:20 p.m.

PERCY TOOK out his Colt revolver and double-checked to make certain it was loaded. It was a soldier's nervous habit. Any veteran knew his life depended upon the proper functioning of his weapons.

From the looks of things, he might soon need his revolver. He squinted into the distance, where he could just make out the fast-approaching column of smoke that heralded an oncoming train. Percy had no way of knowing if the other train was simply headed east to Baltimore or whether it was loaded with Yankee soldiers intent on stopping the raiders.

"At least we're moving, sir," said Cephas Wilson, the engineer, as if reading Percy's mind.

"If they try to flag us down, don't stop," Percy said. "They can chase us if they want, but we're not going to make it easy for them."

Wilson started to ask a question, then seemed to think better of it. "What about the president, sir?"

"If we can't get him to Richmond, our orders are to shoot him. You know that as well as I do, Wilson."

"Yes, sir ... it just don't seem right."

Percy agreed, although he did not tell that to Wilson. To shoot Abe Lincoln, unarmed, seemed wrong, even if he was the president of their sworn enemy, the United States of America. In fact, in Percy's mind it would be murder. If it came down to killing Lincoln, he would do it himself rather than burden one of his men with the assassination of the Yankee president.

Again, Percy checked the cylinder of his Colt. Each of the six chambers was loaded with a paper cartridge of powder and ball. A percussion cap covered each of the six firing cones, waiting for the blow of the hammer. Was one of these bullets destined for Lincoln?

He swung the cylinder shut and holstered the Colt. Ahead of them, on the opposite track, the approaching train had come into view. His eyes were not what they used to be, so Percy strained to see if there were muskets aimed at them from the windows.

"Here she comes, sir," Wilson said.

"Are they armed?" Percy asked, fishing in a pocket for his spectacles.

"Can't tell for sure, sir."

"Give her everything she's got, Wilson. Pour it on."

The engineer opened the throttle wide. Hank Cunningham worked like a fiend, hurling wood into the open maw of the firebox. The task was becoming harder because the supply of cordwood in the tender was getting low. Percy held his breath and kept one hand on his revolver.

The train hurtled toward the *Chesapeake*, spewing smoke and cinders into the sky from its enormous smokestack. In seconds, the locomotive was even with them. The engineer leaned from the window and gave them a wave. Then the train was rushing past, bound for Baltimore. It would not get far. Percy was sure the other train would stop when it spotted the passengers the raiders had put off. But by then, the *Chesapeake* would be far ahead if the other train decided to give chase.

Percy breathed again. And then he whooped. "Ha! They don't know about us, boys! On to Virginia!"

Busy at the *Chesapeake's* controls, Cephas Wilson looked less than elated. They were rounding a bend in the tracks, and he pointed ahead. There, as the curve straightened, was a siding. A locomotive waited under steam. It was a new 4-4-0, the designation coming from the fact that it had four large driving wheels behind four much smaller ones. The huge driving wheels were bigger even than the *Chesapeake's*. The locomotive's new black paint gleamed. *Lord Baltimore* was painted on the locomotive's cab in gold letters a foot high. The engineer leaned out the window and lifted his hand in greeting as they passed.

Percy's smile faded. "That's the same train we saw come through Ellicott Mills this morning."

"What do you want to do, Colonel? We ought to wreck that locomotive."

Percy hesitated, then made up his mind. If they stopped, the eastbound train they had just passed could easily overtake them if it reversed direction. "Keep going, keep going."

A knot of men stood by the new locomotive, watching the *Chesapeake* rush past. The *Lord Baltimore* had only a tender attached. The locomotive would be fast, all right, if it came after them. But there was no sign the crew standing around on the siding was prepared to give chase. They did not appear excited by the sight of the *Chesapeake*. A few even waved.

Hank Cunningham paused in his work feeding the firebox to wave back. He grinned, his teeth showing white against the sooty mask of his face. "Yankees sure are a stupid bunch," he muttered through his teeth. "If this keeps up, we'll be in Richmond the day after tomorrow."

"We're not there yet," Percy reminded him.

Percy knew they were running out of time. Every minute counted. The Yankees might not know the raiders had kidnapped the president, but it was enough that they had seized a train and were running toward the Confederate haven of the Shenandoah Valley. The telegraph wires would come alive, and every Yankee in Maryland would work himself into a frenzy of righteous indignation over the raid.

"More wood, Hank," Percy shouted above the roar of the wind and the engine. "Pile it on. We need speed, man, speed!"

The race for their lives, for the fate of Abraham Lincoln, for the survival of the Confederacy itself, had begun.

CHAPTER 25

Adamstown, Maryland • 2:30 p.m.

MUCH TO HIS ANNOYANCE, Greer watched the *Chesapeake's* smoke trail fade into the vast, violet shadows of the mountains ahead. Even he had to admit they were hopelessly far behind. On foot, there wasn't much chance of catching up again. It could not be a good sign, either, that the second column of smoke from the approaching eastbound locomotive had halted, hovering now on the horizon.

"What's going on, Greer?" Captain Lowell demanded. Only his wounded pride kept him urging his soldiers on. He was anxious to call a halt to what he saw as a futile chase and return to his post guarding the Monocacy River crossing.

"I don't know what the hell those bastards are doing," Greer snapped. "Just keep your men moving."

Captain Lowell was about to argue, but Oscar Schmidt put a stop to that. "You heard him," the big German growled. "Keep marching."

Uncertain of what to do, the captain let himself be swayed again by Greer's tenacity. But he wasn't completely beaten. "Two more miles," he said. "Then we turn around."

Greer only grunted in reply, then started down the tracks.

The soldiers marched on, matching the fast pace set by Greer, in spite of his limp.

Up ahead, the eastbound train's column of smoke began to move toward them again. Greer felt like cheering. After several minutes, the train came into sight.

"Stand near the tracks, wave your arms, flag them down," Greer excitedly ordered the soldiers, bypassing the captain.

"Do as he says," Lowell shouted, but the soldiers were already obeying Greer.

"What if they don't stop?" asked a soldier standing in the center of the tracks.

"They'll stop," Greer said. "Flap your arms like you were trying to fly. Just don't stand in the middle of the tracks unless you're anxious to leave this world for the next."

Greer took up a position in front of the rest of them, waving his stout, powerful arms at the oncoming train. For a moment, the train gave no sign of stopping, and it seemed the soldiers' fears might be justified and they would all face a long walk back to the Monocacy River, empty-handed. The locomotive bore down on them, laboring under a billowing cloud of smoke. Then there was a screech of brakes, the screech of iron gripping iron, and tons of machinery slid to a halt just yards short of where Greer stood beside the gleaming rails.

The engineer leaned out from the cab. "What the hell is going on?"

Greer ran forward. "You're Tom Coker, aren't you? My name's Greer. Some sons of bitches stole my train. You just passed it back there."

The engineer nodded. "I didn't expect to find you out here, Greer. I just picked up some people the Rebs put off your train."

Greer could hardly believe what he was hearing. Rebels! So, the men who had stolen his train weren't just train thieves, after all. The engineer climbed down and joined him on the ground.

"You mean Rebels took my train?"

"That's what the passengers said. Confederate soldiers, led by that Colonel Percy. He's that Confederate colonel I've read about in the newspapers, leading all those cavalry raids."

"Arthur Percy?" Greer said. He had also read about Percy. Baltimore was a pro-Southern city, and the newspapers published lengthy accounts of Confederate exploits.

"The one who led the Buckley Courthouse raid?"

"One and the same. He's the leader of this raid."

"What are the Rebs doing up here?" Greer was amazed they had struck so deep into Maryland. "The payroll for the Cumberland garrison is aboard, and I reckoned they were after that. They're not in uniform."

"Then they'll be treated as spies when they're caught," the engineer said. "Strung up from the nearest tree."

"I'll be damned," Greer said, feeling a new sense of rage spread through him. "Rebels stole my train."

"The passengers said there are eleven men. No rifles that they could see, just revolvers. One of the men is hurt bad. Shot."

"Thanks to this," Greer said, brandishing the shotgun he had managed to save from the wreckage at the Monocacy.

"I've got twenty men," said Captain Lowell, who had been standing quietly to one said. "They're armed with Springfield rifles. I don't think the raiders will give us much trouble."

Coker studied Lowell a moment, taking his measure. He frowned and said, "These are tough customers ... Captain. That Colonel Percy ain't no Bible preacher, from what I've heard of him. He and his men have already murdered at least three passengers. Odds are those Johnny Rebs are all veterans. They know how to fight, and they don't scare easy."

At that point, Greer was long past caution. He just

wanted the thieves caught, his train returned, the payroll money safe. He didn't care if Confederate soldiers or common thieves had taken the train. Either way, soldiers out of uniform or train thieves could all be hanged alongside the railroad tracks and left for the crows to pick at.

"Captain Lowell, get your men aboard," Greer said. "Schmidt! You, me and Frost will ride on the tender."

"Now hold on, Greer," said Coker. "This train is going on to Baltimore. It ain't my job to chase Rebel raiders."

Greer put his hands on his hips and glared at the engineer. He looked as stubborn and immobile as a granite boulder. "Look here, Coker. You work for the B&O Railroad, don't you?"

"You know I do."

"Well, that train is B&O property. It's been stolen. There's government money aboard that's been entrusted to the B&O. As a B&O employee, it is your duty to reverse this train and go after those raiders, whether they are Rebels or ordinary thieves."

The other conductor was not giving in. "Hell, Greer, the way I see it, you're the one who lost that train. It ain't my responsibility."

There was no way Greer was letting Coker's train go on to Baltimore. He needed it to pursue the Rebel raiders, and he would take the train by force if necessary.

"Captain Lowell, will you kindly tell Mr. Coker that you are commandeering this train in the name of the United States Government?"

Coker held up his hands to protest. "Now hold on—"

"Mr. Coker?" Lowell shifted uneasily from foot to foot. "By the power vested in me— "

"You're not a preacher, Captain." Greer felt himself growing more agitated. He took a deep breath. "Just tell him to put his goddamn train in reverse and go after those Rebs."

Captain Lowell nodded, looked at the conductor. "Do as he says."

Grumbling, Coker climbed back on his engine. "I'm going to file a formal complaint with the railroad when I get back to Baltimore, Greer."

"You might not want to do that, considering you'll be a hero for capturing those raiders."

The engine lurched into reverse. It was now pushing twenty loaded cars, instead of pulling them, and the train gathered speed very slowly. With so many cars there was an increased risk of derailing, so Coker refused to give the engine full throttle. They were going after the raiders, but the train was moving so slowly that it could hardly be called a chase. Greer kept looking toward the horizon in hopes of catching a glimpse of the *Chesapeake's* smoke. The sky remained empty.

The Rebels already had a good lead, and the argument with Coker and now the slowness of the reversing train had cost them time. If they didn't move faster, the raiders would soon be close to Confederate-held territory. Greer might never see his train again.

"We'll never catch that damn train at this rate," he said.

"Beats walkin'," Walter Frost pointed out. Like Greer and Schmidt, he was also exhausted from running and then pumping the hand car in the wake of the *Chesapeake.*

"If ya'll don't mind, shut the hell up," Coker said. "I ain't heard as much whinin' from half a dozen young'uns in a candy store as I done heard from the three of you."

Schmidt's big face turned red with anger, and he might have tossed Coker off the locomotive if Greer hadn't stepped between him and the other engineer. "Goddamn fool," Schmidt growled, trying to push past Greer and get at the engineer.

"Anytime you're ready, Dutchy."

The two might have scuffled if Frost had not suddenly pointed ahead and shouted, "Look at that!"

To Greer's amazement, a locomotive on a siding came into view. It was under steam, on the westbound tracks. At first, he thought it might be the *Chesapeake*, abandoned by the raiders. But he could see differences as they drew closer. There were no cars, only the engineer and tender. A small crew stood nearby, clearly curious, but not alarmed by the approach of the reversing train.

Then Greer noticed *Lord Baltimore* painted on the side of the cab in ornate, gold lettering.

He smiled. He recognized the locomotive as one of the B&O's newest, built by the Baldwin Ironworks in Philadelphia. Fast and powerful, the locomotive was on a test run, having left Baltimore that morning well ahead of the *Chesapeake*. The polished edge of the massive driving wheels gleamed in the autumn sun. Greer would wager a month's pay that the *Lord Baltimore* could do seventy miles per hour. The engine was pointed west, under steam, ready to go.

"Stop the train," Greer said. "We just found ourselves one hell of a fast locomotive."

* * *

Sandy Hook, Maryland • 3 p.m.

PERCY WATCHED with a mixture of fear and elation as the cliffs of Harpers Ferry loomed closer. Unconsciously, he let his hand slip to his holster and touch the grip of his Colt. Known locally as Maryland Heights, the towering cliff above Harpers Ferry and the Potomac River might as well represent the odds stacked against them, he thought. The revolver was a puny weapon against so huge an obstacle, not to mention a whole garrison of Union soldiers on the other side of the river.

Harpers Ferry was the town where the Civil War essentially began when the abolitionist zealot John Brown seized the federal arsenal in 1858. Robert E. Lee, then a colonel in the Union army, had ordered his soldiers to storm the arsenal and put an end to the act of rebellion. Stuart's aide, Lieutenant J.E.B. Stuart, led the attack. Just a few years later, Lee would be commanding the whole of the Confederate army and General Stuart would be riding to glory at the head of his famed cavalry.

As the *Chesapeake* raced toward the Potomac River crossing that led to the town on the West Virginia shore of the river, Percy was less worried about history than the current state of affairs in Harpers Ferry. Shadows cast by the hills and bare trees grew long as the November afternoon wore on. It had taken longer than Percy anticipated to reach the Potomac. The challenge now was to cross the river and get as close as possible to the rendezvous point at Romney before darkness fell.

They could still travel after dark—the *Chesapeake* was equipped with kerosene lanterns—but it would be too dangerous to operate at full speed because they would be unable to see the tracks ahead. There was no telling what might be on them—fallen rocks, brush, a stray cow—and Percy had no desire to derail in the mountains ahead without any idea where they were. Also, it would be easy to miss the rendezvous in the darkness. Therefore, speed was of the essence if they were going to reach their destination before nightfall.

Ever since that day John Brown had seized the arsenal, control of Harpers Ferry had changed hands many times between North and South. Stonewall Jackson's troops had sacked the town in September 1863 before the fight at Sharpsburg. The long railroad bridge had been destroyed by flood or soldiers time and time again, only to be rebuilt by the Union's unstoppable engineers. The bridge had to be rebuilt and guarded because the span was part of the vital rail line that linked Washington City with the western states.

The bridge was constructed of iron Bollman trusses, an ingenious bridge-building system that was resistant to fire, but not to the raging waters of the Potomac when the mighty river flooded. The town and crossing were under the protection of Union artillery on Maryland Heights. Percy knew the Yankee gunners could easily blow the *Chesapeake* into oblivion if the telegraph had already alerted them to the stolen train.

Percy realized both his fireman and engineer were watching him expectantly.

"Now what, sir?" Wilson finally asked.

"Open the throttle," Percy ordered. "Let's see how fast we can cross that bridge."

* * *

Weverton, Maryland • 3:10 p.m.

GEORGE GREER WATCHED with satisfaction as soldiers and his own crew swarmed onto the *Lord Baltimore*. "Grab hold of something," he shouted. "This train is going to fly."

"How are we going to get all my men on there?" Captain Lowell wondered.

"They can ride on the tender if they have to," Greer said. As he admired the gleaming new locomotive, it was all he could do not to give a big old war whoop. "Ha! With an engine like that, there's nothing that can outrun us."

The soldiers jammed aboard the *Lord Baltimore*. At first, the conductor for the B&O's new locomotive complained, but his protests were soon drowned out. Red-faced, he jumped down from the cab and shook his fist at Greer. "If you wreck this train, it's on your head, not mine!"

Not all the displaced crew was so hostile. "We saw your train go by," the *Lord Baltimore's* fireman said to Greer. "She was steaming west like a bat out of hell. She's got quite a head start, but if anything can catch her, it's this engine here."

Greer, Schmidt and Frost crowded into the cab, along with the young captain. The soldiers climbed onto the tender or wherever else they could find a perch.

They were just getting underway when a lone, rotund figure jumped down heavily from the train they had been riding and ran toward them with a rolling, clumsy gait.

"Wait for me!" the heavyset man puffed. Greer recognized him as one of the passengers from the *Chesapeake* put off by the raiders. "I want to come along."

"Who the hell are you?" Greer demanded.

"My name's Prescott," he wheezed. "I'm a lawyer."

Greer could not help but laugh. "We don't need any lawyers, Mr. Prescott. We're going to hang these Rebs, not sue 'em—or put 'em on trial, either, for that matter."

"I want to see this thing through," Prescott said. "Besides, I know all these Confederates by sight. I can help you find them if they leave the train and head into any towns."

"He has a point there," Captain Lowell said.

Greer thought it over. "All right, Mr. Prescott, jump on."

Prescott was jogging alongside the engine, which was rapidly gaining speed. The effort left him red-faced and wheezing. Schmidt reached down and helped swing Prescott's bulk aboard. The cab became even more crowded as the fat man squeezed inside.

Not that Greer was paying any attention to comfort. He smiled, watching Schmidt's capable hands work the controls. He had heard about the *Lord Baltimore*, and he knew they were going after the raiders in one of the biggest, fastest locomotives that had ever run the B&O's rails. This was one of the new breed of locomotives that would spin across the rails leading west once the bloodshed of the war was over.

Greer watched an enormous grin appear on the engineer's beefy face as he opened the throttle and felt the power of the huge driving wheels spin, then finally catch on the rails. Frost was busy with a shovel, tossing coal into the firebox. Unlike most of the other trains operated by the B&O, the *Lord Baltimore* was a coal-burner. The new-fangled fuel provided an even, intense heat that helped push the locomotive to greater speeds than her wood-burning counterparts. Thick, black smoke poured from the funnel overhead.

"Now we've got them!" Greer shouted. He felt elated. He had a fast engine under him and a squadron of armed soldiers aboard. Finally, he had a real chance of catching and stopping the Rebel raiders. "We'll hang every last one of the bastards along the tracks and let the crows peck the eyes out of their damn Rebel carcasses."

"We don't have any rope," Captain Lowell pointed out.

"Then we shall have a firing squad," Greer said. "Line up those thieving Rebs and shoot them." He was enjoying himself.

"I'm not sure I can order my men to do that," Lowell said uneasily.

"You can always shoot the Rebels if they try to escape, Captain," Greer pointed out, grinning wickedly, and thinking that Lowell was too soft to be a decent officer. "It might just happen that those Rebs are all going to be shot trying to escape. What do you think of that, Mr. Prescott? From a legal point of view?"

The lawyer was still trying to get his wind back after running to catch the train. "Whatever you say," he wheezed. "You're the conductor."

"That's what I like to hear." Greer clapped him on the

back, then said gleefully, "Open her up, Oscar. Let's see what she can do."

Schmidt opened the throttle wide. The sudden rush of wind tore off the soldiers' hats and howled outside the cab as the engine surged ahead, faster and faster. To Greer's ears, that wind was the sound of vengeance.

CHAPTER 26

Just east of Harpers Ferry, West Virginia • 3:20 p.m.

"AIN'T MUCH WOOD LEFT, COLONEL," said Cephas Wilson, nodding at the tender. Operating at full-throttle, the *Chesapeake* burned terrific quantities of wood. Wilson glanced at a gauge. "And we're low on water."

"No time to stop now," Percy said. "We've got to get across that bridge and through Harpers Ferry. Once we've done that, we'll practically be in Virginia. We can take on wood and water before running for the valley."

"Yes, sir."

"What's the next station coming up beyond the river?"

"Kearneysville."

"We'll stop there."

Wilson looked worried. "If we can hold out that long."

"We'll have to," Percy snapped. "We're too close to Harpers Ferry to stop now and we sure as hell can't go back."

"I'll coax as much out of her as I can," Wilson said.

"I know you will. Now, I am going to climb back and tell Willie Forbes to come up here to help Hank with the wood," Percy said. "Keep her wide open and don't stop for anything. We've got to get across that bridge."

Percy knew the safest course of action would be to stop the train and send Sergeant Pettibone ahead to scout the Yankee position. Were there any obstacles on the track? Did the Yankee gunners have their artillery aimed at the bridge, waiting for the appearance of the stolen train?

There was no time, however, to be cautious. The rapidly fading daylight dictated that.

Not that Percy had ever been known for caution. He smiled to himself. His reputation for military success had been built upon daring and surprise. He would have to hope that his luck held out at least one more time. Sometimes, it paid to be reckless. They would have to run at the bridge full throttle, hoping to rush across before the Yankee sentries could react. By then, they would be in West Virginia, racing toward the Shenandoah Valley and their rendezvous with Confederate forces there.

* * *

AT THAT MOMENT IN RICHMOND, Colonel William Norris was climbing into his carriage in front of the Confederate Signal Bureau. His destination was Libby Prison, where captured Federal officers were held prisoner in the heart of the city.

Built of brick, the three-story prison had once been a tobacco warehouse. Eight cavernous rooms were crowded with prisoners. Sanitation and medical care were practically non-existent. The dead were carried out daily.

Some Richmond residents saw the prison as a disgrace. Corrupt prison officials pocketed the money intended to feed and clothe the Yankees imprisoned there. The mass of prisoners was reduced to eating thin, greasy soup in which a few gray lumps of gristle floated. Water was scarce, blankets scarcer as winter came on. No wonder soldiers held there for any length of time were reduced to mere hollow-eyed skeletons. They wore whatever rags they could to guard against the chill within the prison walls.

Norris believed the prison was a necessary evil. Captured Yankees must be held somewhere. Their sorry condition was the fault of their government, which refused to pay for their keep or to operate any meaningful prisoner exchange.

"Hello, sir," said one of the prison guards, greeting Norris. In the last few weeks, the reclusive colonel had become a familiar sight at Libby Prison. "What brings you here today, Colonel?"

"I've come to check on the progress of the special cell I've ordered prepared."

"This way, sir."

Although it was only early afternoon, the hallways were dim. The guard led the way with a lantern. Norris wrinkled his nose against the smell inside the walls, wondering how the guards ever got used to the stench.

The cell was apart from the others, in an area reserved for high-ranking prisoners. Less fortunate prisoners were held in the cavernous warehouse areas like so much livestock.

Not that the cell was comfortable. It was barely big enough to contain a bed and battered table and chair. The wall facing the hallways was built entirely of iron bars and a single, barred window overlooked the city street below. It was Norris' hope that crowds would gather outside to taunt the man who would be held here. There would be no privacy for the prisoner. In fact, the man held here would be very much like an animal on display.

"Is it suitable, Colonel?" the guard asked.

"Very much so."

"Who are you planning to hold here? He must be important."

Norris smiled. The guard shuffled uneasily, regretting that

he had asked the question. "Oh, he is important," Norris finally answered. "You can't get much more important than the President of the United States."

* * *

"HE'S COMING AROUND!" Nellie cried out, cradling Silas Cater's head. He had been unconscious since being wounded by the shotgun blast. "Quick, do we have any brandy?"

Flynn hurried over. He carried a small flask filled with good Virginia bourbon, which he had liberated from one of the passengers. "Give him a few drops of this. It's not brandy, but it will do."

Cater stirred, groaning, and Nellie trickled a tiny amount of whiskey into his mouth. He coughed and his eyes fluttered open.

"Dear God," he moaned. "But my head does ache."

"You've been shot, Lieutenant," Flynn said. "You're going to be all right."

"It feels like my skull has been split by an axe."

"Pain is a good sign. It means you're alive. And that you've got a thick skull."

"Here, have some more of this," Nellie said, and spilled a few more drops of whiskey into his mouth.

Fletcher wandered over and glared down at Lieutenant Cater's bloody head and face. "So he's not going to die?"

"Shut up, Fletcher," Flynn muttered, then turned to Cater. "You see, Lieutenant, he wants to be second in command, God save us."

"Where are we?" Cater managed to ask, even as he grimaced in pain. "What's going on?"

"We're about to cross the Potomac."

"At Harpers Ferry?"

"That's right."

"Then we'll be that much closer to home, thank God." Cater closed his eyes.

"Stay with us, Lieutenant," Nellie said. She tipped a bottle toward his lips. "Drink some water."

"You're a fine nurse for a volunteer, Miss Jones," Flynn said, smiling impishly.

"He's hurt bad," Benjamin said. "Wouldn't he be better off in a hospital?"

"That he would, lad. The one here in Harpers Ferry would do nicely. But you heard the Colonel. He won't want us to leave Lieutenant Cater here in Harpers Ferry for the Yankees to take care of. We'll take our wounded with us."

"I was just saying he needs a hospital," Benjamin said testily.

Flynn smiled. The boy had regained some of his former bravado since the passengers had been put off. Full of piss and vinegar again. That was a good thing, as far as Flynn was concerned. At this point, all the raiders had going for them was luck, confidence, and several loaded revolvers. Pretty soon, all hell was going to break loose and it remained to be seen if their guns would be enough to save them.

"See if you can't put a few Yankees in the hospital when the time comes, lad."

Benjamin went back to the front of the car, where he had a better view of Maryland Heights looming ahead. Flynn didn't have the heart to point out that the high ground there contained several batteries of artillery which could easily blast the train into pieces. It was doubtful that the Yankees would do that and risk damaging valuable property, such as the locomotive or even the train tracks themselves. Flynn thought it more likely the Yankees would block the tracks with some obstacle to force the raiders to stop.

Then again, the Yankees might not even know they were

coming. They had been lucky so far. That luck might hold for one more river crossing.

"What are you thinking?" Nellie asked.

"That luck is like a shoestring, Nellie. It always gives out at the worst time."

"You could have kept that thought to yourself."

He leaned down near Nellie's ear so that he could whisper. He smelled a hint of perfume and might have even tried to steal a kiss if he hadn't been afraid of getting a knife in the ribs. "That money is going to be ours yet, lass. Just you see. If we can get across the Potomac, we're that much closer to being richer than Queen Victoria."

"It's still a long way to Cumberland," Nellie pointed out.

"We'll get there one mile at a time," Flynn said. "Or not at all. But tell me something. Why are you doing this? Why do you want the money?"

"To be rich, of course."

"Everyone wants to be rich. But what good will it do you?"

Nellie thought it over. "Most men want just one thing from a woman like me. When they're done with that, they're done with me. I'm no better than a slave that way, really. With money, I won't need men, or a man. I won't need to do all the things I've done just to survive. I will finally be free."

Flynn nodded. "No hard feelings about Charlie?"

"He would've just drank up his share and spent it on clothes. What did he know? He's a man."

"What about me? Do you think I'm just as much of a fool?"

"I haven't made up my mind," Nellie said. "It all depends on how this train ride turns out."

"Maybe this train is carrying us to hell."

"What do I care?" Nellie said. "I've already been there."

The door of the car opened and Percy entered, followed

by Sergeant Hazlett. Percy saw Nellie and Flynn bent over Lieutenant Cater and hurried to them, covering the distance in three quick strides. Hazlett struck up a conversation with Captain Fletcher, then wandered toward the door at the back of the car, which led into the baggage car. Nellie and Flynn watched anxiously.

"How is he?" Percy asked, kneeling beside the wounded lieutenant.

"Better. He came around, which is a good sign. But I think the pain was too much. We gave him a little whiskey."

"Silas, can you hear me?" Percy asked.

There was no answer.

"He's out again," Nellie said. "I think he'll be all right. What he needs is rest."

Percy nodded. He hated to see Silas die stupidly, killed as the result of a lucky shot. Then again, Percy had seen his share of men die for no good reason in this war. There was never much sense to it.

He knew this wasn't the time for such thoughts. There were other matters at hand. "Harpers Ferry is coming up," he said. "There may be trouble."

"How does it look for getting across the bridge?" Flynn asked. He knew well enough that crossing the Potomac would be a problem, especially if the Yankees guarding the bridge had any advance warning or became the least bit suspicious.

"We're going across at full speed to see if we can surprise them," the colonel said. He stood up and looked around. "Where's Hazlett?"

The sergeant was gone. Flynn noticed Captain Fletcher had disappeared as well. Somehow, the two had slipped out when he wasn't looking, although he had a pretty good idea of where they were.

"They went into the baggage car," Benjamin answered the colonel.

Flynn's eyes met Nellie's. *Trouble*. Their hopes of quietly spiriting the payroll money off the train would be gone if Hazlett and Fletcher found it.

Just then, they heard a shout of triumph, and Flynn's heart sank. Fletcher came running out of the other car, his face filled with excitement.

"Colonel! We found a whole pile of money in there. It's amazing." Fletcher was babbling. "It's a fortune!"

"What are you talking about?" Percy asked.

"The baggage car, sir. It's full of money."

Hazlett walked in with greenbacks gripped in each fist. He looked, Flynn thought, as pleased with himself as a dog that had caught a rat. He was grinning so hard that the long scar beneath his eye was bunched up into a knot. "There must be thousands of dollars in there," Hazlett said. "Good Yankee greenbacks, not the worthless Confederate scrip we're used to."

Percy disappeared into the baggage car. Flynn chanced a look with Nellie. He expected to see a hopeless expression. Instead, her eyes were bright and cunning. He guessed that she was already trying to think of a way to keep the money to herself.

The colonel reappeared. Unlike Fletcher or Hazlett, who had been so excited about the discovery, Percy looked unhappy. Flynn thought he knew why: so much money complicated their mission, which was to kidnap President Lincoln.

"Must be payroll money," Percy said. "This train's destination was originally Cumberland. It's most likely meant to pay the Yankee garrison there. That would explain the guards back in Sykesville, too. I thought they were for Lincoln, but it's more likely they had no idea the president was aboard. The Yankees probably planned it that way, so that Lincoln would have some extra protection with the guards and they would be more alert, too, to any trouble."

"Not that it did them a damn bit of good," Flynn pointed out.

"Right you are, Sergeant," Percy said. "We still managed to get their president. Not that it will do us a damn bit of good if we don't get across that bridge."

"Forget Lincoln," Hazlett said. "Let's shoot him and be done with it. I say we stop the train, take the money, and slip off into the woods. We might have some kind of chance. The Yankees are about to blow us right off that bridge."

"Damn you, Hazlett!" Percy's face twisted in anger and his eyes sparked. Flynn was amazed by the outburst, which hinted at some deeper anger toward his cousin-in-law. Just as suddenly, the colonel took a deep breath and calmed himself. "Our orders, *Sergeant*, are to bring Lincoln to Richmond if at all possible. We're only to shoot him as a last resort. Our orders include nothing about taking payroll money. Is that clear?"

Hazlett's eyes were hateful, his answer grudging. "Yes, sir."

"Then get back to your post, Sergeant. I believe you're supposed to be in the next car with Private Cook."

Hazlett left without replying. Percy wasn't finished with his orders.

"Flynn?"

"Colonel?"

"That money is to be left alone. Don't let anyone go in there to fill their pockets. Including you. Understood?"

"No one touches the money." If Percy only knew he had just put the fox in charge of the hen house, Flynn mused.

"If there's any trouble, I'll burn that money if I have to, or throw it off the train. We're soldiers, not train robbers."

Percy turned to Captain Fletcher. "Understood, Fletcher? You're to leave that money alone. That's an order."

"Why, yes ... *sir*."

"Benjamin? Understood?"

"Yes, sir!"

Percy looked at Nellie and touched the brim of his hat. "Ma'am, thank you so much for taking care of Lieutenant Cater. He's a good man, ma'am. He deserves to live."

"Anything to help the Cause, Colonel." She sounded entirely sincere.

That made Percy smile. He left the car.

Flynn exchanged another look with Nellie. They couldn't talk, of course, because Fletcher and Benjamin were there. Damn it all! He knew he could trust the lad, maybe even work something out with him about the money, but not Fletcher. The captain would be a greedy bastard, and making a partner of him would only bring trouble.

Flynn's thoughts were cut short because Benjamin shouted, "We're crossing the bridge!"

CHAPTER 27

"FULL THROTTLE, WILSON, FULL THROTTLE," Percy said calmly as the train swept out over the Potomac River.

"Yes, sir," the engineer said. "Looks clear so far."

Chocolate-brown water swirled fifty feet beneath the Harpers Ferry bridge, the current making a creamy froth around the pilings. Autumn wind whistled across the open rivers. Where the tracks had been surrounded by foothills and dense woods, all that fell away as the train reached the open expanse of the Potomac. Two rivers converged near this point, and to their left was the wide Shenandoah River. Directly ahead was the town of Harpers Ferry, built on the bluff overlooking both the Potomac and Shenandoah.

Had the raiders been in the mood for sight-seeing, they might have noticed the incredible scenery. In fact, none other than Thomas Jefferson had once said it was worth crossing the Atlantic just for the majestic view from the bluff. However, the raiders kept one eye on the tracks ahead, and another on the bluff above the river for the first blast of smoke and flame that would mean Union artillery had targeted the train.

"Don't stop no matter what they put on the tracks," Percy said, leaning in close to the engineer to be heard over the wind. "Our only chance is to bull right through no matter what they throw at us. If we can get across the river and through town, nothing can stop us."

The *Chesapeake* roared across with a speed that startled the Yankee sentries, which was just what Percy intended. He knew it wasn't much of a strategy, Percy knew, but sometimes a cavalryman knew all he could do was ride like hell. This was one of those times—only now, his horse was made of iron.

Beneath them, the brown water was deep enough to swallow the engine and cars without a trace if a cannonball derailed them. Percy glanced down again at the churning water far below and felt a hollow pit of his stomach. He could swim, but he had a feeling it wouldn't matter. No one would survive that treacherous current if the train plunged off the tracks.

Then, as suddenly as they had swept onto it, they were across the bridge and on land again. Percy thought it was a small miracle. The second miracle was that the Yankees hadn't opposed them.

They roared through town. Curious faces turned toward them as they rushed between the brick buildings and white clapboard houses. It was a prosperous town, in spite of changing hands so many times during the war.

Percy could see they had taken the Yankees completely by surprise. No one was expecting a train stolen by Confederate raiders. The tracks were wide open. As they reached the limits of the small town, he knew nothing could stop them. They would go on through West Virginia, the pro-Union state which had only recently split away from Virginia. The train would parallel the winding Potomac again just east of Hancock, then race on toward the Shenandoah Valley.

Percy laughed as the dwellings became more sparse. The

town fell away and they entered a country filled with rolling foothills and naked trees as the tracks swung away from the winding Potomac. Later, they would meet the river again.

He wanted to get back across the Potomac before dusk. It did not help that these November days were short. Already, the sun was edging toward the tops of the hills. Shadows flickered past and the bare branches of the trees groped and scratched at the train.

"Colonel?" Hank Cunningham interrupted his thoughts. Percy turned. He immediately noticed the look of concern on the fireman's ash-stained face. "What is it?"

"Look."

A smoke trail stabbed the sky behind them. It had not been there a few minutes before, and Percy wondered how any train could have caught up to them at the speed they were traveling. He hadn't seen any other locomotives in Harpers Ferry.

"That engine on the siding back there in Maryland, Colonel," Wilson said, answering Percy's unspoken question. "She's come after us. She looked to be fast."

Of course. That must be it. Percy cursed their luck, that just when it seemed all they had to do was get across West Virginia before dark, they now had to do it with Yankee pursuers on their heels.

Percy wondered if it was the *Chesapeake's* conductor who was still chasing them. If it was, the man was damned persistent. He had latched on like a bulldog and wouldn't let go. Remembering the stout conductor in his blue uniform, it seemed a good comparison. Why wouldn't the conductor give up? Did he know Lincoln was aboard? Percy decided it wasn't likely. The conductor was probably just stubborn. Percy had run into a few stubborn Yankees during the war, and the smarter ones had all been dangerous.

Wilson and Cunningham were watching him, awaiting an order.

"Run her wide open," Percy said. "Wring every bit of speed out of her that you can."

"What about a stop, Colonel? We need to take on wood and water at some point."

"Goddamnit, Wilson!" Percy shouted in exasperation. "We can't stop now. That engine back there would be on us in a few minutes if we did."

"Yankees on our tail or not, Colonel, we'll have to take on wood and water soon, or we'll be walking to Virginia."

"I know that," Percy snapped. "And we will stop. But we at least have to reach the next depot, don't we?"

"Yes, sir."

"Where would that be?"

"I reckon that would be Kearneysville, sir. It's about ten miles from where we are now."

"Then let's run like hell till we get there."

They raced on toward the Shenandoah Valley, glancing anxiously over their shoulders as they worked, trying to make the locomotive run as fast as possible.

Damn, but she's fast, thought Percy, watching the smoke from the oncoming train. She's too damn fast.

* * *

ABOARD THE LOCOMOTIVE *LORD BALTIMORE*, blue-coated soldiers clung tightly to the tender as the train raced out onto the iron span of the Harpers Ferry bridge. Below them, the brown river moved like a smooth, tense muscle, powerful and deep, nothing at all like the "Muddy Monocacy" they guarded. They held on as the wind off the open water of the twin rivers buffeted them and tried to loosen their grip on the tender. Several lost their hats. They let them go without making any move to stop them, afraid they, too, might spin away into the river below unless they held onto the train for dear life.

"Blow the whistle," Greer ordered. "Clear the tracks ahead."

Schmidt gave three warning blasts on the whistle. On the far bank, a curious crowd had gathered to watch the engine cross the bridge. The first speeding train had caught them by surprise. Now, at the sight of a second racing train, people had come to see what all the excitement was about. Greer didn't want them getting too close to the track. So far, no one had made an effort to block his way. After all, the Union officers expected trouble out of the west, which was where the Confederates still had a stronghold. They would not be looking east, toward the heart of Maryland, which was firmly in Union hands, even if the hearts of all the state's inhabitants were not.

This was a fast engine. The fastest Greer had ever seen. The *Lord Baltimore* was also fully loaded with coal and water. So long as she didn't break down, here on her maiden trip, there was nothing that could stop them. They roared across the final section of bridge and entered Harpers Ferry at break-neck speed.

Captain Lowell saw it first. Greer was too busy keeping an eye on the tracks ahead.

"Greer," Lowell cried. He was pointing. "Look!"

Greer saw it then. Smoke in the sky ahead.

"That's them, all right." He laughed. "We've got them now, boys!"

It could only be the *Chesapeake*. Greer knew instinctively now what the Rebel raiders were doing: running for the Shenandoah Valley. So that was it, he thought. The raiders wanted the payroll money—maybe for the Rebel government, maybe for themselves—and they were running for the safety of the valley, where there would be Confederate cavalry to help them.

Greer knew he could catch them before they reached safety. He knew it because his old leg wound throbbed in the same way it did before a big snow or rain. It was a sign of things to come. The Rebels were like a scent in his nose. Now Greer knew what a hound felt like when it smelled the fox—and ran it down.

* * *

FLETCHER WANTED to see the money again, but he had heard Colonel Percy order Flynn not to let anyone into the baggage car. Fletcher had no doubt the Irishman would welcome an excuse to shoot him, so he left the money alone. Instead, he wandered into the passenger car ahead, where he found Hazlett and Cook lounging on the benches. They were smoking cigars confiscated from the passengers.

Hazlett got to his feet and saluted. Cook did the same. "Captain, sir," Hazlett said.

Fletcher had noticed that, unlike the others, Hazlett always gave him the respect due an officer. He caught himself standing straighter and throwing back his shoulders. Still, the captain didn't waste time with small talk. He decided it was unbecoming an officer. "You saw the money?" he asked Hazlett. There was no need to explain which money he was talking about.

"Yes, sir."

"How much was there?"

"Thousands and thousands, Captain, from the the looks of it," Hazlett said. He raised an eyebrow and the scar on his face danced, as if it had a mind of its own. "You mean you ain't been back to count it?"

"The Colonel told Flynn to shoot anyone who tries to go in there."

Anger flashed across Hazlett's face, making his scar flare like a fire brand. "That goddamn Paddy! He'll do just what the colonel tells him, too, like a good dog would." Hazlett managed to calm himself, and a sly light came into his eyes. "Why, all things considered, sir, you would think Flynn might show you some respect. And that Colonel Percy would, too."

Fletcher was heartened to hear the implied criticism of the colonel. "Percy doesn't want the money touched," he said lamely.

Hazlett snorted. "He wouldn't, would he? The colonel has all the money he wants. He's a rich man back home. It's all well and good for him to say, 'Leave the money alone, boys,' when he's already got his own." Hazlett leaned close and lowered his voice. Fletcher could smell whiskey on his breath, even though Percy had forbidden any drinking during the raid. "What we should do, Captain, is take that money and skedaddle. All of us. We can leave this whole damn war behind, every one of us a rich man."

Fletcher realized he was on dangerous ground, that Hazlett must be testing him somehow. At the same time, he knew he had found a kindred spirit on this raid. He, too, thought they should take the money, abandon the raid, and count themselves lucky.

Not that he didn't have his doubts and sense of obligation. After all, Colonel Norris had sent him to make certain the raid went as it should. Back in Richmond, he had served Norris well. At the same time, he knew he was nothing more than Norris's underling. Norris would never treat him as an equal. What other choice did Fletcher have but to do whatever Norris said? Flynn could act arrogantly and get away with it because he was just a low-born Irishman. If he fell, there wasn't far to fall. Fletcher didn't have that luxury because he held a certain position in society. But without money, or a sense of bravado, he relied on other skills to get ahead.

It was also true that Norris—like Percy—was a member of the Southern aristocracy. He was educated and wealthy. He could afford to turn his back on a fortune in Yankee money in favor of duty. But could Fletcher? Hazlett's words had taken root.

"What about Lincoln?" Fletcher asked. "We're to bring him to Richmond."

Hazlett shrugged. "We shoot Honest Abe, and that's the end of that. Way I see it, we done our duty."

Fletcher realized he had walked into the middle of a mutiny in the making. As an officer, he knew he should denounce the plot and warn Percy, but he couldn't bring himself to walk out. It wasn't that he didn't believe in honor and duty. It was just that he believed in money even more. He wanted to be rich. Fletcher believed money was the only thing that would put him on an equal footing with men like Norris and Percy.

"All right, there's Percy," Hazlett said. "We know he ain't goin' to see it our way."

"Anybody else with us?" Cook asked.

"Forbes will be. He may be a drunk, but he ain't no fool," Hazlett said. "And he's up on the locomotive, which might be helpful when the time comes."

"Now who's against us?" Cook asked.

Hazlett thought a moment. "Cephas Wilson and Hank Cunningham are busy drivin' this here train. They already got their hands full. That leaves Flynn and the kid, Johnny Benjamin. Flynn ain't as tough as he looks and Benjamin, hell, he ain't hardly more than a boy. That fat man almost squashed him."

"He did shoot one of the passengers," Fletcher pointed out.

"It ain't so hard to kill a man." Fletcher noticed Hazlett had stopped calling him "sir."

"What about Pettibone and Hudson?" Cook asked. "You think they might see things our way?"

"They ain't goin' along with us, if that's what you mean," Hazlett said. "They're too loyal to the colonel. Right now, they're guarding Lincoln. We'll just have to deal with them last."

Fletcher remembered the wounded lieutenant and the passenger who had volunteered to nurse him. "What about Lieutenant Cater and the woman?"

"Cater's half dead and we can finish the job easy enough. Hell, back home he's almost as rich as Percy." Hazlett grinned wickedly. "The woman? Why, Captain, I reckon you can pull rank and take her. She does look like a juicy piece. 'Course, Cook and me might want her when you're through. Serious now, you can have her, Captain, just as long as I get Flynn. Nobody else can kill that bastard. He's mine."

Fletcher felt an odd excitement. When he mentioned the woman, it hadn't been to do the things Hazlett hinted at. But then again, why couldn't he have her? To the victor went the spoils. This was war, after all. He felt like a new man, taking what he wanted: money, women, freedom.

Hazlett handed him a flask of whiskey. "Drink on it," he said.

Fletcher drank. There was no going back now. He knew he was in this thing to the end.

CHAPTER 28

East of Kearneysville, West Virginia • 3:45 p.m.

PERCY LOOKED at the trail of smoke behind them, then at the engine's tender. Hank Cunningham and Willie Forbes worked like madmen to feed the locomotive's firebox. Their efforts were quickly using up the cordwood that remained. It wouldn't be long before the *Chesapeake* ran out of fuel.

"How much farther to the next depot?" Percy asked.

The engineer gave the water gauge a worried glance. "Kearneysville is about six miles off," he said. "We'll need to take on water, too, Colonel. We're just about bone dry. We have to stop at the Kearneysville depot if those Yankees back there will let us."

"They will," Percy said. "I have a surprise planned for them."

"I'm glad to hear that, Colonel," Wilson said. "I reckon we won't get much farther if we don't stop in Kearneysville."

As soon as Percy turned his back, Forbes climbed into the tender again with Cunningham and uncorked a bottle of whiskey.

"Where did you get that?" Cunningham asked.

"This is the bottle the colonel made Flynn throw away,"

he explained. "I picked it up. Couldn't let good whiskey go to waste."

"Don't let Percy see you with that," Cunningham warned him. "He'll make you walk back to Richmond."

Forbes shrugged and took a long pull from the bottle, which was already half empty. When Cunningham refused a drink, he hammered the cork home with his palm. "Suit yourself. But this might be the last chance you get to take a drink in this world."

* * *

WITH CAPTAIN FLETCHER OUT of the car, Flynn and Nellie could talk more freely. Lieutenant Cater remained unconscious and Johnny Benjamin was at the back of the car, watching the trail of smoke gradually gaining on them.

"It's not going to be easy to take the money now," Flynn observed.

"We'll find a way," Nellie said. "There's always a way."

"That won't make things any easier," Flynn said, nodding at the smoke. "Those bastards chasing us won't give up."

"The closer we get to Cumberland, the better our chances," Nellie said.

"That damned Hazlett will have his eye on the money," Flynn said. "I'd wager a chunk of what's in that car that he's already scheming how he can steal the money."

"We'll just have to stay one step ahead of him," Nellie said. "I don't trust that Captain Fletcher, either. He's in there talking to Hazlett."

"Hazlett plays him like a fiddle."

Benjamin walked over. "What are you two whispering about?"

Flynn grinned. "Well, lad, if you must know, I'm whispering sweet nothings in Miss Nellie's ear."

"Oh, Sergeant," Nellie giggled flirtatiously and touched Flynn's arm.

Benjamin blushed. He might be a good soldier and handy with a gun, but Benjamin was hardly more than a boy, fresh off the farm and naive about the ways of the world. For this exact reason, Flynn and Nellie already had agreed not to include him in their plans. He wouldn't know what to do with a fortune in Yankee greenbacks, anyhow.

"What do you do back in Baltimore, Miss Nellie?" Benjamin asked. "I reckon you ain't married."

"Why don't it seem like I'm married?"

Benjamin turned a deeper shade of red. "It just don't, is all."

"Well, I'm a schoolteacher," Nellie said.

Flynn had to bite the insides of his cheeks to keep from laughing. He glanced at Nellie, but she had a perfectly straight face. The lass was a smooth liar, yes, she was. A schoolteacher! She was a whore, if ever he had seen one. A fancy whore, to be sure, but a whore nonetheless.

The boy appeared satisfied with her answer. He looked ready to ask another question, but the train began to slow. The drive wheels squealed as the engineer reversed direction. It was no small task to stop a hurtling train. Flynn, Nellie and Benjamin were nearly thrown off their feet.

"Why the hell are we stopping?" Flynn wondered out loud.

Benjamin ran to the windows, fighting to keep his balance as the train rocked and swayed.

"There's a depot up ahead," he reported. "Looks like we're going to stop there."

Flynn stood, drew the big Le Mat revolver, and checked the loads and priming caps.

"Trouble?" Nellie asked.

"Don't know," he said. "But if there's no trouble on the tracks ahead, then it's coming up behind us."

"You're right, Sergeant," Benjamin said. "That other train ain't far behind."

"Come on, lad," Flynn said. "Let's see what all the ruckus is about."

* * *

Kearneysville, West Virginia • 4 p.m.

THE TRAIN ROLLED to a stop at the depot. Within minutes, the lone station agent was tied up and locked inside his office.

The engineer, fireman and Willie Forbes hurried to resupply the locomotive from the water tower and wood pile.

"Hurry, boys!" Percy shouted. "There's not much time."

Every minute brought their pursuers closer. The trail of smoke grew ominously larger in the sky. Percy had no idea who was on the pursuing train or whether it carried any armed men. He was not about to let his own men be captured while they took on wood and water.

"Them Yankees are getting closer," Pettibone drawled.

"All right, listen here," Percy said. "We're going to give those Yankees a surprise."

Quickly, he outlined his plan. His men were soon working to pile railroad ties on the tracks just behind the train. There was a big stack of ties nearby and the men paired off and lugged the heavy timbers and laid them across the iron rails. At the very least, it would take their pursuers several minutes to clear the tracks.

On a siding, they discovered a boxcar loaded with rails and ties meant for repairs. Percy had the men push it into place behind Lincoln's car. They coupled it to the train, then broke out a few boards at one end to make a front entrance. Percy claimed it might prove useful later.

Wilson was busy filling the water tank. It seemed to be taking forever. Forbes and Cunningham slung chunks of firewood into the tender as fast as they could. The tender was little more than a water tank on wheels, with high sides so that firewood could be piled on top.

"How much longer, Wilson?" Percy shouted toward the engine.

"Give us twenty minutes, Colonel, and we'll have enough wood and water to run clear to Ohio if we want."

"We don't have twenty minutes," Percy. "And we're going to Virginia, not Ohio. You've got five minutes."

"Wood's wet, Colonel," Forbes complained, nearly breathless from work. "They ain't got no shed here to keep the wood dry."

"It will burn once it gets in that firebox," Percy said. "It's hot as Hades in there."

Percy looked over his shoulder. The other train was coming on fast. *Too fast*. He wasn't sure now that he could even give Wilson the five minutes to finish refueling the *Chesapeake*. In any case, Percy didn't want to be caught unprepared if the pursuers roared into Kearneysville with a train loaded with soldiers.

"Get ready for a fight, boys!" Percy shouted, running for the barricade. If it came to it, they would use their guns to buy a few more minutes for replenishing the train. Getting a head start on the Yankees wouldn't do them a bit of good if they ran out of steam before the rendezvous point.

Percy deployed his men in pairs. Flynn and Benjamin took positions behind the stack of ties, just to one side of the tracks. Hazlett and Cook took the other side, behind the rough wooden building that served as the stationmaster's office. Pettibone and Fletcher crawled beneath the boxcar, sheltering behind the iron wheels. For a hastily laid ambush, Percy decided, it wasn't bad. The Rebels would be able to pour fire down either side of the train when it arrived. Any Yankees who jumped off would find themselves in the Confederates's gunsights.

The train came on, sounding like a distant thunderstorm approaching.

"If those fool Yankees don't slow down, they're going to slam right into the back of the *Chesapeake*," Percy warned

"Get ready, lads!" Flynn shouted.

The rails hummed. Then, like a great, black beast spitting smoke and sparks, the pursuing locomotive swept into Kearneysville. Iron howled on iron as the *Lord Baltimore* reversed its drive wheels and struggled to stop in time. The locomotive barreled down on the raiders.

"Steady, boys!" Percy shouted from his own position beside the boxcar filled with rails and ties. He cocked the hammer of his Colt. "Keep hidden until I give the word."

* * *

"Stop the train!" Greer cried as the locomotive bore down on the *Chesapeake*. "Do it now, Oscar, now!"

The *Lord Baltimore* hurtled toward Kearneysville station at almost seventy miles per hour. Greer had known they were hot on the raiders's trail, but he hadn't counted on finding the *Chesapeake* stopped dead ahead as they rushed around a bend in the tracks.

Schmidt swore in German. He and Greer had seen the *Chesapeake* in the same instant. Less experienced men might have panicked, but Schmidt's body reacted purely on instinct. He threw the engine into neutral, then reversed the gears.

For a few sickening moments, it looked as if Schmidt still hadn't reacted in time. The massive engine gave no sign of

stopping, but slid relentlessly toward the rear cars of the
Chesapeake, like a sledgehammer bearing down on a spike.
Greer held his breath. The Rebels had thrown some ties
across the rails and he was sure the *Lord Baltimore* would
scatter the piled ties like so many matchsticks and ram the
boxcar.

The driving wheels spun wildly, fighting the weight and
inertia of the speeding train. Then the engine began to slow
amid the scream of iron on iron. A great geyser of steam shot
up. As the wheels gained traction, the locomotive slowed and
crept to a halt with its huge "cow catcher" just short of the
hastily erected barricade.

Greer let his breath out.

Then the shooting began.

* * *

"LET THEM HAVE IT, BOYS!" Percy shouted as he pulled the
trigger and the Colt jumped in his hand.

He could see that the tender was swarming with blue-
coated soldiers. The engine's cab was also packed with men.
There were just too many soldiers. Percy wanted to keep
them pinned down. If the Yankees rushed the train, Percy
knew his handful of raiders would be overwhelmed.

The first shots from Percy's men struck two soldiers, who
fell into the brown grass beside the tracks and sprawled there,
unmoving. The rest took shelter inside the iron-sided tender
and started to shoot back.

The raiders were outnumbered, but their revolvers
enabled them to fire nearly forty shots within the space of a
minute. The Yankees, armed with muzzle-loading Springfield
rifles, returned fire at a much slower rate.

Nothing made Percy's skin crawl so much as the weird
buzz of a Minié ball zipping past his ear. He suddenly heard

several. Splinters flew from the piles of ties behind which his men were sheltering. They couldn't hold the Yankees for long.

After getting off that first shot, Percy held his own fire until his men emptied their guns. Then he fired as his men reloaded. He picked his targets carefully, forcing the Yankees to keep their heads down.

He looked back at the *Chesapeake*, where he could see the train crew working. *Hurry, damn you, hurry*. He shouted to be heard over the gunfire: "Two minutes, Wilson! Then get her rolling!"

The engineer acknowledged him with a wave and Percy turned back to the work at hand. Some of his men had reloaded and were shooting back. Still, one good rush from the Yankees and it would all be over.

A man jumped down from the engine's cab. Percy recognized him as the *Chesapeake's* conductor, still wearing his blue uniform with the double row of shiny brass buttons. Amazed, he realized this man had been pursuing them relentlessly since they had taken the train at Sykesville. How many miles was that? Seventy? Eighty? Percy felt a grudging sense of admiration for the conductor. Not just any man would chase a train that far. The colonel also felt a twinge of uneasiness. It was the stubborn Yankees who were the most dangerous.

As Percy watched, the conductor acted indifferently toward the hail of fire from the Confederates, not even bothering to hurry. As bullets flicked around him, he stopped to shout something at the captain cowering behind the engine. He then stomped angrily to one of the dead Yankees, snatched up the soldier's rifle, and aimed it deliberately at Percy.

Percy swung the revolver up and aimed hastily, but the hammer fell on an empty chamber. Damn. He ducked, and shards of wood exploded from near where his head had been a second ago.

The conductor turned and rallied the soldiers. Bayonets flashed in the late afternoon sun as they fixed them to their rifle muzzles. In a moment, the soldiers would charge and put an end to the raid. Percy's men were outnumbered two-to-one, and would be overwhelmed.

"Here they come, lads!" Flynn shouted in warning.

Beside Percy, the train lurched forward and began to move. Pettibone and Fletcher, positioned behind the wheels of the boxcar, had to roll out of the way to keep from being run over. Yankee rifles spit lead at them as soon as they were in the open.

"Get on the train!" Percy ordered. "Let's get out of here!"

The Yankees charged, shouting *"Huzzah!"*

CHAPTER 29

"SWEET MOTHER OF JESUS," Flynn said. "Here they come."
His revolver clicked on an empty chamber.

"Come on, Flynn," Percy said. "Let's get the hell out of
here."

"Did you think I was going to stay and get a bayonet in
the guts?"

They turned and ran.

Yankees pounded up the tracks right behind them. A tall
Yankee outran the others and lifted his rifle high for a killing
thrust at Percy's back. Hudson jumped from between two
cars, a blazing gun in each hand. Bullets knocked the tall
Yankee off his feet and killed the man behind him. The other
soldiers faltered long enough for Percy and Flynn to swing
aboard the train.

The Yankees did not give up. The *Chesapeake* had not built
enough speed to lose them, even on foot. They were still led
by the conductor, who urged the soldiers on as they rushed
the train, trying to climb aboard the last two cars—the
boxcar of supplies and Lincoln's car. Most of their rifles were
empty, so they jabbed their bayonets at the raiders defending

the cars. The raiders's guns were empty, too, so they could only stomp on the hands of any Yankee who got a grip on the car, while dodging the knife-edged bayonets thrust at them. Legs were sliced open, fingers broke, and both sides screamed curses. The vicious running brawl followed the train down the tracks.

One bearded soldier grabbed hold of the iron railing at the back of Lincoln's car and began to pull himself up. Flynn clubbed him with the butt of his pistol and the Yankee fell away with a strangled shout.

In the boxcar doorway, Cook screamed as a bayonet caught him in the calf and sliced to the bone. Hazlett kicked the soldier in the face and the man tumbled away.

The train gained speed. The soldiers had to run faster to keep up, and one by one they fell behind. Some loaded their rifles and fired. The whine of minié balls followed the locomotive out of range. Aboard the *Chesapeake*, the raiders caught their breath.

"That was hot work, gentlemen," Percy announced. He was bleeding from a bayonet gash near his knee. All four men were bloody and breathless from the fight.

"Those Yankees have a lot of spirit," Flynn said. He, too, had been nicked in a couple of places, but he had taken his revenge. Flynn had felt at least two hands crushed under his boots as the Yankees tried to get onto the car.

Percy nodded at Lincoln's door. "Any sound from in there?" he asked Hudson.

"No, Colonel. All quiet."

Percy was glad Lincoln had not tried to escape during the confusion of the skirmish, because the president surely would have been killed in the crossfire. Percy was determined to deliver President Lincoln alive and well to Richmond. He felt that anything less would mean the raid was a failure.

Pettibone poked his head out from the hole in the boxcar. "Now what, Colonel?"

"Anybody hurt?"

"Cook got cut pretty bad. Hazlett's wrapping up his leg. Other than that, just a few scratches." As usual, Pettibone was the master of understatement. His lower legs were covered in blood from his bayonet wounds. The four men in the last car had suffered the worst of the Yankee attack. Fletcher was the only one who hadn't been hurt, mainly because he had hung back while the others battled the Yankees in the doorway.

Percy glanced at the blood, but didn't say anything about it. "All right. Now listen to me, Pettibone. I want you boys to knock a hole to match this one in the back wall of the boxcar. Use some of those ties in there as a battering ram if you have to."

Pettibone looked puzzled.

"You'll see," Percy said. "When you're finished, tell the other three to keep an eye out, because the Yankees will be after us again like flies on molasses. You come out here with Hudson to guard the president."

"Yes, sir."

Pettibone disappeared into the boxcar, where he relayed the orders to Hazlett, Cook and Fletcher. After the fight, the wounded men weren't happy about the work at hand. Some grumbled as they picked up a railroad tie and began battering at the back wall of the box car.

"The colonel treats us like dogs, you know," Hazlett said.

"Shut up, Hazlett," Pettibone said. Normally, he was too wary of Hazlett to speak up, but the exhaustion and pain from his cut legs had dulled his sense of caution. "Percy has kept us from being caught yet, hasn't he?"

"That was damn close back there," Hazlett snarled. "If the Yankees catch us, you know what they're goin' to do, don't you? They're goin' to hang us right beside the railroad tracks as thieves and spies. You ever seen anybody hang, Pettibone? It ain't pretty. Your tongue gets all swollen and hangs out of your mouth, you shit your pants and if your neck don't snap right off you swing there, kicking your feet."

Beside him, Fletcher paled. "They can't hang us like that," he said, his voice barely audible.

"See if they don't," Hazlett replied.

"I seen men die," Pettibone said flatly. "You're forgettin' I've been in this here war for almost three years. Ain't no way to die that's pretty, 'cept maybe home in bed. Now swing this damn rail, will you?"

Hazlett took hold of his end of the rail. They pounded at the end wall until one by one the boards popped loose and they had created a ragged hole. As soon as they finished, Pettibone crawled out the front of the car to continue his guard duty with Hudson.

Hazlett watched Pettibone go, a crooked smile on his face. "Colonel won't trust me to guard Honest Abe, I reckon. He knows I'd finish the job and be done with it."

Hazlett, Fletcher and Cook were alone in the boxcar. Cook touched the bloody bandage around his lower leg, then sipped at a flask of whiskey to dull the pain. The wound throbbed as if someone was jabbing at his leg with a hot poker. He knew the pain would only get worse.

"If that leg turns bad it will have to come off," Hazlett said. "Some doctor will have at it with a bone saw."

"Go to hell, Hazlett. It ain't goin' to turn bad."

"You get gangrene on us and die, hell, that leaves more of that money for us."

"It ain't turnin' bad," Cook said, a little desperately this time. Every soldier had seen the horror of rotting arms and legs from infected wounds. The only salvation then lay in a doctor sawing off the infected limb. The operation was almost as likely to kill a man as the gangrene. "I know it ain't."

"We've got to get that money now, while the Yankees ain't breathing down our necks," Hazlett said. "If we don't take it now, we ain't goin' to be around to do it. Captain, you still with us? We need to get that money and get off the train now. If we do that, the Yankees ain't goin' to get a chance to hang us."

"I'm with you," Fletcher said. He could almost feel the raw burn of a noose around his neck.

"The colonel won't like it," Cook said. "He's your own kin, Hazlett."

Hazlett snorted and bared his fang-like teeth in a sneer. "He's kin I can do without. Always acts like he's better than me. Besides, once those Yankees catch him, they'll stretch his neck right good. If he gets in our way, I'll save them the trouble."

"So what do we do?" Fletcher asked.

Hazlett took out his revolver. "What we do is load our guns. Then we make ourselves rich."

"GET THOSE TIES OFF THE TRACKS!" Greer barked at the soldiers. "Hurry it up!"

The soldiers worked feverishly, several of them grabbing at once for the heavy timbers and pitching them aside. Some of the men worked with fingers broken in the attack, but they did not complain. The Rebels had killed four of their own. Now, they were bent on revenge.

The ties piled across the tracks were not a huge obstacle, but it was enough to slow them down and buy the Rebels time. Already, the *Chesapeake* was gathering speed, disappearing down the tracks. A few soldiers still loaded and fired after the train, but Greer ordered them to put down their muskets and help with the work.

"Hurry, boys, hurry!" Greer cried. He grabbed the end of a tie and single-handedly hurled it off the tracks.

Panting from the effort, Greer took stock of the situation while he caught his breath. He still had sixteen men, all of them hungry to shoot a Rebel. For most, it was the first action they had seen.

Greer's only regret was that the Rebels had not shot Captain Lowell. The skirmish had left the captain shaken, but he had recovered enough to help the men move the ties off the track.

Greer ordered the bodies dragged into a row beside the stationmaster's office. They would come back later to bury them. There was no time for that now.

How many Rebels were dead? None that he had seen. He had counted just eight raiders altogether, not including the three working to refuel the locomotive. Tough bastards, to have held off more than twice their number. Greer was determined that the Rebels wouldn't be so lucky next time.

With the tracks cleared, the soldiers began to scramble back aboard the train. Up in the cab, Schmidt had already set the *Lord Baltimore* moving. Greer caught the back of the locomotive and climbed up.

"All right, Oscar," he said. "Let's go get those Johnny Rebs."

* * *

Near Hancock, Maryland • 4:45 p.m.

HAZLETT WAS in the boxcar at the back of the train, thinking. The skirmish with the Yankees had been a close thing. He was not so sure he and the other raiders would fare so well if it came to another fight.

His mind made up, Hazlett stood. "It's time," he said.

He crossed over to the president's car, followed by Captain Fletcher and John Cook.

"What's going on?" asked Pettibone, who was standing guard with Hudson. "Your orders were to stay in that boxcar."

"Don't go telling me about orders," Hazlett said, sneering. "We're on our way to see the colonel."

"All three of you ain't got to see him," Pettibone said. "You're supposed to stay here in case the Yankees show up on our tail again."

"Corporal Pettibone, get the hell out of my way," Hazlett snarled.

Pettibone did not move. Behind the corporal, Hudson's massive bulk stood like a wall.

Hazlett knew better than to ask Pettibone and Hudson to join the mutiny. Both were loyal to the colonel, especially Hudson. Besides, Hazlett didn't see why a white man should have to share good money with someone like Hudson.

But this was not the time for a fight. Hazlett knew they had to overpower Percy first. Pettibone could either join him then—or get shot. For the moment, there were other ways to get around him.

Hazlett forced a smile and turned to Fletcher. "Captain?"

"You heard him," Fletcher said. "We have to see the colonel."

Pettibone might oppose a sergeant, but he could not argue with an officer, even if it was only Captain Fletcher.

"All right, have it your way," Pettibone said, then stepped aside.

Hazlett bumped him with his shoulder as he went past and reached for the ladder that led to the roof of the car. "Me and you can talk later, Pettibone."

He started up the ladder. The only way to reach the rest of the train was across the top of the president's car. Hazlett climbed to the roof, clambered onto it, and started across in a wide-legged crouch to keep his balance. Wind sang in his ears and the car swayed dangerously as the train raced down the tracks. He tried not to look down.

The roof sloped away from either side of the ridge only enough to shed rain, so the surface was relatively flat. The ground on either side was a blur and tree branches clawed at him. If he was knocked off and hit the ground at this speed, he would be a dead man. Hazlett scrambled across. Captain Fletcher and Private Cook soon followed.

"I don't want to do that again," Cook said as he reached the safety of the ladder.

"It wasn't so bad," Fletcher said, caught up in the excitement of what they were about to do. He couldn't remember the last time he had felt so alive.

They climbed down the other side and entered the baggage car.

"Here it is," Hazlett said, checking on the money they would soon be taking. If the three men had any lingering doubts concerning what they were about to do, the sight of all those greenbacks put them to rest. It was more money than any of them had ever seen.

"We're rich," Fletcher said. He sounded giddy.

"We've got to get the money off the train first," Cook said soberly. "Then we'll be rich."

Taking the money wasn't going to be easy. They could have thrown the money off the train and jumped after it, but no one could leap from a train moving at sixty miles per hour and expect to live. The ground would hit him like a club.

The only other choice was to seize control of the train from Colonel Percy and force the *Chesapeake* to slow or stop so they could unload the money. They would need to do that before the Yankee train reappeared on the tracks behind them. Hazlett hadn't thought it through, but he knew that any good soldier sometimes had to make things up as he went along.

"We'll take care of Flynn and the colonel, then I'll go forward and stop the train," Hazlett said. "Willie Forbes will see it our way, just as long as we promise him a bottle of whiskey. Come on."

They went out the baggage car, crossed the open platform, and threw open the door to the passenger car.

Percy was there. And Flynn. Johnny Benjamin lounged near the back of the car. The woman, Nellie Jones, was sponging Lieutenant Cater's face with a damp rag. Cater had come around, although his eyes were bright and feverish. His face was pale as a boiled shirt from all the blood he had lost. Hazlett stepped around Lieutenant Cater and the woman to face Percy.

"What's going on?" Percy demanded. "The three of you should be back in the boxcar. What's wrong?"

For a moment, Hazlett just stared at Percy. Then everything happened quickly. Hazlett suddenly had a gun in his hand. Benjamin began to draw his own gun, but Cook hit him with a fist to the jaw that knocked the boy off his feet. Cook took his gun away.

Too startled to move, Percy and Flynn found themselves staring into the muzzles of three revolvers.

CHAPTER 30

"WHAT THE HELL IS GOING ON?" Percy repeated eyes steely with anger. "Have you boys turned into Yankees on me?"

"It ain't like that, Percy," Hazlett said, not bothering to call him "Colonel" or "sir." "We just want to be rich."

"This is about that payroll money isn't it? Damn it all! I knew I should have thrown that money off the train when I had the chance."

"I reckon it's a good thing for us you didn't," Hazlett said. "Besides, the boys and I know this raid will end in some hangings, and we don't want to swing. So, Percy, what you're goin' to do is order the train to stop. We're goin' to take that payroll money, and then me, Fletcher and Cook are gettin' off this wreck."

"You'll do no such thing."

Hazlett thumbed back the hammer on the Colt. "We ain't askin'. We're tellin'. You ain't got no choice, Percy."

"I'm disappointed in you, Hazlett. Truly I am."

Hazlett smirked. "I'm real sorry to hear that. Now stop the goddamn train. I ain't goin' to ask nice again."

"Hazlett, I won't lie to you," Percy went on as if he had

not heard Hazlett's demands and the sergeant was not waving a gun in his face. "I always thought you were no-account back home. You and Cook both. At first I put you in my regiment and made you a sergeant because you're married to my cousin. Thing is, you turned out to be a pretty good soldier. You're good in a fight and the men listen to you." Percy jerked his chin at Captain Fletcher. "Now Fletcher here, I can see him doing this cowardly thing—this *mutiny*. He's not one of us. But I can't understand why you're doing this. Don't turn yellow on me. Not after all we've been through so far. Not now."

Hazlett snorted. "You can save your damned pretty speeches, Percy. You always did think you was better than me. Better than anyone else, to tell the truth. You ain't got all the answers. You're about to get us all killed, for one thing."

"Well, Hazlett, at least I have not forgotten my duty." Up until that point, Percy had been speaking calmly. Now his eyes sparked with anger, and he spoke with stinging truthfulness. "You're a coward. White trash. That's all you are, and that's all you'll ever be."

Hazlett's face twisted in rage, making it even uglier than usual. He raised the revolver until it was pointed at Percy's head. "Damn you to hell, Percy!"

Flynn took a step toward Hazlett, but stopped when Cook leveled a revolver at him. Flynn started to say, "Now, Hazlett, maybe we can work this out about the money— "

"Shut up, Irish," Hazlett snapped, without taking his eyes off Percy. "I want to enjoy watching the high and mighty lord of the manor get hisself shot without listening to you flap your jaw. If Irish here opens his mouth again, Cook, shoot him."

"All right," Cook said. He looked uneasy. It was one thing to shoot a man in battle, but it was altogether different to kill him in cold blood, face to face.

Hazlett's whole arm shook with fury. His finger began to tighten on the trigger. Percy stood calmly, waiting to take the bullet in the chest.

Nearby, Nellie gasped. "My God, he's going to shoot him."

On the floor at Hazlett's feet, Silas Cater lay quietly, forgotten. He raised himself on one elbow and kicked Hazlett just under the knee. It was a feeble kick, but the boot struck with enough force to knock Hazlett off balance.

The gun fired, missing Percy's head by inches. Hazlett swore, swung the revolver down, and shot Cater in the chest. He turned the gun toward Percy as the colonel rushed him. Percy managed to catch Hazlett's wrist and slam his hand into a corner of a bench. The gun slid away under the seats. Percy was just reaching for his own revolver when Cook tackled him.

Flynn drew the Le Mat revolver, but before he could get off a shot he had to dive for the cover offered by the benches as Fletcher snapped off two shots at him. The bullets scattered bits of horsehair stuffing from the seats.

"Damn you, Fletcher!" Flynn shouted. In reply, another shot tore through the seats.

"Shoot him and be done with it," Hazlett snarled at Fletcher. He was trying to help Cook wrestle Percy to the floor.

"I can't see him!"

"Not the Paddy, you jackass! Shoot the colonel!" Hazlett let go of Percy and stepped away.

But Fletcher did not have a chance because Percy and Cook were still wrestling with each other, gouging and punching. He couldn't shoot one without hitting the other.

Hazlett swore. "Take care of him, Fletcher. I'm going to stop the train. We ain't got much time." He dashed out the doorway in the direction of the locomotive.

Flynn popped up and fired at Captain Fletcher, but a

sudden jolt of the train sent his shot wide. Before he could get off another shot, Fletcher yelped and ran out the back doorway, toward the baggage car.

Flynn knew he had to catch Hazlett. Although Hazlett had lost his gun, he might still be able to stop the locomotive, in which case the Yankees would soon overtake them. If that happened, the raiders would all be hanged or shot.

Flynn flung open the door and crossed the platform, rushing into the next passenger car, revolver at the ready.

The car was empty.

Where the hell was Hazlett? He could not have reached the locomotive that quickly. Flynn dashed to the opposite door, threw it open, and ran out. Above the roaring wind, he heard a metallic click.

Flynn ducked.

A searing flash came from the roof of the car and a bullet slashed past his ear, so close he could feel the heat of the lead. He twisted, fired upwards, but there was only empty sky above him.

Hazlett was on the roof of the car. That explained how he had disappeared so quickly. He must have been carrying another pistol besides the one he had lost in the scuffle. Knowing Hazlett, it had been stuffed in his boot. He knew someone would chase him and had planned an ambush. Only the constant lurching of the train had spoiled Hazlett's aim and saved Flynn's life.

"Bastard," Flynn growled, then started up the short ladder that led to the roof.

Carefully, Flynn raised his head above the edge of the roof, expecting another shot at any moment. However, he could see that Hazlett was halfway down the car, moving away from him.

"Hazlett!" he shouted, and pulled himself onto the roof.

Hazlett turned and fired. Flynn snapped off a shot in

reply, but it was nearly impossible to hit anything more than a few feet away on the swaying, wind-whipped roof. The train was moving at sixty miles per hour and wind howled in Flynn's ears. It was like being on the deck of a ship during a storm, with the motion threatening to pitch both men off at any moment.

Flynn had to crouch to keep from toppling off. Branches from trees overhanging the tracks lashed at him, trying to sweep him off the roof. Cinders and hot ash from the *Chesapeake's* smokestack stung his face and eyes.

"Sure, and you picked a fine place to make a last stand, Hazlett," he shouted over the wind.

"Go to hell, Irish."

"Ain't I there already? What do you call this place?"

Hazlett fired again. The bullet sang into the mountain air.

"Listen to me, Hazlett. You would never get far with that money. The Yankees are right behind us. Take a look."

Hazlett glanced over his shoulder. Sure enough, the pursuing train had come into sight. The Yankee locomotive moved like lightning. The *Chesapeake* was running slower than before, although Flynn wasn't sure why. Although the enemy's train was still in the distance, Flynn could see it would gain steadily on them. It was only a matter of time before the *Chesapeake* was overtaken.

"How long do you think we'll last once the Yankees catch up?" Hazlett shouted in reply. "We ain't got a goddamn prayer if that happens. They'll hang every last one of us that don't get killed in the fight."

"You won't have to worry about it, Hazlett, you bastard. I plan to kill you first myself." Flynn raised the Le Mat, but couldn't hold his arm steady enough to get off a shot. Hazlett raised his own pistol and fired two shots. The bullets cracked past Flynn's head, sounding like the flick of a bullwhip.

The hammer of Hazlett's gun fell on an empty chamber.

He tossed the useless pistol away and rushed at Flynn with a snarl. Somehow, he managed to keep his feet. Flynn was busy shoving his revolver back in his belt, trying to get his hands free, when Hazlett butted him in the belly.

The two men fell and rolled. Flynn feared they would go right off the edge of the roof, but he managed to spread his feet, and that braked them. Hazlett tried to bite his ear, but Flynn snapped his own head up and caught Hazlett in the nose. Blood streamed out and flecked them both.

Hazlett hit him so hard on the chin that Flynn's vision swam black and red. He shoved, elbowed, got free of Hazlett.

Both men got to their feet, struggling to keep their balance. Hazlett had the advantage because his back was to the wind, while Flynn faced the front of the train. The rush of air and hot bite of cinders and smoke made his eyes blur. He had to turn his head sideways just to catch a breath.

The train rounded a bend, and the car leaned sickeningly beneath them. Hazlett's position gave him an easier time of it, and he cackled as he watched Flynn scramble to keep his feet. Hazlett's face was streaked with blood from his damaged nose, making him look like a crazed man. He launched himself at Flynn, who hit him with a perfectly timed punch that sent Hazlett reeling.

As the train came out of the bend, Flynn spotted the tunnel ahead. Dark as midnight inside, with a keyhole of daylight just visible at the other end. On the map Flynn remembered it was marked as Indigo Tunnel. Hazlett, his back to the tunnel, didn't see it.

"Let's make a deal, Hazlett," Flynn shouted above the wind, trying to keep Hazlett right where he was. "You and me can split the money."

Hazlett spat away a mouthful of blood. "Not on your life, Irish. I'd as soon burn it as give half to you."

"You need help now," Flynn said. "Fletcher and Cook don't stand a chance against Percy."

"Percy ain't so tough," Hazlett said. "Looked like he was about beat when I left."

The tunnel loomed closer. The *Chesapeake* sounded three short warning blasts, but Hazlett paid no attention.

Just a few more seconds. "Think of it, Hazlett. You and me—we're the only ones who can take that money and get back home alive."

"Go to hell, Irish!"

"You'll beat me there, you bastard!"

Flynn threw himself flat on the roof.

Puzzled, Hazlett stared down at Flynn. Then he turned around.

Too late.

The black mouth of the tunnel was just ahead, with the stone arch four feet above the top of the train. Hazlett had just started to scream when the archway slammed into him and cut his cry short.

Above the noise of wind and train, Flynn heard a sickening *thunk*. Then the train plunged into darkness.

Flynn took a deep breath. He could see nothing but the sparks shooting from the smokestack. The smoke, trapped in the narrow confines of the tunnel, nearly choked him. He held his breath so he wouldn't suffocate. The noise was deafening and his eardrums felt ready to burst. He couldn't see the arch of the tunnel, but sensed it was just overhead, so he kept his face pressed tightly against the roof of the car.

Just as suddenly as the train had rushed into darkness, it burst from the tunnel. Flynn shifted his weight carefully and began making his way back toward the end of the car and the ladder he would climb down to the platform. He took his time, hardly able to believe that he had been standing on the bucking rooftop just minutes ago. Tree branches swept dangerously close to the roof, trying to pluck him off. He had survived this long on top of the train. He didn't plan to be killed in the last few moments on this dangerous perch.

Flynn worked his feet over the rooftop and onto the ladder. He managed to get a look behind the *Chesapeake*, and was startled to see the enemy's train shoot from the tunnel, wreathed in smoke and steam. He cursed, and then he muttered a quick Hail Mary. A prayer now and then never hurt.

* * *

NELLIE WAS in the baggage car filling a sack with bundles of Yankee greenbacks when Captain Fletcher came in. There was only a dusky light in the car, but it was enough for him to spot her.

"What do you think you're doing?" Fletcher asked. He appeared surprised to see Nellie taking the money.

"I'm making myself rich," she said. Nellie turned to him and smiled, although her voice sounded a little desperate even to her own ears. "I could use a partner. How about you? Let's take this money and get off the train."

Fletcher hesitated. He was tempted. All the men on board knew her for what she was, and who could say what besides the money a whore might share with him? Just as quickly, an image of Hazlett's evil, sneering face filled his mind. He shuddered at the thought of what the sergeant might do to him if he tried to cheat Hazlett out of the money.

"No partners," Fletcher said. He moved until he was almost touching her. She wore some kind of perfume that reminded him of lilacs. Fletcher knew it was just a whore's cheap scent, but it was maddening.

"Help me," she said, her voice pleading.

The money was not for her, he thought. But she didn't

have to know that—not yet. Hazlett would soon be stopping the train, but there would be time enough. After casting his lot with Hazlett and helping to oppose Percy, Fletcher felt wonderfully alive, invincible, and he reached out and snatched Nellie's sack of money away. Life, he thought, was about taking what you wanted.

"There's plenty of money here for all of us," Nellie said.

Too late, she recognized the expression on his face. She had seen that same leer a hundred times in various squalid rooms along the Baltimore waterfront, and on tougher faces than Fletcher's. She hated that expression, and Nellie knew that if she managed to take the money from the train, she would never have to see that look of lust again.

He moved toward her.

She tried to dart around him, but Fletcher grabbed her shoulders and pinned her against a pile of luggage.

"Damn you!" She spat at him.

Fletcher was too intoxicated by the day's excitement even to notice. They had outrun the Yankees and kidnapped Abraham Lincoln. He had seen men die. He had lived, and now he would take whatever he wanted, whether it was the money or this whore. He held her down with one hand and dangled the sack of money aloft in the other, laughing.

"Partners? You're a whore! Hell, you'd take me on as your partner and then sell me out to the first bunch of Yankees we came across. Just give me what I want and you can come with us—maybe we'll even let you have some of the money."

She relaxed, and Fletcher interpreted that as compliance. He threw one arm across her chest to keep her pinned down, put the money down, and fumbled at the hem of her long dress with his free hand.

Nellie began to struggle. Her movements seemed weak and awkward. Fletcher laughed.

From the corner of his eye, he saw a flash of steel as she

slipped a long and gleaming stiletto from her sleeve. The blade looked wickedly sharp. The train whistled three times, and then they were swept into total blackness as the train raced into Indigo Tunnel.

He tried to move but his arm was tangled in the folds of her dress. Fletcher felt the tip of the knife probe between his ribs and then plunge deep, burning, slicing, seeking his heart.

He screamed.

Then Fletcher collapsed among the boxes and baggage, a dying man.

Sunlight again. They were out of the tunnel. Nellie stood and straightened her clothes. Some of Fletcher's blood had splashed onto her dress, but that couldn't be helped. She reached down, pulled the knife from the captain's twitching body, and wiped the blade on his coat before slipping it back into her sleeve.

The train had not stopped. Nellie wondered what was taking Hazlett so long. The mutiny had come as a surprise. She had hoped that when Hazlett stopped the train, she might at least be able to escape with some of the money while the raiders fought among themselves.

She knew that to leap from a speeding train in this rugged country would be suicide. Still, she might not have a choice. There was no way she could trust Hazlett if his mutiny succeeded—he wouldn't share any of the money with her. After all, Sergeant Hazlett might not be happy that Fletcher was dead, and even Nellie had to admit she was afraid of Hazlett.

But if the train did not stop, it meant Hazlett had failed. Somehow, Colonel Percy, Flynn, and that boy, Benjamin, had beaten the mutineers. Well, if it came to it, she would much rather deal with Flynn. The Irishman was cunning, but she felt she could trust him. He had a certain sense of honor. The thought made Nellie smile to herself. Honor among thieves?

She didn't know about that, but at least she and Flynn under-stood each other.

Nellie hid the sack of money in a corner, stepped around Captain Fletcher's body, and moved toward the door leading back to the passenger car, wondering what she would find.

The truth was that she didn't care about the war, the Union, or the Confederacy. She just wanted to be rich, and now she would have to wait a little longer.

CHAPTER 31

Near Little Orleans, Maryland • 4 p.m.

FLYNN RETURNED to the passenger car and found Colonel Percy busy tying up John Cook, who lay with his battered face to the floor. He could see it hadn't been an easy fight. One of Percy's eyes had a bad gash at the corner and a split lip dripped blood into his sandy beard. Johnny Benjamin stood nearby, his Colt trained on Cook and a murderous look in his eye.

"I had some help," Percy explained, nodding at the boy. "It's all I could do to keep him from shooting Cook."

"I don't know why you stopped him," Flynn said. He grinned down at Cook's bruised face. "That looks like it hurts."

"Go to hell, Flynn," Cook mumbled.

"Why, those were Sergeant Hazlett's very last words to me."

"What about Hazlett?" Percy asked.

"You might say he lost his head."

Before Percy could ask for any details, Nellie emerged from the back door of the car. Flynn spotted the blood on her bodice and rushed toward her.

"Are you hurt?" he asked anxiously.

Nellie shook her head and slumped into one of the bench seats. Flynn knelt beside her. "It's not my blood," she said.

Flynn glanced at Percy, who shrugged. Benjamin spoke up: "I saw Captain Fletcher follow her into the next car."

Nellie nodded. "I ran out to get away. There was shooting, everyone was fighting. I went into the baggage car to hide. Captain Fletcher followed me. He wanted to—well, it was awful. I had to defend myself."

If Flynn had not known better, he would have believed her. Nellie obviously had taken advantage of the commotion by trying to make off with the payroll cash. He guessed Fletcher was dead because he had tried to stop her. Flynn remembered the touch of Nellie's knife against his throat and almost felt sorry for Fletcher.

"You killed him?" he asked.

"Yes."

"It couldn't have happened to a better man," Flynn said. "You done good, Miss Jones, and I'm glad your honor remains intact."

"Flynn, those are hardly words of comfort," Percy said, looking annoyed. The colonel was no fool. He had long since guessed that Nellie was not an innocent Baltimore belle, but that made him more disposed to be kind to her. Percy had a weakness for whores.

"You're right." He patted Nellie on the shoulder. "There, there, girl. You've been through a lot."

The look in Nellie's green eyes could have frozen water. Those eyes were probably the last thing Fletcher had seen in this life, Flynn thought.

"Now what, sir?" Benjamin asked the colonel. "I was wondering about the money."

"Damn the money!" Percy exploded, losing his temper. "We're not bandits, son. We're soldiers and we're going to follow orders. We do our duty. That's what soldiers do. There are still eight of us, and that's plenty enough to get the job done. Our orders are to get President Lincoln to Richmond, and that's just what we're going to do."

"Yes, sir," Benjamin stammered.

Percy shot a quick glance at Flynn. "There. Will that make your goddamn Colonel Norris happy?"

"It will, Colonel. It will at that."

Duty. To Flynn, it was a word for drawing rooms and politicians, newspaper editorials and fools. Percy, he knew, was just enough of a Southern aristocrat to believe in the concept of duty. He looked again at Nellie, who had a smirk playing at the corners of her lips. There was a world of difference between himself and Percy. On the other hand, he and Nellie knew that words like duty had no place in the real business of life.

A train whistle startled them, the sound cutting the air like the screech of a hunting hawk. They rushed to the windows.

"The Yankees are right behind us!" Benjamin cried.

"They can't be that fast," Percy said in disbelief. "That train was barely in sight just a short time ago."

Flynn gauged for a moment the passing trees and scenery, and did not like what he saw. "We're slowing down, Colonel," he said. "That's why they've caught up to us."

"Damn," Percy said, noticing it himself. "I believe you're right, Flynn. I'll head up to the engine to see what's wrong. I want you and Benjamin to work your way back to that boxcar we picked up back at the depot in Kearneysville. You know those railroad ties in there? Drop them on the tracks behind us. See if you can get them to jam under that other engine. Wreck the sons of bitches." Percy turned to Nellie and gave her a courtly bow "Pardon my language, ma'am."

Flynn doubted that Percy's plan would work. "I don't know, Colonel. It's like throwing sticks at a bear."

"All we need is time, Flynn. Just some goddamn time! If we can hold out a little longer, we'll be closer to the rendezvous. Then it will be the Yankees who are on the run. Throw the ties at them. We've got to try something."

"Yes, sir." They started to move. Flynn stopped. "What about Cook here? You want me to throw him off the train? He might jam up that other locomotive about as good as a railroad tie."

Cook made a desperate noise, as if he were about to start pleading for his life. His eyes looked big and round as silver dollars above the dirty rag tied around his mouth.

"Hush now," Percy told Cook. "Or I will let Flynn throw you off the train." Percy gave Hazlett's gun to Nellie. She swung open the cylinder expertly, checked the loads, and clicked the cylinder shut. Percy smiled. "I believe Miss Jones can handle Private Cook just fine. If he moves, my dear, shoot him."

* * *

GREER COULD SEE THE RAIDERS' train just ahead. They were steadily overtaking the *Chesapeake*, and in another few minutes, the iron "cow catcher" on the front of the *Lord Baltimore* would be touching the boxcar ahead of them. Greer felt elated. He, like the soldiers clinging to the tender, wanted another fight. They would not be bested the second time around.

As if reading Greer's mind, one of the soldiers lifted his rifle and fired at the Rebel train.

Greer whirled around and shouted to be heard over the wind. "Hold your fire! You'll need that ammunition before we're through."

"They're slowing," Schmidt observed.

"I know," Greer said. "This locomotive is fast, but if they weren't losing speed, we wouldn't have caught them already. They had a pretty good head start out of Harpers Ferry."

"I don't like it," Schmidt said. "I don't trust these Rebels. Why go to all this trouble just to steal a train?"

"They want that payroll money."

"Do they?" Schmidt asked. "Then why not just take the money *und* leave the train? If they split up and had a head-start, it will be hard to catch them on foot."

"Hell if I know what's on their minds, Oscar. They didn't ask my advice."

"What else is on that train?" Schmidt pressed. "What is in that car we picked up in Baltimore?"

"I don't know," Greer said, wondering himself. "It's all closed up. No one answered when I banged on the door back in Baltimore."

"Well." It came out as *vell*. Schmidt shrugged his wide shoulders. "Who knows what's in there?"

"Maybe those Rebs do," Greer said. "Looks like we'll be able to ask them soon enough."

* * *

WET WOOD DOESN'T BURN—A fact that was being hammered home aboard *Chesapeake*. Back at the Kearneysville station where they had taken on wood and water, the cordwood had not been kept covered in a shed. Rain had soaked it through and the autumn sun was not sufficient to dry it. It did not help that the wood was also green.

Hank Cunningham and Willie Forbes continued to hurl wood into the red-hot maw of the firebox, but the damp, green firewood only steamed and sputtered. The heat of the firebox was so intense that the wood eventually caught fire and burned, but not with the intensity needed to create the steam needed for outrunning the Yankees.

"Why in hell did you load wet wood?" demanded Percy, who had made his way to the engine to find out what was wrong.

"It was the only wood there was, Colonel," Willie Forbes replied, slurring his words slightly. His bottle of whiskey— well-hidden from Percy—was mostly gone.

The colonel stared hard at him, then finally exploded. "Damn you, Forbes! You're drunk."

"Well, I've been drinking," Forbes admitted.

Furiously, Percy lashed out with his right fist and caught Forbes on the chin. The blow nearly knocked Forbes off the train and he struggled to keep his balance.

Percy whirled on Cunningham. "So help me, Hank, if you're drunk, too— "

The engineer backed up a step. "No, sir."

"How could you let him drink like that?" Percy demanded. "You knew my orders."

"I reckon he's got a mind of his own," Cunningham said. "Besides, sir, that wood at Kearneysville was green and wet, but that's all there was. Drunk or sober, it wouldn't have made no difference."

Percy clenched and unclenched his fists, fighting the urge to strike Forbes again. He knew there was little he could do at the moment to punish Forbes. He needed every man if they were going to have any hope of outrunning the Yankees.

Still fuming, Percy turned to the engineer. "Well?"

"We're winding down like a watch, Colonel," Wilson said. "It wouldn't be a problem if we weren't being chased. We could just take on some dry wood at another station."

"No chance of that. Not with the Yankees right behind us."

"Sorry, Colonel," Cunningham said. He and Forbes looked

exhausted from stoking the engine. "I feel like we let you down."

"Not at all, Percy said. "It's the wood, Hank."

What was done, thought Percy, was done. He knew they had already used up more than their share of luck for one day. Now the only thing that could get them to the safety of the rendezvous point was a miracle—or one hell of a lot of luck.

The train churned through wild country. There were no towns or villages, just groupings of squalid, unpainted frame houses that huddled beside the tracks. The only other sign of human handiwork was the Chesapeake and Ohio Canal, which paralleled the tracks of the B&O. This time of year, however, there wasn't a great deal of boat traffic.

Mostly there were just empty mountains rising steeply beyond the rail lines. The tracks lay on the West Virginia side of the Potomac River, and across the water was Maryland.

As they approached the head of the river, the Potomac was now shallow enough to wade across. The current was swift and the river foamed white as it passed over the rocky riverbed. Hard to believe this was the same river they had crossed three days ago near Washington, where the Potomac was so vast that steamboats could navigate. These lonely mountains struck Percy as a forlorn place to make a last stand. Sometimes a soldier didn't get a choice.

FLYNN AND BENJAMIN were climbing to the roof of the president's car. "Once we get to the top, get across and be quick about it, lad," Flynn said. "Don't get to thinking about what you're doing, or you won't do it."

The car bucked beneath their feet and on either side the rocky ground far below was just a blur. A slip would mean death, but they scrambled across, trying not to think about that. The soldiers riding on the pursuing train were quick enough to get shots off, but the bullets buzzed harmlessly past. Then Flynn and Benjamin reached the ladder on the other side. They climbed down almost on the heads of Pettibone and Hudson.

"Any word from the president?" Flynn asked.

"Not a sound out of him. It's quiet as the grave in there," Pettibone said. "What happened to Hazlett and the rest? They said they had to go see the colonel. I told him to stay, but he wouldn't listen."

"You heard the shooting?"

"A little." Pettibone shrugged his bony shoulders. "I reckoned Benjamin here was taking potshots at the Yankees behind us."

"The truth of the matter was that we had a mutiny on our hands."

"Goddamn Hazlett. I knew he was up to no good," Pettibone said.

"Those three decided they wanted to take the payroll money in the baggage car and asked the colonel to stop the train so they could get off."

"Those bastards." Pettibone shook his head in astonishment. "I reckon Colonel Percy didn't like that plan."

"There was a disagreement," Flynn said, grinning. "Hazlett and Fletcher are dead. Cook is tied up good and tight so he won't cause trouble."

"I'll be damned," Pettibone said in his slow drawl. "What happened?"

Flynn quickly detailed the brief mutiny. "I won't miss Hazlett," he added.

"Neither will I," Hudson announced. "He didn't have much use for negroes."

"That leaves fewer of us to fight the Yankees," Pettibone said.

"Hell, it just evens the odds," Flynn said. "Now, if you'll excuse us, lads, the boy and I have work to do."

Flynn crossed the open space between the two cars and ducked into the boxcar, with Benjamin right behind him.

"I ain't a boy," Benjamin said, once they were inside the car.

Flynn looked at him, saw a face that could not yet grow more than a few scraggly whiskers, and suppressed a grin. Benjamin really *was* just a boy, but there was no denying he was doing a man's work.

"Right you are, Private," Flynn said. "My apologies. Now, grab hold of the other end of this tie. Let's give the Yankees something to chew on."

The railroad tie was carved from black locust, a species whose dense wood was naturally resistant to rot. It was six inches square and almost as heavy as iron. They maneuvered it toward the hole in the back wall of the boxcar, stumbling every time the speeding train swayed on the tracks.

"When I say the word, give her a big push," Flynn said.

He eased the tie out and balanced it on the edge of the opening. Flynn knew what they were doing was purely desperate, but it still had some small chance of success. If they could get the tie to land on the tracks in just the right way, it might get caught up in the machinery of the wheels and driving rods of the pursuing locomotive. They might even manage to derail the train.

"Now!" he yelled, and with a powerful shove, they sent the tie shooting out of the boxcar. It missed the tracks altogether and bounced, turning end over end until it landed in the river with a tremendous splash.

"This might take some practice," Flynn said. "Let's try again."

They manhandled another tie into position. The soldiers aboard the *Lord Baltimore* were now firing at the boxcar.

Fortunately, a speeding train wasn't the most stable platform to shoot from. The soldiers were also hampered by their own engine ahead of them, which blocked a clear shot. Still, the Minié ball drilled through the boxcar with disturbing ease. Splinters showered down upon Flynn and Benjamin. They had no choice but to go on working as the bullets zipped past with hair-raising, high-pitched whines.

They hurled the tie out. It bounced and rolled, then came to rest across the iron rails, perpendicular to the oncoming train. The Yankee train's cowcatcher swept it aside like a toothpick.

"We may be in trouble, lad," Flynn conceded. A bullet cracked between them. Benjamin flinched, but Flynn ignored it. "You'll never hear the one that kills you. Now, let's give it one more try."

They wrestled another tie into place. Both of them sweated from the effort of moving the heavy lengths of wood. Another minié ball punched through the wall. It seemed to Flynn that their train had lost even more ground to the Yankee engine. He maneuvered the tie closer to the edge.

"If this one don't do it, lad, our goose may be cooked. Give her a good shove. Now!"

This time, the tie came to rest inside the tracks, parallel to the iron rails, making a kind of wooden third rail. It slipped beneath the oncoming locomotive's cattle guard and suddenly the train jolted as the locust tie entangled itself in the train's undercarriage. The whole engine swayed and shuddered.

"Ha, ha!" Flynn shouted triumphantly. "Look at that!"

The locomotive lurched to one side. Chewed wood spit from between the churning iron wheels. The train gave one last spasm and rushed on. Flynn felt his hopes sink.

"I reckon we're in trouble, Sergeant," Benjamin said. More bullets plucked at the boxcar, and both men hunkered in the shelter of the stacked ties. Lead spattered against the wood with a sound like June bugs smacking into window glass on a summer night.

Flynn clapped Benjamin on the shoulder. "Well, boy—I mean, *Private*—the fight ain't over yet."

Flynn looked around the boxcar. There was still a good supply of ties remaining, but another attempt to derail the oncoming train would be suicide. Since the last tie had been so effective, the Yankees were now pouring fire at the boxcar. If they stayed, it was only a matter of time before one of them was shot.

He spotted an oil lantern on the floor by the sliding side door. It must have been left behind by the workmen who used the boxcar while making repairs to the tracks. The sight of the lantern gave Flynn an idea. He smiled.

"Get out of the car, lad," he ordered Benjamin. "I'm setting it on fire."

CHAPTER 32

FLYNN GRABBED the lantern and smashed it against the wall. He splashed kerosene generously around the boxcar, letting it soak into the wood. His nose wrinkled against the acrid smell.

Bullets hammered through the walls. Flynn kept his head down. The Yankees must be coming closer, he thought.

Flynn took out his revolver, held the muzzle close to a spot on the floor that was slick with kerosene, and pulled the trigger. The muzzle flash set the kerosene burning. Flynn waited until the small flame lept higher and began to spread. Fire licked across the floor and up the walls, and the car began to fill with choking, black smoke. Coughing, Flynn scrambled out and jumped to the platform of Lincoln's car, where Pettibone, Benjamin and Hudson waited.

"What the hell are you doing, Flynn?" Pettibone demanded as smoke began to billow from the boxcar.

"Making things hot for the Yankees," Flynn replied. "Now unhitch her, lads, unhitch her."

Wind from the rush of their passage fed the flames, which soon poured from the car's openings. Unless they all wanted to be burned alive, they had to detach the burning car. Petti-bone got down on his belly and reached for the pin that held the coupling between the two cars in place.

"It won't come loose," he said. Orange tendrils of fire whipped over his head, beating at the air. "It's no good."

"Let me help," Flynn said, and climbed over the side. The coupling between the two cars was like an iron handshake, gripping them together, and the iron bars that ran from the coupling to the undercarriage of each car were like the wrists. Flynn edged out onto the closest of these bars, keeping one hand on the platform railing for balance. It was a perilous place to be, balancing on the three-inch-wide bar, because each jolt of the train threatened to throw him beneath the wheels. Flames fluttered within a few feet of his face.

Carefully, Flynn reached down and took hold of the coupling pin. He tugged and tugged again, but the pin wouldn't move. Friction and pressure held the coupling pin in place. He would have to find a moment when the weight of the cars shifted enough so that the pressure on the pin eased and he could pull it right out.

"You're a damn fool, Flynn," Pettibone shouted. The burning boxcar was rapidly becoming an inferno, and the flames had driven the men up against the side of Lincoln's car, where they covered their faces against the heat. "You're going to get us all burned up."

Flames lashed at Flynn, singeing the sleeve of his coat. The heat was like standing in front of a blast furnace.

Flynn reached for the pin, grabbed it. A sudden lurching of the train threw him off balance and he lost his grip on the pin. He would have fallen and been ground to sausage under the wheels, but Hudson sprang forward and caught Flynn's coat, steadying him. Flynn nodded his thanks, then bent again to tug at the pin. If he couldn't get it out and separate the cars, the whole train might burn up, President Lincoln included.

He slipped his fingers around the iron nub, and lifted straight up. The pin slid free this time as easily as a ramrod out of a musket barrel. Flynn tossed the pin away, then kicked at the coupling to break the grip between the two cars. Nothing moved. Flynn hid his face in the crook of his elbow to protect it from the flames. The heat from the burning car was making it difficult to breathe and the hair sticking from under the edges of his hat burned away. Finally, the train jolted over some rough place in the tracks, the coupling separated, and the flaming boxcar drifted back toward the Yankees.

Behind him, Pettibone let out a Rebel yell. "Chew on that, you Yankee sons of bitches!"

* * *

"Here it comes!" Greer shouted in warning.

Then he watched in horror as the fireball rolled toward them. At first, Greer wasn't sure what the raiders were up to, setting the boxcar on fire. The next thing he knew, the *Lord Baltimore* was rushing headlong into the flames. He realized then that the raiders must have uncoupled the car.

"I can't see!" Schmidt shouted as fire swept around the locomotive, licking at the cab. The impact sent a tornado of sparks swirling into the sky.

Schmidt reached for the Johnson bar to reverse the locomotive. Greer grabbed his wrist. "Oscar, you will not stop this train," he growled. "Keep after them."

"We'll be burned up!"

"This locomotive is made of iron, and iron doesn't burn. Now keep that throttle wide open."

The train rushed blindly into a world of flame. The wind

fanned the burning car into an inferno. Ribbons of fire whipped and curled around the locomotive. The four men in the cab—Greer, Captain Lowell, Schmidt and Prescott—sheltered inside as flames swept past the windows. They wouldn't be able to continue the chase much longer before the inside of the cab became a death trap, hot as an oven.

* * *

WALTER FROST HUDDLED with the soldiers. He was able to see ahead of the engine as it rounded a slight curve in the tracks. Smoke and heat enveloped the train, threatening to choke them. The *Chesapeake* was no more than two hundred feet ahead and Frost could see four raiders standing on the platform of the last car, looking back at the flaming boxcar. They were a tough bunch, he thought, but the second time around, they wouldn't stand a chance against a whole squad of soldiers. The raiders had just been lucky back at Kearneysville.

Frost felt rage burn within him, hot as the flames filling the sky. Those Rebel bastards had caused him, Schmidt and Greer a lot of trouble, maybe even good jobs with the railroad, and, like Greer, he was all for hanging the raiders alongside the tracks.

If they could catch them. Frost's rage gave way to glee when he saw their chance to leave the burning boxcar behind. The men in the locomotive's cab, he knew, couldn't see anything but flames. Frost crawled forward.

"Greer!" he shouted, keeping his head beneath the billowing sheet of flame and smoke. "There's a siding about two hundred yards ahead. Slow it down and we can lose the boxcar."

Schmidt, too, had heard the fireman. He had already begun easing back on the throttle, and at a nod from Greer, he used all his strength to pull back the Johnson bar and reverse the engine. Frantically, Frost grabbed the brake wheel and screwed it down. The train ground to a halt, spewing steam, smoke and flames. Frost jumped down from the tender and ran to the siding. While they waited for Frost to throw the switch, Schmidt backed the engine away from the fireball.

The siding had an abandoned air about it. Most likely, it was used only a few times each year to load timber or hogs or corn. The switch was stiff with rust, and Frost heaved with all his might at the lever. Greer jumped down and ran over to help. Grunting and cussing, the two men finally got the switch to move.

Schmidt eased the locomotive forward until he once again came in contact with the burning car. He pushed it onto the siding, then reversed the engine. Once the locomotive was back on the main track, Frost and Greer moved the switch again so the train could bypass the siding. The boxcar was left alone, filling the sky with smoke and flames. Some of the soldiers whooped and hollered as the car burned.

The delay was maddening. By the time Greer and Frost were done and back aboard the train, the raiders had disappeared from sight. Nearby, the boxcar hissed and popped as flames poured from it.

Greer swung aboard. Frost took his place on the tender. "After them!" Greer barked. "The next time we stop, we're going to have ourselves a hanging party."

* * *

"WE LOST THEM," Johnny Benjamin reported as he peered into the distance.

"You did it, Flynn. I reckon your crazy plan worked, after all," Pettibone said with a grin. "For a while there, I thought you was goin' to roast us."

"They'll be after us again," Flynn said. "All we did was get a little extra time. The closer we get to the rendezvous, the better our chances."

Far off, they could see the smoke from the burning car. Because the smoke was now rising straight up, it appeared the boxcar had brought the Yankees to a halt. They noticed, too, that the eastern horizon was getting dark as night came on, although the sky to the west was still bright blue above the mountain peaks. The river that the tracks followed was deep in shadow, cold and misty.

Around them, the country had changed considerably. The flat, Maryland farm country they had crossed that morning was long-gone, as were West Virginia's gently rolling hills. They were now in the Allegheny mountains—the name for that portion of the Appalachian range that ran like a bony spine through Virginia, West Virginia, Maryland and up into Pennsylvania.

The Alleghenies were from two-thousand to nearly five thousand feet high, not tall compared to the huge mountain ranges in the west, but rugged country nonetheless, with steep slopes studded with rocky outcroppings that angled sharply toward the river.

The tracks followed the flat river bed as it wound through the Alleghenies, twisting and winding on itself like a copperhead snake. Gone, too, was the languid Potomac they knew so well. Here in the mountains, it had become a wild thing, foaming over boulders and fallen timber. The water was swift and shallow, clear and cold, and the river had narrowed to the point where a man could easily pitch a stone across.

It was a cruel country, especially with night coming on. The kind of place that would be glad to see a man die. There was nowhere to run except the river and mountains. The raiders had their backs to the wall.

"Here they come," Flynn said.

Behind them, the smoke trail of the pursuing engine looked like a banner in the sky. Then the train itself appeared, thundering up the tracks as if the locomotive itself were angry and bent on revenge. The tracks began to climb slightly. The *Chesapeake* had slowed to the point where a man could run alongside and keep up. The wet, green wood in the tender could keep the train going, but it was impossible to build any speed without a full head of steam. There was no longer a boxcar to set ablaze or railroad ties to heave off.

"Looks like this is it, boys," Pettibone said.

Benjamin nervously licked his lips. "You reckon they'll hang us if they catch us?"

Flynn checked the Le Mat to make sure it was properly loaded. "That's a possibility, lad. But there's no surer way to end up dead than being afraid of dying. Fear freezes a man up worse than any winter cold."

Pettibone shook his head and grinned. "Why is it you Irish have something to say about everything?"

" 'Tis a gift," Flynn said.

Benjamin checked his guns as well. He had taken Cook's revolver, so that he was now armed with two Colts. "Well, I reckon if I'm goin' to die, I'm goin' to take a few Yankees with me."

Flynn clapped him on the shoulder. "That's the spirit, lad. Everything's going to be all right. Just make each shot count."

The Yankee train thundered up the tracks, gaining on the raiders every minute.

All at once, they became aware of someone running beside their car. Benjamin swung both pistols at the runner.

"Don't shoot, lad!" Flynn shouted, and leaned down to help Colonel Percy onto the car. The *Chesapeake*, which had once hurtled down the tracks awesome speed, had slowed to the point where a man could jump on or off if he was quick. One misstep meant being ground to bits beneath the wheels.

"What's happening, Mr. Arthur?" Hudson asked, dropping Percy's military title to call him by the name he had known long before the war, back home in Virginia. "Why are we going so slow?"

"Wet wood," Percy said. "Goddamn wet wood, Hud. It's green and it's damp and it won't burn worth a damn. We can't keep up a decent head of steam."

"Looks like we've got another fight on our hands," Flynn said.

Percy shook his head. "We're not fighting this time, Flynn. We wouldn't stand a chance, out here in the open. No, we're running." He gestured at the door to the president's car. "Get Lincoln out. We're taking him with us."

"Sir?"

"Do as I say, goddamn it!"

Hudson was the first to move. He threw one of his massive shoulders against the door. Most doors would have flown off their hinges. The door to the president's car barely moved.

"Stand back, Hudson," Pettibone warned. He stepped forward and fired two quick shots into the lock. Iron and wood flew. Before the smoke from the shots even cleared, Hudson had his shoulder to the door again.

There were more shots, this time from the opposite side of the door. The bullets punched two holes in the door, the new wood suddenly showing bright where only dark planks had been before. Hudson stared down, dumbfounded, at the bright red stains spreading across his chest.

"I'm killed, Mr. Arthur," he said, locking startled eyes with Percy. "I done tried to open the door."

Hudson started to fall, and Percy lept forward to catch him. Hudson was a big man, but the colonel held him as if Hudson was a mere child, and he gently eased him to the floor of the platform.

"Hud!" he cried. "What have they done to you?"

But Hudson's eyes already were turning glassy. Blood bubbled from the two holes in his chest.

Percy held him a moment longer, until his old friend was gone. Slowly, he let go of Hudson's body. Then he stood.

"Colonel?" Pettibone asked.

Percy did not appear to have heard. He drew his Colt revolver, aimed at the door, and cocked the hammer.

Flynn spoke up, gently but firmly. "Colonel, sir, maybe it would be best if you asked President Lincoln to come out. You know how to do it, sir. Gentlemanly, like. We are supposed to bring him to Richmond."

For a moment, it looked as if Percy might turn the Colt on Flynn. He glared at him, but at the same time seemed to look right through him. His angry expression faded. "For once, Flynn, you're talking sense."

The colonel approached the door, stood to one side, cleared his throat, and spoke: "Mr. Lincoln? Mr. President, sir? This is Colonel Percy again. I ask you to open the door. You have already killed one of my men. If you don't come out, we will have no choice but to open fire on you. Frankly, sir, it will be like shooting hogs in a pen." His tone grew threatening as anger over Hudson's death edged back into his voice. "Not that you don't deserve it. You're a damn Yankee coward for shooting through the door."

Percy heard voices inside. Lincoln and his bodyguard arguing? From what he had heard of Lincoln, the man probably would not give up easily. Then again, Lincoln was no soldier like the Confederate president, Jefferson Davis. He was used to contests of wills, not of arms.

"We're waiting for your reply, Mr. President," Percy pressed.

Finally, a high and reedy voice answered from within. Was it Lincoln's? "You realize, Colonel, that we can see out the windows. There's an entire train carrying Federal soldiers just behind you. You're out of time, sir. If you weren't, you wouldn't be knocking on the door. Might I even suggest that you surrender to prevent further bloodshed?"

Percy never had a chance to reply. No sooner had the voice that must be the president's finished speaking, than rifle fire began to pour from the oncoming Yankee train. Although the Yankees were still several hundred feet away, the four fully exposed Rebels on the platform of last car made a tempting target. Minié balls buzzed like fat bumblebees. Most of the shots went wide, but one stung Pettibone, cutting a bloody swath across his arm. Another bullet struck Hudson's body with a sickening <u>thunk</u> that shook the corpse.

Back at Kearneysville, there had been eight raiders to fight the Yankees. Now there were just four. The enemy soldiers were hungry to avenge their own dead companions and the fire increased as the train roared closer.

Percy jumped down, raised his Colt, and fired a single shot straight into the air. He had arranged this signal with Cephas Wilson. No sooner had the shot been fired, but the *Chesapeake* ground to a halt, reversed direction, and began to creep toward the oncoming Yankee train.

"Now what?" Benjamin wondered.

"Unless those Yankees stop in time, there's going to be one hell of a collision," Flynn said.

CHAPTER 33

Near Paw Paw, West Virginia • 5 p.m.

"Get the hell out of here!" Percy shouted. "You might have a chance to reach the valley if you keep out of sight and follow the river west."

Then Percy was gone, running toward the front of the train. Flynn was left on the car with Pettibone and the boy.

Flynn turned to Pettibone. "What are you going to do?"

Pettibone answered with a humorless smile and glanced down at his arm. For the first time, Flynn noticed that Pettibone's sleeve was soaked in blood. His leg was bandaged from the bayonet wound back at the depot. He must have been in a great deal of pain, but he bore it stoically. "I'm staying right here," Pettibone said. "If Abe Lincoln comes out, I aim to shoot him."

"That would be a fine plan if we weren't about to ram that other train," Flynn pointed out. "I do believe the colonel intends to assassinate the president with a train collision."

"I'll jump before that happens," Pettibone said. "I'll keep Abe from doing the same."

"I'm staying with you," Benjamin said.

"No, you ain't," Pettibone said. "Go with Flynn, boy. That's an order."

Flynn hesitated. In spite of the fact that everything had gone about as wrong as it could, he couldn't help but remember their mission. If Lincoln would not be going to Richmond as a captive, then he must be assassinated. Those were the orders. Normally, he would not have cared much for orders. But he could see the importance to the Confederacy. Already, good men had lost their lives for this foolhardy enterprise. He had to at least try to finish what they had begun.

However, there was no way they could get to the Yankee president so long as he was locked up tight inside the rail car. They could always set it on fire, just as Flynn had done to the boxcar, and smoke Lincoln out. But they were fresh out of kerosene lanterns—and time. They were heading right for the Yankees.

Of course, the collision with the Yankee train might kill the president, but Flynn couldn't count on that. Also, if he ever saw Colonel Norris again, he could honestly tell him he had tried to assassinate the Yankee president.

"Give me your pistol, lad," he said to Benjamin.

The boy did as Flynn asked. Flynn held the Le Mat in his left hand, the Colt in his right. As Benjamin and Pettibone watched in surprise, he took a step back and emptied both guns into the door of Lincoln's car. Splinters flew and smoke filled the air before being whipped away in the wind. The echoes from the gunshots rolled away across the mountaintops. He handed back Benjamin's pistols. "Better reload these."

"What the— "

"That should settle Honest Abe. If the bullets missed him, then he's a lucky man and deserves to live," Flynn said.

He turned to Pettibone. "Sure you don't want to come with us now?"

Pettibone shook his head. "I'll stay, just in case. I wouldn't get far with this leg, anyhow."

"Good luck to you," Flynn said.

Pettibone nodded grimly, then turned to face the oncoming train.

Flynn jumped. Benjamin followed. The train was moving so slowly that they landed easily enough. Benjamin started toward the river, but Flynn caught him by the shoulder.

"Where you going, lad?"

"The colonel said the river— "

"You come with me, or the Yankees will have you strung up within the hour."

They ran alongside the train, which was still moving slowly enough for Flynn to catch a handhold on the side of the baggage car. He grabbed Benjamin by the back of his coat and swung him bodily onto the car's steps, then climbed aboard himself.

"Why are we getting back on the train?" Benjamin asked. "It's headed right for the Yankees."

"You'll see, lad. You'll see."

"We ought to be running."

Despite his protests, Benjamin followed Flynn as he flung open the door of the car. They found Nellie stuffing a sack with the last of the payroll money.

"I thought you might be here," Flynn said. "Planning to carry all this yourself, Miss Jones?"

"I knew you would show up, Flynn. Here." She tossed a sack of money at him. "I'm glad you brought some help along. There's a lot of money to carry."

"We're stealing the money?" Benjamin asked.

"It's not stealing, lad. It's the spoils of war. No sense letting the Yankees have it back. Now get to it."

They carried the bags out and crowded onto the platform. The train was barely moving faster than a man could trot. Flynn threw the money off, being careful that the bags didn't land too far into the underbrush, and then they jumped themselves.

Flynn came down in a tangle of brambles. Benjamin helped pull him free. Nellie landed expertly, hitting the ground running.

"Come on," Flynn said, picking the worst of the thorns from his clothes and ignoring the scratches on his hands and face. "Let's get out of here. There's going to be one hell of a bang-up in a moment."

In the distance, there was a shriek of iron on iron as the Yankee train tried to reverse itself as the *Chesapeake* rushed toward it. The *Chesapeake*, moving backwards, swept past Flynn, Benjamin and Nellie. They had a glimpse of Cephas Wilson standing at the controls. He was leaning from the cab, trying to see where the train was headed. Willie Forbes and Hank Cunningham were in the cab, too, but the three men didn't even notice the trio staring up at them from beside the tracks.

They grabbed their sacks of plunder and started running, searching for a place to cross the C&O Canal so they could reach the towpath on the other side.

Flynn looked back just as the trains were about to collide. "Mother of God," he said.

* * *

WITH A NOISE LIKE A LONG, ragged rip of thunder, the trains crashed with bone-wracking force: CRAAAACK. Metal screeched, couplings snapped and popped. Steam gushed and filled the air with a hot, metallic smell. Even at a safe distance, Flynn felt his bones shudder. President Lincoln's car

derailed. It did not overturn, but tilted perilously on the edge
of the bank that sloped toward the river.

The Yankee train was still on the tracks, although the iron
cow-catcher grate in front was bent upward much like the lid
of an opened tin can. The silenced that followed the crash
seemed to roar in the survivors' ears. Steam hissed like a
dying groan.

Then the shooting started. Pettibone, who had managed
to ride out the collision unhurt, appeared on the platform of
the president's car. Armed with Hudson's revolver as well as
his own, he poured shot after shot at the blue-coated soldiers
swarming out of the tender.

Greer was bleeding from a nasty cut above his right eye.
In the crash, he had lost his balance and struck a sharp corner
of the cab.

Walter Frost was not so lucky. He was busy shoveling coal
when the trains struck, knocking him off his feet. As he fell
between the locomotive and tender, the iron wheels cut him
in two. Captain Lowell saw the bloody heap of intestines and
organs spilling from the dead man's torso and vomited.

A trickle of blood from the gash on Greer's forehead
reached the corner of his mouth. The taste of his own blood
made him go into a sudden rage. He pointed at the lone
Rebel unloading his pistols at them from no more than thirty
feet away. Already, the man had shot three soldiers. "Kill the
bastard!"

Four soldiers fired a ragged volley. At that distance it was
almost impossible for a rifle to miss. The heavy .58 caliber
bullets struck Pettibone all at once, throwing him back into
the wall of the car. He raised his pistol and fired a final shot
as he slid down, leaving a smear of blood on the wall.

A dozen soldiers were still on their feet. Greer led them
forward. "Fix bayonets," he snapped. Captain Lowell came

running up and joined them, his sword drawn and his pistol out.

Greer did not know how many raiders might be left to fight. He abandoned caution and rushed ahead because he didn't want any of the Rebels to escape. He vowed there would be some hangings before dark. He would make damn sure of that.

They encountered no one until they reached the tender. There, they surprised two raiders trying to uncouple the tender from the first passenger car. Greer guessed they were hoping to run on, leaving the wreckage on the tracks behind them as a barrier.

The soldiers shot one raider. His ash-covered face and clothes marked him as the locomotive's fireman. He fell in a heap beside the tracks, quivered, and went still.

The second man, who was small and wiry, took off running.

He did not get far. A soldier caught him in the back with a bayonet. He fell, screaming, and the bayonet plunged again to finish the job. The soldier had to kick at the body to get the blade free, and it came out, red with blood to the hilt.

Greer ran on. Aboard the locomotive, the Rebel engineer was waiting for them with a Colt in his hand. He shot the first soldier to appear. Then three rifles fired. The engineer's lifeless body slumped over and hung out the cab window.

"Search the cars," Greer ordered. The soldiers fanned out. There were two bodies on the platform of the derailed car, one white man, one black. They found another body in the baggage car. Curiously, it appeared the man had been stabbed in the heart. Another corpse turned up in a passenger car. His head was bandaged, but he had obviously died from the gaping bullet wound in his chest. Greer wondered what had happened aboard the train.

He was disappointed that they found only four dead. Some of the Rebels must have escaped into the woods.

One Rebel was found alive, hog-tied, in a passenger car. He claimed to be a passenger taken as a hostage by the raiders. Greer didn't believe the man's story, so he called in the lawyer, Prescott.

"He's a Rebel, all right," Prescott said. "His name is Cook."

Greer smiled down at the man. "You're going to hang, you damn Johnny Reb train thief. But before you do, you're going to tell me all about this raid. I want to know how many got away, so we can start looking for them. We'll put the local home guard to work."

Desperate to save his life, John Cook told them everything. He twisted the story of the mutiny, playing up his own role and trying to make it sound as if he and the other mutineers had been trying to stop the train so they could all surrender.

"You're not soldiers," Greer said. "You're thieves. You wanted that payroll money."

"We weren't after that money at all," Cook said.

"Then why did you take the train?" Greer demanded.

In spite of the trouble he was in, Cook laughed. "Why, you don't know, do you?"

"Know what? Don't laugh at me. I know you're a goddamn Rebel son-of-a-bitch."

"I reckon I am," Cook said proudly. "And I also know that President Lincoln is aboard that last car—if the wreck didn't kill him."

Greer's eyes grew wide. The mysterious car added during the night in Baltimore, the train being stolen by Rebels—it was all beginning to make sense. Still, it was too overwhelming for him to believe it.

"You're lying, Reb."

"Go see for yourself," Cook said defiantly.

Greer stared at Cook for a long moment. "Boys," he finally said, not taking his eyes off Cook. "Look after this Johnny Reb here. Captain Lowell, you come with me. Let's see if he's lying or not."

They left Cook under guard and ran out. He and Lowell arrived at the last car just as a tall, gaunt figure emerged.

He was dressed all in black, with a white shirt, and his beard nearly covered his deeply lined face. Although neither Greer nor Lowell had ever seen him in person, there was no mistaking the man before them.

Greer managed to stammer: "Mr. President ... sir." He and Captain Lowell saluted. Lowell stood frozen in the salute, but Greer managed to ask, "Are you all right, sir?"

"Fine, thank you, although I feel like a tomcat that's been rolled in a barrel," the president said. A uniformed bodyguard stood with him. The president observed the wreckage and the bodies with a detached curiosity. Eventually, he turned back to Greer and said simply, "Well done."

"Thank you, sir."

"What's your name?"

"George Greer, Mr. President. I am the conductor."

"This is Major Rathbone," the president said, nodding at the officer accompanying him. Rathbone still had his revolver out and looked as if he wanted nothing more than to shoot someone. He was bleeding from a wound in his upper arm, where a bullet had grazed him. "You're probably wondering what I'm doing here."

"The thought had crossed my mind, sir."

The tall man's faint smile played again at the corners of this thin lips, and then he explained that he needed to reach Gettysburg, Pennsylvania by morning.

"Gettysburg?" Greer said, astonished. "Why, that's several hours' ride from here."

"Then we had better get moving, Mr. Greer," the president said. "We'll have to take our time in the dark."

Night was already beginning to fall, cloaking the mountains around them. Only the very highest of the peaks stood out against the fading sunset. Oscar Schmidt began to light the lanterns that hung from the *Lord Baltimore*. Despite the force of the collision, there was little damage to the B&O's new locomotive. Even more miraculous was the fact that the train had not derailed.

"Mr. President, sir, why did no one tell me you were aboard? How did you expect to get to Gettysburg?" Greer asked.

The president held up a hand. "All in good time. Now let's talk about how I'm to complete my journey. I have to be in Gettysburg tomorrow to help dedicate the new national cemetery."

They quickly agreed upon a course of action. Once Greer explained the route the president must take to reach Gettysburg, Major Rathbone gave orders. Greer was glad to let someone else take charge. A feeling of exhaustion settled over him, weighing down his arms and legs. But it was not yet time to rest.

"Mr. Greer, we would appreciate it if you and Captain Lowell would stay here and continue to search for the remaining raiders," Major Rathbone said. "Colonel Percy does not seem to be among the dead."

According to the lawyer, Prescott, three raiders had escaped, including Colonel Percy, and they had taken one of the passengers with them, a woman who had agreed to stay aboard to care for a wounded Rebel officer, now dead. On foot, here in the mountains, Greer doubted they had gone far and was sure he and the remaining soldiers could quickly track them down.

Oscar Schmidt would operate the train carrying the president to Gettysburg. Prescott would accompany them, as would two soldiers. Schmidt would reverse the *Lord Baltimore* all the way beyond Harpers Ferry to Weverton. From there, a branch line of the B&O known as the Washington County Railroad would carry them north to the Western Maryland Railroad at Hagerstown, and from that Maryland town to Gettysburg. Barring any unforeseen problems, they would reach Gettysburg by morning, hopefully in time for the president to make his speech as part of the dedication ceremony.

"Getting to Gettysburg by morning will not be easy. Not with having to backtrack through these mountains," Schmidt said. He looked as tired as Greer felt as he climbed up to the cab of the locomotive. "But we must try."

* * *

THE MEN STANDING to one side of the tracks were so involved in making plans that they did not see Percy emerge from the underbrush. He crouched and held himself very still, his Colt revolver at the ready, his gray suit nearly blending with the late autumn twilight. He had hidden himself there seconds before the two trains collided. Helplessly, he had watched Pettibone die making a valiant last stand, then seen the Yankees slaughter the engine crew.

As he saw his men killed, it was all Percy could do not to make a wild, desperate attack, but he knew that would only be throwing his life away. Crouching there in the darkness, Percy considered giving up and trying to slip away. No one would blame him. But he could not do that. Five of his men had died for the sake of this mission, and he would see it carried out—or die himself in the attempt. It was his duty.

Seeing his men cut down by the Yankees left him feeling hollow and empty. They were his men, and he had led them to their deaths.

Some might call what the Yankees had done murder, considering the raiders were not given a chance to surrender. Percy was reluctant to put a name to it, because he had seen the same killing done many times before. This was war. It was a cruel and brutal business. Besides, what would someone call what he was about to do?

Assassination was just another word for murder.

Percy held his breath as he edged away from the shelter of the brush and edged closer to the tracks and the engine the pursuers had ridden. He had seen the president come out of the car, but there were too many soldiers milling around for him to have a chance with a mad rush at Lincoln. He would have to be stealthy.

The conductor, Yankee captain and the president himself stood on the other side of the tracks, screened from view by the iron hulk of the locomotive. Several soldiers stood nearby. If the Yankees spotted him now, he would be shot to pieces.

The *Lord Baltimore* was just a few yards away, still under steam, and he ran toward it in a crouch. It was dark, but lanterns now cast a circle of light around the locomotive. No one was guarding the train itself. Most of the soldiers were busy hunting Percy's remaining raiders. The nearest Yankee was a dead one, his mangled body cut in two by the train's massive iron wheels.

A stone clattered under Percy's foot, but he kept going. No turning back now. Those few yards were the longest he had ever run. It felt like crossing half a mile of open country. At every step he kept expecting a shout to go up or to feel the thump of a bullet between his shoulder blades.

The train was ten feet away. *Five*. Percy reached the train unnoticed and slid beneath the tender. He was safe for the moment, out of sight.

It was obvious, now that the raid was over, that the president would be leaving. Percy just wasn't sure whether Lincoln would go on to Gettysburg or return to Baltimore. All that Percy knew for certain was that the President of the United States of America would not spend the night in a Godforsaken stretch of mountains with only a handful of tired soldiers to guard him—not when Rebel cavalry patrols might be just miles away. No, Lincoln would be leaving, and wherever the president went, Percy would go, too. His orders were to bring Lincoln to Richmond or shoot him. His mission had reached the point where assassination was the only option.

From between the tender's wheels, he chanced a look at the president. He stood head and shoulders above the other men, but he was too far away and surrounded by too many men for a clear shot. All the men except Lincoln had guns in their hands.

There must be another way. Percy studied the underside of the tender above him and quickly made up his mind.

The bottom of the tender was not even two feet above the tracks. The car had been strongly built to carry huge loads of coal, and the underbelly was crisscrossed by a framework of wooden beams. Percy intended to hide in that framework. Someone glancing under the tender would never see him.

Percy was able to work his body into a space between two beams that ran the length of the car. Another wooden stringer ran the width of the car to create a kind of shelf. There was just enough room to wedge himself between the makeshift shelf and the floor of the car above. It was an incredibly tight squeeze, and he wasn't sure that he would ever be able to get himself out again. Still, he had to try.

Voices.

The sound of talking men came closer. He heard men walking toward the locomotive and tender. Get small, he told himself. Get very small. He gave a final grunt, squeezed, and was suddenly jammed into place as tight as a walnut in its shell. Percy held himself still as boots crunched on the gravel just feet away from him.

"I'd like to stay for the hanging," said a voice, so close it could have been in Percy's ear. "I want to see that Reb colonel get what he deserves."

"I've seen enough men die for one day," the other soldier said, then spat a gob of tobacco juice on the rail near Percy's head. It landed inches away with a wet splat. "I'll be glad to leave."

Once the men climbed aboard, Percy squirmed in hopes of settling into a more comfortable position, but it was impossible—iron rivets dug into his back no matter what he tried. Wherever they were going, it was going to be a cramped, miserable ride, but when the train stopped, he planned to settle this business once and for all. He vowed that he would make sure his men had not died for nothing.

After a few minutes, more men climbed aboard. The train began to steam in reverse, going back the way it had come and leaving the wreckage of the Rebel train behind. Percy tried not to look down, where the railroad bed was a blur beneath his face.

Duty, he reminded himself. *I do this in the name of duty*.

CHAPTER 34

FLYNN, Nellie and Benjamin hurried along the canal towpath. From the direction of the train, they heard a series of gunshots. Then all was quiet.

"You reckon the Yankees got Pettibone and the others, Flynn?" Benjamin asked.

"I reckon they did, lad," Flynn replied, puffing under the weight of the sack of money he carried.

"Even Colonel Percy?"

"Percy's a sly one. I wouldn't number him among the dead just yet."

"Do you reckon you got Lincoln when you shot through the door?"

"I must have. There's not many men who can dodge a dozen bullets."

"Stop talking and hurry it up," Nellie snapped impatiently.

"I never thought money could be so heavy," Benjamin said.

Flynn laughed. "I can think of worse burdens."

The towpath was a well-worn dirt road, a good twelve feet

wide, and they covered the ground quickly. Flynn couldn't help thinking that the soldiers, who wouldn't be weighed down by sacks of money, would have an easy time chasing them down along this road.

It was growing dark. Overhead, the bare, intertwined branches of the trees served to block what light remained, so that it was as if they were moving through a tunnel. Nightfall would work both for and against them. The soldiers would have a harder time following them in the dark, but on the other hand, Flynn, Nellie and Benjamin would be traveling blindly down unfamiliar roads.

"This way," Nellie said, leading them toward a road that emptied into the towpath near one of the canal locks. Nobody was in sight.

"Where are we going, Nellie?" Flynn asked, amused that the woman had taken charge. "You act like you know this road."

"Any road is better than this towpath," she said. "As soon as the soldiers are finished with that train, they're going to come after us, and they'll make better time."

"I was just thinking the same thing," Flynn said.

"How do we know we won't run into a Yankee patrol on this here road?" Benjamin asked.

"We don't," Flynn panted. "But Nellie has a point. The more distance we put between ourselves and the railroad tracks, the better. We've got to cover all the miles we can tonight. The roads will be swarming with troops looking for us at first list. Anyhow, lad, keep that gun of yours handy."

They hurried on, with Nellie in the lead.

Benjamin stumbled. "Go ahead," he said. "I'll catch up in a minute."

Darkness was falling quickly, especially on the roadway, which ran beneath a canopy of overhanging trees. It had grown cooler, too, although they were moving so fast that they barely noticed the damp chill that crept up from the river.

"What are you going to do with your share of the money, Nellie?" Flynn asked.

"I'm going to buy a big house in a fine neighborhood in Baltimore and I'm going to have lots of Irish servants."

"Irish are too much trouble," Flynn said. "I'd look for a good English butler, if I were you."

Benjamin had caught up again. He managed to laugh, despite his heavy load. He cut himself short and stared down the road into the gathering darkness.

Nellie and Flynn saw them, too, and stopped.

Four horsemen waited up ahead, blocking the road. They were hard-looking characters. They wore wide-brimmed hats pulled low over their eyes, shading their faces. All were armed, their hands within easy reach of their guns. There was no hint of any uniform, either blue or gray, and Flynn wished he had seen the horsemen in time to duck off the road. Flynn had the uneasy feeling that the horsemen were expecting them. He was afraid they had walked right into a trap set by the Yankees.

Flynn dropped his money bag and reached for his gun. "We may be in for a bit of trouble."

GREER INSISTED ON THE HANGING. It would have been easier simply to shoot the captured Rebel, but Greer would not be cheated out of his revenge. After all, Greer had chased his stolen train across two states, seen his fireman and friend Walter Frost killed, and probably lost his job with the railroad. Hanging the lone raider they had caught was a small consolation. No one even bothered to suggest that the Rebel be taken back to Baltimore so that he could be sent to military prison.

A rope was found, a noose made, and John Cook was marched at bayonet point to a suitable tree not far from the tracks. An uncomfortable silence had fallen over the soldiers. It was one thing to talk about a hanging, but now that they had the rope and the noose, no one was eager to carry out the task at hand.

"Let's string him up," Greer ordered.

"You ain't got no right," Cook protested. He was close to tears. Several of the soldiers looked away, not wanting to meet Cook's eyes. "I'm a prisoner of war. You can't hang me."

"You're a thief and a spy, you damn Reb. Now shut the hell up or I'll have a gag put in your mouth."

Cook decided to die quietly. He choked back a sob and shuffled toward the noose. His hands were tied behind his back, but his legs weren't bound.

Night was coming on fast. The train carrying Lincoln and the others had already steamed away. Greer could scarcely believe his train had been secretly carrying the president to Gettysburg when the raiders struck. He felt angry, too, for not having been told the president was aboard. He understood the need for secrecy, but if he had only known what an important passenger his train carried, he might never have stepped off the train in Sykesville for breakfast. None of this mess would have happened. As it stood now, he would always look like a fool because of the day's events. That thought snuffed any spark of mercy he might have felt toward the Rebel about to be hanged.

"Let's get to it," he growled. "There's not much daylight left."

The soldiers threw the rope over a branch, put the noose around the Rebel's neck, and tightened it. Cook was standing on an upended crate dragged out from the train for just that purpose. When everything was in place, all eyes—including the doomed Rebel's—looked to Greer.

Greer had never witnessed a hanging before, much less overseen one. He supposed there was some proper ceremony, some prayer he was supposed to utter, but he decided it really didn't matter, so long as the result was the same.

"God have mercy on your soul," he said, making an attempt at a proper hanging. He couldn't help adding spitefully, "Not that you don't deserve what's coming to you, you damn thieving Johnny Reb."

He nodded at the soldier who was the appointed executioner, and the man kicked the box out from under John Cook.

The rope went taut.

Death did not come quickly. Cook's neck didn't snap because the box wasn't kicked hard enough and he stepped into space, rather than fell with the full weight needed to make a clean break. His face turned blue and he made horrible strangling noises. His legs kicked wildly, trying to find a foothold that was no longer there.

Disgusted, Greer strode forward. This was supposed to be a hanging, not a torture, and he grabbed the man's dangling feet and tugged down mightily. The body suddenly went still.

"Amen," someone said.

"Let him hang for a minute, then cut him down," Greer ordered. He felt satisfied, watching the limp body swaying in the dusk at the end of a rope.

That's for taking my train, you Reb bastard. It's also for Walter Frost.

Greer had the captain send his men out to search for the remaining raiders. At most, they had half an hour before night settled over the mountains. It would be futile to fumble around in the dark, so unless the soldiers found something right away, the search would have to resume in the morning.

With any luck, Greer thought, they would have need for more rope.

* * *

"LOOKS LIKE HOME GUARD," Benjamin said, referring to the quasi-military patrols that roamed the roads, upholding the law as they saw fit.

"Once you start shooting, lad, don't stop," Flynn said. "Ready—"

"No!" Nellie put a hand on Flynn's arm as he was about to draw his revolver.

"Let me handle this," she said. To Flynn's astonishment, she walked out to meet the horsemen.

"We reckoned we'd find you hereabouts, Nellie," said a man wearing a long duster coat, leaning forward in his saddle and glaring at Flynn, whose hand was firmly on the butt of the Le Mat. "Where's Charlie?"

"He's dead."

"Dead? What happened?"

"We got ourselves mixed up in the middle of a train raid by some Reb soldiers." She jerked her chin at Flynn and Benjamin. "That's two of them."

"You want us to shoot them?" The horseman leveled a rifle at Flynn's chest. He was barely twenty feet away, and Flynn knew the man wouldn't miss. He held his breath and stared at Nellie, amazed.

She turned. Even in the gathering dark, Flynn could see Nellie's cold smile. She held his life, and Benjamin's, on the tip of her tongue.

"No," she finally said. "They helped me get the money off the train."

One of the men slid off his horse, and while the others

covered Flynn and Benjamin with their guns, he relieved them of the sacks of money.

The man carried it back toward the horses, and as he divided the greenbacks among the saddlebags, the man with the long duster coat explained how they had come to find Nellie. They had dragged some trees across the tracks a short distance ahead as planned, in order to stop the train. But the train never arrived. Instead, they heard a crash and then gunfire. Leaving three men at their makeshift barricade, the rest had ridden the roads that paralleled the tracks, intending to find out what all the commotion was about.

"Knowing Charlie, I reckon he must have gotten itchy under the collar and raised hell," the man in the duster said. "I suppose it was enough to get him killed."

"Yes," was all Nellie said. Flynn was glad she didn't point out that he was the one who had done the killing.

"We done brought your horses along," the leader said. "Just in case we had to help you make a getaway."

Nellie walked over to one of the horses and the man still on the ground helped her swing up into the saddle. She straddled the horse, skirts and all, just like a man.

"Give them Charlie's horse," she said.

"We ain't giving them a horse," the leader protested. "These horses cost good money."

"There's Yankee soldiers on our trail," she said. "You want these two to get caught and tell those soldiers about us?"

"It ain't too late to shoot them," he offered. "They won't talk much then."

"Give them the horse."

One of the men led the animal forward and offered the reins to Flynn. He took them gladly, but couldn't take his eyes off Nellie. She had played him for a fool and outfoxed him all the way. Damn the woman.

"Might we request a few of those greenbacks for our troubles?" Flynn asked.

"I don't think so." Nellie laughed. "You have a lot of brass for asking, though. See you in hell, Irish."

The thieves turned their horses and quickly rode back the way they had come, leaving Flynn and Benjamin alone on the dark road.

"Well, it all makes sense now," Flynn said, watching as the horsemen were swallowed by the oncoming night. He sighed. "She never wanted to split the money with me in the first place. Nellie just needed someone to carry it off the train for her, so she could meet up with her friends there. That's why she wanted to make sure we were bringing the train this far. It was where those fellows were setting their ambush."

"Ain't you mad?" Benjamin asked.

"Mad? Hell no, lad. We're alive, which is more than some can say tonight." He looked back toward the river, where the railroad tracks ran, somewhere in the distance. "All the rest weren't so lucky."

"Maybe she ain't as smart as you think," Benjamin said.

"What do you mean, lad?"

Benjamin opened his coat, revealing several bundles of greenbacks stuffed into his belt. He reached into his coat pockets and pulled out more money. "Back when I pretended to stumble, I took some of the money out of the sack and put in a couple of rocks so it wouldn't seem any lighter."

Flynn stared, astonished, then threw back his head and laughed. "There's hope for you yet, lad."

He hooked a foot in the stirrup and pulled himself up onto the horse, then reached down and helped the boy up behind him. "If those Yankees chase us anything like they chased that train, they won't give up. Come morning, they'll be riding all over these mountains looking for us and that money. Only we're going to be in Virginia by then. Nellie saved our lives twice tonight, first by telling her friends not to shoot us, and then by giving us this horse. We can't ride fast or far, not with two of us, but we'll make better time than walking."

Flynn headed the horse south, toward the Confederacy. He and Johnny Benjamin were going home.

CHAPTER 35

Gettysburg, Pennsylvania • November 19, 1863

The train crossed the border between Maryland and Pennsylvania sometime after dawn. Wedged into his hiding place beneath the coal car, Percy felt more dead than alive. *Stiff as a corpse*, he thought. His whole body was numb and cramped, but he didn't dare relax his grip for a moment because the spinning wheels of the coal car were just inches away, ready to cut him to ribbons if he fell.

The first leg of the journey, from where the trains had collided to the spur at Weverton that ran north, had taken hours. The train rolled backwards, slowly, because operating too fast in the mountains at night would have been disastrous.

The train stopped briefly during the early morning hours in what Percy guessed was Hagerstown. Another car was added, evidently so that Lincoln could ride comfortably, instead of in the locomotive's cramped cab. Percy considered carrying out the assassination while the train was stopped, but the station was pitch black and he heard the voices of many men on the platform. He could only imagine himself stumbling around in the dark, trying to find the Yankee president. Under those circumstances, he doubted that he could succeed.

Wait, he told himself. *Be patient.*

The train would stop again at Gettysburg, and there would be no mistaking Abraham Lincoln by the light of day.

The day dawned sunny and unseasonably warm for November, perfect for the crowds that would gather to hear the president's remarks. The pleasant weather seemed to be at odds for the dedication of a national cemetery where thousands of Union dead lay buried at the edge of town. The new national cemetery was an attempt to bring an added measure of dignity to all those who had sacrificed themselves in that decisive battle.

That wasn't to mention the more practical reasons for the cemetery. In the wake of the battle, nearly every field around town had become a boneyard. Something had to be done.

The cemetery was laid out on a low ridge within sight of where the center of the Union lines had withstood the high tide of the Confederacy. It was arranged something like a Greek amphitheater, with designated sections for each Union state. At the center, where an amphitheater's stage would be, there was instead a towering monument. The new headstones were flush with the newly turned earth. It was ground steeped in men's blood, and dignitaries like Lincoln and the scheduled orator, the famed Edward Everett, could say little to further consecrate the cemetery. Those buried there had already done that.

Percy had little room in his mind for such grandiose thoughts as the train steamed into Gettysburg. He hadn't slept all night. He was cold and stiff, and he wondered how in hell he was ever going to extricate himself from the iron skeleton of the train's tender without being seen.

When the train finally arrived in Gettysburg, the platform was nearly empty because almost everyone had gone to see the ceremony at the cemetery. In fact, the whole town was deserted. No one was there to meet the train except a handful of soldiers left behind on guard duty.

Once the train stopped, Percy slowly freed himself from his hiding place. He felt like a snail sliding from its shell, so tightly was he wedged beneath the car. His feet, when they touched the ground, had no feeling. He was forced to wait for several minutes as the blood began to circulate again.

He longed for a cup of hot coffee, warm biscuits, and a fire. He crouched under the belly of the train, rubbing his numb hands together until he had enough feeling in them to work a revolver.

No one at the station noticed him under the car, half-hidden by the tender's wheels. The guards would not be expecting trouble. Gettysburg was deep inside the Union and there was little reason for the sleepy-eyed soldiers guarding the station to expect anything out of the ordinary. Robert E. Lee had invaded just last summer with his entire Army of Northern Virginia, but because of the sacrifices of the men buried in the cemetery, it wasn't likely the Rebels would ever return this far north.

Finally, the president emerged from one of the cars. Percy looked out from behind a wheel and saw him up close, a tall, bearded man, thin to the point of emaciation, dressed in black and looking as tired as Percy felt. In the bright autumn sunshine, he looked even more gaunt than he had in the mountain twilight the night before.

The president clutched some papers in his long hands and looked puzzled about what to do next. He wore a stovepipe hat that made him tower over the men nearby.

A few others got off the train. There was a sturdy-looking officer Percy recognized as Major Rathbone, the bodyguard who had ridden with Lincoln in the car from Baltimore. Percy spied on him from his hiding place under the tender, and held his breath as the major glanced back at the train. Rathbone's gaze didn't linger on the train, however. Instead, the major carefully studied the station, but, seeing nothing out of the ordinary, appeared to relax. There was also a short, fat man Percy recognized as one of the passengers from the *Chesapeake*.

With stiff fingers, Percy drew the Colt revolver from his pocket and thumbed back the hammer.

* * *

ON THE PLATFORM, one of the soldiers nudged the corporal next to him. "I'll be damned but that tall fellow looks just like President Lincoln," he muttered.

"It can't be him, though," whispered the corporal, who had also noticed the resemblance. "We saw him ride past here this morning on his way to dedicate the cemetery."

Still, there was an air of dignity and command about the tall, bearded man. If this was Lincoln, the corporal briefly wondered, then who was at the cemetery?

"Damn peculiar, if you ask me," the first soldier said, staring at the man in the stovepipe hat.

"You there—where is everyone?" the major asked the soldiers.

"They're all up at the new cemetery, sir, watching the dedication," the corporal answered, offering a ragged salute. He was staring at the tall man in the black suit beside the major, still not quite sure what to make of him. "They're listening to Edward Everett, the orator ... and President Lincoln."

"Mr. Everett is a good speaker," the president said. "As for Mr. Lincoln— " He raised his bushy eyebrows quizzically and a glance passed between the president and Major Rathbone.

Percy decided it was now or never. He slipped out from

under the tender and moved, stiffly and slowly, toward Lincoln. His right hand was wrapped firmly around the grip of the revolver. Percy walked toward Lincoln with as much dignity as he could muster after the long, cramped ride.

Strangely, he felt nothing. No fear. No excitement. Just a sense of calm. Only his heart, thumping in his chest, betrayed any emotion.

A lifetime of memories washed over Percy as he crossed the depot toward the president. He thought of home: green fields in springtime, sweethearts he had known, the first time he jumped a fence on horseback—

Duty.

One of the guards saw Percy and elbowed his companions.

"Look what the cat done dragged in," the corporal said, just loudly enough for Percy to hear. The men laughed quietly at the figure in the dirty coat. "You reckon he's left over from the celebration last night?"

A great crowd had come to town for the ceremony and some men had caroused to excess the night before. Although the man on the platform looked as if he had crawled out of some alley after a night of hard drinking, there was a determined quality about him. He strode deliberately toward the tall, bearded man in the stovepipe hat. His face was hard and set. The laughter stopped, the soldiers exchanged worried looks, and they nervously held their rifles at the ready. Something was going on, but they didn't know what.

Percy crossed the platform. None of the men in the knot immediately surrounding Lincoln had spotted him. He was thirty feet away, but he didn't trust his aim in the condition he was in. He walked closer. Twenty feet. Fifteen feet. *Close enough*. He raised the Colt.

* * *

PRESCOTT, the fat lawyer, saw him first. His eyes went wide as he recognized Percy.

"Look out!" Despite his surprise, Prescott managed to shout a warning. "It's one of the Rebels!"

The men surrounding Lincoln did not have a chance to react. Percy's revolver was aimed at Lincoln's heart by the time Prescott managed to shout a warning. Too late, Major Rathbone lunged forward, trying to use his body as a shield in front of the president.

"Assassin!" Rathbone shouted.

Rifle fire cracked. Three bullets struck Percy all at once. The force of the bullets spun him around and Percy fell, sprawling, the revolver still gripped tightly in his hand. Percy had never pulled the trigger. His body rolled in the dust and lay still.

The soldiers on the platform had been watching the strange man intently, sensing trouble, and they reacted when they saw him run forward with a revolver. Now they stood with smoking rifles, staring at the body. Silence fell over the train station.

Calmly, the president broke away from the small group of men surrounding him and walked over to the figure on the ground. He stood for a moment, staring down at the body. He stooped to pick something up, his long body seeming to take a long time to bend toward the ground. He stood back up holding a pair of eyeglasses, the frame twisted and one of the lenses cracked.

"He was one of the raiders?" the president asked Prescott, without looking up.

"Yes, sir. He was the leader of the train raid, Mr. President," Prescott replied. Normally, he would have felt a pompous importance at providing information for the president, but the sudden violence had left him shaken. "His name was Colonel Arthur Percy."

"Ah. I remember that I spoke to him through the door," Lincoln said. "How did he get here?"

"I've been wondering the same thing, sir," Major Rathbone said. "He must have hidden himself aboard the train somehow. I don't know where—it's possible he was under the tender. That's about the only place he could have been."

"Remarkable," the president said. He added, as if to himself, "Why must we kill such men?"

"Because he was a Rebel, sir," the major said. "And he was about to kill *you*, from the looks of it."

The president nodded. Already, the incident at the train station was starting to draw attention. The dedication ceremony was ending, and people were beginning to drift back into town. Some townspeople looked curiously at the dead man on the ground, while others gawked at the tall figure in the dark suit and stovepipe hat, pointing him out to their companions.

Major Rathbone immediately ordered two of the soldiers who had shot Percy to take the body away. He then touched the president's arm, guiding him back toward the train.

A throng of people was just reaching the train station as the crowds spread through town. One of the passersby, a bony man with a black patch over his left eye, stopped to stare after the body being carried away. "What happened to that one?" the one-eyed man asked the lone soldier left on the platform.

The corporal was about to explain, but stopped when he saw the sharp look Major Rathbone gave him. "He just went crazy and got himself shot," was all that the corporal said.

"Is that right?" the man with the eye patch said. He looked doubtful.

"Well, that's what happened," the corporal insisted, although he didn't sound too sure of himself.

"Move along, sir," Major Rathbone said pointedly. "The excitement is over."

"I'm sorry I missed it," the one-eyed fellow said. "I suppose it was more interesting than the speechifying."

"Move along," Rathbone repeated.

"That Mr. Everett gave a fine oration, but awful long," the man said, ignoring Rathbone and using his one good eye to peer closely at the figure in the stovepipe hat. "President Lincoln hardly spoke at all. He got up there and sat back down before you knew it. We couldn't even hear him in back. Why, for all we know it could have been anyone making that speech."

The tall, gaunt man was listening intently. People stared at him with puzzled expressions. A low murmuring swelled among the citizens at the depot.

The major touched his elbow again. "Mr. President?"

Abraham Lincoln put his folded sheaf of papers in his coat pocket, took a last look at the dead Rebel being carried away through the crowd beginning to fill Gettysburg's streets, and climbed back aboard the train.

-The End-

ABOUT THE AUTHOR

David Healey lives in Maryland where he worked as a journalist for more than 20 years. He is a member of the International Thriller Writers and a frequent contributor to *The Big Thrill* magazine. Visit him online at:

www.davidhealeyauthor.com
or www.facebook.com/david.healey.books

Thank you for reading! If you enjoyed the story, please consider leaving a review on Amazon.com.

Made in the USA
Columbia, SC
29 September 2023